THREE GENERATIONS OF WOMEN WHO LIVED AND LOVED AT

MOORHAVEN

CORDELIA came to the big stone house by the sea as a governess for Jonathan Moorhaven's young nieces and nephews. She soon became Jonathan's bride and Moorhaven's first mistress.

DORINDA was Cordelia and Jonathan's beautiful young auburn-haired daughter. She fell in love with her own adopted brother and was determined to marry him despite family opposition.

CASSIE, Dorinda's daughter, is the third mistress of Moorhaven and the last to inherit its curse. She and the man she loved would eventually unravel all the mysterious and sinister events that had befallen three generations of the Moorhaven family.

DAOMA WINSTON
MOORHAVEN

AVON
PUBLISHERS OF BARD, CAMELOT, DISCUS, EQUINOX AND FLARE BOOKS

MOORHAVEN is an original publication of Avon Books. This
work has never before appeared in any form.

AVON BOOKS
A division of
The Hearst Corporation
959 Eighth Avenue
New York, New York 10019

ISBN: 0-380-00244-2

First Avon Printing, February, 1973.
Eleventh Printing

AVON TRADEMARK REG. U.S. PAT. OFF. AND
FOREIGN COUNTRIES, REGISTERED TRADEMARK—
MARCA REGISTRADA, HECHO EN CHICAGO, U.S.A.

Printed in the U.S.A.

FOR JAY GARON

MOORHAVEN

Chapter 1

The first time Cordelia Davis heard of Moorhaven was when her guardian Henry Ward said, "Imagine, Cordelia. In just ten days, we enter the twentieth century. We stand on the threshold of a new era, portending great changes for mankind. It is only fitting that you should begin your new life at Moorhaven at the New Year."

The words did not quite register at first because she was thinking, with affectionate amusement, that Henry sounded as if he were dictating one of his essays that would, after months and months of labor, appear within the covers of the *Atlantic* or *Harper's*. But then, like a distant echo she heard the words again. *Begin your new life at Moorhaven.* That was what her Uncle Henry had said.

Her slightly slanting, green eyes widened. Her slender body contracted within the protective arms of the big wing chair next to the fireplace that had been hers, as far back as she could remember, for schooling, storyreading, and rare moments of discipline. She folded her hands into the fullness of her skirt, and waited.

Henry stroked the round bowl of his pipe, and gave her a faint smile. "Aren't you going to ask me any questions, Cordelia?"

She swallowed against the lump in her throat. She

would have preferred to flee the room she had always loved rather than speak. She did not want a new life in a new place in a new century. She was, she thought hopelessly, exactly where she belonged and where she wanted to remain.

She had come squalling into the world in the small room just off the kitchen of this old country house. Her mother had died there, and been buried in the family cemetery in the oak grove just up the hill.

She did not want this new life Henry had planned for her. She only wanted everything to continue as it had in the past. Yet she knew that this could not be.

She had no claim on Henry. For the past nineteen years, from the moment of her birth, he had given her care, sustenance, and love. But he owed her nothing. She called him uncle out of respect, although he was no kin of hers. She considered him her guardian, as he did himself, because he had raised her, but he was not bound to her legally. He had taken the responsibility for her out of the goodness of his heart. And now he wished to lay that responsibility aside.

He watched her, making the soft humming noise with his lips that meant he was uneasy.

She said faintly, "I'm afraid I don't quite know what questions to ask, Uncle. I am overwhelmed."

The firelight danced on his gold-rimmed spectacles, and shone on his hairless head as he nodded. "I've been unfair to you, my dear. I meant to pleasantly surprise you, not to shock you into speechlessness."

Yet it should not have been all that much of a shock, Cordelia supposed. There had been signs of what would come. There had been murmurs that stopped when she entered the parlor. There had been certain narrow-eyed looks, and changes in the routine of years which had left her displaced, her hands suddenly emptied of chores that had always been hers.

Henry made the soft humming noise again, and then went on, "Now you must understand, Cordelia. This is for you, for your own good. I must consider your future. Ryetown is small, a backwater. Though I did want to keep you nearby, I saw no opportunity for you there. So I have done what I think is best." One of his pudgy pink hands reached up to tug at his sand-colored sideburns, another symptom of unease, Cordelia knew. Then he went on, "On my last trip to New York, when was it? Some three weeks ago? I met an old acquaintance of mine. A physician who comes from Tembley. His name is Peter Van Nuys, and he is a solid person. He happened to mention the Moorhavens, friends of his, who are greatly in need of a governess for two young children. As he spoke, I thought of you. It seemed a very proper situation, and so I investigated the family thoroughly. I am completely satisfied, as Peter Van Nuys assured me I would be, that the Moorhavens are good and substantial people. They have been shipbuilders for two generations at least, although they are now involved in railroads, I believe. Anyway, I have contacted Jonathan Moorhaven myself, and made the arrangements."

She swallowed again, and managed to breathe a single word. "When?"

"You are expected just after the turn of the year. So you will have Christmas here, at home with us."

"Ten days," she said. Her wide green eyes shifted from his plump, rather uneasy face, to the tall bookcases behind him. "You mean I'm to leave in ten days."

"Is that too difficult for you?" he asked quickly. "Clara assured me that it is a simple matter of preparing what you shall need, and packing, and that . . ."

Four months earlier, Henry had set out on a research trip to New York. He had been a fifty-year-old bachelor, pudgy, pipe-smoking, and somewhat absent-minded. He had returned a bridegroom, attentive at last, but no match at all for the woman who was his bride.

Clara Ward was quite tall, thin, and flat-chested. Her black hair was worn in two braided coils over her large ears. Her face was long and narrow, its flesh thin and without color. When she arrived she wore a dark brown traveling suit with a high-necked white percale blouse, an outfit that gave her a look of crisp efficiency, which she soon proved to be reality.

She pressed her dry lips to Cordelia's cheek, and murmured, "How wonderful that we meet at last. Henry has told me so much about you."

Cordelia had not then recognized her cold kiss to be a declaration of war, nor had she realized that the small skirmishes that followed were part of an organized campaign. Only now, when Clara's victory was complete, and not to be undone, did Cordelia understand that Clara had been determined to displace her from the beginning.

"Tell me," Henry was asking anxiously. "Is ten days too soon?"

She said in a steady voice, "No, no. It's quite all right. I can be ready by then."

"But, my dear," Henry answered, his round face sagging with relief over his high stiff collar, "you oughtn't to look so sad. It is change, you see. Changing means growing up. And if you don't find it to your liking at Moorhaven, then you must come home, you know."

Cordelia nodded, smiled. "Of course. I understand."

But she knew it was only common courtesy that made him offer her reassurance. Her days in his house were over.

"Clara will help you. And Aunt Berthe, of course." Henry's hands described circles in the air, and a bit of burning ash flew from his pipe to the brown rug.

Cordelia leaped to her feet, swooped down and caught it between thumb and forefinger, feeling its sting as she pressed the ember out between them. Sharp-eyed Clara would have noticed one more scorch mark among the many others, she knew.

When she regained her feet, Henry said with a sigh, "I don't know how I shall manage without you, my dear."

But he would manage, of course. Clara would see to

that. Already she had taken Cordelia's place in this very room. It was she to whom Henry now dictated his pompous prose, to whom he directed his thoughtful remarks on woman suffrage and the temperance movement, subjects of major interest to him these days.

Cordelia forced a smile. "Changes, Uncle," she answered lightly. Then, excusing herself, she left him peering thoughtfully at the fire.

The hall was dim, an inch of pale light showing beneath the parlor doors. Cordelia wondered if Clara lingered there, hoping to hear what had happened between her and Henry.

She thrust her small chin high, refusing to look, but as she turned toward the kitchen, she blinked back hot tears.

It was not fair, she thought, that what was good should come to an end. It was not fair that she could no longer belong in the one place to which she did belong. Yet who had promised her that life would be, must be, fair?

She thrust open the kitchen door.

Aunt Berthe, also a title of respect rather than relationship, was at the big stove. She was a small woman, gray-haired, hunch-backed, wearing a long gray dress under a heavy canvas apron.

Until this very moment, Cordelia had never realized Aunt Berthe's age. She had been a day-to-day figure, as much a part of Cordelia's life as Henry. Now the young woman saw that Berthe Hunt was old, and, since she had not changed in all the years Cordelia had known her, she must have been already old when Cordelia was born.

She slipped into a chair and watched Berthe stir a steaming pot with a big ladle. She watched as the old woman banged the ladle on the stove edge, and banged it again, and muttered angrily to herself.

Aunt Berthe already knew. That much was plain.

Cordelia said, "I'm to leave in ten days."

"It will be a good thing. That's what he says. A good thing for you to go off among strangers. If only his mother were here . . . If she heard it, saw it. If she . . ."

Cordelia cut in gently, "Aunt Berthe. Please. It's done. Could you come now and sit with me for a minute? Could you tell me about it just one more time?"

Berthe lurched over the stove, and banged her ladle down. She turned, and came stamping heavily across the room, her boots thudding on the hardwood floor. "Just one more time," she repeated, lowering herself into a chair. Her tongue came out to touch her pale withered lips, and suddenly two bright tracks appeared on her wrinkled cheeks. She rubbed them away with a gnarled hand. She drew a deep shaky breath, and said, "It was an August night, in the year 1880. Henry was just thirty-one then, but very settled indeed. His mother, your Aunt Bessie, was well into middle age. And I, I myself . . . let's say I was certainly much as I am today. There was a storm that night. A storm that came with terrible hot winds from the south, and great torrents of rain. By late afternoon it was dark as midnight, and we had the lamps lighted and burning brightly." Aunt Berthe went on, her slow voice telling the tale she had told so many times before.

Cordelia no longer had to listen to the words. She knew them by heart. She knew them well enough to picture the late afternoon that was as dark as night, with the great oaks bending in the hot southern wind, and the sheets of rain turning the dirt road outside into a morass through which a pair of fine black horses struggled to pull a small cart.

The first Henry knew of it was when there was a loud hammering at the door.

Aunt Bessie said, "Ah, some poor soul is lost on the way to Ryetown. Do let him in, Henry." She turned to Berthe, "You might go and see about tea. He will need it."

Henry had gone to open the door, holding a lamp. Its dim rays fell on a man whose face was white with desperation. His dark auburn hair, curly and thick, gleamed with rain. His green eyes were filled with terror.

"Can you help me?" he cried. "For the love of God, can you help me? It's my wife. She's in labor. And we can not go on. We dare not go on."

Henry stared, stared hard at the man for a moment, seeing his one arm, and the pinned-back sleeve where the other had once been. Then he caught up a heavy cloak and hurried outside.

Between the two of them, the men managed to bring the woman indoors. She was burning with fever, half out of her head with pain, yet she managed to murmur thanks when she was dried and wrapped in blankets and put to bed in the room off the kitchen.

"We must have a doctor," her husband said. "It's too soon for her time, and something's not right."

"In Ryetown," Henry told him. "If you can get there."

"I will," the man answered grimly. He bent to kiss his young wife. Then, refusing tea, refusing a change of clothes, he set out on one of his black horses.

None of them ever saw him again. He had disappeared into the storm, and never returned.

No one knew what had happened to him, but the dirt road had been a river at flood, completely washed away in many places. It was assumed that the one-armed man had drowned.

"It wasn't that he didn't want to come back," Aunt Berthe said. "It was only that he could not. For he loved her, you see. That much was plain even in those few moments. He loved her, and would have given his life for her. And he did."

During the night, while the hot winds howled, and the house shook, his wife seemed somewhat improved. She lay limp in the feather bed, smiling, and told Aunt Bessie that she and her husband were on the way to her family down South. She said that her name was Cordelia Davis, and that her husband was George. She spoke proudly of how he had lost his left arm when he was a fifteen-year-old drummer boy in the War Between the

States; and what a good and brave man he was. By dawn the storm was over. Cordelia had given birth to a small lusty girl, and had kissed her and named her Cordelia, too, before the fever returned. She lasted only a few hours into the calm sunny morning, and then, whispering her husband's name, she died.

Henry thought at the time that George Davis would still find his way back somehow. He believed that for the first few days, and then continued to pretend to believe it for the next few weeks.

Aunt Berthe and Aunt Bessie had known otherwise, and set out to make the child a joy rather than a problem to be dealt with. It was, they had told Cordelia many times, one of the easiest tasks they had ever undertaken. Henry was smitten the first time she blinked her green eyes at him. He was outraged when a neighbor suggested that the child be turned over to the town constabulary for disposal. He never considered any place for her other than his own home, with his mother and Aunt Berthe to care for her.

She didn't remember just when she had first been told the circumstances of her birth, but she knew that it had been early enough for her to have grown up with the knowledge, with new details added as she grew old enough to understand them. It had been Henry's way, she was certain, of giving her a past, antecedents, parents who had loved her. She could never think of herself as an unwanted or deserted foundling, because she knew Cordelia and George, and knew they had loved her. When she was twelve Henry gave her the small heart-shaped locket that had been her mother's, and she saw the two likenesses from which she had been blended. She had, even then, her mother's firm round chin and curled lips, and her father's wide eyes and thick wavy hair. Henry had also given her the wedding ring from her mother's hand, and she wore it, along with the locket, around her throat on a thin gold chain.

The few clothes that had been in her mother's trunk had been cut down to make clothing for her when she was a child, and the cart eventually wore out and was taken apart and used for kindling. The fine black horse, whom she still faintly remembered, died when she was four. Of her past, she had the locket and ring, and memories. Memories which were not actually hers, but which she considered a precious gift. It was on them that she based her daydreams. She imagined that her father was related to Jefferson Davis, that her mother grew up in a big, white-columned house, and danced in great swinging skirts of silk. On the bare bones of the past she built the expectation of an exciting future.

It was when she was twelve, too, that Aunt Bessie died, and was buried in the oak grove on the hill. But the untroubled years continued until Henry brought Clara home with him.

"And now," Aunt Berthe finished, with a quaver in her thin voice, "and now, my dear child . . ."

Cordelia summoned resources she had not known she had. She smiled widely, "I'm very excited about it, Aunt Berthe. Imagine, in no time at all I'll be a grown woman earning my own keep. It's something I've always dreamed about."

The words were untrue. She had never had such dreams. She had always imagined she would live with Henry, helping him with his essays, keeping house for him until one day she would somehow meet the man with whom she would fall in love. She would know him, she believed, the moment she saw him. He would be tall and dark. A quiet man, interested in the same subjects as Henry—knowledge of the past, the shape of the future to come.

Now Aunt Berthe's rheumy eyes misted. She was too wise to argue with Cordelia. She simply sighed and shrugged her hunched shoulders. "The next will be me," she said softly. "I know how the wind is blowing, it will blow me far from home, too."

Then and there Cordelia made up her mind that it must not be so. She was herself young. She could bear the burden of departure. But Aunt Berthe was old. What would happen to her? Where would she go?

That evening, after a supper of soup and hot bread, and a pudding made from leftover rice, with Clara's narrow face unaccustomedly animated by joy, and Henry's accustomedly thoughtful, Cordelia tried to find a moment to speak to him alone.

It was impossible, she soon saw.

Clara firmly ensconced herself in the chair by the fire and plied her embroidery needle with a patience that could not be overlooked.

Henry read and yawned, and read again.

Cordelia listened to the winter wind beat against the windowpanes, and planned her words. Then, having forgotten her careful planning in worry, blurted out, "Uncle Henry, what do you mean to do about Aunt Berthe? She is terribly frightened. She thinks that you intend to send her away, too."

Henry blinked behind his gold-rimmed spectacles, and closed his book firmly. He hummed between his lips, and tugged his sandy sideburns. "What's that, Cordelia? Where did she come by that foolish idea?"

Cordelia had no opportunity to explain.

Clara's needle flashed steadily as she said, "She is old, poor thing. She finds the work most difficult. She would be better off in some quiet place . . ."

"No," Cordelia cried. "You can't do that. Not to Aunt Berthe. This is her home."

Clara's voice went on, inexorable, cold. "It is not for you to decide." She didn't look at Henry, Cordelia saw, as she went on, "I will not have my perogatives usurped by a young and spoiled snippet. This is *my* home now. It is *my* decision, who goes, or who stays."

Henry cleared his throat. "What's this now? I never thought . . ."

Clara continued as if he hadn't spoken. "But, of course, as long as she can do her work to our satisfaction, there is no question but that she will remain with us, Cordelia." Dark eyes flashed resentfully at the young woman. "It is you who are creating the problem.

And not for the first time. I regret that you feel you must do so."

Plainly there was no more to be said. Cordelia bade Clara and Henry good night, and withdrew.

She took a lamp to light her way up the dark stairs, and undressing quickly in the chill of the familiar room, she blew out the flame, and climbed under the down quilt, and cried herself to sleep.

Chapter 2

A great billow of cindery black smoke hung over the train, and white jets of steam shot out from beneath it. There were shouts, and clatters, and quick conversations. Cordelia felt dazed, beyond the reach of the stirring excitement around her.

The past ten days had gone by so quickly. There had been preparations to make. She and Aunt Berthe had readied her clothes, while Clara stood by to observe and comment. "Now remember," she said. "You'll be an employee in the Moorhaven household. You must learn your place quickly." And a few moments later, "You'll hardly need that Spanish shawl, Cordelia. I doubt a governess would wear one." Cordelia put the shawl, a Christmas gift from Henry, aside, and later, when Clara had left the room, Aunt Berthe carefully packed it.

The small carpetbag that Cordelia was to take with her on the journey was soon full. The trunk in which the rest of her belongings would be shipped separately was half empty when she and Aunt Berthe lowered its lid. She had had a small wardrobe and no need of a large one in a country house. She was certain it would be the same at Moorhaven, and wasn't troubled by the thought.

At the last moment, having undergone Clara's final

inspection, she wrapped herself in a heavy brown cloak, deciding that if Clara's intent had been to make her appear plain then Clara must have her way this one last time.

She wore a heavy brown woolen dress, the neck as high as her chin, the sleeves an inch past her wrists, the hem at the tip of her ankle-high black boots. Her auburn hair was brushed high off her neck, thickly rolled, and anchored at the back of her small head with heavy pins. The green ribbons, a gift from Aunt Berthe, intended to be woven through her waves, were folded into the string purse on her wrist. Clara had objected to them as frivolous. The hat she wore instead was small, flat, and completely unfashionable.

Now she stood shivering in the station, Henry beside her, until the lanterns were swung, and the "All aboard," was passed along from man to man. Then, with Henry leading the way, she climbed on the train.

He settled her on a stiff seat near the velvet-curtained window and placed her carpetbag beside her.

"Remember, my dear. You must write and tell me how you are. And if . . . if you should prove to be unhappy, then . . ."

She smiled tremulously, promised. But she knew she would never see Henry again.

As he stepped off, the train's long, drawn-out whistle signaled its departure. With a jerk that very nearly threw her to the floor, it began to move.

She sat back with a sigh, and then, for the first time, began to think ahead. What would she find at the end of the five-hundred-mile journey? What would the Moorhavens be like? Would she meet Dr. Peter Van Nuys to whom she owed this dubious adventure? It was now somehow unnerving to face what lay before her. She decided not to allow herself to dwell on it.

The train bucked and jerked and fought its way along the long weary miles. It passed through the busy little towns strung like jewels along the snowy coast.

Cordelia ate the sandwiches Aunt Berthe had made for her, dozed, had an apple she herself had picked in

the orchard the September before, and then dozed
again. The coach was crowded with traveling men, who
eyed her, and with a few women, who ignored her. An
infant in arms cried fretfully through the long night.
Cordelia spoke to no one. She found herself thinking of
Ryetown's bells, tolling out the old year and the old
century, tolling in the new. She wondered if Tembley's
bells had rung at the same time.

It was almost noon the next day when the train
wailed at a grade crossing where two wagons and a
carriage waited, horses rearing and snorting, and slowed
for a tiny station.

Cordelia gathered her things quickly, the purse con-
taining the ten dollars given her by Henry, the carpetbag that held her few dresses and the Spanish shawl. As
she stepped off, she touched the locket and ring on the
chain at her throat, smiling faintly at the thought of
Henry's disapproval. He did not hold with superstition,
nor with talismans for good luck.

She stood next to the train, bathed on one side by its
hot steam, and on the other by an icy wind. The few
passengers who got off with her soon disappeared.
Within moments, the train wailed and jerked and
clattered away. She remained alone, bewildered, not
knowing quite what to do.

Beyond the open area where the tracks and platform
lay, across a snowy block rutted by muddy wagon
tracks, there were two huge abandoned warehouses.
The name Moorhaven appeared in fading black paint
on both of them.

The sky was blue and clear, the sun sharp and
brilliant on the single street that must be, she realized,
all that there was of Tembley.

If Henry thought Ryetown was a backwater, what
would he call Tembley?

Shivering with cold and with the beginnings of fear,
too, she wondered what she would do if the Moorhavens did not soon appear. Perhaps there was a shop
where she could warm herself. Perhaps there was a
church where she could ask for help.

But from where she waited, nothing of this sort was visible. And she was afraid to move away lest she miss the Moorhavens when they came.

An hour passed. Her hands within their brown mittens were numb. Her feet were ice within her boots. Her teeth chattered together. She was so withdrawn inside herself in an attempt merely to survive, to wait, that she didn't, at first, hear the voice that addressed her.

"You there," it whined shrilly. "Are you deaf and dumb, too? Can't you hear me? You there, miss. Do you plan to put down roots and remain there forever in this cold?"

Cordelia started, blinked back stinging tears. Tears, she assured herself, caused by the biting wind. Her cold lips attempted a smile. "I'm waiting," she explained.

"Then go into the waiting room," the whining voice retorted.

"The waiting room?" Cordelia repeated. Now that the tears were blinked away, and she could see clearly, she found the source of the suggestion.

It was a woman, small, bent, wrapped in a black shawl that covered a worn black dress. Beyond her, Cordelia saw, was a dismal wooden shed. She had noticed it before, and thinking it was for storage, had not ventured a closer look.

"Come along." A thin, wrinkled claw fastened itself around her wrist. "Come along, I say. Otherwise you'll freeze to death before they come from Moorhaven on the Marshes for you."

Cordelia, allowing herself to be drawn toward the shed, asked, "But how do you know that I'm waiting for the Moorhavens? How do you know who I am?"

The old woman cackled. "I don't know who you are. Only that you're to go out there. To them."

She thrust the door to the shed open, pulled Cordelia in with her.

Blessed warmth, steamy and comforting, though not pleasantly scented, enfolded her.

There was a red-hot pot-bellied stove in a corner.

Four men surrounded it, working men to judge by their bibbed overalls and heavy shirts, with big scarred hands held out to the warmth.

The old woman pushed her way in amongst them. "Here now. Let the young lady have some of that. She's about frozen to death."

The men muttered among themselves, but fell back. One of them, thick-shouldered, tall, with thin black hair, asked, "Why, Mother, who do you have here?"

"I don't know her name. But I know where she's bound," the old lady retorted.

Cordelia hastily introduced herself and expressed her gratitude at being led to the warmth.

"And where *are* you bound?" the thick-shouldered man asked.

"Moorhaven," the old lady cackled. "She is going to be governess there, poor child, and I doubt very much that she deserves it." Dark eyes peered from under shaggy white brows. "They didn't tell you, of course. They didn't say they were bringing you to doom, did they?"

A small chill crept over Cordelia's thawing flesh. She wondered if she had heard the word right. Doom? Was that what the old woman had said?

"Now, Mother," the thick-shouldered man laughed, "the poor girl's only just come. Must you start that?"

"My son. Arley. The oldest. I have only two children left. Yes. The oldest. Arley. And the youngest." The blue lips twisted. "I am Daviette Jones. Now when you speak of our meeting, and surely you will, you'll know who it was that warned you."

"Warned me?" Cordelia echoed. Her green eyes went anxiously from the withered old face to the younger but work-worn one.

Arley shook his dark head, and shrugged his thick shoulders.

But one of the men behind him muttered a gruff, "Yes, yes. She might as well know the truth. And be prepared."

Daviette Jones didn't seem to have heard him. She

stared at Cordelia, her black eyes burning like coals in the wrinkled parchment of her face. "It's the curse, you understand. It's what must be. Here was a town. Busy, young, joyful. Work to do, a life to live. Here was Tembley, where the ships came in, and the ways were long, and the docks crowded, and the warehouses filled to bursting. Here was a church with never enough pews, and shops, and markets, and gas lamps on the street corners. And now . . ."

She stopped. Her shawl-wrapped shoulders moved in a shrug. "You saw it with your own eyes. Where is it now? Where did it go? What happened to Tembley? Now there are no ships. No stores. No markets. It is gone, all life is gone."

"Now, Mother," Arley said, "you know why the port died. It was when the ships stopped coming in."

The words were sensible enough, but they held no conviction. What Arley Jones said, he did not himself believe. Cordelia was sure of that, if of nothing else.

Daviette Jones said firmly, "It was when the Moorhavens pushed the sea back. When they pushed it back four years ago."

There was a murmur of agreement from the men around her. There was a shuffling of boots and a heaving of shoulders.

The small room was suddenly too warm. There was no air to breathe. There was not enough light to see by.

Cordelia wished herself in the cold out of doors. She turned, but the withered hand tightened on her wrist.

"You must hear it all," Daviette Jones said.

"Never mind," Arley cut in. "She'll hear it soon enough. It needn't be now."

"Now," the old woman whined. "Now is the time. While she can still turn back. Now. While there is still a way to save herself."

"Leave it," Arley answered. "You're frightening the child out of her wits."

But again, Cordelia noticed, there was no real conviction in his voice.

"I want to frighten her," Daviette answered. "To

frighten her out of her wits, and then into them. So she will be saved."

Cordelia's small slender body shrank within the folds of her heavy brown cloak. She managed a bewildered, "But I don't understand."

"And no reason why you should," Daviette retorted sharply. "At least not yet. What do you know of the Moorhavens? Nothing. Nothing. How could you? But it is they who destroyed Tembley. That is what you must know. They sold off their ships. They closed down their ways and warehouses. They moved off to the marshes, and built their home there. And then, when they no longer needed it, they pushed the sea back. They drove the sea away. Our sea. Which nourished us, kept us, gave us hope. They thrust away the sea. But it will return, you know. Mark me, remember it. The sea will one day return to claim its own."

The door behind Cordelia opened. Chill air swirled through. She started, as if, in that moment, she expected to be seized by an incoming tide. Seized and flung away. It was, she knew, the strength of Daviette Jones' whining voice, her burning eyes, that had seemed to turn what was nothing but a draft into the reaching sea.

She swung around.

A short, heavy-set man forced the door shut behind him, then gave the room a quick glance. He came directly to her. "Miss Davis?"

"Mr. Moorhaven?" she asked.

There was a gruff laugh from somewhere behind her near the stove.

"I'm Joshua Sawyer," the short, heavy-set man told her. He gave her a quick warm smile, white teeth flashing in the iron gray of his beard, as he pulled off his cap. "I'm sorry I was held up. There was a great deal of snow on the road after what fell last night. I had to stop and shovel two or three times. I'm glad you found the place to keep warm while you waited for me."

"And someone to talk to," Daviette Jones said bitterly.

He gave her a brisk nod. "I'm sure of that, Mrs. Jones."

Daviette cackled. "As well you might be."

Joshua ignored her. He took up Cordelia's carpet-bag. "Is this all?"

"I have a trunk coming. But it will arrive later," she told him.

"Then, if you're ready, the carriage is outside."

Daviette's hand clasped Cordelia's cloak. "No," the old woman whispered. "No, girl. Don't go to Moorhaven."

"But I must," Cordelia said. "I am to work there."

"The curse is no concern of yours," the old woman continued. "Not yet. Don't go to Moorhaven."

How Henry would frown, Cordelia thought, if he knew the chill she felt at the old woman's words, if he knew how fear made her hands clammy within her mittens.

She hesitated, not knowing what to say, nor how to free herself from the old woman's grasp.

Joshua resolved the matter for her. He took her by the elbow, edged her around. She had time only to call out her thanks, before she found herself once more in the cold.

He stowed the carpetbag, helped her up, and climbed up beside her. With a flick of the reins, he started the two big bays.

They trotted briskly down the empty street, carriage wheels jolting in the frozen ruts.

"I hope the old lady didn't upset you," Joshua said at last. "That was a rare welcome. But remember, she's in her dotage, and has been for years."

"Of course. I understand," Cordelia said. And added, "But she's right in that there isn't much to see in Tembley."

His beard split in a smile, and his blue eyes twinkled. He was, she decided, in his mid-forties, about the same age as Arley Jones.

"Oh, the old woman's not completely mad, you know. She's right enough about the town, and the cause of the town's trouble, too." He stopped, then in a lighter tone, he said, "Now this, through which we pass, is called Washington Avenue. It is the main street of Tembley, and the only street."

She smiled her appreciation of his dry humor, but returned to the subject he had dismissed. "What happened to the town, Joshua?"

He shrugged. "Over the years, the tides caused a change in the harbor depth. It happened slowly, so slowly that no one saw it going on, or knew what it would eventually mean. As the channels grew more shallow, fewer and fewer ships could come in. And then, at the same time, through the same forty years or so, the trade itself began to die. That happened slowly, too, I suppose. And then, about eight years ago, the results were final and inevitable, and there was nothing to do but accept the verdict nature had laid down."

"But why does Mrs. Jones blame the Moorhavens?"

"They had the biggest shipbuilding firm in the area. The older Moorhaven closed the yards, the ways, and warehouses. He got out in time."

"And no one else did?"

"There was, once the yards and docks were closed, nothing for anyone to do. Those that could went elsewhere to look for work. Those that couldn't or wouldn't, stayed here." Joshua shook his head. "Some insisted the trade would pick up again, the harbor somehow become deep. Some just couldn't believe what had happened to them."

"And so the Moorhavens . . ."

"You mustn't be troubled about that. Mrs. Jones means you no harm. Or the Moorhavens either. She's had terrible losses, and no way to explain them, so she's become afraid."

Cordelia thought Joshua's calm explanatory voice was very much like Henry's, and what he had just told her was what Henry would have said if he had heard the old woman. It should have been quite enough to put her at ease. Yet, Cordelia still heard the shrill whin-

ing voice saying, "It's the Moorhaven curse. The sea
will return to claim its own."

Joshua chuckled with a quick sideways glance at her
face. "Yes. Washington Avenue is Tembley's main
street and only street. And we're about to come to the
end of it. If you look there, back among the blue
spruce, you can get a quick look at the Van Nuys
place."

She craned her neck, saw a big house, one much like
that she had left behind. Three stories high, with huge
windows. A wide porch. It looked roomy and comfortable. She was pleased. She said, "That's where Dr.
Van Nuys lives."

"Yes," Joshua agreed, as they left the blue spruce
behind.

They passed a huge open field. It was covered with
deep unmarked snow. At the back of it, way back from
the road, a tall dark chimney reared against the sky.

She studied it, then asked, "What's that, Joshua?"

He didn't seem to hear her. He urged the horses on
and after a moment or two, he nodded toward another
house. "The Falkland place."

It was a house much like that belonging to the Van
Nuys. She mentioned that to Joshua, and he nodded.

"The Falklands, and the Van Nuys? Are they friends
of the Moorhavens?" she asked.

"Yes," he said. "Friends and neighbors for a long
time. And friends still."

She thought of the way they had just come. The Van
Nuys house in the grove of blue spruce. That vast
empty lot where the stained chimney reached for the
sky. Then the big Falkland house.

"Neighbors, you said?" she asked Joshua.

He grunted, shrugged. Then, "The Moorhavens were
between the other two. You saw the chimney. It's all
that remains. The house itself burned down last year."

"Burned down?" she cried. "But how . . . why . . ."

"It had been vacant for years," he said quickly, and
went on, "And that's the last of Tembley. It'll be
country all the way from now on."

She shivered under her cloak as the carriage jolted over icy ridges, and slipped in and out of frozen tracks. The horses labored, breaths steaming in white plumes over their heads, up steep hills, while Joshua pointed out the places where he had foundered earlier and had to dig out. At last they rolled over a final high knoll, and the road curved down toward a strange and glittering flatland.

"You mentioned Dr. Van Nuys," Joshua said. "Do you know him?"

"No. But my guardian does. It was Dr. Van Nuys who arranged this position for me."

"You'll meet him soon enough," Joshua said dryly. "And, unless I miss my guess, you'll see a good bit of him thereafter."

"What do you mean?"

Joshua's beard once more split in a grin. "I'll let you find out for yourself."

The carriage jolted down and down and the strange glittering flatland always lay just ahead of them.

She stared at it, bewildered. It seemed to heave and strain. It seemed, even, to be breathing. There was something oddly frightening about that gleaming, icy mass.

At last she remarked on it.

He said, "Yes. Those are the marshes that Daviette Jones was telling you about. The place where she believes the sea was pushed back."

"You mean the place where the sea withdrew," Cordelia retorted.

He chuckled. "Right enough. I'm glad to see you understand."

Then, before she could answer him, she saw off to the left, a big stone house, and rising behind it, a snowy cliff.

She made some small inarticulate sound.

"That's right," Joshua told her. "That's it. Moorhaven on the Marshes."

In the same moment, a single small cloud appeared

in the hard blue of the empty sky. It drifted across the shining face of the sun.

A deep shadow fell on the house, on the gray stone, the empty windows, the slanting roof.

While all the world around glittered with an unreal brilliance, Moorhaven lay still in the dark.

Chapter 3

Cordelia felt a threat in the spreading shadow, and put her hands out in a blind thrusting-back gesture, as if she were shielding herself from some wicked force.

Joshua pulled the reins sharply and the horses stopped so suddenly that the carriage bumped and slid in the snow.

"Well, miss?" he asked. "What is it?"

She turned wide green eyes to his bearded face. How could she tell him that the dark over Moorhaven gave force to the maunderings of the old woman in Tembley? She drew a deep breath, smiled. "Joshua, would you do me a favor?"

"If I can."

"Then please do call me by my Christian name." She did not go on to explain that Clara had always called her 'miss', an appellation that had no affection in it, and no interest either.

"I should have explained. I'm the hired man here."

Now she knew why someone had chuckled in the shed when she had addressed him as Mr. Moorhaven.

He was saying, "And my wife is the housekeeper."

"And I am to be the governess, Joshua," she answered. "So . . ."

He smiled at her. "Shall we go on, Cordelia?"

"Wait a moment, please." She turned back now to

Moorhaven. The cloud was gone from the face of the sun. Brightness lay across the fields, the gray stone.

Now she saw that the huge rectangular building was completely unadorned except for carved cornices over the big windows.

"The rock came," Joshua said, "from the cliff above. We cut it out ourselves and brought it down on carts."

The house had a raw, brooding ugly look to it, even with the shadow of the cloud gone. It needed paint and planting, Cordelia thought. Black shutters and shiny black doors with brass fittings to match the two gas lamps that graced the entrance way. And rows of lilacs that would bloom in April, such as those she had left behind her.

Then, forgetting what she would do if the house were hers, she saw the great long hump of the dike that circled the area in a crescent as far as her eye could see.

"Should the marshes rise," Joshua explained. "Jonathan put it in four years ago."

"The marshes rise?"

"We are prone to heavy storms here."

She nodded, thinking of those that often lashed the Ryetown area, and the one that had turned the road into a muddy river the night she was born.

"Storms," he was saying, "with driving coastal tides. They generally come in the fall of the year. When they do, the marshes seem to swell. They've done no real damage so far, but Jonathan believes that one day they could. Hence the dike."

"But the area seems so static, Joshua. So frozen."

"No," he said. "It isn't frozen. There's a skim of ice on the surface. If you were to go over the dike, walked down, you'd see what I mean."

She shivered slightly. "I am not likely to do that, I think."

He moved the reins. The horses stepped out.

"Tell me about the Moorhavens," she said.

"You'll see them soon enough now," he answered.

"Yes," she agreed. "But it would be nice to know

what to expect. I've heard only of Mr. Moorhaven, and
that there are two children. But what of his wife? Will
she like me, do you think?"

Joshua turned his head to stare at her for a moment.
Then he said slowly, "You've been told nothing of the
family I see."

"As I said."

"Jonathan Moorhaven is the head of the house. He
is unmarried."

"But the children ... Mrs. Moorhaven ..." Cordelia
said.

"Elena Moorhaven is Jonathan's sister-in-law, the
widow of his older brother Dennis. Dennis died on San
Juan Hill about two years ago. The children are his.
Lena is eight years old. Sam is ten. The older Jonathan
died soon after Dennis."

"And the older Mrs. Moorhaven?"

Joshua frowned. "She was killed in a carriage accident while this house was being built." He went on
after a pause. "Then there is Ralphine. She is Jonathan's sister. A spinster. About thirty, I'd suppose.
There are two younger brothers. Gregory is twenty-six.
Denton is twenty."

Cordelia wished now that she had not asked for
advance information about the family. She was caught
up in a sudden whirl of names and ages and relation-
ships. She was not sure that she would ever be able to
sort them out.

Joshua grinned at her. "You look frightened."

She didn't reply, but she admitted to herself that it
was true. She *was* frightened. During the flurry of
preparations she had had no time to think ahead, to
conjecture much about what she would find at Moorhaven. Now, as if transported to another world, although she had come only five hundred miles, she was
here.

The carriage rolled to a stop before wide stone steps.

Joshua climbed down, then helped her to alight.

She turned, looked down the long snow-covered
slope to the hump of the dike. Beyond it, she could see

a rim of the glistening, heaving mass that was the marsh. She drew a slow breath of the icy air as she turned back toward the house.

There was a movement of white lace at one of the windows. She saw it from the corner of her eye and repressed a smile. Someone inside was of the same anxious turn of mind as she herself.

The door swung open just as she reached it.

The girl who stood there was no more than sixteen, Cordelia was sure.

She had black hair and narrow black eyes. Her chin was pointed, and her mouth very straight. She wore a long black dress of coarse cotton fabric, and a white apron. A small white cap sat on her head like a bird about to take wing.

She made a small curtsey, said, "Come in. Mrs. Moorhaven is waiting for you in the drawing room."

The vestibule was very large and bare except for a few heavy pieces of furniture. A long shining table on which a potted plant seemed to be dying. A clothes tree hung with a variety of cloaks and coats. A big, gilt-framed mirror, in which Cordelia caught a glimpse of herself as she removed her cloak and took off her hat.

She was tired after the long journey, and there were faint smudges of soot on her face. Her hair was every which way and wisping into curls. The green ribbons were still in her purse. She would have liked to tidy up before the coming interview. But there was plainly to be no time for that.

She turned to the girl who had greeted her, struck by a vague feeling of familiarity.

She could not have seen the girl before. It was impossible. Yet there was something in the chin, the eyes, the straight mouth ... She said, "I'm Cordelia Davis."

"And I'm Mary Jones," the girl answered.

"Jones?" Cordelia smiled quickly. Then, "Does your mother live in Tembley by any chance?"

Mary sighed. "Yes. She does. And I see that you

have hardly set foot in the place and you already know her."

"We met briefly," Cordelia answered. "She was kind enough to show me the shed while I was near frozen waiting for Joshua."

Mary's straight mouth curled. "I cam imagine how kind she must have been. Knowing that you were coming to Moorhaven."

"I believe I met your brother, too," Cordelia said hastily. "Arley, isn't it?"

"Arley it is." Mary gave her a long look. Then, "I suppose you think my mother's daft."

"I have no opinion. I only know she was kind to me."

"They are all daft," Mary said. "Believe me. Mother, and the rest of them in Tembley. But that doesn't stop me. For I'm not."

A door opened at the end of the vestibule.

A tall, slender figure stood there in the shadow. A cool voice carried clearly over the distance.

"I believe I heard the carriage some time ago, Mary. What's the delay? Why are you dawdling out there?"

"Coming just now," Mary said, flicking a look at Cordelia.

She went ahead, and Cordelia followed. Her heart began to beat very quickly. This would be Mrs. Moorhaven, the mother of the children who were to be her charges.

The tall, slender woman moved back into the room as Cordelia approached. She was a thirty-three-year-old woman with hair braided and wrapped into a high coronet on her narrow head. Her face was pale, and her blue eyes and thin lips were pale, too. She wore a soft black gown with a large collar of fine white lace. There were falls of matching white lace at her wrists.

She sank onto a dark brown love seat, then gestured to Cordelia.

Cordelia took the straight chair indicated. She thought that if Clara had begun to make her feel dowdy the day before, the woman now facing her had completed the task. She felt like a country girl in her brown dress and heavy winter boots. She reminded herself that that was what she was. A country girl. She sat very still under the long silent scrutiny to which Mrs. Moorhaven subjected her.

At last the woman said, "I am Elena Moorhaven. My two children, Lena, and Sam, will be in your care. I would like to know something of your credentials. But, first, tell me how old you are."

"Nineteen," Cordelia answered. "I will be twenty this coming August."

"It is very young, isn't it? To be responsible, I mean, for two young children?"

"Young?" Cordelia's brows rose. "Why, I shouldn't think so. Many women are mothers at my age."

Elena smiled faintly. "Mothers. Yes. But that isn't quite the same." She shrugged. Then, "Never mind. Why did you leave your last position?"

"I've had none before. This is my first."

Elena's pale eyes narrowed. "Your first. Indeed. Then you'll need to learn, won't you?"

"I hope to."

"And I hope that your learning won't be at my children's expense," Elena said sharply.

Taken aback, Cordelia was silent. She felt, with quick alarm, a certain animosity in Elena Moorhaven. Unaccountably Clara came to mind.

Elena went on after a moment. "Why did you leave home?"

Cordelia thought of Henry, of Clara. But she said, "It was time."

"Time?" Again Elena's eyes had narrowed.

Cordelia hesitated. She pictured the firelight glinting off Henry's hairless head and gold-rimmed spectacles. She thought of his plump hands making circles in the air as he explained his decision to her. Finally she said, "I am a grown woman now. I must make my way in the world."

"Indeed," Elena said softly. "And what way is that?"

"I don't know yet. But it seemed to my guardian that this would be a good place for me, and a job I could do well."

"Let us hope so," Elena answered softly. She rose to her feet, turned toward the door.

At that moment, it opened.

"Jonathan," she said, her voice soft and gentle now, her narrow pale eyes shining. "I was just about to call you. Here is Cordelia Davis. If you should care to interview her . . ."

Jonathan Moorhaven paused at the threshold.

He was a tall man, with big broad shoulders and a wide chest. His hair was very dark, cropped at collar length. His face was clean shaven, and his sideburns were short and well-trimmed. He had a ridged brow, square jaw and jutting nose, and his dark eyes seemed to burn with hidden fires. A raw and angry scar breached the flesh of his right temple.

It seemed to Cordelia that time had stopped while he stood on the threshold. She slipped backward into her dream of the man that she would some day love. She buried the recollection deep, and made as if to rise.

"No," he said quickly. "Don't get up." He moved into the room, limping noticeably. He went to stand before the fireplace, hands clasped behind his back. "I hope you had a good journey, Miss Davis."

"Yes, I did, thank you."

He gave her a quizzical look. "What am I supposed to ask you? It is all settled. It has been since Peter, that is, Peter Van Nuys, spoke to me of you, and of Mr. Ward."

Cordelia clasped her hands in her lap. She glanced sideways at Elena, still standing, her tall slender figure wrapped in black. "Mrs. Moorhaven mentioned my credentials."

Jonathan shrugged. "You have them in adequate measure. I went into that with Peter, and with Mr. Ward." He smiled faintly. "As I said, it was settled some time back. And we're glad to have you. My sister-in-law is not well." His dark eyes touched Elena expressionlessly. "She finds the care and training of the children a debilitating chore." He paused, dark brows rising, as Elena made a sudden movement. When she didn't speak, he went on, "And in this isolated spot it is difficult to find anyone with education."

Cordelia relaxed. "Then it's all right?"

Elena interposed in words she had used before, "Let us hope so."

A peculiar tremor touched Cordelia. It did not sound to her as if Elena really meant the hope to come true. She brushed the feeling aside. She must not allow herself to imagine what could not be the case. And in any event, she was here in Moorhaven. She had passed the first test. It was decided that she would stay. Her relief was overwhelming, although, surprisingly, it had never occurred to her until she stepped into this vast room, that there was any question but that she would stay.

"Of course you're all right," Jonathan was saying. "Surely you didn't expect otherwise. And now, you would like some tea, wouldn't you, before you meet the children?" He didn't wait for her answer, but turned to Elena.

She took a small brass bell from the marble-topped table beside her. She shook it briskly. Its clatter had barely begun when the door burst open.

A small, dark-haired girl dashed into the room and came to a quivering stop. "She's here, isn't she? Mary said . . ."

"Lena," Elena said. "Lena, my dear. What an exhibition of bad manners."

The small face tightened mutinously. "Well, I want to see her. I want to talk to her. Why do you keep her a prisoner in here? She belongs to us, doesn't she? Then why don't you . . ."

Jonathan, a quizzical look of amusement on his face, cut in quietly, "That will do. What will Miss Davis think of you, of all of us, at this behavior? Now then, suppose we begin anew."

Lena drew a deep breath. She turned to Cordelia and smiled.

It was impossible not to smile back. Who could resist the melting warmth of that look, of those dark, dark eyes?

"I'm happy to meet you," Cordelia said.

Lena dipped a not very steady curtsey. "Thank you, ma'am. And I'm glad to meet you, too. I thought you would be very old and ugly. Wait until Sam sees you. Just wait. Why, what we thought . . ." She stopped, added ingenuously, "That's why we didn't want a governess, Mother. We were so certain . . ."

Jonathan again interposed. "And where is Sam?"

"Hiding upstairs," Lena laughed. "He thinks if he pretends it's not happening then it isn't. But that's not so. Of course not. For all our pretending Miss Davis is here."

Elena said, "I would like you to go and find him at once." And, "Tell Mary we'll have tea."

Lena grinned, skipped from the room, her blue skirt flying around her.

"You see that you have your labors prepared for you," Jonathan said.

"She seems a very nice child," Cordelia answered. "And clever, too."

"They are both exceedingly clever," Elena told her, without an ounce of pride in her cool voice. "Perhaps too much so. They need a firm hand, and much supervision. I'll expect you to supply both."

Moments later, Lena returned. She was followed by a tall, dark-haired boy. The children both resembled their father, Cordelia supposed. For they were so clearly Moorhavens. Dark hair, dark eyes, quick lithe bodies.

At the introduction, Sam nodded his head, but did not speak.

Cordelia said, "I'm glad to meet you, Sam," and waited.

He said nothing.

Elena murmured, "Sam, Sam, what is it now?"

He raised dark eyes to Cordelia's face. "I suppose you will make us study very hard."

"I hope that you will want to," she retorted.

Jonathan laughed, "The answer will give you something to ponder, Sam, while you work on your small inventions."

Cordelia was about to express interest in those inventions, but Mary came with the tea tray.

Jonathan excused himself, and left the room.

It was as if the quality of the air instantly changed. The light went out of Elena's pale eyes, and the sweetness from her voice. It was as if a certain strength had been withdrawn. Cordelia felt diminished, tired.

She quickly drank the tea Elena served her, then rose.

Lena cried, "Let me take you up. Sam and I will show you the way."

She raced to the door, Sam following more slowly.

Cordelia looked at Elena. "If that is all then . . ."

"For the moment," Elena answered quietly.

Chapter 4

"We'll go straight up," Lena said impatiently.

But Cordelia stopped in the vestibule before two huge portraits.

"Grandfather and Grandmother," Sam said.

No one could have mistaken the older Jonathan for anything but a Moorhaven, Cordelia thought. He was big, with a rough-hewn face, and the dark far-seeing eyes that he had passed on to his son. The older Mrs. Moorhaven was dark, too, wasp-waisted in a low-cut velvet gown, smiling faintly over a bouquet of roses.

Lena danced up the broad staircase, making muffled sounds on the heavy dark green rug.

Cordelia followed her, with Sam at her side.

The wallpaper was patterned with white flowers on a green background and the high ceilings were painted white. Scrolled cornices marked each doorway she passed.

It seemed a long way up to the third floor, to the large room into which Lena at last led her.

"There's a playroom and a school room," Lena informed her. "And my bedroom and Sam's, too."

Cordelia nodded, went to the big window that was curtained in heavy blue velvet. She saw, below her, the glittering marshes, and a rim of the horizon, the blue horizon that must arch over the retreating sea.

She shuddered. From here the humped dike seemed an immense battlement, thrown up as protection against an enemy whose might had already been measured time after time.

Lena leaned at her elbow. "We'll go down there. I know a lot to show you."

"It looks dangerous," Cordelia answered.

"Only if you don't know your way. But I do. Don't I, Sam?"

Her brother shook his head slowly from side to side.

"But I do," she cried. "And so do you."

Mary appeared in the doorway then. "Oh, leave off, the both of you. Miss Ralphine wants you. So go to her, and give this poor girl a chance to catch her breath and unpack."

Lena's small face stiffened. Her cheeks burned red. "I won't. I'm tired of Aunt Ralphine. We have Miss Davis now. We don't need Ralphine any more."

Mary's straight mouth curled with a bitter smile. "Go tell her that."

Sam edged toward the door and disappeared without a word or backward look.

Lena held her spot. "I will not. If you want to repeat it, you may, of course. But I'll say I didn't mean it." Her eyes gleamed. "I'll say I didn't even say it, Mary."

Cordelia cut in gently, "That would be an untruth, Lena. I'm sure you don't intend any such thing. Now, I have some small chores to do. I'll see you later."

Lena sulked, waited, then gave up with a grin. "All right. Later."

When she had gone, Mary laughed, "You'll have a job to do on her. She never heeds the first time, and you'll soon see it. The both of them ... I tell you, I don't envy you."

Cordelia didn't answer. She surveyed the room again, more carefully this time. There was a big four-poster bed covered by a ruffled blue canopy. A heavy wardrobe of light oak nearly covered one wall. The fireplace had a white mantel, its sole decoration two pewter candlesticks with half-burned white candles still in them. A small rocking chair, and a knee-hole desk completed the furnishings. It was a cold place, without much comfort or character. She sighed to herself. Her room at home had been a projection of herself, built up over the years. The curtains she had made with her own hands, the stuffed animals, the bits and pieces that Henry had brought back from his travels. She thought that when her trunk arrived and she put her quilt on the bed, and her animals on the mantel she would feel more at home.

But then she found herself wondering if she would ever feel at home at Moorhaven.

Mary said, "You're hardly older than I am, are you?"

"I'm nineteen," she answered.

"And a teacher, too, " Mary said admiringly. "Well, I expect you had lots of schooling." She tossed her head so hard that it seemed as if her white cap must take wing like a bird but it remained fixed to her black hair. "Not me. The little I had was more than I wanted."

"Do you like it here?" Cordelia asked.

"Like it?" Mary looked surprised. Then, "Oh, you mean because of what my mother told you."

"No. I mean you. Yourself. Do you like it."

"I like having my keep and my pay, and though they're after me in Tembley, all the time, too, they like having the small things I can give them. Is that answer enough?"

"That's answer indeed," Cordelia said. She wished that Mary would remember the admonition given to the children. She would like to have been alone now, to do a few small chores, to collect herself and her thoughts, to change the clothes which she had worn for more than a full day.

But Mary was disposed to linger. She said, "Is there any help you need?"

Cordelia thanked her, said that she would manage herself.

"If there is . . . I'd be glad . . ."

Cordelia smiled her gratitude. Then, "I'll just

change, and put my few things away. And then I'll come down."

"To meet the rest of the family," Mary finished for her. "You have no great treat in store," she went on. "There's Ralphine, and Gregory and Denton. And then you'll know the lot of them." She went to the door. "And, of course, Mrs. Sawyer, Joshua's wife. She's another one to watch out for."

"Watch out for?"

Mary grinned. "If you're smart enough to be a teacher you must know what I mean."

"But I don't, I'm afraid."

Mary opened the door, looked out, turning her head to check both ends of the hallway. Then she closed the door again. "Elena. You'll have to keep her in view all the time. And Ralphine, too. And now I've told you about Meggy Sawyer."

"I don't understand," Cordelia protested.

"None of them wanted a governess. The talk over it was loud and long, believe me. But Jonathan got his way. He always does, as you'll see."

There was, Cordelia saw, a certain brightness in Mary's eyes, a softness in her voice, when she spoke Jonathan's name.

But she asked, "Why did he want a governess? If there were three women, four including you, to attend to the children . . ."

"Attend to them, yes. But that's all. You can see how they mind me, and why should they? I'm only the maid. And I don't know enough. Ralphine . . . well, you'll understand when you meet her. And as for Elena . . . she's too busy playing the mistress of the manor. And having her sick headaches." Mary giggled. "And besides, she's got other things on her mind."

"What things?" Cordelia asked curiously.

"Mrs. Sawyer let it slip one time. Long ago, when Elena married Dennis, the one she really wanted was Jonathan, you see. But he was much too young then. So Elena settled for what she could get. But now that she has a second chance . . ."

Cordelia decided to ignore that bit of ancient gossip. She asked, "Isn't Elena very well?"

"Well enough. Except when she wants an excuse. Which happens often. Maybe that's why she's easy and strict by turns with the children." Mary, leaning against the wardrobe, appeared ready to remain for some time, but before she could go on, she was displaced by Mrs. Sawyer, who, with a cold, no-nonsense smile, remarked that there was silver to be polished below, and if Mary did not find that sufficiently occupying, then she, Mrs. Sawyer, could no doubt discover some cut glass that needed dusting.

Mary grimaced at Cordelia, and sauntered out.

Mrs. Sawyer sighed. "That girl . . ." Then she shrugged. "Are you quite comfortable here? Is there anything you need?"

Cordelia assured the housekeeper that she was certain the room would suit her.

"If not, then tell me. I'll be glad to do what I can." A faint smile curled her lips. "My husband tells me this is your first job."

Cordelia nodded.

"He says, too, that you didn't have the best introduction to Tembley and Moorhaven."

"Oh?"

"Daviette Jones," Mrs. Sawyer explained. "Mary's mother."

"She was kind to me. She took me into the shed so I would be warm."

"She had her reasons, no doubt."

"Perhaps," Cordelia agreed.

"To tell you of the curse. That was her purpose." Mrs. Sawyer sighed. "Do you know, with Mary here, the village of Tembley is as well informed of the business of this house as we are ourselves?"

"I'm sure she means no harm," Cordelia said hurriedly.

"As I am," Mrs. Sawyer agreed. "But it contributes to Daviette's madness, you see. If it *is* madness."

"If?" Cordelia's eyes widened with surprise. "Do you mean that you believe what she says?"

Mrs. Sawyer was silent, her square face expressionless, her gray eyes thoughtful. At last she said, "And what is it that Daviette says?"

"That the Moorhavens pushed back the sea, and the sea will someday reclaim its own," Cordelia whispered.

Again a faint smile curved Mrs. Sawyer's lips. "That's a way of speaking only. Another would be to simply admit that since this house was built, and even while it was being built, it has been touched by tragedy. There was Janina Moorhaven, who died on the road between here and town, when her horse bolted and turned her carriage over. And then later, when we moved here, Dennis was killed in Cuba, and Jonathan was injured there . . ."

"Jonathan?"

"With that still-raw scar on his forehead, and the limp he'll have to the rest of his life, to prove it, too," Mrs. Sawyer said. Then she went on, "After that, the older Jonathan died. And now Jonathan's master. And the house left behind in Tembley burned down to the ground last year."

"Trouble comes in bunches," Cordelia said, thinking of Henry. How he would fume at this conversation. How he would insist on disproving . . .

Mrs. Sawyer's small smile broadened. Her gray eyes suddenly glowed with approval. "Exactly, Cordelia," she agreed warmly. "Joshua and I have been with the family for years. We've seen the children born and grow up. They've hurt no one. And . . . and there's no curse on this house." With that, Mrs. Sawyer nodded, and left Cordelia alone.

It was that message, those final words, that Mrs. Sawyer had come to deliver, Cordelia was sure.

As she busied herself unpacking, she wondered why the housekeeper had considered her errand necessary.

She did not know then that very soon she would begin to glimpse the reason for the housekeeper's concern.

It was late the same evening. Gaslight cast a soft and flickering glow over the long table. Small shadows danced on the snowy linen, and small glints sparkled in the fine cut-glass tumblers.

The elegant dining room was a far cry from the huge old kitchen in which Cordelia had always dined with Henry Ward. She sat uneasily on the edge of her chair, wishing now that she had been allowed to have supper with the children, although she realized that it had been kind of the Moorhavens to insist that she join them. It was their way, she supposed, of resolving her somewhat equivocal position in the household. She was the governess for Lena and Sam, but she was to be in no way considered a servant. She sneaked a quick look at Jonathan's scarred face, and wondered if the decision had been his. Or if it had been Elena's.

She didn't look toward Elena, who presided over the table from where she sat opposite Jonathan.

Earlier she had unpacked. She put her comb and brush on the washstand. She spread the Spanish shawl on the bed to smoothe its wrinkles. She stacked the two books she had brought with her, leather-bound copies of the poems of Emily Dickinson and the stories of Mark Twain, on the kneehole desk. After washing, she had changed to a dark green wool dress. Then she had brushed up her hair and run through the burnished waves the green ribbons Aunt Berthe had given her.

She had found her way down to the drawing room, and, hesitating at the big doors, had been accosted immediately by Denton Moorhaven.

He had a round, dimpled face, and sandy hair. His eyes were as dark as Jonathan's, but not as deep-set. His somewhat short, bulky body was clothed in a red brocade jacket and black trousers. His black boots had scuffed toes.

He had bowed to her, and grinned, and said, "Welcome to Moorhaven. I'm Denton. And you're Cordelia Davis, of course."

She smiled at him.

"Are you loitering here because you don't want to go

in? If so, I'm your man. We can take a quick run through the snow. Or, if you like . . ."

"I just came down," she answered, trying for dignity.

"Then you *want* to go in." He bowed, pulled the door open.

Once in the drawing room, he retreated to a chair in the corner, and left her quite on her own.

Elena made languid introductions.

Gregory, suave and smiling, had murmured, "How do you do? I understand you know Peter Van Nuys. He should be along after dinner."

"No," Cordelia said. "I don't know him. It is my guardian, Henry Ward, who does."

"Then you shall meet him." Gregory's eyes twinkled. "More's the pity, too. I'd sooner that you didn't."

Ralphine gave Gregory a disapproving look, then turned it on Cordelia. "We aren't certain that Peter will be coming. He works so hard, you know. He is a very dedicated doctor. But he will bring his sister with him if he does."

Ralphine had the Moorhaven coloring, but in her it seemed to have somewhat faded. Her skin was sallow, her eyes like chips of agate. She wore a gray dress, and had a matching gray shawl around her narrow shoulders.

Gregory's small smile widened. "Oh, he's a dedicated physician, all right. But I imagine he will manage to visit us tonight. Unless his batteries run down, or out, or whatever you call it." He winked at Cordelia. "Our good Peter has an electric brougham. It purrs nicely when it runs. Which is not always." Gregory's dark eyes, resting on Cordelia, indicated what he thought the special attraction would be that night. And to make sure that no one missed his point, he went on, "He'll be anxious to see how his recommendation appears to us."

"You're embarrassing Miss Davis," Ralphine said tartly. "Do mind your manners, Gregory."

Denton made a sound between a groan and a laugh. Ralphine turned and quelled him with a single look.

Jonathan came in just as Mary announced that dinner was served.

Gregory went in with Cordelia and seated her.

Mrs. Sawyer and Mary served the meal, a roast decorated with potatoes, deep bowls of carrots, and creamed onions.

Now Cordelia became aware of Denton's gaze, following every movement that she made. She found it difficult to swallow. She found it difficult to sit still. His intense concentration embarrassed her, too. She wondered if the family was always this quiet, or if it was her presence that restrained them.

At last Elena said, with a smile at her, "Jonathan, Cordelia told me this afternoon that she believes a woman must make her own way in the world. And that is why she has come to Moorhaven. What do you say to that?"

Heat burned in Cordelia's cheeks, dried her lips, as Jonathan's dark eyes suddenly turned to her, alight with amusement. "Is that what you believe, Cordelia?"

She nodded, unable to bring herself to speak.

"What have we here?" Gregory cried. "A suffragette? A career woman? A . . ."

Cordelia caught her breath, then plunged in. "Wait, Gregory," she said. "You're mixing two things up. One is the vote for women. Which they should have, of course. The other is something else. If a woman must earn her living . . ."

Jonathan's deep voice interrupted her as she had just interrupted Gregory. "Women should have the vote, of course?" There was an amused twist to one of his dark brows. "Did I hear you rightly?"

"You did," she answered, although she was fully warned.

"I don't believe in woman suffrage," Jonathan answered. He leaned back in his chair, smiling at her. "I don't think women do either. Except for some angry few."

Elena rang a small brass bell.

Mary came in with a tray of ices.

The subject was dropped, but through the rest of the meal, Cordelia was aware of Jonathan's dark eyes fixed on her, of the amused quirk in his brow.

They had just adjourned to the drawing room when Peter and Felicia Van Nuys arrived.

He was a tall, very thin man, about thirty years old. He had light brown hair and a small, very trim light brown beard. His eyes were a strange amber color, and very sharp. On entering the room he came directly toward Cordelia.

"I am so glad to see you. I feel as if I already know you, of course. Through your uncle. A fine man, Cordelia. A probing mind."

"Who," Jonathan said dryly, "most probably believes in the vote for women."

Peter Van Nuys grinned. "Why not?" He turned back to Cordelia, "I hope you'll be happy here."

"I'm sure I will be," she told him. "And I thank you for your part in bringing me to Moorhaven."

Felicia Van Nuys was small and slim, but with her older brother's coloring. She said, "I think you must wait until you've lived here a while before you form any judgments, Cordelia."

Gregory laughed softly. "Felicia is prone to a jaundiced view."

"I am not," she flashed. "I'm simply aware that no one can, in a few hours, decide how one will feel. About anything."

Cordelia pretended not to have understood the implied rebuke.

Felicia continued, seating herself on the brown love seat, "I hope you won't find Tembley too isolated for your tastes. It is such a tiny town, and so far away in any case."

"I'm quite accustomed to living quietly," Cordelia told her.

"Oh, yes. Of course. Peter explained that you have been near Ryetown. But still, you may not find this quite what you expected."

Cordelia smiled faintly, agreeably, but didn't answer.

She did not see that she had to explain to Felicia that she had expected nothing. She had not known what she was coming to when she came to Moorhaven that afternoon. She still did not quite know. But she sensed something cool and strange in the air. She raised her head.

Elena was staring at her, her slim face impassive, her eyes glittering under straight brows.

There was something in her look that chilled Cordelia.

"How did you come out?" Jonathan was asking.

"I very much feared you would want to know that," Peter laughed. "We came by carriage, which I think you already suspected."

Jonathan grinned. "Oh? What happened this time?"

"The batteries. And without them, the brougham . . ."

"I think I'll settle for a Packard, powered by gasoline. Your experience, Peter, has saved me some trouble."

"I'm glad to hear it," Peter said sourly. Then, as Cordelia rose, "You must come in to see us in Tembley, Cordelia. We'll arrange it."

She thanked him, and then pleading fatigue from her long journey, she went up to her room.

She felt, as she slipped inside, closed the door behind her, and leaned against it in the dark, as if she had at last reached sanctuary.

She was tired. It had been so long now since she had waved goodbye to Henry in Ryetown. It had been a strain to meet so many strangers at one time. She had no reason to feel as if she had just come through some fearsome ordeal, but that, she admitted to herself, was just what she felt.

At last she pushed herself away from the door and picked her way through the dark to the mantel. There she found the matches she had seen there earlier. She lighted the two gas jets, and then knelt to light the heater on the hearth.

When she rose and turned, she realized that something was wrong.

Chapter 5

The room looked as if a whirlwind had spun through it.

The big oak wardrobe had been emptied, and her few dresses had been tumbled out, and lay crumpled on the floor in an untidy pile. Her petticoats and chemises had been flung in a corner. A stocking was draped around one of the pewter candlesticks on the mantel. The Spanish shawl was still on the bed where she had left it, but now, ripped up the middle, it was in two shredding pieces. Her books lay on the rug beneath the desk.

The gaslight suddenly jumped, and her heart beat harder, faster, at the way the shadows danced and glided around her.

Someone had been here, moving through the dark, guided by malice, to destroy her few poor belongings. This was surely the work of human hands. But whose?

Pulses pounding, she knelt to touch the books. The brown leather, stamped in gold, was torn. Mark Twain. Emily Dickinson . . .

The tears stung her eyes, beaded her lashes. She blinked them away, and rose, suddenly angry.

Whose hands had done this?

She went on quick tiptoe out into the dark of the

hall, and then into Lena's room. The small girl was barely visible under the heavy mound of quilts.

Cordelia moved quietly to her side.

Lena's head was burrowed into the pillows, but a part of her face was visible. A single closed eye. A portion of relaxed mouth. A lock of hair moved gently with her breath. She was sound asleep.

Cordelia backed out, closed the door behind her, and went on to Sam's room.

He lay on his back, arms flung wide, the quilts half fallen to the floor, with one leg thrust out into the cold. He, too, slept soundly, the lashes making dark crescents on his cheekbones.

She covered him with care. He stirred and mumbled and then relaxed again.

The anger was fading now, the hot temper cooling. Cordelia returned to the chaos of her room, certain that the childish mischief to which she had been subjected had not been the work of a child.

Had it been Lena and Sam, one or the other of them would surely have been awake to observe, to listen. Of what use was mischief if it afforded the doer no pleasure? Having convinced herself that the children could not be responsible, she righted the rocking chair and sat down to consider further.

If there was no pleasure in such malice then what motive was there?

Mary's words came back to her. Neither Elena, nor Ralphine, nor Mrs. Sawyer had wanted her at Moorhaven. Though why Mary had not explained.

Could either of the three women have slipped into her room some time while she herself was downstairs? It seemed possible. Mrs. Sawyer had surely been on this floor in that three or four hours. Ralphine and Elena had both left the drawing room after dinner on different pretexts. But so had Gregory, and Denton, and Jonathan himself. Yet it was impossible to imagine any of them slipping up the stairs quietly to do this work. The same held for Felicia and Peter Van Nuys.

Still, the work had been done.

It was meant to tell her that she wasn't welcome here.

She rose, sighing, and went to gather her tumbled dresses. What she had done once, she could do again. As she busied herself putting her things away, she asked herself who did not want her here, and why.

The gas heater on the hearth did little to soften the chill of the room. Shivering, she took up the two pieces of the Spanish shawl.

She had been in Moorhaven hardly more than eight hours. What did this beginning portend?

"I hate numbers," Lena said fretfully. She flung herself back in her small straight chair and scowled at Cordelia.

"And I hate spelling," Sam grumbled, leaning his square jaw on his doubled fist.

In the week since her arrival, and the settling into the routine that she had established at Elena's direction, Cordelia had had time to recognize the ploys offered by the children as avenues of distraction. They were not so different from the ploys Henry had used when, baffled as how to proceed, he had left off dictating to her and begun to complain. But she believed that it was as good for the children to have talk and discussion, as it had been for Henry. She considered it part of her job to encourage them. And besides, she found them interesting. More interesting, she confessed to herself, than she had thus far found the adults in Moorhaven.

Now she smiled at Lena. "You only hate numbers because you're afraid of them."

Lena considered, a scowl wrinkling into her smooth round brow. "It may be that," she admitted finally. "But why am I afraid?"

"Perhaps you don't like the thought of making an error."

"Perhaps. But why are numbers so hard?"

Sam had listened long enough. He said, "When I'm master here, there'll be no need for me to spell."

"Oh?" Cordelia asked. "Then how will you attend to your business affairs? Your Uncle Jonathan spends hours and hours in his office each day, working away at letters and books. How will you manage if you write no better than a dockworker?"

"There are no dockworkers any more," Sam told her in heavy tones of disgust. "And we no longer build our ships, or sail them either."

A faint ripple of uneasiness touched Cordelia. She wondered if Sam knew of Daviette Jones' awful prophecy. She wondered if he had somehow heard of the curse. He was only a ten year-old boy. She did not believe it would be good for him to grow up with that false shadow over his head.

"But we don't need our ships," Sam went on, and if he was thinking of the curse, nothing of that showed on his face. "We have shifted to rail transport, and to other investments. I've heard Uncle Jonathan discuss it with Mr. Alderson from Boston. Uncle Jonathan is very enthusiastic, and wants to go out to the West, to oversee the setting up of the lines. But he is stuck here. With us."

"Why do you say that?" Cordelia asked.

"Someone must run the house, the family," Sam answered, giving her a wise look. "For all of our sakes, you know."

Cordelia had no doubt that he was parroting Elena, and no doubt either now that Elena did not want Jonathan gone from Moorhaven. No more did she herself, Cordelia admitted in her thoughts. For increasingly in this past week she had had to remind herself, on those rare occasions when she had seen him that he was her employer. Her employer. Nothing beyond that. She had had to struggle with a strange hunger that she could repress, but never deny.

Now Lena, tired of being forced into silence by Sam, burst out, "Oh, you don't know anything, Sam. You'll not be master here. What if Uncle Jonathan marries? What if he has children? Then where will you be?"

Sam's face grew round and puffed and red, so that

his burning eyes seemed to shrink to dark pebbles. "Hold your tongue, you infant," he roared. He kicked back his chair and lurched to his feet.

Cordelia rose quickly. "That'll do. Both of you are at fault."

"It's the truth," Lena cried.

"He won't," Sam snarled.

"Numbers," Cordelia said briefly. "And spelling. The both of you. At once, if you please . . ."

Sam crumpled into his chair, bent his head over his desk.

Lena said, "But I hate numbers, and I . . ."

"You're afraid of them," Cordelia corrected, "and the only way to deal with that is to learn them. Now go ahead."

Lena sighed loudly and disgustedly. But after a moment, she, too, settled down to her work, a small tongue thrust from the corner of her mouth as she labored over her sums.

Cordelia watched the two of them.

She did not feel that she knew Sam. It would take longer than a week, longer than a month, to learn Sam Moorhaven. He had a few moments of being relaxed, out-going, but most of the time he was silent, withdrawn. It was hard to guess what he was thinking. She had tried to draw him out about what Jonathan had called his small inventions. But Sam didn't want to speak of them. Only the day before, by accident, she had learned one of them. She had been having a cup of coffee with Mrs. Sawyer in the kitchen, and had heard a shrill bell suddenly go off.

Mrs. Sawyer rose instantly. "That'll be the drainage bucket under the ice box. Sam has saved me many an hour of floor scrubbing. He's rigged a bell and a lump of sugar on a string. When the water melts the sugar, the bell rings. And I know I must empty the bucket."

It was, Cordelia thought, an impressive idea for a ten-year-old boy. She had mentioned it in her letter written the night before to Henry, thinking he would be amused. She hoped, gradually, to gain Sam's confidence.

Lena was something else again. A completely open rebel, who wanted her way, and would have it, as long as she could get it without alienating the affection she wanted. She knew when she would push too far and had learned how to retreat gracefully but in time.

Now, with the first seven days behind her, Cordelia was more certain than ever that neither of the children had crept into her room that first night and scattered her belongings and torn the Spanish shawl that now lay carefully mended on the wardrobe shelf. She was glad that she had not accused them wrongly, glad, too, that she had told no one of her misadventure. It was a mystery that continued to trouble her from time to time, but she tried not to dwell on it. It had happened. It was over. She supposed that some day she would learn what it meant. If it meant anything at all.

Meanwhile there was much to think about. It had become increasingly apparent that Elena's deeply courteous manner covered an inexplicable animosity. Cordelia was certain now that she had not imagined the coolness in their first meeting. She had had fresh evidence of it in one way or another ever since. Not that Cordelia could point to any single word or phrase. But she had seen the long narrow eyes study her reflectively, and sometimes blaze with the cold fire of dislike.

It was hard to understand since Elena certainly gave no evidence of desiring to rear and educate her children herself. She rose late in the day, spent hours at her toilette, and more hours in simple wandering about the house.

It was the same with Ralphine, who had responded to Cordelia's small overtures of friendship with a chill that was positively freezing, and who examined the children each day as if she had expected them to grow horns and tails during the night as a result of Cordelia's instruction. That, at least, Cordelia believed she understood. Ralphine was a spinster. She had, until Cordelia's coming, taken full responsibility for the children in the absence of Elena's interest. Now she felt displaced. Cordelia sympathized with her, knowing how painful such a feeling could be. Did she herself not feel the same toward Clara? Was she not anxiously awaiting a letter from the place she still thought of as home though it was no longer home and never could be again?

Mary had been quite right to warn her of those two. The burden of Elena's concealed dislike, and Ralphine's open disapproval, was a heavy one to bear, to live with day after day. And Cordelia knew that she must live with it, until, in some way she could not now see, she had managed to win them to her side. If that were possible. And she did not know how it could be.

And there were the others to consider, too. It seemed that, rather than making new friends, she had fallen into a nest of those determined to dislike her. Felicia Van Nuys had amply demonstrated a mysterious resentment the first night they met. The reason for it had become obvious the evening before. Felicia and Peter had come to Moorhaven, bringing with them young Helena Falkland, for a few hours of games. It became evident then that Felicia considered Gregory her personal property, for she had grown very tart when Gregory had offered his usual pleasantries to Cordelia.

Ever since her arrival, Cordelia had tried to avoid him as much as possible. She had not found it as easy as she would have liked. Gregory managed to appear the moment she set foot downstairs. If he had lain in wait for her, he couldn't have been more successful. There was absolutely no occasion when he did not appear to smile at her, to banter, to suggest a walk through the snowy fields. She had made it as plain as she could, without being offensive, that she had no intention of granting him anything more than the most superficial politeness.

It was the same with Denton. He would appear just two steps after Gregory, giving her long soulful looks. . Cordelia considered his open admiration sweet, but it was embarrassing and annoying, too. For she had no desire for his company, and his interest in her plainly had angered Helena. She was sixteen, with her hair just up, but her manners did not quite match that symbol of maturity. She had flirted sulkily with Denton, while he tried to make conversation with Cordelia. And at last, Helena had cried, "New faces are best it seems," and flounced away to sit with a disapproving Elena.

Fortunately, with the routine that Elena had established, Cordelia was forced into little association with the adults.

The children had their meals on their own floor, and spent most of their time there, too. They visited with the grownups in the drawing room at tea time, which day after day, had proved to be something of an ordeal. Sam was always more quiet than Elena wanted him to be, and Lena was more obstreperous. Cordelia supervised their meals, but took her own in the dining room. It was only then, and for a few hours afterwards each night, that she saw the others. Gregory and Denton were always in attendance, much as she wished them elsewhere. Elena and Ralphine, too, were always there, and twice now, the Van Nuys.

It was Jonathan who absented himself more often than not. He seemed to avoid the others, as well as Cordelia herself. He worked in his office, rode daily into Tembley, and with Joshua, walked the dike each day. If he had an interest beyond his business affairs and Moorhaven, Cordelia could not guess what it was. Yet he seemed to be an interesting and vital man. One that Henry had approved of. And his approval was never given lightly.

A tall, dark man, Jonathan. With the scar lending an odd interest to the rough-hewn face.

With a start, Cordelia heard, "You're daydreaming."

It was Lena, peering across the desk at her.

She came back to the schoolroom in spirit as well as in flesh. "Have you done your sums?"

"I have," Lena said triumphantly.

Cordelia held out her hand for the somewhat rumpled sheet of paper.

The door opened just then. Ralphine stood there, looking into the room for a moment before she came in, without awaiting an invitation. "Hard at work?" she said.

"I've done numbers," Lena cried. "And I won't do any more today."

Ralphine took the paper the child had been holding out to Cordelia. She examined, studied, frowned. Then she gave her dark head a single shake. "Oh, Lena, you do seem to be getting worse than ever. What a sorry sight this is. You have more errors than I can count. And you've blotted and marked over. You know I don't allow that. You know what you must do."

There was a small cold silence.

Then Lena cried, "You're not my teacher any more," and jumped to her feet.

Cordelia said gently, "Lena, please sit down." She held her hand out for the paper.

Ralphine thrust it at her with a grimace of disgust. "I find it hard to see how a child could retrogress so badly in a week. Peter Van Nuys will be surprised."

It was the mention of his name that brought to mind something that had happened the evening before. Cordelia, observing Peter's arrival, had seen Ralphine go to meet him. He had given her a small silver music box, saying casually, "I thought you would like this, Ralphine." She had tipped back her dark head to smile at him, a sudden pink in her sallow cheeks, but before she could speak, he had turned away to take Cordelia's hand, his amber eyes gleaming. She had thought then how kind he was, and forgotten the look on Ralphine's face. Now, in her thoughts, she saw it again.

Ralphine was saying, "I shall discuss this problem with Elena, of course."

Cordelia repressed a surge of anger. She said quietly, "It must take us some time to become adjusted to each other, you know."

Ralphine retorted, "My brother would like to see you in his office." She drew a deep breath. "If you don't

object, I'll stay here with Lena and Sam. We have a
great deal to talk about."

Cordelia rose, her heart suddenly pounding against
her ribs. What was wrong? Why had Jonathan sent for
her?

She rushed to her room, smoothed her hair, and gave
her dark dress a quick brushing. It was somehow important she look right for this meeting. She did not ask
herself why.

Chapter 6

He sat at his desk before the big window. His face and form were in shadow.

She stood on the threshold, waiting.

He looked up, said, "Oh, yes, come in, Cordelia. I hope I didn't interrupt anything too important in the schoolroom."

"Arithmetic and spelling," she answered. "It can be picked up on my return."

"Then sit down please." He bent his head over the papers before him.

She took the seat he had indicated, a big horsehair chair that had thick arms covered with white lace antimacassars. It reminded her of the chair that had always been hers at home. Her throat tightened. It was still not easy to think of that.

She forced herself to look around the room. She had never seen it before. The window was covered with a white lace curtain and hung with thick velvet draperies. The white walls had a tall set of oak bookcases. From where she sat she couldn't read the titles, but she hoped that some time she would be able to examine them.

Jonathan said, "There. Sorry to keep you waiting."

Her attention, forced away from him before, was now permitted to return. Her throat tightened even more. But no longer with homesickness. He looked so grave, so stern. It was, she had already learned, the way his face set in repose. But now she asked herself if he were about to send her away? Could he, after only one week, and before Ralphine's complaint was even registered, have decided that she was not fit for the position he had given her?

He said quietly, "What is it? You look so ... so frightened."

She swallowed, murmured, "Oh, no. No. It's just that . . ."

"I sent for you only to say that I've brought your trunk from Tembley. It has been sitting in the shed for two days. Joshua found it there after a careful search. He has taken it up to your room."

"Oh, thank you," she gasped, and started to get to her feet.

"A moment please. Or are you in such a hurry to return to the children that you've no time for me?"

She sank back into the chair. "I'm sorry. I . . ."

He leaned his elbows on the desk, and folded his hand under his chin. He stared at her steadily. Then he asked, "What is it, my dear?"

She wished that he would not speak to her as if she were a child, but she blurted, "I thought you were going to tell me that I must leave Moorhaven."

His dark brows drew into a frown. His dark eyes narrowed. "Why would you think that?"

She drew a deep careful breath. She couldn't tell him of the burden of animosity that lay on her, a weight that could not be removed. She couldn't say that Elena watched her the way a cat watches a mouse, that Ralphine detested her. She could not say she was friendless and alone, and had begun to think that she would always be. So she said, "It's not such an illogical thing to think. I have never taught children before. Nor been responsible for them. I feel sure that I can be a satisfactory person, but who really knows until they try?"

A flash of understanding seemed to light his eyes momentarily. She wondered if he were aware of her position in the house, if he knew of the opposition to her. Then he said dryly, "You are here, and here you shall stay. But let me tell you, even if that were not true, it would not be the end of your life. You're very young, and perhaps you don't realize yet how it must be. If you fail at one thing, then you try another. It's as simple as that."

"Yes," she agreed. But she thought that he didn't understand. If she failed here, she had no place to go. She couldn't return to the country house outside of Ryetown. She couldn't ask Henry for help. Then what would she do?

He said, "You said you were fearful that you'd be sent away. Now tell me, is that the case? Or is it that you're not content in Moorhaven?"

It was the perfect opening for the discussion of the truth. Yet Cordelia knew that she must not give way. If she were to stay here, she must not complain against Elena and Ralphine. Nor against anyone else. And what complaint could she truly make? It was a problem for her to deal with. She must win them, or fail to win them, on her own. She couldn't ask his help with that. Nor whine to him that she was friendless and alone.

He said, and his voice was very deep now, "You haven't answered me. And I want an answer."

"I am content here," she told him at last.

A smile suddenly warmed his hard face. "It would be rude of me to call you a liar," he retorted. "But I will tell you that I don't see how you can possibly be content. To spend all your time, day after day, with Lena and Sam, can't be the most enjoyable occupation."

"I assure you," she began, "I don't . . ."

"And then, an hour or two after supper in the drawing room . . ." He straightened up, leaned back in his chair. "I don't consider that the routine you have established in this past week is a good one. Not for you, nor for the children. If you did establish it, that is." He paused, apparently expecting some comment from her. When she offered none, he went on, "I am

not a slave driver, and I didn't bring you here in order
that you spend twenty-four hours a day every day with
the children. Elena and Ralphine are perfectly capable
of being with them some of the time. There is also Mrs.
Sawyer and Mary. You are the governess, however you
must have time for your own interests."

She said, "That's kind of you."

"I've arranged that Mary and Mrs. Sawyer will be
available to oversee Lena and Sam after school hours
whenever you like. And that Joshua will take you into
Tembley if you just ask him. Peter and Felicia will be
very glad to have you, and the Falklands, too, of
course."

She had no intention of taking advantage of Jonathan's arrangements, but she saw no reason to tell him
that. She said only, "Thank you. I appreciate your
concern."

He stared at her for a full minute. Then suddenly he
straightened. He pulled the papers toward him, and
picked up his pen. "That's all," he said curtly.

She felt heat rise in her cheeks, and fled before he
could see her blush. She wondered, as she hurried up
the three flights of stairs to the schoolroom, just what
had happened. She didn't know what she had said, or
not said, that had displeased him. But that something
had she was certain. That dark, sudden-cold assessing
look had to mean something.

"I like her," Lena was saying. "She has beautiful
hair."

Cordelia crossed the threshold in a whirl of skirts.

Ralphine sat at the desk now, hands folded under
her chin in a position exactly like that of Jonathan only
moments before. She gave Cordelia a faint questioning
smile, but her eyes were cold and measuring and dark.

"My trunk has arrived," Cordelia explained

"And he needed to tell you that in person? My
brother can be very surprising indeed."

"Why, we spoke for a bit, too, about the arrangements."

"So I should imagine," Ralphine said dryly.

Cordelia would liked to have asked that the older woman remove herself from Cordelia's place. But it seemed both unkind and impolite to do so. Ralphine had had that particular place for her own for years.

Cordelia drew up a chair, settled herself, and told the children, "If you like, we'll unpack together. I have a few small things that might amuse you."

"Now?" Lena demanded.

"When Sam is finished with his spelling," Ralphine interposed.

Sam said, "I'll never be finished at this rate. How can I think with this continuing talk?"

Ralphine rose instantly. In a cold voice she said, "I'm sorry to have intruded and distracted. It didn't occur to me that I was no longer welcome here." But she was not looking at her nephew. She was looking at Cordelia, hate in the twist of her pale lips, in the gleam of her dark eyes. Then she turned, stalked out, slamming the door behind her.

"Why, Sam," Cordelia said faintly.

"You didn't know how to get rid of her," Lena said. "So Sam had to do it."

"Oh be quiet," he told his sister. "I want to finish so we can go and unpack."

That afternoon, Cordelia found that she had been quite mistaken when she had thought that she could pretend to agree to Jonathan's instructions and then not follow them.

She and the children had no sooner finished emptying the trunk when Mary appeared.

"You're to come with me," she told Lena and Sam.

"But where?" Lena demanded. "Cordelia has some stuffed dolls, and we're . . ."

Mary shrugged. "If you think this is my idea then you're daft. No, no. It's no use pouting at me. And I won't look anyhow. Your uncle says Cordelia is to have some free time each day, and you are to come down to the kitchen with me and Mrs. Sawyer. She is baking bread, and you can learn a thing or two, or bother me if you like. But that's how it's to be."

"I don't want to," Lena said.

Sam went to the door, disappeared into the hallway.

"I've nothing I planned to do," Cordelia offered.

"Then go and tell Jonathan. I'll not tell him for you," Mary retorted.

Lena gave a last wistful look at the dolls on the bed, and then followed Mary out.

Cordelia sighed, went to look out the window. She supposed she should have known that Jonathan would see to it that his injunctions were obeyed. But what was she to do with herself?

She had already unpacked the trunk, and shoved it, with Sam and Lena's help, against the wall. The mended Spanish shawl thrown over it turned it into a small table on which she had set the additional books just arrived. The dolls were on the bed with the stuffed animals. She moved them to the mantel, displaying them between the candlesticks. The sight of them sent a chill of remembrance through her. Just a week before she had found her stockings draped over one of them, and the shawl torn in two, and . . .

She shrugged the memory away, and turned to the mirror. It was framed in molded plaster, thick curling roses covered with gilt. She saw her reflection in the glass. There was a very definite smudge of chalk dust on her uptilted nose. She brushed it away, wondering if it had been there during her interview with Jonathan. She repressed an inward giggle of amusement. How could he have looked so stern while she sat before him with that smudge on her nose? She found herself going over in her mind every second of that meeting, while she looked deep into her own green eyes. She saw the shadow on his face, saw the flash of understanding. She saw the hardness in his mouth as he dismissed her. There was a sudden thrum of pain deep inside her. What had she done to induce that coldness? Why had he become angry with her?

She sighed, turned away from the glass, and went back to the window to stare at the glittering marshes, the small stunted trees that seemed to move with the ever-present wind.

A man walked alone on the humped dike. She knew by his height and form, by his limp, too, that it was Jonathan. She realized that he walked there often. She wondered if he went to check the dike. Did that mean he believed in the curse? Did he think that one day the sea would return to claim its own?

The wind ruffled his dark hair. Now, suddenly, she wanted that wind on her hot cheeks. She snatched up her cloak, and found her mittens in the wardrobe. She bundled herself well, and hurried downstairs.

Yes, yes. That was what she needed. To be out in the air, to escape Moorhaven for a little while at least. To escape Moorhaven . . .

She saw no one in her quick journey, and when she had quietly closed the heavy door behind her, she drew a deep breath of relief.

The air was sharp, but sweet. The January sun was brilliant, blinding. She waited for a moment, then went down the path cut through the snow, straight along the slope toward the great dike.

The cold wind pulled at her. The blue of the sky pressed on her. Halfway down, she turned to look back.

The house loomed against the wall of the cliff, huge and still, windows sparkling like great empty eyes. It was easy somehow to believe that it was a place accursed. A shiver touched her.

She turned her back on the house, and on the thought. She wished now that she had never met Daviette Jones in Tembley. It seemed that what the old woman had told her on that other cold afternoon would never fade from her mind.

From here, climbing the ice-slick stones to the top of the dike, the marshes were not visible. It was as if one would reach the top of the world and then step off into a void, perhaps into the nothingness that those before Columbus had pictured as the edge of the world.

Breathlessly, with a last careful step, she at last rediscovered earth. She stood at the top, braced against the wind, and saw the marshes spreading out below her. Mile after mile of glittering ice, thin as paper, Joshua had warned her, and stands of reeds and stunted black trees.

This was the system Jonathan had devised for holding back the sea should it rise again. This was the cause of the curse of which Daviette had spoken.

Cordelia shivered again. She told herself that the wind was too cold. But she knew it was not the wind that had caused the chill in her flesh and deep in her bones. It was the memory of Daviette's words, the memory of the hands at her wrist, the memory of those burning eyes . . .

There was the sound of crunching footsteps.

Cordelia turned quickly, expecting that Jonathan had seen her, come to join her.

But it was Gregory who climbed up to stand beside her, his wide smile releasing his breath in a white plume. "You were quite engrossed in the view, Cordelia. You'll soon tire of it, you know."

"It's strangely exotic to me still," she answered. "But I must go in. It's very cold after all."

He put a hand on her arm. "Not yet. You always run away. Stay a minute please."

She hesitated.

He said quickly, with a laugh, "Are you afraid of me?"

"Oh, no. Of course not. Why should I be?"

"Then why do you avoid me so?"

"Avoid you? I have hardly managed to do that, Gregory."

He laughed softly. "Then you admit you do try?"

It seemed pointless, and useless, to her, to attempt to dissemble. She said directly, "I am an employee in your brother's house. Any attentions you pay me are embarrassing. I'd hoped you would understand that without my saying so."

There was no laughter in his voice when he asked, "Embarrassing? But how?"

Her cheeks burned hotly, but she answered, "You don't realize, Gregory. If others become jealous . . ."

He answered, "What of it? I owe nothing to anyone, nor do you."

Chapter 7

She wished now that she had been less forthright. She didn't quite know how to proceed. Nothing in her past had prepared her for a moment like this, and she didn't know how to deal with it.

At last she said, "It's not a question of owing. If I'm to live here, it must be with people who like and approve of me."

Gregory cut in roughly, "We all do, Cordelia. And you mustn't imagine what isn't there. No one has a claim on me."

But Felicia's eyes, manner, said otherwise. Cordelia couldn't say that. She saw now, suddenly, that what mattered wasn't fear of Felicia's dislike, but Cordelia's own unwillingness to pretend to an interest in Gregory. Her eyes sought out the place on the dike where Jonathan had been. She wished with all her heart that it was he who had met her.

But Gregory caught both her hands in his. "I'm free to do as I choose. And I can offer you a great deal. I'm not Jonathan, pulled down by a pack of yammering women. Elena, curled up with her smelling salts and migraines, so that he feels compelled to stay in Moorhaven when he'd rather go out himself to set up the depots in the West instead of letting Alderson do it. And Ralphine making cow's eyes at Peter, and hanging on Jonathan as if he were father instead of brother to her. And even poor little Mary, going pink when he looks at her. I'm not Jonathan, no. I'm free. I can take you to San Francisco, to Chicago, to St. Louis. With me, you'll see all of our beautiful country. You'll . . ."

She pulled away from him, knowing that her own cheeks were pink. She felt the heat in them. She said faintly, "Gregory, no, please . . ."

"Are you promised to someone else? Is that it? Do you have a sweetheart? Is that why you were sent here?"

"No," she said sharply. "No. To all of your questions. Not that it's any concern of yours, nor ever likely to be."

Gregory started to speak, then stopped as Denton shouted from the path below.

"Come down," he called. "Helena just rode over from the Van Nuys. We're all meeting there for tea."

Cordelia took the interruption as a good opportunity to evade Gregory. She slipped and scrambled down the stony path, then turned toward the house.

Denton stopped her. "You, too, Cordelia. You're especially invited."

The fur collar of his coat was turned up at his neck, like a heavy brown ruff. From it, his plump face beamed.

She smiled at him. "No, thank you. I've chores to do."

Gregory leaped the last few feet and landed heavily beside her. "This girl has taken it into her head to refuse to associate with all male Moorhavens. Excepting Sam, that is."

"Lucky Sam then," Denton laughed. "But he's not here. And we are." He grinned at Cordelia. "I think we'll carry you off by force. I've already promised Helena that you would come, and she's started back to the Van Nuys."

"I'm sorry for that, but . . ."

Gregory cut in, "Denton, don't argue with the lady. Just go up and ask Jonathan if he ordered her to refuse our company and to stay here on the property forever."

Cordelia gasped, "That's ridiculous. You mustn't do any such thing."

Gregory raised his brows. "Why not? You don't offer a reasonable explanation of your unfriendliness. So I have the right to guess what I will, and ask what I will."

Denton looked at his brother's face, then at Cordelia. His prominent eyes were full of bewilderment. He passed a thoughtful hand through his sandy hair. At last he said, "Gregory, you carry your teasing too far. Cordelia must do as she wishes. I just want her to know that she's welcome to come with us."

She wondered just how hard Helena had pushed the invitation, but she said, "I wish to return to the house."

Gregory gave her a small bow, and turned away.

Denton, frowning, trudged up the slope beside her.

Just as they reached the house, Joshua drove the carriage around from the back.

"You won't change your mind?" Denton asked.

"Another time," Cordelia said lightly, and went indoors.

She didn't know then that very soon she would wish she had gone to the Van Nuys, that she would wish she had delayed the return to her room for a little while at least.

She climbed the steps slowly, trailing her hand along the broad polished bannisters.

The stillness of the house seemed complete. It was as if the very walls themselves breathed softly, absorbing all the usual sounds. There was no bustling about, no laughter, no footsteps.

With a sinking feeling in her heart, she wondered how badly she had erred in trying to deal with Gregory's flirtatiousness in an honest way. It frightened her to think that she might, unwittingly, have made an enemy of him. And perhaps Helena, and the Van Nuys, too, would misunderstand her refusal to visit them that day.

As she reached the long corridor that led to her

room, she heard a very distinct cry. She forgot her thoughts, and broke into a run.

Mary was standing at the threshold of her room, clinging to the partly-open door as if she needed it to brace her failing legs.

"What is it?" Cordelia cried. "Mary! What's wrong?"

And then she saw. There was no need for Mary to explain.

The dolls that she had so carefully unpacked with Sam and Lena's help, and then set up on the mantel shelf between the pewter candlesticks, were now scattered over the floor.

They lay on the blue rug like dead things. Each one had been split neatly down the middle. Bits of gray cotton wadding lay scattered about. Pieces of brightly colored fabric, once gowns and hats in miniature, littered the destroyed bodies. The plump little velvet animals had been dismembered of tails, legs and head. The mended Spanish shawl she had left on the trunk, was torn into four pieces and spread on the quilt that Aunt Bessie had made for her. The books, leather bindings cut, were thrown in a corner.

There was something sickening in the wanton destruction. It was as if a blow had been struck at her, her own body damaged. She shivered, and blinked back tears.

Mary cried, "I didn't do it, Cordelia. I came up just now to turn down the bed for the evening and to light the gas heater, and when I saw it, I became weak all over."

Cordelia stepped into the twilight-filled room. She lighted the gas jets, sank into the rocking chair.

She tried not to see the torn dolls, the ripped book covers. She stared down at her hands.

"I'll go tell Mrs. Sawyer," Mary said.

Cordelia looked up quickly. "No, Mary. Come in and close the door."

With an obvious shudder, Mary stepped over the threshold, pulling the door shut behind her. She made a wide detour around the dolls, and stopped before Cordelia. Her black eyes were anxious as she said, "You didn't do this. And I didn't. Then someone . . ."

Cordelia shook her head slowly. "Hush, Mary."

"But it's wicked. You must tell."

"You saw no one?"

"I was upstairs, doing the Sawyers' room. And then . . ." Mary's voice trailed off. She blinked. "Well, then, I . . ."

Cordelia waited.

"I might as well tell you. You won't give me away. I sneaked off to my room for a bit of sewing."

"So you were in your room upstairs," Cordelia said. "And you heard no one down here?"

"No one," Mary agreed. "But of course I wasn't listening, you see. Except for Mrs. Sawyer to come up. If I'd heard her, I'd have made a run for the dust mop."

Cordelia grinned. "I'm sure of that."

Mary looked at the dolls again. "Wicked. There's a sick mind at work here." A sudden flush touched her cheeks. "Perhaps my mother's not as daft as we all like to think."

"Perhaps not," Cordelia agreed thoughtfully. She found, without knowing how it had happened, that her fingers had reached for the locket and ring that hung at her throat, reached for them and now clung to them for comfort.

"You must tell Mrs. Sawyer," Mary said. "She'll know what to do. Or tell Jonathan himself."

"No, no," Cordelia answered quickly.

"But why not? Are you afraid?"

"Afraid?" Cordelia asked. "Why should I be afraid?"

"I would be." Mary's shoulders hunched under the black uniform. The white cap on her dark hair quivered. "I'd be afraid to find this mess in my room, and afraid to accuse anyone, too."

"There's no one to accuse," Cordelia said. "That's why I must say nothing. And I insist that you do the same."

Mary gave her a doubtful look. "If you're sure that's what you want."

"I'm sure," Cordelia said firmly. "And I want you to promise."

"I will. You mustn't think I want to get mixed up in this. Whatever it is. It's wicked and I want no part of it. I think you'd best consider it for the warning it is and whose hand offered it."

Cordelia nodded, said, "I think you'd better get back to your work."

Mary turned back the quilt on the bed, left the room with a final glance at the dolls on the rug.

Alone, Cordelia sat looking at them, too.

It was curious that on the very day when Jonathan had told her she must spend less time with the children, have more opportunity for her own interests, that this should have happened.

First, on the night of her arrival ... And now, just after Jonathan had given her those particular instructions.

But who could have done it, and why? The same questions that she had asked herself on her first night in Moorhaven presented themselves to her now. For all she knew it could have been anyone in the house.

She had left the room and walked alone on the dike for some time. She had not seen Jonathan after the glimpse she had had of him through the window. Gregory had come down later, and Denton, too. As far as she knew, all the others had stayed within.

But what motive would have led a person to creep in, perform these mad acts of destruction, then creep away, unseen, unknown, to gloat in silence over what had been done?

She could not believe the children responsible.

But what of Ralphine's open rivalry for their attention and affection?

What of Elena's cold, unspoken animosity?

Or Denton's revenge for her open discouragement of his shy attempts to interest her?

Cordelia sighed. She just didn't know what to do, or to whom she might safely turn for advice.

At last, she found her sewing kit. She took up the four pieces of the Spanish shawl, and squinting in the gaslight, she went to work to once again repair the damage that had been done to it.

The snow fell from a leaden sky. It drifted past the window in thick fleecy flakes. On occasion, it drew attention to itself by tapping like quick impatient fingers against the glass.

The sound made concentration difficult, Cordelia knew. Even she found herself looking out, listening, and yearning to feel those flakes on her cheeks.

Lena stirred restlessly, and twisted to look.

Sam simply put down his pen and stared out the window.

It was school time, and not pleasure time, and neither of them suggested otherwise. But the expressions on their faces, and the tense muscles in their bodies, spoke of the same yearning that Cordelia felt.

They had, the three of them, been working hard these past two days. It seemed to be the moment for an adventure, a break in the routine, for the refreshment of change.

Cordelia closed her book. "What if we were to stop now?"

Lena yipped happily and slid off her chair.

"And do what?" Sam asked, with that same curious suspicion Cordelia had seen in him before.

She said, "We might go out of doors. We could build a snow man."

"Or go for a ride in the cutter," Sam suggested.

"Is there one?" she asked, smiling. The thought was in her mind of the cutter Henry had had, of the many rides they had taken, bundled in robes, flashing through the sunlight to Ryetown. The thought of Henry reminded her, also, however, of the letter she had written to him just the night before, answering one of his. He had said that Aunt Berthe grew more feeble daily, but had said no more. Cordelia had pleaded with him in her letter not to send the old woman away. Now, although it was more than a week too soon to expect a reply, she was already anxiously waiting.

Sam was saying disgustedly, "Of course we have a cutter. What do you think?"

Cordelia got to her feet. "Then wrap up warm. I'd love to have a ride. We'll ask Joshua if it's all right."

"It is. Why not?" Sam was already at the door. "I'll tell him to harness the horses." He disappeared, running, down the hall.

Lena went to get coat and mittens while Cordelia did the same. They met at the head of the stairs and descended together.

Jonathan stood in the office doorway. "Where are you off to?"

"We're going to build a snow man," Lena cried. "We're supposed to be in school, but Cordelia declared a holiday because of the snow."

Jonathan grinned. "If you take holidays each time we have a snowfall, you'll never be at your books."

Cordelia wondered if that were an oblique reproach. She said quickly, "This is the first one in a long time."

"And we're going to have a ride in the cutter. Sam is having Joshua harness the horses."

Jonathan looked at Cordelia. "You can handle it safely?"

"Oh, of course. I'm a girl from the country, you know. And we had no servants." Just speaking of it brought back her worry for Aunt Berthe, and her homesickness, too ... A memory of the fire-lit room, and Henry's deep pompous sentences rolling on while her pen scurried across the page, trying to keep up with his dictation ...

"Then have a good time," Jonathan was saying. His dark eyes seemed to linger on her face.

She had the feeling that he might see the hunger for home written there. She thanked him, turned away quickly.

As she and Lena passed the open double doors of

the drawing room, she saw Elena and Ralphine. They sat in opposite chairs, their heads bent over books. Neither of them looked up.

Lena shouted, "We're going out," and scampered by.

Still neither responded with so much as a look or a quiver.

It was, Cordelia thought, as if the two women were made of stone.

She dismissed the thought of them when she stepped outside.

The soft flakes brushed her cheeks with feathery fingers, and the cold air brought a high color to her smooth skin, and a sparkle to her green eyes. The wind cuffed and buffeted her. She raised her face to the leaden sky and laughed aloud.

Joshua brought the cutter through the drifts, tied the horses to the post, and returned to the stables behind the house.

Sam, trailing him, shouted for Cordelia to follow with Lena, to where he had begun the snow man.

It was a good flat spot, not far from the windows of the office where Jonathan was working.

She helped the children mold a fat round body for the man that was to come, and at the same time, she found herself sneaking quick glances at that window. Was Jonathan standing there, watching from behind the lace curtains? Was he admiring her? Her wind-reddened cheeks, and her bright auburn hair against the brilliant whiteness of the fresh snow?

"Hurry," Sam cried. "Hurry. I want to ride in the cutter."

"First the man, as we said it would be," Lena insisted.

The body was done. It took longer to form arms. Twice they broke apart, when they were pressed into place, reminding Cordelia of the torn dolls she had tried to mend. At last, they managed it however. Sam thrust a rake against a smooth round shoulder, and dashed off to return with a bucket which he asserted made a fine hat. They used lumps of coal for eyes, for nose, for smiling mouth, and finally they were done.

Sam allowed them only moments to admire their handiwork before he was off to the cutter.

He climbed in, impatiently waited for Lena and Cordelia to follow. Just as they had joined him, Ralphine came out of the house.

She called, "No, no, children. You must come in now. Your mother wants you this instant."

Lena howled, "We're going for a ride."

Ralphine moved quickly to the horses' heads, seized the bridles. "Your mother wants you this instant. If you don't come I shall go to Jonathan."

Lena's mouth opened on a great rebellious roar of denial.

But Cordelia whispered, "Go on. We'll do it later. Go on, Lena. And you, Sam. No arguments now. Please."

Her whispered plea was successful. The children, grumbling still, climbed down from the cutter, and stamped their way up the steps.

Ralphine released the bridle.

For a moment, Cordelia hesitated. And then, in the same spirit of rebellion that had seized Lena, she started the horses. They stepped out briskly into the snow, with the cutter moving smoothly behind them.

They had gone no more than a dozen yards when the reins were suddenly too slack in Cordelia's grasp. What had begun as an adventure turned into a nightmare. She sawed desperately at the reins, yanking and tugging, but it was no use.

The horses bolted, and leaped free.

The cutter spun on, wildly out of control for another dozen yards, then bounced in a rut and tumbled over.

Chapter 8

Cordelia fell sideways, with the leaden sky slipping over her. She landed on her shoulder and rolled hard, entangled in her cloak.

She pulled herself to her hands and knees, and felt the quick ache of bruises and a burning in one palm. When she moved it, she saw red blood against the white of the snow.

Sam and Lena had come hurtling down the steps and the slope, shouting.

"What happened?" Lena cried. "I thought you knew how to drive a cutter. You told Uncle Jonathan you did."

"You're not hurt, are you?" Sam asked.

"No." Cordelia got to her feet, stood swaying, with snowflakes melting on her cheeks. "No. I'm not hurt. It's all right."

Ralphine, at the door, shouted, "What happened?"

Elena appeared behind her. She stood silent for a moment, then thrust Ralphine aside, and ran to where Cordelia stood with Lena and Sam. She swept them into her arms, then glared angrily over their heads at Cordelia. "Well, what do you have to say for yourself? What did you think to do to my children? If I had not asked that they be sent in to me, they would have been with you. They would surely have been injured."

The cold hand that clutched Cordelia's heart was colder than all the snow around her.

She saw the terror and rage in Elena's face, and did not know how to answer it.

Ralphine said, "What an extraordinary thing to happen. Who hitched the horses? I want to know who hitched the horses, Cordelia."

Sam said, "Joshua did as always. What did you think? That Cordelia did it herself?"

"You are not fit," Elena cried. "I told him so, and now I tell you to your face. You're not fit to care for my children. Why if they'd . . ."

Her voice was shrill, thin, as cutting as the cold wind. It carried far. It carried so far, Cordelia thought, that it drew Joshua from the stables, and Jonathan from the house.

Joshua took one look, his mouth hardening in his beard, and went down to the dike where the horses having run off their panic, huddled together.

Jonathan stood beside the overturned cutter, and looked at it, and then at Cordelia.

"It was a strange mishap," she said helplessly. "I don't quite know how it could have happened. The reins went slack suddenly, and then the horses ran. I don't know . . ."

"But the children could have been killed," Elena said. "Ralphine," she turned to her sister-in-law. "Ralphine, you must know. You were out here to fetch them for me. Why did she drive off that way alone when I asked that the children come in? Why did she behave so wildly? She's not responsible, Jonathan. Something terrible will happen."

"But, in fact, nothing has happened to Lena or Sam," he said quietly. "Nothing except perhaps to Cordelia herself." He smiled faintly at her. "Are you hurt, Cordelia? It seems no one in this family will think to ask."

She put her cut hand behind her back, and shook her head.

He glanced down at the bloodstain in the snow. "Are you quite sure?"

She nodded.

"Nothing happened this time," Elena cried. "But what about next time? She says she can drive the cutter, and immediately has an accident. Thank God, and my own instincts, that Lena and Sam had come inside. But what about next time?"

"Accidents happen," he said, "and there's no harm done. You can't wrap the children in cotton wool, Elena. Until a few moments ago, I heard nothing but laughter."

"Laughter! Oh, yes. She was laughing. I heard it. I saw it, too." Elena gave Cordelia a bitter look. "How terribly amusing to risk the necks of my children. Of your niece and your nephew, Jonathan. Of Dennis' only children, and his heirs."

In the small silence that followed, Cordelia heard Ralphine's muted gasp, and the shuffle of Sam's boots, and the sound of the horses' hooves slipping on ice as Joshua led them back to the stable.

At last, Jonathan said, "All of which has no bearing on what remains no more than a small accident, Elena. One in which neither Lena nor Sam were in any way injured. Since they were in no way involved." He paused, then went on deliberately. "It's too cold. You must all go indoors now."

Elena looked as if she were about to speak.

He said in a low hard voice, "Now, Elena. And you, too, Ralphine."

Elena swept Lena and Sam with her, and, followed by Ralphine, she went into the house.

"I hope you understand that Elena shows the panic of all mothers when she believes her children have been threatened," Jonathan said quietly. "You must not take what she says too seriously."

"But she seemed to think that I would have deliberately . . ."

"No. No, of course not. She is only upset. She takes her widowhood hard, you know. It is as if she has come to fear life itself. Because Dennis was taken from her, she expects whatever she loves to be taken from her as well."

Cordelia wondered, but she didn't argue. She said, "I'm sorry. And I don't know how it could have happened."

"You've nothing to be sorry for. You did nothing. Except have a fall yourself." He took the hand that she had hidden behind her back, and looked at it, frowning. "And cut yourself as well. You'd better go in and wash this off."

But she looked toward the stables. She wanted to speak to Joshua. She wanted to ask him if he was certain that the harness had been secured, the cutter secured when he tied it to the post outside the front door.

Jonathan said, "Go on, Cordelia."

She suddenly had the notion that it was no use in talking to Joshua. He had, of course, made certain all was well before he left the cutter and went back to the stable.

But it had been there, unattended, just outside the house, while she and the children built the snow man well out of view. From where they had been under Jonathan's office window, they would have seen no one, heard nothing.

A shudder shook her, rocked the ground beneath her feet. What was she thinking? Did she suspect that someone had tampered with the harnesses? Did she think that someone had done that, and then Elena, by some strange coincidence, had called the children inside, lest they be harmed in the arranged accident?

"What is it?" Jonathan asked, putting a hand on her shoulder.

She felt a queer warmth at his touch, a tingling. It startled and shocked her. She turned quickly toward the house, saying, "It's nothing, nothing."

She knew, she could feel, that his gaze followed her all the way to the steps. There, she turned back. He was standing where she had left him, still watching her through the softly falling snow. As she looked, he turned away. She knew that he must be going to speak to Joshua.

She took what must be her only opportunity to examine the ground near the post. The boot prints were filling in with snow. Hers, Lena's, Sam's. And there were other ones, too. Small narrow ones. Elena's? Ralphine's? Had they stopped here at the post on their way out to the overturned cutter? Or had one or the other of them been here before. Before the accident occurred?

As Cordelia went inside, she felt snowflakes melting on her cheeks, coursing down her cheeks like falling tears.

Nothing more was said about the incident with the cutter. But Cordelia did not forget it. She remembered it as she remembered what had happened to her clothes on her first night in Moorhaven, and the ripping of her dolls, seven days later. She knew that if the accident had been a planned one it had been, at the most, designed to leave her injured or dead. At the least to make it appear that she was unfit to care for the children. She had begun now to be afraid. But of what, and whom, she did not know.

It was easiest to suspect Elena, but that was too easy. What of Ralphine? What of Gregory, and Denton? Anyone of them could have stepped outside, gone to the hitching post. And one of them could have waited to see the cutter run out of control.

She was certain only that her presence in Moorhaven was anathema to someone. She was certain that she walked in danger. What had been malice had become hate. She kept her own counsel however. There seemed no one to whom she could turn, no one she could trust.

It was a dark afternoon in mid-February when Cordelia stood at her window considering these things.

Ralphine had triumphantly borne off Lena to do some sewing, and Sam was with Joshua at the stables.

Felicia and Helena had driven out from town together. Cordelia imagined them, gathered before the fire with Gregory and Denton, whispering so as not to disturb Elena who had another of her migraines.

But Cordelia wanted to avoid them. She dressed warmly and slipped out through the kitchen, smiling at Mrs. Sawyer's cautioning, "Be careful, Cordelia. There's been a bit of a thaw."

The cliff behind the house was steep, and snow-covered, and thick with tall blue spruce. She made her way toward it, and then up, moving in slow and careful stages.

She thought that there, on the high bare summit, she would be free of the spell of Moorhaven.

She would be able to look at the horizon, perhaps even gaze on the distant sea. The sea that Daviette Jones swore the Moorhavens had pushed back, the sea that Daviette swore, in her mad way, would some time return to claim its own again.

It was a laborious climb, and took much longer than Cordelia had thought it would.

Sunset colored the lowering clouds by the time she reached the dark bare windswept point.

Below her, the house seemed small and insignificant on the broad plain that gently sloped to the glittering marshes where the dark trees stood sentinel against the sky.

The horizon was darkening. She had no view of the rim of ocean as she had expected. She rested for a few moments, stamping her numb feet, before turning back.

It was when she started down that a strange unease filled her.

The mauve sky shown through the heavy limbs of spruce like bits of stained glass, and beneath them where Cordelia struggled on the trail, the shadows were darkening. The wind had grown strong now, ambushing her from behind tall snowy boulders and through narrow ravines. The trees rustled and sang and whispered, and from every direction there were unidentifiable sounds. Very quickly it became hard to see well enough to find her way.

Yet, she reminded herself, just below, and not very

far now, the windows of the house must shine from the decorated globes of the lamps that Mrs. Sawyer would have lighted by now. The fire would be leaping high on the hearth. Elena would be presiding over the tea tray if she had recovered enough to do so. Cordelia fixed the vision in her mind, and moved quickly from boulder to boulder, tree to tree, skidding once and catching her balance only with good luck. The sounds grew louder now. Her own breath rasping in her throat. And crackles of ice, and thuds and rushes.

And then, from somewhere behind her and higher up, there came a peculiar booming echo. It seemed but an instant later that a vast crack of thunder exploded around her.

Even as she identified the noise, and knew it for what it was, the source of it was upon her.

It came roaring down the hillside, a huge wall of snow that seized her and shook her, and threw her sprawling. She fell with it and under it and was rolled and rocketed down, and down, until the limbs of the trees opened wide and the mauve sky fell upon her . . .

"Get the horses ready," Jonathan was saying. "We'll take her in to Peter."

Those were the first words Cordelia heard. His voice, concerned, frightened even, was the first one that she heard. There were others, faint twitterings from far away. But his low hard tone was the only one that mattered to her.

She opened her eyes to find him bending over her. His hands were on her shoulders, partly raising her from the snowy ground, while Joshua tried to slip a robe around her, and Gregory and Denton pushed forward to see her.

She said faintly, "I'm all right, I think."

"Be quiet," Jonathan told her. "Save your breath, and don't move."

"But I am all right," she insisted. "I think I may have bruised every bone in my body, but I'm sure none are broken."

Jonathan sat back on his heels. His frowning face seemed to soften. "Then you're very fortunate. Do you realize how reckless it was for you to climb the cliff alone? That snow fall could have . . ."

"Jonathan," Gregory cut in, "are you certain this is the time for a lecture?"

"What about Peter?" Denton asked.

Jonathan nodded, rose. "Joshua?"

The heavy-set man hurried off into the darkness.

Denton picked up a lantern and it was only then that Cordelia began to realize that the men could not have stumbled upon her by accident. They must either have been out searching for her, or seen her as she fell.

She would have asked, but Gregory bent to raise her to her feet. Jonathan brushed him aside, and swept her up into his arms.

"But I can walk," she protested.

"You'll try that on steadier ground," he answered.

"I'd like to know what happened," Gregory muttered.

"And you will," Jonathan retorted. "But later."

Cordelia closed her eyes. She felt safe now. She felt secure with his arms around her. She wished to stay within their encircling warmth forever.

The footsteps of the others crashed ahead. Holding her, Jonathan followed, limping carefully along the path she had earlier climbed alone.

Too soon the lamps of the house cut through the darkness to dim the rays of the lantern swinging from Denton's hand.

Inside, Jonathan put her on the sofa in front of the fire, while Ralphine and Elena demanded to know what had happened.

"Cordelia was on the cliff. There was an avalanche," Gregory explained."

"Is she hurt badly?" Elena asked in a cold even voice.

Cordelia raised her head. "No. Just shaken up." She smiled faintly. "And perhaps still a little frightened."

"Joshua's hitching the horses. We're going to take her in to Tembley," Gregory said, ignoring her words.

She pushed herself up, sat trembling on the edge of the sofa. "It isn't necessary," she protested.

"You hardly know," he answered. "If you could see your color, or rather lack of it, and the cuts on your face, you would be less insistent on your being all right."

"But what on earth happened? Felicia and Helena waited for you to come down, Cordelia . . . and then I sent Mary up, but you weren't in your room. Mrs. Sawyer said you'd gone for a walk . . ."

Cordelia put shaking hands to her cheeks, to her damp hair, darkened by melting snow. "I climbed the cliff to see the view. And it got dark. I could hardly find my way down." Her voice trailed off.

She was remembering the rustling sounds around her in the dark density of the trees, the sudden echoing boom, and the thunder of rushing snow hurling itself at her.

"Really," Elena said disgustedly. "You could try the patience of a saint, Cordelia. What a foolhardy thing to do when we've had a thaw these past few days. I think you surely tempt the Moorhaven curse."

It was then that Jonathan, silent since he had carried Cordelia in, spoke finally. "That will be enough, Elena." And to Cordelia, "I hear the carriage outside."

Chapter 9

"Wait," Ralphine protested. "If Cordelia is injured Peter must see her. But we all know what we know. And if you take her to Tembley the talk will start all over again."

"I have no interest in town gossip," Jonathan retorted. "And neither should you." He bent his dark head to Cordelia. "All right?"

She nodded, rose, and looked with wondering eyes from the narrow pale face of Elena to the cold hard face of Ralphine. They both believed in the Moorhaven curse, she thought. Or they pretended to believe in it.

But it had been no curse that had brought the avalanche crashing down upon her. It could not be anything but a natural force. Some loose stone, working free. Or an animal trotting across the cliff at some weak point in the frozen snow. And somehow she herself had just managed to be in the right place, at the right time. Somehow . . . Just as somehow the horses had come loose from the cutter . . .

A shiver touched her, stirring deep and primitive fears. There was light, and against it, the dark. There was good, and against it always, evil. Evil . . . the faint stirring became suspicion.

She had wondered if someone had tampered with the horses' harnesses while the cutter stood tied just outside the front door. Now she wondered if someone, unseen, unknown, had climbed the cliff behind her, circling away, always out of sight, to the summit? Had someone silently watched her while she looked at the house below? Had someone waited until she began her descent? Had someone deliberately rolled a log down the incline to start the avalanche that had come down at her out of the darkness?

A wave of dizziness swept her. And the pale light of the room seemed to fade away into glimmering shadows.

She was aware of Jonathan's arms around her, and heard, as from a distance, his quick, "Gregory, ride in for Peter at once."

She was aware of being eased to the sofa, of being covered. But the shadowed room still seemed to spin around her. She clenched her fists, fighting to retain consciousness, while questions whirled through her mind. How was it that Denton and Gregory and Jonathan had been together when they found her after she fell? Had they come out in a group? Or had they been separate and then met by chance? And what of the women? Had Felicia and Helena stayed in the house with Elena and Ralphine? Or had any one of them, told by Mrs. Sawyer that she had gone for a walk, slipped out to follow her?

Trembling shook her. She felt a touch on her shoulder, and opened her eyes.

"Are you in pain?" Jonathan asked.

"I'm sorry. I felt faint. Perhaps now . . ."

At that moment, Mary swept into the room like a leaf blown on the wind.

Her dark hair was disarrayed, and her white cap had slipped to one side. Her face was white with fright, and her eyes were rimmed with tears.

"Denton just told me what happened," she cried, and flung herself down beside Cordelia. "He said you were knocked senseless by a snow fall and might have frozen to death if you hadn't been found."

"But I'm not hurt," Cordelia said. "It's nothing."

"Not hurt," Mary wailed. "But you could have been."

Elena interposed, "Mary, what is this? You must try to exert some control. Why have you hurled yourself in here shouting and weeping? Cordelia has had a small accident. It is nothing. She says so herself. She . . ."

Mary wailed, "My mother warned her."

Elena murmured through thin lips, "You sound as mad as she is, Mary."

But Mary implored Cordelia, "Why don't you tell him?"

"Really," Ralphine said quietly, "this is no concern of yours, Mary. Tell what? Tell whom? You make no sense at all."

Jonathan moved slowly until he stood over Mary, his big body interposed between Cordelia and the others. He said, "I want to hear Mary out. Will you, Ralphine, and you, too, Elena, leave us for a little while?"

"This is no time to consider a servant girl's whims," Elena cried.

"Please, Elena."

Ralphine said, "I'll stay and attend to Cordelia."

Jonathan turned his dark head and regarded her silently for a moment.

She shrugged, raised her brows, and left the room. Elena followed her.

Jonathan turned back to Mary. "Now then. What is this that you want Cordelia to tell me?"

"Let it be. Please," Cordelia whispered. "No, Mary. Don't."

"But I can't," Mary said. "This much is my fault, you know. For not saying. And if anything else happens, it will be my fault, too. He must know, Cordelia."

"I must know what?" Jonathan demanded, his dark eyes on Cordelia's drawn face.

She shook her head, bit her pale lips.

Mary said, "Why, from the first day she came she has been . . . has been . . . Oh, I don't even know the words. But my mother warned her. And then it began

to happen. It did. It did. You may sneer at the mad old
woman in Tembley, but she was right in a way."

"What began to happen?" Jonathan asked harshly.

Mary gulped. Her sallow face turned red and then
white. "Tell him," she pleaded.

But Cordelia said nothing. She couldn't. She couldn't
even explain why she was so sure that to discuss the
events that had taken place since her arrival would be
to open the door upon a danger she couldn't name.

Mary said, "The first I knew of it was the day she
came. Though she never mentioned it to me. She had
unpacked and put her things away. Then someone went
in and tore her shawl; ripped her books, and threw her
dresses on the floor."

Jonathan looked down at Cordelia. "Is that true?"

She nodded, but didn't speak.

Mary, having opened the gates, allowed the flood to
pour forth. "And then I saw it with my own eyes again.
Right after the trunk arrived. She unpacked it with the
children helping, and set her stuffed dolls and animals
on the mantel. She had done up the room just right, her
own little place, I thought. And Mrs. Sawyer thought
so, too. Then that evening, when I went up to turn
down the bed for the night, I found everything destroyed. The dolls and animals cut to pieces, the pretty
shawl that she'd mended torn again, too. The books . . .
everything, everything . . . And now . . . now she's been
hurt. Someone wants to hurt her, and she has been."

There was a brief silence.

Then Jonathan said, "Thank you very much, Mary.
You may go now."

She mopped her tearful face with the edge of her
white apron, and though Cordelia knew that Mary
considered herself grown up at sixteen, the look that
she turned on Jonathan was a child's hopeful, trusting
one. And yes, yes, it was a loving one, too, Cordelia
realized.

"You will make him stop it, won't you?" Mary
asked.

"Make *him* stop it?" Jonathan repeated.

"Him, or them, or whoever it is," she whispered. "Or whatever it is. You must stop it. Or else send Cordelia away at once."

Jonathan went to the door, opened it. He jerked his head toward Mary.

She slipped by him, hurrying now, and disappeared into the shadows of the hallway.

He closed the door firmly, returned to where Cordelia lay.

She looked up at his stern face fearfully.

"Did you think," he asked coldly, "that I would not care, or be concerned? Could you possibly imagine I would have no interest in what happens to you in this house?"

She swallowed hard. She knew that he expected, demanded, some answer. But she didn't know what to say. She had been afraid to tell him of the malice that had beset her. Afraid because of the words Mary had just spoken. If she were to admit what had happened, he would send her away. And where would she go? What would she do? There was no place for her in Henry's house, not as long as Clara was there. There was no place for her in all the world, it seemed suddenly.

And yet, yet, what had she done? Why had this malice turned against her? It was easier to believe in the curse on Moorhaven than to understand what had befallen her.

He said, "I am completely responsible for those who live under my roof. I will deal with this, Cordelia. You need not be afraid any longer."

She wondered if it had occurred to him to consider the incident with the cutter as well. Mary had made the fall from the cliff seem part of the whole by telling of it all together. Had Jonathan noticed that? Did he realize that what had seemed to be an accident might not be an accident at all?

At last she said aloud, "I've brought trouble here. Not meaning to, nor wanting to, nor understanding why, but I've brought trouble here. I'm sorry for that."

"Let's be honest with each other," he said quietly. "You didn't speak of these things. Were you protecting someone? Who do you suspect has been subjecting you to these . . . these indignities?"

"I don't know."

He sighed, asked, "Is it the children? Do you think Lena and Sam . . ."

"No," she said quickly. And realized at once her error. If she didn't think it Lena and Sam then she must suspect one of the adults. Children might be guilty of mischief, but they could not be guilty of the kind of planning that caused the cutter to overturn, or the avalanche to engulf her on the cliff.

"You don't think it was the children," he said gently.

She shook her head. She wouldn't shield herself behind them by accusing them. She mustn't do that. She mustn't be that unkind. She knew, though, that her denial would lead Jonathan to consider further. She watched his still face

He surprised her by saying, "There is more to this than you imagine. You, with your youth, your protected life, could not dream . . ."

She thought then that he must know, see, understand that which she herself didn't understand. Though he didn't speak of it he must link those first assaults on her property to this apparent assault on her person, even on her life.

"All right, Cordelia. I'll see about it," he said.

"You won't make me leave?" she pleaded. "If only there were some way . . ."

"We'll not talk of that now."

She closed her eyes to conceal her relief. She did not want him to realize the strange conflict in which she found herself. She was frightened. But at the same time she had discovered that the thought of going away, of leaving Jonathan behind, induced pain which she had never before experienced. No, not even when Henry had told her she was to leave home had she felt such pain. In these weeks something had happened to her.

Perhaps it had happened the very moment that she first
saw Jonathan.

She allowed herself to drift, aware of his presence
beside her in the warmth of the firelit room.

She allowed herself to dream, remembering how it
had felt to be wrapped in the strength of his arms . . .

Peter smiled down at her, but his amber eyes remained serious. "You're fit enough," he said. "Though
I shouldn't have expected it. I gather you're a hardy
enough girl, Cordelia. Even so, people bowled over by
avalanches don't usually come out of them so well." He
sat back, ruffling his light brown hair. "A few cuts and
bruises easily attended to, and that's it. I pronounce
you undamaged, sound in mind and in limb."

Suddenly his smile was gone. He said, "Cordelia, I
want to be your friend. Is it possible for you to think of
me that way?"

She nodded, giving him a quick look.

"There are many hazards in Moorhaven. Hazards, it
appears, for which you haven't been prepared."

"What do you mean?" she asked quickly.

"You know, I think." He lowered his voice, added,
"I thought you'd think of me as your friend. Then you
must trust me."

She didn't answer him.

He went on, "You must realize that I am responsible
for your being here. I, and I alone. If I hadn't spoken
to Mr. Ward, told him of the position here, you would
still be safe at home."

"Oh, I doubt that," she contradicted him. "I expect
I'd have been somewhere else by now."

"Whatever the truth of that, it's my doing that you
are here. Now. What is this all about? What frightens
you so?"

She shook her head slowly. "Peter, I'm afraid I don't
know."

"When Felicia returned to Tembley this evening she
was disturbed, Cordelia. She said that she and Helena
felt that you were deliberately avoiding them. That

you'd gone out for a walk rather than visit with them. Is that true? Is there some reason for it?"

She had learned from her experience with Gregory that to be too forthright was to make trouble. She knew that she mustn't tell Peter that Felicia had plainly indicated her jealousy over Gregory's interest in Cordelia. That Helena was openly angry that Denton rode in to Tembley less frequently since Cordelia's arrival at Moorhaven. She found herself wondering now if either of these young women had left the house, and knowing that she had climbed the cliff, followed her.

Peter, his amber eyes narrowed, said, "Gregory told me that this isn't the first time you've had a misadventure. There was that business with the cutter."

"It wasn't my fault," she said angrily. "No matter how it might appear to you, or what Gregory or Ralphine told you . . ."

"Ralphine felt you had been reckless. Nothing more," Peter retorted. "But that wasn't my concern. I just don't like two such accidents happening. Perhaps lightning does strike twice in the same place. But a doctor is not inclined to think so when his experience has taught him otherwise."

She didn't know what he meant, but she wouldn't ask him. It seemed to her that every bone in her body had begun to ache. Though she was warmly wrapped, and the fire was high, there was an untouched lump of ice within her. She wanted only to be left alone now, to sleep, to forget the booming echoes of the snow wall racing after her.

Peter went on, "And this thing that happened this evening . . ."

"That was not my fault either," she said finally.

"It was perhaps a bit reckless for you to go out alone into an unfamiliar terrain."

She sighed, raised her eyes to meet his. "What are you suggesting?"

"You're too pretty a girl for the place," he said gently, smiling at her. "I think you're too tired for any more of this discussion as well. So I suggest, for the moment, that you go to bed, with a sleeping draught that I will give you. Take one packet, and one only, along with a cup of good strong tea. Then, in a few days, when you're completely recovered from the shock, we'll talk about it again."

The door opened as he got to his feet.

Felicia thrust her head in. "Well, what is it? Is the consultation to go on through the whole night, Peter? Is something wrong with Cordelia that none of us knew about?"

"I'm finished," Peter said. "Cordelia is all right. I've told her to go to bed. If you'll call Mary to help her upstairs, and have Mrs. Sawyer make up a pot of tea, I'll speak to Jonathan, and then we'll start back to Tembley."

"All right," Felicia answered. "Jonathan's in his office, waiting for you."

Peter nodded at Cordelia and left the room.

Felicia came and stood over her. "You've had a bad time. It must have been frightening."

"It was." Cordelia smiled faintly. "I'm lucky." Her fingers crept to the locket and ring at her throat.

Felicia frowned. "Luckier than you deserve, I think. Whatever possessed you to climb the cliff alone? It's a dangerous place at best. And today wasn't best."

"I didn't realize it then," Cordelia answered.

"You might think of it as an omen," Felicia said softly.

"An omen?"

"Of what is to come. You already know, of course. Daviette Jones told you all about it. And I suppose others have, too. The Moorhavens are doomed, and those who are tied to the Moorhavens are doomed with them. Think back over these last few years, and you'll see that it's so."

With that, Felicia turned, and flounced from the room, leaving Cordelia alone.

Chapter 10

Were it not for the aching in her bones, Cordelia would have thought her terrible struggle the evening before could have been nothing except a dream from which she had at last awakened.

She had taken the sleeping draught Peter gave her, had fallen into the big bed and slept so heavily that it was well into the morning before she awakened.

Now, up for a little while, aware of her bruises, but driven from bed by a deep restlessness, she finished dressing. She swept her auburn hair up, anchoring its loose waves with pins.

Outside her door, there were voices.

"Shh, Lena. If you wake her up, Uncle Jonathan will tear your head from your shoulders and throw it into the marshes."

"He won't. He likes me. Besides, I'll tell him that you were the one who woke her up."

"Ralphine said we're to go into the schoolroom and stay there."

"But Ralphine doesn't really care what we do, Sam."

"I know. I know. That isn't the point though. She said . . ."

"But I want to see Cordelia," Lena cried. "Cor . . . de . . . lia!" The name was a loud squeal.

Cordelia smiled to herself as she hurried to open the

door. She must admit to having been listening in order to prevent more mayhem.

When she stood before them, the children turned eager faces toward her.

Sam dropped his hands from Lena's shoulders.

She said, "You're all right, aren't you? You're not sick, are you?"

"I'm fine," Cordelia assured her.

"We've been instructed at least forty times. First by Mary, then Mrs. Sawyer. After that it was Mother, and Ralphine, and just now, Uncle Jonathan stopped us on the steps. To say we must be quiet and leave you alone." Lena gave a small giggle. "But I wanted to see you. I wanted to be sure that you were really here."

"Certainly. Where else would I be?"

"You might have run away," Lena said wisely, tossing her dark curls.

"But why would I do that?" Cordelia asked.

Lena's eyes sparkled. "It's supposed to be a secret. But I heard them. Mary told Mrs. Sawyer. She said if you'd any sense at all, you'd run away as far as you could. Run away to save yourself."

Cordelia repressed a shudder. The children must know nothing of what she suspected. She said, "You have extraordinarily large ears. And it is very rude indeed to listen to adult talk and then repeat it to others."

"Maybe," Lena agreed. "But is what Mary was saying, and Mrs. Sawyer agreeing true? Are you in danger?"

Cordelia forced herself to laugh. "I think that's quite obviously not so. Here I am, and here I stay. And you may very well regret it, because I think it's time for your lessons, and I see no reason at all for you to avoid them today."

"Ralphine said . . ." Sam began.

"Oh, yes. I understand. But I'm well, and up, and determined that we shall go to work together," Cordelia told him firmly.

She had turned towards the schoolroom when Denton appeared at the top of the stairs.

"Jonathan asks how you are this morning," he said.

"I'm fine. We're about to take up the usual routine."

"But didn't Peter say you were to rest for a few days?"

"I have no reason to," she answered. She didn't explain that the worst thing she could imagine at the moment would be to remain alone and unoccupied in her room, with her mind seeking answers it could not find.

He came down the hall, frowning, with odd new lines in his plump face and his prominent dark eyes full of uneasiness. He sent the children off with a curt, "Go along for a minute. Ralphine will be up any time. I want to talk to Cordelia."

Lena balked, but when he gave her a hard look, she went. Sam followed her, without protest, but turned twice to look questioningly over his shoulder.

When the two of them were alone, Denton said, "Cordelia, I've something to say to you."

He looked as if he were about to step into her bedroom. She blocked his way by standing in front of the door, then reaching back to close it firmly behind her. She was determined not to permit even the appearance of an impropriety, nor did she want him to see the mended stuffed animals that were displayed on the mantel, and the repaired dolls. These were her things, the room her own private place. She didn't intend to share it.

She said, "Yes, Denton. What is it?"

"I don't like what happened last night. I know that you, and the others, believe it to have been a freak accident, perhaps due to the thaw. But I don't. I can't somehow." He waited, tugging at his embroidered vest. But when she said nothing, he went on, "I rode into Tembley earlier, and spoke to Helena's parents. They offer you a place in town with them. They'll be good to you, Cordelia. And you . . . you will be safe there."

She supposed he was right. The elder Falklands

would have her, and she would be safe. But what of Helena? How would she like Cordelia living with her? But it didn't matter. Cordelia knew that she wouldn't leave Moorhaven. Not unless she was forced to.

She said steadily, "Thank you, Denton. It was thoughtful of you to worry about me. But accidents do occasionally happen. I've no reason to leave here."

A chill touched her, ran through her flesh. The night before Felicia had told her that she wasn't safe in Moorhaven. Now it was Denton.

And she found herself wondering if it was an altruistic motive that moved him to seek help for her, a place for her, or if there had been some other motive. Why did he want her gone from Moorhaven? Was it he who had circled her on the cliff to start the slide that had almost killed her? Was it he who had maneuvered the accident with the cutter so that she would appear reckless, or perhaps be injured? Was it he who had hated her from the first moment she set foot in Moorhaven?

"You've reason enough," he said quietly.

She looked into his face. No. No, she thought. It was not hate that she saw now in his eyes. Regretfully, she recognized the pain there, the shy hunger. A young man's hunger.

She said, "Denton, we're good friends. Truly. You know that, don't you?"

He smiled slightly. "Friends, Cordelia? Well, all right. Let it be that then. I am willing, grateful even. If you're willing, too." He was plainly disappointed but also uneasy. "But we're not all made the same, Cordelia Gregory . . ."

"Let's not talk about him," she said quickly.

"I'm sorry. I think we must. He isn't like me. He won't be friends with you. He and Felicia were very nearly engaged before you came. Since your arrival he is much less interested in her, and . . ."

"Do you mean that Gregory would . . . would harm me? Harm me because I don't want his attentions?"

"Harm you?" Denton gave her a blank look. "Oh,

no. No. I only mean that he'll not allow you to be friends with him."

Was that intended as a warning? Cordelia wondered. Did Denton mean her to understand, without spelling it out more clearly, that Gregory was her hidden enemy? Or was the implication that Felicia threatened her? Felicia? Could she have left the others, slipped away to the cliff? But what of Helena? Elena? Any of the women might have done it. Or, she thought, any of the men.

At last she said, "I think we must all do the best we can, Denton."

"Then you won't go to the Falklands?"

"I can't," she answered, slowly shaking her head.

"Be truthful with me, Cordelia. Is it because of Jonathan?"

A quick hard anger swept through her. Yes, yes, it was true. She did not want to leave because of Jonathan. She had no reason to stay, stay where she was plainly unwanted, and perhaps in danger, except for what she felt for Jonathan. Yet how dare Denton speak to her like that? He had no right to.

"That's no concern of yours," she flashed. And realized the admission she had made with her words. She went on quickly, "It would be no concern of yours, that is, if it were true. But it's not. Jonathan is my employer. Nothing more."

"Of course," Denton said, with the same ironic tone of voice that she had often heard in Jonathan's. "Of course, Cordelia. Forgive me." He moved away, then turned to add, "If you should change your mind, be certain to tell me. About going to the Falklands, I mean."

She stepped back into her room, closing the door gently behind her.

She went to the window. From there, she could see the circular hump of the dike, and the sparkling marshes beyond it. She could also see Jonathan's tall black silhouette against the sky as he moved slowly along in his usual inspection tour with Joshua.

She wondered if, as he limped there, he heard in his mind the words that Daviette Jones had pronounced. That the sea would return to claim its own. She wondered if he believed, as Felicia did, that the Moorhavens were doomed.

She watched until he and Joshua both disappeared from sight. Then she decided to go to the schoolroom. The children would be waiting for her. There was nothing to be gained by remaining alone, and much to be lost in admitting fear to herself.

Lena was crouched mutinously in her chair, eyes flashing.

Sam had his nose buried in a book, plainly detaching himself from his surroundings.

Ralphine was at Cordelia's desk, tapping her long white fingers impatiently. She ignored Cordelia's entrance. She said, "Lena, you will and you must. If you do not, then I shall discuss it with your mother."

Lena gave a triumphant shout when she saw Cordelia. She cried, "You see. I told you. She's up and about. She'll take us today. Not you."

Ralphine turned to glare at Cordelia, then said to Lena, "I remember when you were glad enough to have me help you with your tables. I remember when you were happy enough to climb into my lap and eat sweets from my fingers."

"But that was then," Lena cried. "Now Cordelia can help me."

Cordelia said quickly, "Thank you, Ralphine. It was good of you to take over for me. But I do think I'd prefer to be up and about."

"Then you're quite recovered from last evening?" Ralphine asked.

"Oh, yes."

"I thought you were told to rest for a few days. And Jonathan was quite specific . . ."

"There's no need."

"How nice that you're so sturdy," Ralphine went on reflectively. "Anyone else would have suffered a broken bone or two. At the very least."

Was there regret in Ralphine's thoughtful voice? Was she concealing disappointment that she had not accomplished the task she had set for herself? Cordelia didn't know the answers to these questions.

Aloud, she said, "Perhaps I am more fortunate than sturdy." She went to the blackboard, picked up a piece of chalk. "Lena . . . what about the multiplication table?" And then, "Sam, it is time for spelling, and you know it, and not time for reading Washington Irving. So please . . ."

Ralphine rose without a word, and without a word she left the room.

"She's angry," Sam said quietly, but with an obvious note of satisfaction in his voice.

"She's going to complain," Lena told him, more in joy than in fear.

"There's a letter for you," Joshua said, and grinning through his beard, he put it into Cordelia's hand.

The family was gathered for tea.

Ralphine sat grimly in the big horsehair chair, while Elena presided over the silver service from her usual place on the sofa.

Cordelia was aware of both women watching as she accepted the letter, and slipped in into her pocket. Although she was anxious to read what Henry had written, she had no intention of opening her letter before curious eyes.

"Jonathan said he'll be in shortly," Joshua told Elena.

She nodded. Then, "And the others?"

"Denton and Gregory rode in to Tembley a little while ago."

Elena nodded again, and Joshua left the room.

Ralphine said softly, "Then Gregory has gone to see Felicia, Elena."

Elena smiled. "Yes. I'm sure of it. And I think it will be all right." She slid a glance at Cordelia. "One can make too much of momentary diversions which mean absolutely nothing." In exactly the same tone, she went on, "I am dissatisfied with the children's progress, Cordelia. We must discuss it, I'm sorry to say."

"Of course we must, if you are dissatisfied," Cordelia answered, remembering the earlier incident with Ralphine. "But what's the trouble?"

"Trouble?" Elena smiled. "Why, simply that you don't give either of them the firm hand that they need. Not that you don't try, I'm sure." Her smile widened. "You are very young. Perhaps it's just too difficult for you."

Cordelia leaned back. She clasped her hands into the folds of her dress. "I doubt that age has anything to do with your complaint. It's a matter of point of view, I think. I was raised to believe, and I do believe, that a child will learn most when he is interested. Rote, yes, for tables and spelling, but for general knowledge, there must be some interest, some excitement that stirs the imagination."

Elena cut in smoothly, "Why that's very interesting. But I can't accept it. Sam must be prepared for Andover, and Lena for Miss Porter's, when the time comes. I suspect that you were taught yourself by a very advanced sort of teacher."

"My uncle was my teacher, as I think I told you when I first came."

"And you believed that you learned well from him?"

"I think so."

"But not all that you needed to know obviously," Raphine put in.

There was a feline purr in her voice that very nearly made Cordelia laugh.

It was not her ability to teach, or to control the children, that was being discussed now. It was something else entirely.

She was glad when Jonathan came into the room, bringing with him a whiff of the fresh outdoors, and forcing a change in the conversation, though the subject itself was not much to Cordelia's liking.

He said, with a frown to her, "You were supposed to

rest today all day, and you haven't, have you? Don't you believe in following doctor's orders?"

"I'm fine," she said stiffly, at the same time aware of the various bruises that still pained her.

Ralphine sniffed. "Some people have no appreciation for concern. And I was driven from the schoolroom like a pariah. The children's manners are growing worse and worse. I was telling Elena, and I tell you now, Jonathan, I can't imagine what will become of Sam if he doesn't learn respect for his elders. And as for Lena . . . well, she's just impossible."

Jonathan grinned. "I'm sorry that they offended you, Ralphine. But perhaps you concern yourself with them too much."

Elena put in, "You know so little of these matters, Jonathan. I wouldn't expect you to understand. But I wouldn't expect you to make light of them either."

He accepted the tea she offered him with a nod of thanks, then he went to stand before the fire. "I think the thaw is continuing. It will give us all a chance to get the chill out of our bones."

Elena sighed faintly, acknowledging his refusal to listen any further to her complaints.

But Cordelia saw the tightening of her narrow lips, the white line of anger that appeared around them.

Chapter 11

Cordelia was curled up in her rocking chair, legs folded under her, the quilt Aunt Bessie had made for her over her knees.

All was well in Ryetown, Henry had written. There was little news, except that Aunt Berthe was ailing. It seemed unlikely that she could do her share of the chores around the house much longer. Clara was busy, what with taking his dictation, and correcting it as she chose without consulting him.

Cordelia repressed a smile at the thought of that. How Henry despised changes in what he had dictated.

But what of Aunt Berthe? Henry had not answered Cordelia's anxious plea that she be allowed to stay with him. That he ignored her words, wrote only that the old woman was not well, must be a bad sign. And where would she go? What would she do? How would she find a new home when Henry's house had been her own for so long. A shiver touched Cordelia. Aunt Berthe had been right. First Cordelia, then she herself. They were both displaced.

And Cordelia, although she had been set securely in a new spot, didn't know how much longer it would be hers, or even how much longer she could endure it.

The window was black with night, and since the avalanche had thundered down from the steep path on the cliff she had begun to suspect the dark of a special menace.

She tried not to think of it.

She looked down at the letter again. Henry wrote that he had taken out, in her name, subscriptions to *Harper's* and the *Atlantic*. She would, therefore, soon be able to read his latest work. Just because she was in Moorhaven teaching children was no reason to allow her mind to go to seed. She must press on with her education. She must prepare herself for the new century and the new world to come.

The letter slipped from her lap to the floor. She sighed and allowed it to stay where it had fallen.

Henry, the house outside of Ryetown, all seemed so far away.

The new century was here, and what had she to show for it?

She supposed, if she used Henry's long view, she was expecting more than she had a right to expect. Time moved at its own pace. But she wasn't Henry, and she didn't have his long view. She was lonely and surrounded by currents of feeling she didn't understand and against which she had no defense. What did it matter that great things were happening in Washington and Boston and New York? She was in Moorhaven. There seemed to be no real world beyond Moorhaven.

A tap at the door interrupted her despairing thoughts.

She went to open it, throwing the quilt on the bed.

Mary said, "You're to come down. Jonathan says so," she added, as Cordelia began a protest.

Cordelia shrugged. It was, she imagined, one more sign of his sense of obligation toward her. He seemed to believe she must spend a certain amount of time with the family in the drawing room. She wished that the thought had never occurred to him. Not that she was actually adverse to his company, although it troubled her that she felt that way. But the less she saw of the others, the better, she was sure, it would be for her.

Mary said softly, "I'd better tell you, Cordelia. I'm

going to be away for a bit. I don't know how long. But I want to warn you to be careful."

"You're going away?"

"You see," Mary went on, "Arley came out a while ago. My mother's ill. She needs me. Jonathan said I might go and be with her. Arley is waiting while I pack a few things, and I'll go back with him."

"I'm sorry about your mother," Cordelia said quickly. "I hope . . ."

"Thank you. You're the only one in Moorhaven to say so, or think it, Cordelia."

"Oh, no, no, Mary. The Moorhavens don't wish her any harm."

"Wish her harm? No. I didn't mean that. But she frightens them, you know. And people don't like to be frightened."

"Is there any way I can help you?"

Mary shook her dark head. "I don't think so."

"Then will you give my good wishes to your mother?"

Mary's eyes suddenly filled with tears. "You would do well to heed what she told you that day, Cordelia. They sold the yards, and ships, and built the house here. The older Mrs. Moorhaven died before the family even moved in. Then Dennis. too. And the older Jonathan. It must mean something."

"But Mary," Cordelia protested, "you yourself are willing to work here. And I'm not different from you."

"But you are," Mary whispered. "I knew that the moment I saw you. Perhaps my mother did, too. You're of this place. And I am not, nor ever will be."

"Of this place?" Cordelia repeated. "No, no. I have a position here. That's all."

"But is it?" Mary asked. "Is that all?" Then she went on, whispering still, "Be careful, Cordelia." With that she hurried down the hall.

Cordelia straightened a few curls before the rose-carved mirror, pinched her cheeks to brighten them, and went down to the drawing room.

Her heart was heavy. With Mary away, her only ally

would be gone. Who was there now to turn to? Who to be her friend?

"I can't say I'm sorry," Ralphine was saying when Cordelia entered the room. "I suppose it's unchristian of me, but that woman has bandied her foolish ideas about for too long as it is. And too many people have listened to her."

Elena gave Jonathan a warm smile. "Don't you agree that we must all be sorry for her?"

"Of course," he said absently. And then, to Cordelia who was hesitating on the threshold, "Come in. We're speaking of Daviette Jones. Arley's come for Mary because the old lady is very ill."

"Yes. Mary told me." Cordelia remained where she stood. "Is that why you sent for me?"

"Sent for you?" Jonathan's brows arched quizzically. "You make an invitation sound like an order. I didn't intend that. I thought you might spend an hour or two with us. I don't like the thought of you sitting alone in your room, perhaps brooding a bit on your narrow escape."

Ralphine's long thin hands twisted the lace at her throat. She said, "But that's what servants usually do, Jonathan. I mean, sit in their rooms when they're not at work. Perhaps you could explain to me how Cordelia is any different."

Cordelia took a step back. It was as if Ralphine were repeating Mary's words, but with different intentions.

"Wait," Jonathan ordered. And then, turning to his sister, he said, "But Cordelia is not a servant, as you know. That was not the arrangement, nor my intention when I discussed her situation with Henry Ward."

"There is no need for all this heat," Elena interposed gently. "Cordelia knows she is more than welcome. Ralphine is upset and means nothing." She smiled at Cordelia, "Come in. Do. Mrs. Sawyer is preparing coffee and will bring it in soon."

Cordelia took a chair as far from Ralphine and Elena as possible. She sat with her hands folded in her lap, trying to stifle her rebellious feelings. Ralphine had called her a servant, which, in a manner of speaking, she was. And not ashamed to be considered so, either. Yet Elena had denied it, siding with Jonathan, winning for herself an approving smile from him. But it was Elena whose animosity, now hidden, was the most clear when the two of them were alone. Was Elena the person she was to fear? Or Ralphine whose dark eyes now looked at her with hatred.

Jonathan, with a disgusted look at Ralphine, said, "I'm sorry, Cordelia. I apologize for my sister. I'm afraid we're all too much alone together here. It leads to unpleasant outbursts."

Ralphine said coldly, "You needn't apologize for me. I can do it myself. I'm sorry, Cordelia. I didn't mean to be offensive, although I know I was. It's just that ... that I don't understand Jonathan."

Cordelia smiled faintly, shook her head, wishing herself anywhere else in the world at the moment.

She found herself wondering about Jonathan. Why had he brought her here, knowing as he must have, that neither Elena nor Ralphine had wanted a governess for the children? What had made him decide that she should be more a member of the family than an employee? Wasn't he aware of the warm possessive looks that Elena gave him so frequently, and her open desire to please him? Had he decided to use Cordelia as a buffer between Elena and himself?

It was a provocative thought, but a painful one. No woman would want to feel used in that fashion. It made of her an object, nothing more. A pawn in a game. It deprecated her worth.

Mrs. Sawyer brought the coffee, and Elena, acting as the mistress of Moorhaven, as she always did, poured it, then allowed Mrs. Sawyer to serve it to the others.

"Where are Gregory and Denton?" Jonathan asked, from his place near the hearth.

"They'll be down in a moment," Mrs. Sawyer said.

"I'll pour for them in that case," Elena decided. "Gregory likes his coffee cool."

"He'll probably cool it with brandy," Ralphine observed.

"He'll certainly do that," Gregory announced, with a grin for his sister, as he entered the room. He took a decanter from the sideboard and waved it triumphantly. "May Ralphine never be wrong."

Denton soon followed. He was given coffee and took a place near Cordelia.

She sipped her cup slowly. The brew was bitter, stronger than she liked it, but she felt obliged to drink it regardless.

The others spoke of Jonathan's impending visit to Alderson's in Boston, but Cordelia followed their conversation with only half her mind.

She was remembering evenings in Henry's house when she had curled up in her own big chair, reading by kerosene lamp, while he had worked at his desk, puffing on his pipe so hard that bright embers fell in a shower around him, leaving brown scorch marks on the rug. She was remembering the evenings when she had gone with him into Ryetown and been enchanted by the bustle of the gaslit streets. Those had been days of contentment and safety, though she had taken them so much for granted that she hadn't known it at the time.

She paid little attention when the others moved around her now.

Ralphine, going to the big windows to pull aside the heavy curtains, looked out into the starry night. "I had thought Peter would come out this evening. If for no other reason than to see Cordelia again."

Elena, placing her cup on the silver tray, answered, "He is probably with Daviette Jones."

Denton shrugged, rose to pace the room in long slow strides. "There's not much he can do for her, I think."

It was Gregory who refilled Cordelia's cup, and brought it to her. Later, she was to remember that.

But now she accepted it with insincere thanks, and drank it quickly. Soon, with a false yawn, she rose, made her excuses, and went up to her room.

Mrs. Sawyer had drawn the curtains, lighted the gas

fire on the hearth, turned down the quilt, left fresh water in the jug, and clean towels on the washstand.

Cordelia threw open the window, then undressed quickly and got into her nightgown. She was suddenly tired. Her eyelids were too heavy to keep open. Her arms and legs were thick and clumsy with fatigue. She lowered the flame in the gas heater on the hearth so that it burned a small peak of pale blue, then turned off the gas jets over the mantel and hurriedly climbed into bed.

Sleep came with the instantaneous effect of a quick hard blow. Dreamless. Thick. A black binding weight . . .

What awakened her, she did not know. She had no idea how long she had slept.

The house was silent. She felt cold on her face, the cold of an unheated room. But her eyes and lips stung, as if burned with flame. Her lungs struggled for breath, and found none.

She pushed herself up, peered into the darkness.

No air.

No breath.

Utter darkness.

The blue peaks of flame were gone from the heater on the hearth.

Yet now she heard clearly the hiss of gas.

She tried to get up, and fell. She slid from the bed to the floor, and crawled on hands and knees across the room. It had grown larger, a big huge endless distance, a choking desert with no end in sight.

At last she found the heater, her fingers slid over it, searching, seeking. The jets were open to full strength. She coughed and choked as she turned them off. The hiss was fainter now, almost gone. She dragged herself to her feet, and leaning on the mantel felt for the light jets. They, too, were open. She turned them off carefully. The hiss was gone.

The room was utterly silent now, but for the sound of her panting.

She gathered all her strength, pulled herself along the mantel toward the door. At last she reached it, opened it. There was a sound on the stairs, a whisper of movement.

She fell back, instantly terrified, and groped her way to the window. She pulled the curtains open, and found it firmly closed.

Closed.

Throwing it open, she remembered that she herself had opened it before she climbed into bed. Just as she had herself adjusted the gas heater.

Bewildered, dizzy, sucking in the fresh clean air as hungrily as she could, she clung to the washstand, peering down at its marble surface.

Clean towels, basin, soap. Something else had been there. She had noticed it that morning. But had she noticed it just before she fell into bed? The small twist of brown paper in which Peter had given her the sleeping draughts. She had only used one of them. There had been one left. Now it was gone.

She thought of the bitter taste of the coffee, the sudden and terrible fatigue that had overtaken her, the black clouds of dizziness that had swept around her as she climbed the stairs.

Someone, she was certain now, had introduced the sleeping draught into her coffee. Someone had intended her to sleep so deeply that she would not hear the window being closed, the small peaks of flame being blown out in the heater, the hiss of the gas pouring freely into the room. Someone had intended her to sleep forever.

The cold wind blew her hair, touched her cheeks.

Her flesh prickled and fear seemed to melt her bones. She couldn't move. There had been a sound on the stairs. She knew she must go and close the door. She must lock it against whoever lurked there, waiting.

But she couldn't move.

Was it Gregory, turned against her because she had rejected him? Was it Denton, pretending friendship and hiding hatred behind a smiling mask? Or had Ralphine, enraged because she was displaced in the children's affections, put the draught in her coffee? Or Elena, who smiled at Jonathan so sweetly, and had, according to Mrs. Sawyer, once wanted him? And then came an intense and unbearable pain. For another name presented itself to her mind. What of Jonathan? Jonathan ... why had he brought her here? Why had he said she mustn't be afraid, said, too, that there was so much she didn't know? What did he intend?

At last, in desperation, she forced herself to creep to the door. She closed it softly, locked it. She returned to the open window, breathed in the cold clean air in slow, deep breaths.

Having felt the wings of death brush her, she knew how sweet it was to be alive. She determined that no one should know what had happened.

She, she alone, would unmask the would-be murderer. He, or she, was the curse of Moorhaven. And Cordelia herself would lay aside that curse forever. She must. For Jonathan's sake. For her own.

How she would do it, she didn't know. What weapons she would use, what her means would be, she didn't know. But she would free Moorhaven, or die in the attempt.

Chapter 12

The evil must be unmasked, the wickedness that planned her murder must be destroyed.

But Cordelia didn't know how to accomplish its destruction.

Several weeks had passed, and nothing further happened. A lull seemed to have settled over the house.

Under the circumstances it would have been easy for Cordelia to doubt herself. She could have decided that perhaps, after all, the children had damaged the things that belonged to her. That the avalanche on the cliff had been an accident. That she herself had absent-mindedly taken the sleeping draught and closed the window the same night that by some freak the gas heater had died in the hearth. She could almost have begun to believe that her imagination, over-excited by her stay in Moorhaven, had led her to the wrong conclusions. That was how strong and calm the lull seemed to be. And yet, in spite of that, she never considered it. She sensed always an ominous quality to the tenor of the days. There was some kind of undercurrent, hidden beneath the usual courtesies, that oppressed her.

But she couldn't quite identify it, nor its source. She couldn't point her finger at anyone and say, "You, you're trying to destroy me. You're the curse of Moorhaven."

Mary returned from Tembley, eyes swollen, face

pale. Her mother had died and been buried, but she had sent a message to Cordelia.

Whispering, Mary delivered it. "She told me, Cordelia. With nearly her last breath. Told me that the sea will come and destroy us all. The Moorhavens are doomed, she swore, and all who stay with them are doomed as well."

Cordelia shook her head, said gently, "Mary, we're modern young women. We don't believe in such prophecies."

"Don't we?" Mary asked. "Then let me tell you that you're wrong. At least in this. Everything that's happened to you proves that my mother is right."

"It proves nothing," Cordelia said. And wondered at the coolness and firmness of her voice. For she felt less certain than she wanted Mary to think.

Though she didn't believe in the sea's revenge, she believed in the evil of the human heart, the evil that would destroy Moorhaven if it went unchecked.

When Mary left her alone, shrugging at her refusal to agree, Cordelia asked herself from which direction, and when, the evil would strike next.

The children were restless, Lena argumentative, and Sam so withdrawn that he seemed more often than not to be in a world of his own. It took all of Cordelia's ingenuity to keep them at their studies, to amuse, and at the same time, instruct them, in their free hours.

She managed to avoid any more than the most brief and superficial contact with any of the adults in the house, yet as the weeks passed, she realized that, except when she was in her room, she was very rarely alone. One or another of them was always there. She would look up from her desk in the schoolroom to see Gregory peering in at her. Or she would take Lena and Sam for a romp in the melting snow, and Denton would invite himself along. She asked Joshua to take her in to Tembley one afternoon and found Jonathan in the carriage. It had been an odd ride. He was grimly silent while she forced herself to make conversation with Joshua.

There had been no mail for her that day, and she had been silent all the way home.

But the next afternoon, Joshua had brought her a letter from Henry. He wouldn't have to accept or reject her plea to keep Aunt Berthe with him. Aunt Berthe had died.

Cordelia read the words, and wept, and then, listening to the muted whisper of the house, could bear it no longer.

She wrapped herself in her heavy cloak, pulled on her boots, and stepped outside.

There had been a sleet storm the night before, and now the stunted trees in the marshes were silvered with thin gleaming layers of ice, and the marshes themselves were frosted over.

There had been voices in the drawing room when she passed, but she hadn't paused to listen. Now, as she stood just outside the door, it opened.

Ralphine looked out. "Oh, I thought it was Elena. Where are you going?"

"Just for a walk."

"But isn't it too cold?" Ralphine asked. And then, with a narrow glance at the sky, "And won't it be dark soon?"

"I shan't be long," Cordelia promised.

Ralphine went inside, and Cordelia trudged slowly down the slope.

At the bottom, she looked back. She had the feeling that someone was watching her, that from some place of concealment eyes followed her as she went. But she could see no one. She supposed that she was allowing her nerves to affect her, and went on slowly, her thoughts returning to the small hunched woman who had been her friend. She could hear in her mind the careful voice saying, "He would have come back if he could. For he loved her. He loved her enough to give his life for her. And he did." Aunt Berthe describing her parents ... Aunt Berthe folding the Spanish shawl carefully and slipping it into the carpetbag. Aunt Berthe weeping as she said goodbye for the last time ...

The melting snow crunched in cadence with her step. It was a little while before she realized that there were other crunchings, hurrying ones, that she couldn't possibly be making. She stopped, looked about her.

A shadow moved in the grove just beyond. A tall, slim shadow . . .

Cordelia's heart began to beat more quickly. Who was walking there? Who had followed her from the house?

She felt for the locket and wedding ring at her throat. She clasped them in her hand, drew them to her lips.

The tall slim shadow moved closer. It was Elena. She wore her long black cape, its fur collar turned high around her throat. She walked so lightly now that she seemed to drift inches above the ground.

Cordelia wanted to turn, to run away. But she stood frozen, waiting.

At last, close, within arm's grasp, Elena said, "I thought we might walk together," and smiled faintly. "Unless you'd rather not, that is."

There was something inexorable in the cool polite voice, and the cool polite words. Cordelia would have preferred to avoid walking with Elena, but there seemed to be no way of saying no. She simply nodded, walked on.

Elena fell into step beside her. "I wanted to speak with you privately anyway."

Cordelia was sure now, sure that her instincts were right. Elena had been watching for just such a moment as this. She had slipped outside, watched Cordelia, and then, seeing that she was alone, had followed her. It was Elena's intense gaze that she had felt on her back earlier, though, when she turned, she had not seen Elena herself.

After a moment's silence, Elena said, "Men can be strange." A smile curved her narrow lips. "You're perhaps too young to realize that, Cordelia. But it's true. They'll seem to be attracted by a pretty face. They'll do their very most to win it. And then, quite suddenly, when they do, they are no longer interested."

Cordelia didn't see where this was leading, but she didn't say so. She held her tongue, waiting.

Elena continued, "I suppose you've not much experience with men, so you wouldn't know that they tend to collect women's hearts the way children collect toys."

"I've no experience at all," Cordelia answered. "But that seems an odd generalization to me. Men are human. They're as different from each other as women are different from each other."

"It would seem so to you perhaps," Elena agreed. "Still, I know that I'm right. Particularly about the Moorhavens. I've known them for years now. My judgment is sound you may be sure."

"Perhaps," Cordelia agreed.

"The proof is in Denton," Elena smiled. "How madly he pursued you in his shy and backward way. And now . . . ?" She shrugged. "He's at the Falklands every day. Why, in a year or two, he'll be determined to marry Helena."

It was true that Denton rode into Tembley frequently. But he was just as frequently at home, Cordelia thought.

All she said, however, was, "They'll make a good couple, I think."

"And Gregory, of course he still casts sheep's eyes at you occasionally, Cordelia. I'm quite aware of that. But it's habit, rather than interest. He'll wed Felicia. You can be sure of it."

It was true that she had often noticed Gregory's eyes watching her, but they were no longer sheep's eyes, Cordelia thought. And after the night she had been drugged, left to die in the gas-filled room, she had no longer suspected Felicia. Felicia had been in Tembley. It would have been impossible for her to gain entrance to Cordelia's room, find the drug, administer it, and then close the window and blow out the flames in the gas heater. No, Felicia's jealousy hadn't driven her to such an insane act. Nor could it have been Helena, so childishly open in her unreasoning resentment. The culprit belonged to Moorhaven.

Cordelia slid a careful look at Elena's long pale face, and knew within her heart that the culprit walked beside her at that moment.

She wanted to run, to flee, but to turn her back on danger would not resolve it. She knew that she must stay and learn the truth. Stay here, with Elena, under the darkening sky, with the breathing marshes just beyond, agleam with the ice-sheathed trees.

Elena was saying, "I must say, Cordelia, that you handled both men extremely well. But as a woman, I must also say that I think you were very unwise. You're nineteen years old. You ought to have thought of yourself."

"Thought of myself?" Cordelia repeated. But she knew what must be in Elena's mind now.

"Of course. Or do you want to be another Ralphine? A hungry-hearted spinster, always adoring another woman's children?" Elena laughed. "No, no. I simply don't see you that way."

"I don't either," Cordelia agreed. "But I have time to think of that."

"Not much," Elena retorted. "And that's why you must leave Moorhaven. There's no one here for you. No one with whom you can think to build a future."

Cordelia didn't answer. She thought of Jonathan. Jonathan, who had somehow managed to claim her heart, without having tried. Jonathan, who viewed her as a young girl in his house, deserving of his protection and interest, but nothing more than that.

"Unless," Elena said silkily, "unless you've some interest in Peter Van Nuys. I think, were you to concentrate in that direction, you might win him. But of course Ralphine would never forgive you."

"I've no interest in the doctor," Cordelia said.

Elena touched her elbow lightly, maneuvering her along the hump of the dike. "This way. There's a fine view. At the bend there. You'll see." She drew Cordelia with her, still holding her by the elbow.

Cordelia would have liked to have drawn back. The twilight had faded into the deep purple gray that always preceded the dark. But the hand at her elbow had tightened into a steely claw, reminding her of Daviette Jones' hand on her wrist as she spoke of the Moorhaven curse.

"Come," Elena repeated insistently, and her fingers tightened more.

But as Elena drew her along with her, she turned to look back at the house. It lay still, silent, against the cliff. The brass lamps that flanked the door glowed with light now, and pale yellow edged the windows.

Inside, the others would be sitting down to tea. They would no doubt assume that Elena lay abed with one of her migraines, and that Cordelia was in her room. They would perhaps send Mary to look for her. But Mary wouldn't find her. And what would they do then?

Elena caught her by the shoulder. "Don't look for help from him. You won't have it. There's no help for you now. I've made sure of that."

Cordelia tried to step back, but now she couldn't move. Elena's hands gripped her too tightly.

But what was in Elena's eyes gripped her as well, chained her within the older woman's grasp. It held her immobilized. For here, now, was the truth she had sought.

Elena said, "You'll not have Denton, nor Gregory, nor Peter. Because it's Jonathan that you're scheming for. Tell me, it *is* Jonathan, isn't it?"

"I didn't come here to find a husband," Cordelia said gently. "You mustn't think that, Elena."

Her eyes went back to the house again, measuring, wondering. But she knew it was quite hopeless. From where she and Elena stood, on this bend in the dike, no one could see them. A stand of glistening trees, now turning black, stood in between.

"I mustn't?" Elena sneered. "Why, it may be that you plotted it all out with Peter. You, your uncle, whoever he is to you, and Peter Van Nuys himself. It may be that once you've got Jonathan and Moorhaven, you and Peter . . ."

Cordelia said steadily, "That's not true, Elena."

"But you'll not have Jonathan," Elena said. "He's mine. And always has been mine. Whatever he thinks today, or wishes today, or told me today, is of no matter. He is mine, I tell you."

Cordelia stirred slowly in Elena's grasp, bracing herself. "What did you Jonathan tell you today?"

But the older woman ignored the question. Her thin arms were surprisingly strong. They rose from the folds of the black cape and clasped Cordelia to her in what might have seemed an embrace to anyone watching, but what was capture instead.

"Look," she whispered. "Look to the marshes. They take and they give back. Did you know that? Did anyone ever tell you that?"

But Cordelia's gaze remained fastened to the white face whose pale blue eyes seemed to burn with a mad fire. "Was it because of Jonathan that you tried to drive me away, even from the first day I came here?"

"For him, of course. I'll see him marry no one but me. I've loved him since I was a girl your age. I'll not give him up now. And the moment I saw you, I knew what would happen. I know him well, better than he knows himself. I saw you, and I set out to drive you away. I thought if I could frighten you, make you dislike the children, then you'd pack up and run. So I slipped into your room, and left it a shambles. It seemed to have no effect on you. When I saw that I felt I must discredit you. I unbuckled the harnesses on the cutter, sent Ralphine to fetch the children in, and then watched you from the window. Regrettably, you weren't hurt, and Jonathan didn't seem to realize how reckless a girl you are. So . . ." She shrugged. "I followed you up to the cliff, and when you started down, I rolled a rock at you. The avalanche was good luck for me, though it did you no real harm."

"The gas heater, the jets . . ." Cordelia breathed.

"My work," Elena boasted. "What a pity you didn't

die then. It would have been so much better. For now,
Jonathan . . ." She stopped herself, though her pale face
twisted with fury. "But it doesn't matter. When you're
dead, and gone, he'll turn back to me. And you'll be
gone. Gone . . . gone . . ."

The movement was so sudden, so strong, that it
caught Cordelia before she could save herself.

Elena's grasp loosened. She thrust forward with all
her raging strength.

Cordelia stumbled back on the narrow rim of the
dike. She stumbled and fell backwards down the rounded stony hump of the slope to sprawl breathless and
stunned on the thin crackling ice of the marsh.

Elena stood above her, the wind blowing her cloak,
her pale hair loosened by the struggle. "You won't
come back," she said triumphantly. "Never. You won't
come back now."

Cordelia struggled to rise, but the thin crust broke
under her weight. Her cloak and dress were instantly
soaked, weighing her down into the icy water. She
fought it, screaming, and heard Elena's mad laughter
from above her.

Then Elena's laughter became a scream, too.

Cordelia, struggling still, heard the sliding fall of dirt
and stone. It poured around her, and threw Elena,
flailing the empty air, very nearly on top of her.

Above the two of them, she saw the ragged edge of
the bank where the dike had crumbled from beneath
Elena. But she had only one thought. To escape, while
Elena, panting, reached to seize her, to force her head
down into the icy water.

Struggling, fighting, screaming, with the ice breaking and crackling under her thrashing body, she knew
that she was lost.

And then, suddenly, over her own panting aching
breath, while Elena grabbed the gold chain at her
throat and tried to strangle her with it, she saw through
the misty darkness a gleam of light.

A golden gleam swung along the dike. Another approached from the shade of the trees. A third seemed to drift in from the marsh.

Elena twisted the chain at Cordelia's throat, but at the same time, she rose, listening, looking. And then, with a great wail of anguish, she cried, "Here, here. Help me. Help me, Jonathan."

The dark crept back under the glow of the three lanterns.

Jonathan was there, big, dark, his face grim, the scar at his temple livid.

"Jonathan, here. Help me," Elena cried again.

He bent over, gave her a single cold look. "You madwoman!"

Elena cried, "What are you saying, Jonathan? She . . . if you hadn't . . .

It was Gregory who answered, "We heard, Elena. All of us know."

She gasped, stumbled back, fingers still clinging to the locket at Cordelia's throat. The gold chain broke. She moved beyond the circle of lantern light. She was there for one moment, wavering, her face pale as the snow on the cliff, eyes wild, and then, quite suddenly she was gone.

There was an explosive crackling of ice. Close by, then farther away, then farther still.

They never saw her again.

But they didn't know then how it would be as they stared at each other in the dark.

In the next instant Gregory shouted and went plunging across the marsh with his lantern. Denton and Joshua followed.

Jonathan drew Cordelia to her feet, held her trembling body close. "Cordelia, can you forgive me? Will you try? I took a terrible risk with your life."

She leaned against him tiredly, "But you couldn't have known."

"I did, you see. From the moment Mary told me those first things that happened, I was sure. But I had to have proof, Cordelia. Elena is my brother's widow, the mother of his children. I couldn't drive her out, not unless I had absolute proof of her intent. Poor woman, she has always been possessive towards me. She didn't want anyone else at Moorhaven. She opposed my idea of a governess for the children from the beginning, and when she saw you she was more opposed than ever, so she first tried to drive you away, then to kill you. I watched her. Denton and Gregory watched her, too. When the time dragged out, I began to be afraid that something would happen that I couldn't prevent. I decided to test her. I told her that I was going to marry you, Cordelia."

"Marry me," Cordelia repeated. "You told her that, Jonathan?"

"It was a test," he explained. "If she ignored it, then I would know I was wrong. I would have to look further for whoever threatened you. But I wasn't wrong."

Cordelia shuddered, touched her throat. "She tried to strangle me. She . . ."

"She wanted to make sure that you died here. No one would have known. You'd have been missing, but who could have accused her?"

He drew Cordelia with him, up the crumbling hump of the dike to its top, drew her away from the place where the bank had caved in beneath Elena.

From there they could see the light of the moving lanterns.

They could hear the voices shouting, "Elena, Elena, this way. Don't move off. This way, Elena!"

But no answer came through the night.

And further search by day was no more successful.

When, finally, it was admitted that Elena was lost, Jonathan came to Cordelia and said, "I told her that I would marry you. I think I ought to have asked you first." He smiled faintly. "Have you considered your answer?"

She leaned her head against his shoulder and whispered, "You must know the answer is yes."

Chapter 13

Now Jonathan sat across the table from her reading his paper. His dark brows were drawn together in a frown, and he made some wordless sound of disapproval.

"What is it?" she asked.

"Some archduke has been assassinated in Europe, and the German kaiser is rattling his saber again. I think I had better go to Boston and speak to Alderson."

"Yes," she answered absently. "Yes. Perhaps."

But she was thinking, not of the sudden death of royalty, but of the moment when she, too, had come face to face with that same threat, and Jonathan had lunged from the dark night to save her.

It had been fourteen years ago but there were times when she still remembered and the blood seemed to run cold in her veins, and Elena's distraught and enraged face rose before her mind's eye.

A breeze shifted the white lace curtains at the window.

She leaned back in her chair, thinking of the house on the outskirts of Ryetown. How far away it seemed now. Not just the five hundred miles that lay between, but in time as well. It had been so long since she had seen it. She supposed she would never see it again. She didn't even know if the old house stood, or who occupied it. Bessie, and Henry, and Berthe, part of that place, who had been so dear to her, and given her so much, were all gone now.

But she had Jonathan. How little he had changed. His wavy hair was still dark, his eyes still held their glow. He was as straight and lean as the day she had first seen and fallen in love with him. Only the scar on his temple seemed to have faded a little. A small smile curved her lips.

He put down the paper. "Do you want to go into Tembley with me to meet the train?"

"Yes, I'd like to. It's been a long time since Gregory went away."

Jonathan grinned. "You're showing all the signs of feminine curiosity."

"Why not?" She went on, "I only wish that Jon and Dennis were here, too."

"Perhaps for the weekend. If you insist."

"But it's a long drive to Andover, and I don't like to interrupt their routine."

"It's not so far that I can't take the time to do it." Jonathan rose, stretched. "We owe Gregory a good deal, Cordelia. It's fortunate for us that he has always been the restless sort. St. Louis, Chicago, San Francisco. If it hadn't been for his willingness to do that job, I'd have felt compelled to do it myself. And I wouldn't have wanted to be away so much from you and the children."

But she wondered. He had planned, before his father died, to take advantage of the opportunities the West offered. When Moorhaven came to him, he didn't feel free to leave it. Then they had married . . .

The small church in Tembley. She had worn a long white lace gown and a long veil. She had written to Henry to ask him to give her away. But he was unwell, Clara had written in return, and the journey by train would be too much for him. So Peter Van Nuys had led her down the aisle, and Gregory had stood up with Jonathan.

Outside, standing on the steps, Gregory had smiled, kissed her cheek. "Be happy, Cordelia."

Two days later, he was gone. He had never returned, though they heard from him weekly over the years, and occasionally through Aldersons. He had never married.

Cordelia had sometimes wondered if she were the cause of his bachelorhood. She hoped not. She wouldn't have wanted it that way. She had expected that he would turn to Felicia, but he hadn't. Soon after his departure, Felicia had left Tembley and moved to New York, where she was now a successful career woman, much to the amusement of Jonathan and her brother Peter.

Gregory would be forty years old now. It was hard for Cordelia to imagine what the years might have made of him. She was somewhat ruefully aware of the changes in her.

Her hair was still the same deep auburn that it had been when she first came to Moorhaven, her eyes the same clear green. Yet the small delicate figure had rounded with each of her four children. Jon, her first son, then Dennis, then Harris, and, just four years ago, Dorinda, a tiny replica of what she herself must have been at the same age.

It seemed that so much had happened in the years since Gregory had gone. And yet, when she thought of it, she couldn't really put it all into words. Gregory would ask the right questions, she supposed, and then she would know the answers.

Jonathan said, "I suppose Denton and Helena will be here this evening."

"Yes. At about seven." Cordelia hoped that it would be a pleasant visit, for Gregory's sake, as well as her own. Childless Helena had developed a bitter tongue in the past few years, and she had begun urging Denton to leave Tembley, to go with Gregory. But Jonathan had felt that Gregory must decide if Denton would have a contribution to make, since it was Gregory who had made a success of that branch of the transport concern.

Jonathan, as often happened, seemed to read her

mind. He grinned. "Helena will be on her best behavior tonight." Then, "I'll be in the office. We'll leave in about two hours. All right?"

She nodded, sighed. She would have a great deal to do in order to be ready on time, yet she didn't feel disposed to begin. She imagined that Gregory's coming had unleashed the memories of the past that crowded her now.

What had happened between Elena and Cordelia that terrible night on the marshes had never been discussed. It had been said only that Elena had gone for a walk in the marshes, had probably lost her way, and been drowned.

Those who knew the truth buried it deep within themselves for Lena's and Sam's sake, as well as to avoid the scandal that would have ensued with public knowledge.

Cordelia had raised Elena's children as if they had been her own, and they weren't displaced when her own were born. Now Sam was twenty-four, a graduate of Harvard and working with Aldersons, too interested in a girl to return frequently to Moorhaven. Lena was twenty-two, and still at home, but restless, and spending more time in Tembley than either Jonathan or Cordelia would have liked.

When one had six children, it was to be expected that there would be problems, and yet Cordelia, when she thought of Lena always had a peculiar twinge of the heart. Perhaps she saw in Lena's face something of Elena.

Now she sighed, pushed herself to her feet as Harris trotted into the room.

"Dad says you're going to Tembley with him. Can I come, too?"

"Did you ask him?"

"Yes."

"Then what did he say?"

Harris sulked. "He said no."

That was typical of Harris. He would try first father,

then mother, playing each off the other, to get his own way.

She said sternly, "Why, Harris, if Dad said no, then you have my answer."

"I don't see why."

"If you go, then we'll have to take Dorinda and Lena. And it will be too much confusion. Your Uncle Gregory will have one look at us and hop back on the train and run away for more long years."

Harris grinned suddenly. "Aunt Ralphine says he's got a surprise for us. That's why he's coming back. She said that must be the case. What do you suppose it is?"

"I wouldn't hazard a guess." Then, "Why aren't you at your books?"

"It's early."

"Not that early."

Cordelia sent him up to the schoolroom. It was plain, she thought, that Jonathan was right, and she was wrong. Jon and Dennis had gone away to school when they were ten at Jonathan's insistence. But she had clung to Harris, insisting that he study at home until he was twelve. Plainly, though, Harris needed the discipline of teachers he couldn't wrap around his little finger as he found it so easy to do.

It would have been so much better if the children had been able to go to school in Tembley. But Jonathan was adamantly opposed to that, and she knew he was right. They were Moorhavens, and the people of Tembley still spoke of them as accursed. The death of Daviette Jones, fourteen long years ago, hadn't changed that. The words had been passed from his mother to Arley, and were no longer a madwoman's explanation for depression and need, but a fact of life. Jonathan would not have his children exposed to it. So each of them had to go away when they reached the proper age. It was a parting that Cordelia dreaded, having experienced it so many times before.

She knew what the preparations were like, and what the long months between vacations were like, too. Still, she accepted the necessary, and forced herself to wait patiently for the letters that came at weekly intervals, and for the holidays that brought the family together again.

She rose now, went into the hall. The portrait of Jonathan, just recently finished, hung over the wide mahogany sideboard beside the one done several years before of his older brother Dennis. Sam's and Lena's father. The Dennis she herself had never known. It had been her idea that the painting be done from the old brown photograph that was all they had left of him. And her idea, too, that Elena's portrait be done at the same time, though she felt a shiver each time she looked at that long pale face with its coronet of pale blonde hair.

Remembering though, how she had clung to the story of her own birth as told to her by Bessie and Berthe, she had felt that the children must have some sense of their pasts, their parents. The dark shadow that Elena had cast over them, over Moorhaven, must be banished.

So Dennis had been painted by George Watson, and then Elena, and she had managed to sweet-talk Jonathan into the portrait of himself. Now George, at Jonathan's insistence, was painting the portrait of her. She was not much interested in it, and resented the hours of posing. But it would soon be finished to her relief. And to Jonathan's as well, she knew. For he, secretly, was beginning to be surfeited with George's company, and the attention that he paid to Cordelia.

A June breeze swirled through the vestibule as the big front door opened.

Mary cried, "Dorinda! Wait," as Dorinda hurled herself across the threshold to throw herself at her mother's knees, babbling excitedly.

Cordelia kneeling, hugged her, said, "Hold on. I can't understand a word you're saying. You can talk. Stop blathering."

"There's a robin," Dorinda cried triumphantly. "On the tree. I want cookies. I want candies."

Mary shrugged. "I don't know what's come over her.

She wants. That's all she can say this morning. She wants."

Cordelia laughed. "Wanting won't help. She won't have cookies or candies. Not now." She gave Dorinda another hug. "Go find Aunt Ralphine. She'll tell you a story. Mary has work to do."

Mary Jones had lost her sixteen-year-old thinness. She was plump now, her dark hair piled on top of her head in a heavy bun, her sharp black eyes lost in the roundness of her face. She had never married, nor seemed to want to. She rarely saw her brother Arley, or the people of Tembley. She had become a true part of Moorhaven.

"Joshua was asking which of the cars you want for the ride to town."

"The Packard, I suppose."

Mary grinned. "Joshua will be pleased. He loves to drive it. Have you seen his face when he passes Dr. Peter in that old electric brougham of his?"

Cordelia laughed. "For a middle-aged man he is very adept at adjusting to modern things, isn't he?"

"He's one of those men that grow younger over the years."

Cordelia didn't say it aloud, but thought to herself that Joshua's new lease on life had somehow begun with the death, two years before, of Meggy Sawyer. Since then Joshua had seemed to walk with a lighter step, though anyone would have expected a man of fifty-six to be slowing down and not speeding up.

It was fortunate for Jonathan that it was so. Without him it would be hard to imagine the changes that had been effected in Moorhaven.

Joshua, as a younger man, had helped to build the house. And as an older man he had overseen the construction of the new wing and the terraces. It was he who had agreed with Cordelia that the great front door must be black, with brass fittings to match the lamps that hung on each side of it. He who had done the shutters in the same shiny black. He, who many springs ago, had put in the lilacs because she said she remembered them from her earlier home. The man could do nearly everything, Cordelia thought. From making her feel safe the first moment he saw her in the shed in Tembley to learning the secrets of the electrical wiring that had been installed ten years before.

He had his own little apartment over the garage, converted from the stables when most of the horses had been sold off, replaced by the two automobiles that Jonathan had waited six months after ordering to obtain.

Dorinda cried, "Auntie," and climbed two steps, and fell back three. She sprawled, her face turning red, her mouth stretching wide.

Mary picked her up, set her on her feet. "Go on, baby. I'll be right behind you," and directed her up the staircase."

Cordelia watched until they disappeared into the shadows of the second floor, then turned away, making lists in her head.

The train steamed its way to a stop.

Two people got off, stepping into the waiting arms of relatives, and hustled by porters anxious for the few cents they could get for handling the luggage.

Jonathan said, "You don't suppose he's missed the New York connection, do you?"

Cordelia answered, "I don't think so, no," and with the next breath cried, "There he is."

Gregory stood on the step, grinning. He raised his hand, then turned back into the train for a moment. When he turned again, he was carrying a child.

Chapter 14

Cordelia blurted, "Perhaps that's the surprise Ralphine meant," and hurried forward. Gregory swung the small boy to the platform and held him firmly by one hand, while with the other he reached to hug Cordelia.

"You're as lovely as ever," he said, grinning under his heavy black mustache. "And you're a sight for sore eyes, Jonathan."

In the confusion of greetings, the boy stood quietly, patiently. Then Gregory said, "Let me introduce Delaney."

Jonathan's dark brows rose. "We'd no idea, Gregory. Why should you keep him a secret?"

"What you're thinking is quite wrong." Gregory's grin widened. "Delaney is not my son. I found him in the Dearborn station, and brought him along with me."

"You what?" Jonathan demanded.

Gregory said, "Shall we go? I'll explain along the way."

Cordelia knelt, put her hand out. "Hello, Delaney."

But the boy ducked his sandy head, and shrank back against Gregory's thigh, staring at her through wide tan-colored eyes.

"He's five, I believe. But he hardly speaks. Though he can if he wants to," Gregory explained. And to the boy, "It's all right, Delaney. This is an uncle for you.

His name is Jonathan. And here is a beautiful aunt.
Her name is Cordelia. You'll get used to them after a
time."

The men collected the luggage, loaded the car with
Joshua's help.

When they were on the way out of Tembley, Gregory said, "Yes. In Dearborn station. Last year, it was.
I've kept him with me ever since."

"You mean he was abandoned?" Cordelia asked.

"Just so."

"But didn't you try to . . ."

"Of course I did. My dear Cordelia, I contacted the
police the day I saw him, but they knew nothing, and
had very few ideas. The child was simply left there, not
hungry, not badly dressed. He was sitting on a bench,
as patient then as he is now. He knew his first name,
and that was all. So . . ." Gregory shrugged. "I saw no
need to turn him over to an orphanage. You know
what those places are. With my resources, I manage
nicely, I think. What do you say, Delaney?"

The boy's thin solemn face was suddenly alight with
a smile.

Cordelia found herself remembering her own beginnings. She, too, had been taken in by strangers. She
looked at Gregory with new respect.

He was no longer the dapper dandy who had
courted her so assiduously fourteen years before, and
then, perhaps concealing a broken heart, had gone
away. Now he was a man, solid, kind. How else to
explain his concern for Delaney?

When they arrived at Moorhaven, Dorinda was sitting on the front steps.

Joshua pulled into the driveway and stopped.

She scrambled to her feet, hurling herself at the car
as Cordelia got out.

Gregory lifted Delaney down. Dorinda stared at him,
her round green eyes shining. Then she laughed. She
thrust a pudgy hand into his. "You come," she ordered.

Delaney cast one look upward at Gregory, then followed her up the wide stone steps.

They had had dinner. The men had withdrawn to Jonathan's office for brandy and cigars, and Cordelia sat in the drawing room with Ralphine and Helena.

"A foundling," Ralphine said through tight pale lips. "Do you really believe that, Cordelia?"

"Of course," she retorted. "If that's what Gregory tells us. Why should he lie?"

"More likely the child is Gregory's bastard," Ralphine answered tartly. She patted her thick gray hair. "I see no good in taking a child whose parents are unknown, whose background must be of the lowest, to raise and cherish. Why, who knows what illness, madness, is in his blood?"

Cordelia said firmly, "Ralphine, you have no right to say such things. Gregory is a grown man. Surely the choice is his."

"Then why did he bring the boy here?" Helena asked. "You'll find that he he his reasons."

"Of course he did. He wanted the child to meet his new family."

"If he were Gregory's," Ralphine said, "that would make sense. Otherwise it doesn't."

"Perhaps he's planning to adopt the boy," Cordelia told her. "And if he does, then he has the right to ask us to accept him."

"Adopt him? What for? Unless, as Ralphine said, the boy is his." Helena cast an annoyed look at the closed door of the office. "Why are they taking so long, do you think? I want to go home. And I'd just as soon Denton had less brandy before the drive. I've no trust for that automobile. I always have the feeling that we'll bounce off into the marsh before we get out into that awful road."

"I suppose they have a great deal to talk about," Cordelia said.

Ralphine grimaced. "I expect Gregory is about to launch the surprise."

"Surprise?" Cordelia asked. "You mentioned it to Harris, didn't you? But he didn't know . . ."

"I'm sure there will be changes," Ralphine told her.

Helena nodded agreement. Then, "And did you notice how he kept talking about the possibility of war in Europe?"

"Everyone does these days," Cordelia answered.

"Not me. I don't care what happens there," Ralphine snapped. "It's not our problem. Let the Kaiser invade England and sit on the British throne for all I care."

Helena rose, whirled restlessly, so that her dress belled out, showing her slim ankles and a bit of her slim legs. She was still pretty, still young, though two lines of discontent were scored around her mouth. "I wish you wouldn't talk of war. I wish I didn't have to listen."

The office door opened.

Cordelia's eyes went anxiously to Jonathan's face. The talk of changes had troubled her. What she saw now in his face troubled her, too.

He looked worried, his dark eyes narrowed, his brows drawn together so that the scar stood out on his temple.

But Gregory had a gay expression on his face. He glanced around, then his gaze settled on Helena, "My dear, I hope this is going to make you happy. Denton tells me that this is something you've wanted for some time."

"What?" she looked suddenly suspicious. Her mouth turned down. Her eyes glinted behind their long lashes as brightly as the diamonds that hung at her ears. "What have I wanted?"

Denton cut in quickly, "We're going to San Francisco, Helena. We leave as soon as we can be ready."

Her eyes widened. She was suddenly very still. "What do you mean? Why? Why are we going?"

It was Gregory who answered her. "You might thank, or, if you're so inclined, you might blame, me. I . . ." His dark glance touched Cordelia now, "I've felt for several years that I'd had enough of the West. We're a going concern now. We've our depots, and warehouses, and the newest transport will be with heavy duty trucks. Our managers are established. I want out.

Denton has promised to take the San Francisco office to relieve me."

"But what will you do?" Cordelia asked.

He smiled at her. "I'm going to England," he said.

"But if there's a war. . ."

"That's *why* I'm going."

"You?" Ralphine cried. "It has nothing to do with you."

"It has to do with all of us," he answered. "But then, that's not something we must discuss. I've decided. It's done. There's only one more detail." He smiled at Cordelia. "And it depends on you, Cordelia."

"What detail is that?" she asked. But she already knew. It would have to do with Delaney. She wondered what Jonathan would say. Or what he had already said.

Gregory went on, confirming her thought. "It's the boy. I can hardly take him with me."

"Then send him to a home," Ralphine cried. "There's no need . . ."

"I couldn't," Gregory said simply. "He's been with me a year. I couldn't turn him out now, I'd have to set up an establishment, find a housekeeper nurse. Which is what I'm prepared to do, unless . . ."

Cordelia cut in quickly, "No, Gregory, you mustn't do that. We've plenty of room for Delaney here. We want him with us until you come back."

"That's what Jonathan told me. And he assured me you'd say the same. But are you certain you want the responsibility of one more?"

"Dorinda has already made him welcome," Cordelia laughed. "He'll be a brother to her, they are so close in age, while the others are so much older."

"I think," Ralphine said, "that if you are really to ask this grotesque favor of the family, you must be honest in what you say."

Gregory stroked his dark mustache, stared at her coldly. "I don't think I know what you're talking about."

"Where did you really get the boy?" she demanded.

"I found him in Dearborn station," Gregory grinned.

And then, the amusement fading from his face, he said coldly, "And I'll thank you to remember that from now on."

Ralphine's eyes glittered at the rebuke, but she said nothing more.

Delaney was moved into a room on the third floor, and soon knew his way about the house as if he had been born in it.

He spoke little, and no one saw him cry until the day Gregory left. Then he wept for hours, while Dorinda tried to divert him, and Cordelia promised him that Gregory would soon be back.

But, at the end of the year, Gregory was dead in France, and Jonathan formally adopted Delaney and made him another son, though Dorinda never considered him a brother.

It was Delaney, thirteen years old, a tall thin boy with tan-colored eyes and thick sandy curls, who first saw the lights in the marshes.

No one else in the house would have known about them except that Dorinda caught him at the window very late one night.

The summer of 1922 was hot and still, with frogs croaking in the sink holes, and weeds growing along the hump of the dike that Jonathan walked each day.

It happened that Cordelia overheard her two youngest talking about the lights, and set herself to observe the marshes that same night.

She was heavy and slow-moving in her unexpected pregnancy, and slept badly. She saw no reason to trouble Jonathan with what was probably nothing more than children's imaginary adventures.

But she herself saw the far-off glimmerings in among the stunted trees. She watched them for an hour or two, and was still watching when they disappeared.

In the morning, she told Jonathan about them.

He frowned. "I don't understand. Could you have seen fireflies?"

"I doubt it." Then, vaguely troubled, "Could there be people . . ."

Harris, tall now, dark as his father, laughed. "You've probably been dreaming, Mother. Nobody comes to the marshes. Why would they?"

"I'll have a look tonight," Jonathan answered.

Harris sighed, openly exasperated with his father. At eighteen he was in a state of continual excitement with growing up, Cordelia told herself. It was to be expected that he contradict his father whenever and however he dared.

She wished that Jon and Dennis were still at home. They would be steadying influences, she thought. But Jon, having graduated from Harvard, was visiting Denton and Helena for the summer in San Francisco. Dennis, exploiting the artistic talent he had discovered early, was on a painting trip in the Rockies. Sam, married, with a son named Dennis, ran the Chicago branch. Thus, only Lena, and the two youngest were still at home. And Moorhaven seemed empty.

But, when the baby came in a few months, they would all be busy again. Ralphine was already doing her perfect embroidery, and Mary had begun preparing the nursery.

That night Cordelia heard Jonathan stirring. She sat up. "What is it?"

"I'm going out to see if there's anything to this story of Dorinda's and Delaney's." He pulled on his shoes. "I don't like the idea of anybody being out there. I want to take a good look."

She sat in the chair, watching the dark swamps until she saw the single light that she knew must be from Jonathan's flashlight. Then, rising, she stood waiting, and remembering again that night when she and Elena struggled there.

At last he returned. "No one was there now," he said heavily. "But I saw traces that suggest someone has been. Cigarette butts and packets, on a hummock, and some footprints under the trees." He yawned. "I'll have another look by daylight."

He told her, late the next afternoon, that he and Joshua, after a long search, had found nothing more.

The next day he made one of his monthly visits to
Alderson and Sons in Boston, planning to be gone for a
week.

At twilight one evening, Cordelia sat on the terrace.
Her needles clicked between her fingers as she knitted a
small sweater.

Lena, her long legs looking even longer due to her
very short skirt, tapped her foot restlessly and smoked
one cigarette after another.

Suddenly Dorinda and Delaney came racing up the
slope.

"Mother, there's a man hurt on the other side of the
dike. We saw him. Come and see."

Cordelia put aside her knitting and pushed herself to
her feet. "Where exactly?"

Delaney pointed off toward the stand of marsh trees.

"But no one would go in there," Cordelia protested,
thinking again of the lights she had seen, the search
Jonathan had made. "Are you quite sure?"

Delaney nodded. "He's got blood on him. I saw it."

"Run for Joshua then," Cordelia ordered.

Lena's eyes sparkled. She was no longer the moody
thirty-year-old who pretended to be ten years younger.
She was a child, excited by a new amusement. "Let's go
down," she cried happily.

Chapter 15

Cordelia thought briefly of the guns in Jonathan's office.

Two years before, Sam, on a visit, had built a special safe concealed behind a mirror. She supposed they were still there. But the thought of going armed frightened her.

She said, "Lena, had we better call the police?"

"Since when do we call to Tembley for help?" Lena demanded.

"Peter then," Cordelia said. "Go phone him and tell him that we need him right away."

"You don't know what we need," Lena said impatiently. "Hadn't we better see if the children are right, and if so, if the man is alive or dead?"

"Then get Harris. He and Joshua can go."

Lena looked as if she were going to protest. But for once, she didn't. She ran inside, called loudly.

Harris came on the run. He first made light of Delaney's and Dorinda's discovery, but when Cordelia insisted, he agreed to go into the swamp with Joshua.

Cordelia and Lena followed the two men, although Harris warned them to stay on the terrace and wait. Thus they were there when Harris bent over the young redhead who lay sprawled under one of the trees, soaked, muddy, and bloodstained. Thus they heard him mumble, "So you came back, did you? Damn your eyes!"

Joshua looked up, mouth tight in his gray beard, his sharp blue eyes cold as ice.

Cordelia pretended not to have heard. She wasn't sure that Lena had. The girl was down on her knees in the mud cradling the young man's head in her lap, crying, "We *do* need a doctor. We must get him back to the house."

He said, "No. No doctor. No law."

"What are you doing here?" Cordelia demanded.

The young man groaned and closed his eyes.

Joshua and Harris got him back to the house and settled into bed. The two of them cleaned him up, examined his wounds, while Cordelia directed them.

Peter Van Nuys soon arrived, plainly frightened that the summons had been for Cordelia herself.

When he saw the young man's wound, he whistled through his teeth, then asked for hot water and bandages. When he was finished, he told Cordelia. "You should have him moved to a hospital somewhere, and report this to the police."

"I can't," she said faintly.

"You can't? Why not?" There was gray in his light brown hair and in his small, well-trimmed beard. He was still very thin, his wife Bettina having failed to fatten him up as all had predicted.

Cordelia shook her head. "No, Peter. I think we must take care of him here."

"But why?"

"I can't explain that to you," she said quietly. "Just believe me when I say it would be better. At least until Jonathan comes back."

"Then call and tell him to come now. I don't like this."

After Peter had gone, she called Harris into the office. She sat behind Jonathan's desk, her hands folded into her skirt. She said, "You know that man, Harris."

Harris nodded, grinned. "I guess you heard him after all."

"I did. What's his name?"

"Marty Brown." The face so like Jonathan's looked partly defiant, partly ashamed.

"Marty Brown," she repeated. "And what was he doing in the marshes?"

"You're not going to like this," Harris warned.

"I already don't like it," she said steadily. "But will you tell me?"

"Bootlegging whiskey."

"How did he get shot?"

"I don't know. He says he was hijacked. Lost everything he had."

"You're involved," she said faintly.

"It was just a lark, Mother."

"A lark," she said sadly. "And what shall we do now? Because of your . . . lark."

"See Marty on his feet and on his way," Harris retorted. "He won't blow the whistle on me. Not unless he gets turned in to the police."

"I'll talk to your father and let him decide," Cordelia said thoughtfully.

Harris laughed softly. "I think, if you'll forgive me, Mother, it would be better not to explain *all* of this to father. He's going to be very angry at my playing smuggler."

"As I am myself," she said crisply.

"But he's very likely to throw Marty Brown out, and me with him."

"I doubt it," she said. But she wondered. She couldn't predict how Jonathan would react to news that Harris had aided a bootlegger, even shown him the marshes, led him right to the Moorhaven front door.

"Who else is in it with you?" she asked.

Harris looked even more embarrassed, but then he gave her a deliberately wide-eyed look. "What do you mean? No one. No one else."

She shook her auburn head. "Harris, please. I'm not so much a fool. Who handles the whiskey in Tembley?"

"I have no idea," Harris protested.

"Someone did the hijacking, as Marty Brown calls it. Wouldn't it be a Tembley person?"

Harris shrugged. "That's nothing to do with us. All we have to do is wait until Marty is well enough to travel, then send him on his way. After that we can forget it."

"But can we?" she asked. "Can you?"

"Why, of course," he assured her. "There's no reason why not."

She remembered those words a month later.

It was the day that Marty Brown had at last decided that he was well enough to leave Moorhaven.

That was the first that Cordelia realized what had been happening. She blamed herself for it, for not listening to Jonathan, forever after.

She had called him in Boston, and he had come back at once. When the story was laid before him, he said immediately, "Turn this Brown over to the police. What else is there to do?"

"And Harris?"

"If he's involved then he must pay for it."

Cordelia felt the blood leave her face, felt her whole body go limp. She whispered, "Jonathan, we can't let that happen. We mustn't."

He gave in when he saw how deeply she was affected. He allowed Marty Brown to stay through the month, and at the end of it, Marty told Cordelia, "I guess you'll be glad to see the last of me," and grinned impudently.

"Yes," she answered. "We all will."

"Not all, lady."

"What do you mean?" she asked sharply.

"I guess you just haven't noticed."

She stared at him, her heart sinking. "I want you to tell me. Your innuendos are meaningless."

"Ask Lena," he said quietly, but with his eyes flashing triumphantly.

There was no need to ask Lena. The situation was suddenly clear to Cordelia. Lena had cared for Marty through most of the month. She had fetched and carried and sat with him. She had blushed when she spoke about him. And now, with her bags packed, she tossed her dark curls defiantly. "You can't stop me, you know. I'm a grown woman. I'm thirty years old. And if I don't marry Marty I'll marry no one. Do you want another old maid like Ralphine on your hands?"

Cordelia had tried reason, and Jonathan tried orders. Neither would change Lena's mind.

She went with Marty, and it was only after the two of them had gone, that Cordelia discovered that Harris had left, too.

That night Cordelia struggled through a miscarriage, and Peter told Jonathan that she must not become pregnant again. She refused to accept Peter's orders, nor Jonathan's pleas, and managed to become pregnant after three years of hope on her part, and three years of anxiety on Jonathan's.

She was expecting the baby within days when Harris suddenly turned up at Moorhaven again.

He was a gaunt, exhausted-looking twenty-one-year-old, but there was still something very childlike about him.

After the first shock, as he sat with Cordelia, twisting his hands on his knees, she began to see that he was troubled. She waited for him to tell her what was wrong. At last he blurted it out.

Lena was dead, Harris told her in an agonized whisper. Marty had deserted her sometime before. She had taken a job as a cigarette girl in a Chicago speakeasy and had been shot in a gang war. The police had not yet established her true identity, but they no doubt soon would. Harris wanted Cordelia to be prepared when the word came, and that was why he had returned home so unexpectedly.

"And you," she asked at last. "What about you, Harris? Will you go on this way?"

"I'm through with it."

"Will you stay home now?"

"If you'll have me," he told her.

"Of course," she whispered. "You belong here."

That night she dreamed that the sea had risen. It crawled silently up the long slope to engulf the house. Moorhaven was doomed.

At dawn the next morning, she went into labor. She struggled hard, sweating in pain, to deliver. By noon, she had had a stillborn boy. An hour later, she was dead, with Jonathan leaning over her, whispering in anguish, "Cordelia, Cordelia, no."

Chapter 16

Dorinda awakened suddenly. Something, she didn't know what, had jerked aside the merciful waves of sleep and pulled her back into painful consciousness.

She lay very still. She could hear nothing. Nothing but the pounding of her heart against her ribs. She tried to tell herself she must relax. There was no reason for the peculiar fear which welled up in her. There was no reason. Yet the fear grew stronger and stronger.

She tried to tell herself that she was a grown woman. She was twenty years old, surely no longer a child who was afraid of the dark.

But at last she rose. She could no longer cower under the thin summer coverlet in growing terror.

She saw the clear sharp outline of her body as she crossed the thick blue rug, and staring at it, she felt her eyes widen. If there was shadow, then somewhere there must be light. But the room was in utter darkness. She reached out to switch on a lamp, then drew her trembling fingers back. It was, she realized, from the window that the faint light came. She went to it, opened the heavy brocade curtains.

From her vantage point she could clearly see a triangle of terrace and the part of the long low building called Jonathan's wing in recent times.

A shadow limped slowly past the window, falling on the terrace stone beyond. Then it limped slowly back.

A wave of pity swept through her. Poor man, she thought. He couldn't sleep. He had no rest at all. What would happen to him?

Then reality touched her. She bit back a scream of disbelief.

Yellow light poured from the window. A tall black shadow moved, limping, on the ground below. Someone was pacing the floor in that brightly lighted room.

But no one could be there. No one.

Dorinda closed her eyes, clung to the sill with trembling fingers.

That was Jonathan's wing, Jonathan's room. But he was no longer there.

Just two weeks before, she had found him sprawled on the floor of his study. His big lean body was unmoving. His haggard face was colorless, the scar on his temple an odd blue. She had known instantly that he was dead.

She had wept, the tears streaming down her cheeks as she knelt beside him. But there had been no surprise. In the five years since Cordelia had died, Dorinda had watched Jonathan's grief and feelings of guilt destroy him.

The day Cordelia had been buried, he had withdrawn to the wing. He had stayed there, seeking out no one, taking no part in family life. Dorinda, still a child of fifteen, had watched him walk the dike daily with Joshua at his side, and tried to understand.

Now she remembered standing beside his grave in the brilliant sunlight. Standing with Jon on one side of her and Delaney on the other. If it hadn't been for Delaney's quiet presence, she didn't know how she could have borne it. He was her strength, and had always been, just as she was his, and had always been.

Delaney had put his hand on her arm and said, "Come away now, Dorinda," and she had followed him.

She was aware of the look that tall, dark-haired Jon

exchanged with Sam. She knew what it meant. But she refused to think of it then. She clung to Delaney, allowing him to lead her to the black limousine, and she had clung to him since. The same way, if the truth were told, that she had clung to him all her life.

She liked to believe that she remembered the first time she had seen him, though when she had told Cordelia that years before, her mother had laughed, "No, darling, that's not possible. I'm sure what you remember is hearing me talk about it."

"But I see it so clearly in my mind," Dorinda protested. "Uncle Gregory lifted him down out of that big green car we had then, and set him on his feet. He looked so small and scared, standing with the grownups around him. I was sorry for him, and I liked him, and I went down to him."

"Yes. You did that," her mother had agreed. "You were always the most tender of my children, Dorinda."

"I've always wondered," Dorinda had said, "why nobody wanted him but you. And why, when you and Dad adopted him, Aunt Ralphine was so upset."

Some of the brightness went out of her mother's face. She said gently, "You seem to remember more than I would have thought." Then, "But it was nothing, dear."

"It was, you know. I remember it. You just don't want to tell me, I think."

Cordelia smiled. "There's nothing to tell. What you remember is a distortion of how it was. There was some discussion. I expect the others felt that we had a large enough family. But your father and I believed there was room for one more. And time proved that there was. Delaney has always been a joy to us."

And he was a joy to Dorinda now.

She would never let anything stand between them.

But Jonathan's shadow limped past the window. And Jonathan was dead.

She strained her eyes, staring down.

It was there. Yes. Real. She wasn't in some strange

waking dream which created an image of something that didn't exist.

It didn't occur to her to cry out, to call for help or company.

She snatched up a light robe, and fled into the hall.

The sounds of her own movements seemed overloud in the thick silence. They trailed after her as she raced down the steps.

It was as if the house were suddenly empty, as if no one alive breathed there. It was as if Moorhaven were suddenly haunted by the memory of life, but not filled by life.

The sensation was familiar. She had known it occasionally while she was growing up. She had told no one about it. No one. Not even Delaney. But there had been moments when she thought that the house spoke to her and if she were able to listen hard enough she would understand. There had been moments when she felt that secrets were hidden within the walls and if she were able to stare hard enough she would see them. But she was twenty years old now, and such romantic imaginings were well behind her.

But still part of her mind insisted that she alone was alive in Moorhaven, though she knew perfectly well that her brothers were asleep in their beds. That Delaney was in his room. That Ralphine slept as soundly as always.

She eased the front door open, and stepped out onto the stone steps from which she had first seen Delaney.

The brass lamps on either side of the big black door were off as was usually the case at that time of night.

She turned quickly to look at Jonathan's wing.

The window was dark. The pacing shadow was gone.

She drew a quick hard breath, a gasp of fear, but determination, too.

She raced past the lilac bushes, done flowering now and without the scent that she always associated with late spring.

She reached to open the door. Her hand shook on

the brass knob. She heard from somewhere near by a whisper of movement. She strained to listen. Her whole body made the effort to identify the source of what she was certain she had just heard. But it was gone. Just as the limping, pacing shadow was gone.

She drew a deep careful breath and turned the door-knob. It clicked in response, but held fast.

It was locked, as it had been since the day she had found her father in his office. She turned the knob again, pushed the door hard, throwing her whole weight against it. But it held firm. Yes. It was still locked.

Yet she had seen a light in the study window. She had seen the shadow of someone who paced the floor there.

Was it Jonathan's ghost? Had he come back from his newly-dug grave to haunt Moorhaven?

She shrank back from the unyielding door.

She forced herself to take the six steps that brought her close to the office window. She eased her way through the bushes, and rose up on tiptoe to peer over the sill. Inside all was blackness except for a tiny pinpoint of light, a faint reflection in the mirror that hung on the opposite wall. Nothing. No one.

A breeze stirred around her, and she felt the damp breath of the marshes touch her. The Moorhaven marshes that lay beyond the circle of the dike, and spread to an invisible horizon, A place of bogs and quicksand, and hummocks on which the small ugly trees rose like gnarled fingers pointing to the sky.

The breath of the marshes touched her and turned her. It moved her away from the wing, back toward the house. She remembered when she and Delaney had seen the man lying, bloodstained and unconscious, under the trees. Marty Brown, with whom Lena had run away. Dorinda thought she alone had understood the need that had compelled Lena. A woman must have love. She would go where it led her. For Lena love had meant death.

The breath of the marshes seemed suddenly chill as

Dorinda crept up the steps. What, she asked herself, would love mean to her?

The big black door was closed now. She paused, frowning. It seemed to her that she had left it wide open, that she had fled through it from the dark within to the dark without on a single breath. But now the door was sealed against her.

It was an omen, warning her that she must not re-enter Moorhaven. The thought flashed through her mind like lightning. She rejected it instantly. Moorhaven was her home.

She pushed the door, but it didn't open. Bewildered, she tried again, then once more. But the door held firm, as firm as the one she had tried in the wing. It, too, must be bolted now.

She was still certain that she had come through it, leaving it open. But since then it had been closed and locked.

The breath of the marshes chilled her even more, and built a strange new terror in her. She felt as if the moist darkness was rolling over her, swelling beyond the dike and up the landscaped slope to the terrace itself. She flung herself against the door, and pounded with her small fists.

Then the door suddenly swung open. She fell across the threshold into the blinding brightness of the vestibule.

Sam, in the act of belting his brown robe, stood on the bottom step. "Dorinda, what's the matter?" he asked, his voice level. "What were you doing outside?"

He was a tall man, but very heavy-set. His black hair was receding, giving a tonsure effect to his hairline. His face was full, jowly, and always somewhat pink, as if the blood were too close to the surface. His voice was deep, rasping, as if rusted with the long silences habitual with him.

She crouched against the door, holding to it, her fingers white-knuckled. In the instant of silence between when he questioned her and when she answered him, she came to a rapid decision. She would not tell him of what she had seen. "I . . . I went out for some air," she stammered. "And I suppose the door closed behind me. I . . . I couldn't . . . I couldn't . . ."

"Went out for some air?" he repeated, dark brows rising quizzically. "At this hour of the night, Dorinda?"

"As I said, I just couldn't sleep."

"But why were you pounding at the door?"

"It wouldn't open. It was locked," she told him quickly.

"It was locked?" His brows rose again. "Then how did you get in?"

She blinked at him. "But, Sam, didn't you . . ."

"I haven't touched the bolt," he told her. "I heard the pounding and came down. I was where I am right now, at this moment, when you burst in as if the furies of hell were behind you."

She said, "But . . . I thought . . ." Then she stopped herself. She made a shame-faced grin, a pretending grin, hoping that he would accept the lame explanation she was about to offer him. "I suppose, being half asleep, I just didn't push hard enough. And I . . ."

He said quietly, "Never mind, Dorinda. I understand. You're simply overtired. These last weeks have been too much for you. Perhaps you had better go back to bed."

She nodded silent agreement, and went past him, carefully holding her robe tight around her. She moved up the steps slowly, feeling his eyes follow her. Midway she stopped, looked down into the vestibule. He was still standing at the foot of the steps. Beyond him, along the walls, she saw the row of family portraits. The Moorhavens looking out of their gilt frames. Grandmother Janina smiling faintly over a bouquet of roses. Grandfather Jonathan. Her father, Jonathan, too. Sam's parents. Dennis, in cavalry uniform. Elena, pale blue eyes, pale coronet of hair. Her Uncle Gregory, who had brought Delaney to her. Uncle Denton, dead in San Francisco, leaving no children behind him. They were all there, and more. And as she looked at them, the faces seemed to change, to lean out of the frames, frowning at her.

What were they saying?

But it was Sam, his voice raspy, saying impatiently, "Dorinda, do go to bed."

She went on. Then suddenly the lights went out.

She heard him coming up behind her, his step heavy, firm and even.

She hurried to her room, went in, closed the door softly behind her. She leaned against the panel, listening as his footsteps, muffled by the thick rug, faded away up the second flight toward his room.

She waited there until she could hear absolutely no sound. Then she turned and went to the window.

She peered out. Jonathan's wing lay in darkness now.

She shuddered. Had the light she had seen, the pacing shadow, been no more than a dream? Had she imagined that the ghost of Jonathan walked in his study?

It had been dark when she went to investigate.

The room had been still, empty, shadowed.

The door to the wing had been locked as always.

Then what had she really seen as she looked down from her room? What had been there, projected out of her mind, or, and she found that she couldn't believe that, what had been there in actuality?

The big front door had been open when she went down the steps. How had it closed so soundlessly? How had the bolt been thrown?

And how had it opened so suddenly?

Sam's look had been quizzical. It wasn't hard to imagine what he had been thinking when he saw her standing there, heard her stammering partial explanation.

She was glad now that she hadn't blurted out the truth. He would have laughed at her. He would have said she was mad.

And perhaps ... perhaps a waking dream was a form of madness.

She shuddered with a new chill of fear. Were the

secrets of Moorhaven she had always suspected concerned with a hidden madness?

At last, with dawn almost breaking, she went back to her fourposter bed.

She rose tired, her face, even at twenty, showing the marks of sleeplessness under her clear green eyes.

She brushed her short-cropped auburn hair back from her high brow.

She was, she knew, almost all her mother. The same small triangular face. The same short narrow nose and faintly pouting lips. But her brows, dark, straight and very expressive, were completely Moorhaven.

She dressed in a navy blue skirt, a short-sleeved white blouse with a big square collar, and went downstairs.

Her brother Jon was saying, "I don't understand it . . ."

"And I don't either," Sam answered. "But I'm very much afraid . . ."

They both fell silent as she entered.

Ralphine looked up at her, smiled tightly with pale lips bracketed with lines of discontent, and narrowed dark eyes. "Good morning, Dorinda." And then, with a faint frown, "Are you well? You're terribly pale this morning."

"I'm fine." She slipped into her chair with a quick smile for Delaney.

He was slim, very tall, his sandy curls stubbornly falling over his brow no matter how often he brushed them back. His mouth was finely-cut, sensitive. His eyes were a pale tan, and strangely old for his twenty-one years.

She noted, with a glance around the table, that he was the only one who smiled at her.

Her older brothers, Jon, Harris and Dennis, were staring at her with the same solemn expressions. Though it was hard to take Dennis seriously, with that smear of green on his jaw, a sign that he had been at his easel early that morning.

Sam's son, young Denny, who was twelve, was a replica of his father. Dark, flushed of face, he sat quietly, looking as if he wished he were somewhere else. Dorinda supposed that he did. Or perhaps he was still missing his mother, who had died two years before.

Jon's fiancée, Estella Beckett from Boston, was smiling faintly. She was a small girl, but very shapely. Her blonde hair was cut short, and she still wore those tiny curls over her ears and on her forehead that had been fashionable when she was twenty, but she was twenty-six now.

Yes, Dorinda thought, they were all regarding her oddly. She knew why the conversation had stopped when she came into the room. Sam had been telling them what had happened the night before.

A faint heat rose in her cheeks. She said brightly, defiantly, "Well, what is it? More bad news on the radio about the stock market?"

Ralphine said reproachfully, "I don't consider that a proper subject for levity, Dorinda. We're all very fortunate that your father was wise enough to do as he did. We got out just in time. Just, Dorinda. And if Alderson and Alderson had not been able to invest safely for us, all of our lives would have been changed."

Dorinda grinned. "Sorry, Aunt Ralphine. I know how lucky we are." She shrugged. "Well, if it's not that, then I guess it must be me."

"You?" Ralphine said coolly.

"The way everybody is staring at me," she retorted.

"Staring at you?" Estella's laugh tinkled through her red lips, and she shot a look at Jon. "Whatever do you mean?"

But Jon, his dark brows drawn together, said heavily, "Dorinda, I think you should go in and see Dr. Peter this morning."

Chapter 17

The heads nodded in solemn unison, as if they had each of them discussed it, decided it, before she came into the room.

Only Delaney abstained. Now he smiled at her again.

She sat straighter in her chair, narrow shoulders braced, chin high. She said. "Why should I see Dr. Peter? I'm perfectly all right."

"But are you?" Sam asked.

"Of course." The faint heat in her cheeks became a definite burning. She knew that she was blushing under his questioning look.

She had grown up with Sam, and they were first cousins. But he was just twice her age. She never felt she knew him. And, of course, in truth, she didn't. He had gone away to school, worked in Boston with Alderson and Sons, and married there. He had returned to Moorhaven only for rare and brief visits. He had been widowed two years before, having left Aldersons to go into private law practice some time earlier. Just a month ago, he and Denny had come to Moorhaven for an indefinite stay. He and Dorinda had no relationship, save the one of kinship. And suddenly that seemed hardly to matter.

He said, "I felt it my duty, Dorinda, to speak of what happened last night."

"I guessed that. But nothing did happen."

"I'm afraid that I can't agree that nothing, or what you call nothing, happened," Jon told her. "Plainly something did. You said you went out. But why would you do that in the middle of the night?"

Mary came in with a platter of scrambled eggs and pork sausages. She set them on the table, said to Dorinda, "Oh, there are you. I'll get you your coffee right away." She went to the door, hesitated for a moment. The sharp black eyes in her plump face touched each member of the family. She gave an audible sigh as she disappeared. A moment later she returned with a pot of coffee. She filled Dorinda's cup, then patted her shoulder fondly. "Be sure and have some eggs," she ordered.

When she had gone, the door closed behind her, Jon said, "Well, Dorinda?"

"I couldn't sleep. So I went out for a breath of air."

"Oh, really?" Estella's blue eyes moved from Dorinda to Delaney. "Is that the real reason? Or did you have something else in mind?"

"Just that," Dorinda retorted, wishing that Jon's fiancée would remember that she was not, yet, Dorinda's sister-in-law, not a member of the family.

"And that business with the door," Sam asked. "The way you were pounding on it. It sounded like sheer panic. I could hear you all the way up to my room and through a sound sleep." His dark eyes glowed. "It seemed as if you thought you were being chased."

She said faintly, "Well, it just surprised me that it was stuck, closed." And she wondered how it was that Sam had heard her all the way up on the third floor, while none of those sleeping closer had heard her.

He gave a shrug of open disbelief, and turned his flushed face away.

Denny, thin face alight with laughter, said, "Is there any sleepwalking in the family?"

"Certainly not," Ralphine said sharply. "If anyone would know I would. The Moorhavens are, and have always been, perfectly normal people."

"He's just joking," Sam grinned.

Ralphine tossed her gray head, answered grimly, "This isn't a joking matter."

It was typical of Ralphine to react that way. She had a thing about the family. Dorinda supposed that it was because she had never married, and now, at sixty, had nothing to occupy her but the family, the estate, and her cabinet of mementos over which she puttered constantly.

"No," Jon agreed heavily. "Not a joking matter at all."

Dorinda sipped her coffee, her eyes fixed on Delaney. She wouldn't listen to the rest of them any more. She wouldn't think of what they were saying. She wouldn't explain what had happened. A shiver touched her. What would they say if they knew she had seen a light in Jonathan's study window? What would they think if she told them about the slowly pacing shadow with its limp?

But she decided she would go into the wing. She would examine Jonathan's office and would see if anyone had been there.

Jon told her, "Dorinda, I'm going to insist on this, you know. I do want you to see Dr. Peter this morning."

She moved her glance to his face. "But why? Just because I got up during the night?"

Ralphine cut in, "No, dear. It's because you seem not quite yourself."

Dorinda looked back at Delaney. He smiled faintly. She knew that he understood just what she was thinking then.

They were making an issue out of what Sam had told them because they needed an issue. What had happened the night before wasn't important. They had something else in mind.

Delaney and she knew what it was.

Now he said suddenly, "Dorie, I think Jon's suggestion is a good one. I'll drive you into Tembley right after breakfast."

She put down her coffee cup. She said tiredly, "All right, Delaney. If you think I ought to."

Ralphine said, in a voice thick with satisfaction, "There. That's settled. I'll call and tell him that you're coming in this morning."

Dorinda repressed the need to laugh. Poor Aunt Ralphine, so delighted to have an excuse to speak to Dr. Peter. It was funny to think that a woman her age could have a crush on a man his age.

Dorinda finished her coffee, left the room. Delaney, following, caught up with her in the hallway. His warm hand curled around her shoulder. "Hold it, Dorie. Don't run away from me, too."

She turned quickly, accusingly. "Why did you agree to it? I'm not sick. I don't want to go to Dr. Peter. I have nothing to complain about, and I . . ."

He grinned at her, his tan eyes gleaming. "It'll give us a chance to be alone, won't it?"

"Oh," she said. "Oh." Then she grinned, too. "Now why didn't I think of that?"

"You were too busy resenting them, Dorie. You mustn't waste your time and strength on that."

"But what else can I do?"

"Just be firm. Trust me. We'll bring them around, you know."

"Never," she said bitterly. "Never."

He hugged her to him. "Wait and see, Dorie."

She wished she could believe him. With all her heart she wanted to accept his reassurance. But she knew she mustn't.

She had known it since the evening just a week before when she told Jon what she and Delaney planned.

It should have been no surprise to her older brother, but she had been startled by his reaction when she said, "Jon, Delaney and I are going to be married."

Jon had said, "Oh, no you're not!"

She'd stared at him, bewildered. "But we are."

His dark brows had drawn together. He had gotten to his feet, stood over his desk, looking so much like their father that she gasped with the pain of their recent loss. Then he'd said, "Dorinda, put the idea out of your mind for good. Delaney's a brother to you, and he can't ever be anything else."

She shook her head adamantly from side to side, and set her jaw. "Delaney's not my brother. And you know it. When he was adopted . . ."

Jon answered, "We won't talk about it. It's out of the question."

She lost her temper then. She snapped, "I'm afraid that you don't understand. I wasn't asking for your permission. I'm not asking for it now. I'm twenty years old. I thought it only polite to tell you, but I certainly have the right to make up my own mind."

"Twenty," he said patronizingly, "as if that makes you all knowing, and all wise."

"Then thirty doesn't either," she retorted.

He'd said, "Send Delaney in here, Dorinda. I want to talk to him."

"Oh, no," she'd cried. "You're not going to talk to him alone."

Jon rose, went to the office door. He opened it with an angry jerk. "Delaney," he shouted. "Get in here, will you?"

Without waiting for an answer, Jon returned to his desk. "All right, Dorinda. You can stay and hear this if you want to."

"We've always loved each other," she said, more quietly now. "You know that, Jon."

"As brother and sister."

"No. Not at all."

Delaney came in. His grin faded as he looked at Jon. "Something wrong?" he asked quickly.

"Very wrong," Jon retorted. He drew a deep heavy breath, then let it out as if it pained him. "I'd have thought that after all this family has done for you, you'd have some gratitude."

That was too much for Dorinda. The small grasp she had on her self-control broke. She cried, "Stop it, Jon. You have absolutely no right . . ."

Jon went on remorselessly. "You were adopted by my parents. You were treated, always, as one of the family. You owe us all something for that."

The color had gone from Delaney's face. His jaw had hardened. He asked quietly, "What's all this about, Jon?"

Dorinda said, "I told him. And he . . ."

Again Jon cut in, "I am opposed to this marriage of yours. The idea of it disgusts me. That either of you should even think of it disgusts me. And I blame you, Delaney. You ought to have had more . . . more sense . . . and more gratitude, as I said."

"If Dad were here . . ." Dorinda said angrily. "If he . . ."

"But he isn't," Jon answered. "And I'm the head of the family now."

Delaney said quietly, "There's no reason why Dorie and I shouldn't marry. We're in no way related by blood. You know that we've always loved each other."

"In no way related by blood," Jon said bitterly. "How freely you say that. And you don't even know. You don't have the faintest idea . . ."

"But I do. And so do you and the rest of us. Gregory brought me here, and when he died, your parents . . ."

"But where did you come from?" Jon demanded. "Who are you?"

Delaney's tan eyes narrowed. "You know as much of that as I do, Jon."

"Then we both know nothing," Jon said in a heavy whisper.

"Jon, Jon, what's this all about?" Delaney asked, quiet still, bewildered. "I don't understand you."

"Of course you don't. Or else you're pretending not to."

Delaney looked at Dorinda, shrugged. Her heart quivered in her breast as she saw a curl fall across his forehead, and she yearned to brush it back for him.

Jon went on, "Gregory brought you here. He was very inexplicit about how he'd found you. You were

five, but spoke very little somehow. You only knew
your first name."

"Yes," Delaney drawled. "And so . . ."

"You might have been Gregory's natural son, his
illegitimate son," Jon said deliberately.

"Oh, no," Dorinda cried. "That's quite impossible.
You've absolutely no reason . . ."

"Then why else would our parents have adopted
him?" Jon demanded.

"For Gregory's sake," Dorinda cried. "Because that's
what he would have done."

Jon said coldly, "Dorinda, you were too young to
remember, but I do. I was fourteen. I heard the talk.
Dennis, too. Aunt Ralphine was quite beside herself
when our parents decided on the adoption. She was
concerned about it then. Just as she is, and I, too, am
concerned with it now."

"That was no more than a bit of malicious family
gossip," Dorinda cried. "You've no real reason to think
such a thing."

Jon ignored her. "If you're Gregory's son, then
you're Dorinda's first cousin. That's too close, Delaney.
Too close by blood for the two of you to marry."

"But I'm not Gregory's son," Delaney said. "I've no
cause to think it, and neither have you."

Jon leaned back, closed his eyes. "We're not going to
argue about it. The whole thing is out of the question. I
refuse to discuss it any more."

It was that scene that had been behind Jon's concern
for her at the breakfast table. Memory of her defiance
had driven him to insist that she see Dr. Peter.

Since that night she had found it almost impossible
to be alone with Delaney. Where they had once been a
part of a family, they were now both suddenly two
outcasts, observed, judged, watched, in every move that
they made.

"If you're ready, we can go now," Delaney said.
"Before somebody decides to come along with us."

"I am . . . but . . . but wait." She had remembered
the one thing that she had wanted to do that morning.

She turned toward the door, then remembered that she would need a key. "I'll be right back," she told him, and hurried to the kitchen.

Mary frowned when she asked for the key. "What for, Dorie? Why do you want to go in there now?"

"Just for a minute," Dorinda answered.

Mary took the key off a hook behind the kitchen door, said, "Bring it back, will you, Dorie?"

Dorinda hurried back to Delaney. They went outside together. She hesitated on the steps, looking at Jonathan's wing. Then, "I want to go inside."

"Okay. But why?"

She hesitated. Should she tell Delaney what she had seen the night before? What she had seen, or what she had dreamed? Should she explain why she had gone out into the night while the house slept?

What would he think? What would he say?

He took her hand, repeated, "Why?"

How could she doubt him? He was her love, her whole heart. All that she wanted and needed of joy.

Quickly, in half sentences, she told him what had happened. She described the sight from her window, her trip down the steps and out onto the terrace. She told how she had found the door locked as it should have been, and peering in the window had seen nothing. She described how she had returned to the house, and the door had been closed against her, and when finally she had gotten it open, Sam had been on the steps, asking her what was the matter.

Delaney's sensitive lips pursed in a soundless whistle. "You're sure, Dorie?" he asked finally. "Of what you saw, I mean."

"I think I'm sure, but how can I . . ."

"Then we'll go and have a look," he told her decisively.

It was different to pass the huge lilacs by daylight, to cross the terrace with Delaney beside her.

A faint haze hung over the marshes, and Joshua, still heavy, but bent now, stamped along the hump of the dike with his white beard blowing in the breeze.

Delaney took the key from her, unlocked the door. They entered the stillness of the front sitting room.

"The window of Jonathan's office," Delaney said.

She nodded. She held her breath as they paused before the open door of that room.

The curtains were pulled back, allowing the sunlight to fall on the rug where long streaks in the nap showed. Long uneven streaks. Like footprints, she thought. But surely Mary had vacuumed in here before closing the wing, Dorinda thought.

Delaney said quietly, "There's nothing to see, Dorie."

"No way to tell," she breathed.

"To tell what?"

"What I saw," she explained. "If I saw anything."

He looked at her silently for a moment. Then, "Dorie, let's not make too much of this. Whatever happened last night is over now."

She agreed with a thoughtful nod, but felt her heart sink within her.

Chapter 18

The road to Tembley was narrow and bumpy. It curved over the cliffs and through the deserted countryside.

Delaney drove fast but carefully.

It was one of the qualities Dorinda admired in him. Harris handled a car as if he were a demon and it his chariot. Jon was terribly slow. Dennis rarely bothered to drive at all.

They passed no other cars on the way, but as they reached the town itself a yellow roadster hooted its horn at them.

"Old Arley Jones," Delaney said.

Arley raised his hand and smiled. His black eyes glittered under an unruly thatch of dingy white. His sallow wrinkled face was a map of his years. There was no friendliness in the curve of those narrow lips, only a familiar knowing mockery.

She forced herself to smile in return.

Delaney said, as he drove on, "Old Arley's done all right by himself in the two years he's been out."

"I suppose it went right on while he was in jail," she answered.

Delaney nodded, turned into Washington Avenue.

A man sat on the curb in the sunlight. He had a

small box of apples on his knee. His clothes were worn, his face thin, haggard.

Dorinda wondered who in all of Tembley would stop to buy his wares.

Delaney slowed suddenly, jerked the car to the curb. She bit back a protest.

He got out, spoke to the man for a moment. He took an apple, put a quarter into the man's outstretched hand.

The man squinted at it, rubbed it, then gave Delaney a twisted grin. In a voice loud enough for Dorinda to hear, he said, "Why, thank you, Mr. Moorhaven."

The words were commonplace, but the tone in which they were uttered, the tone of exaggerated gratitude, was loaded with that peculiar antagonism that she had recognized since she was a small child, riding with her parents on an occasional errand into Tembley.

She had never really understood it. She didn't understand it now. But it made her heart shrink within her. To live, to try to be young and happy and loving, when surrounded by hate, by unacknowledged and unexplainable hate, was difficult indeed.

Delaney swung back into the car, drove on.

She said, "You oughtn't to have done that."

He smiled faintly. "I know it. But he needs the quarter."

"You heard how he sounded."

Delaney shrugged. "He still needs the quarter. And as for how he sounds . . . well, we're used to that, aren't we?"

The Moorhaven warehouses, burned out husks now, still stood across from the railroad station, but hardly anything remained of the family name on the charred walls.

As Delaney drove past the small church, a group of children playing on the street looked up. They stared, drew back, eyes big and watchful in small faces.

Delaney ignored them, but Dorinda, turning for a second look, saw the ragged clothes they wore and the bitterness in the angle of small heads and rigid shoulders.

Delaney said, "Stop it, Dorie. They're nothing to you, nor you to them."

"Yes," she agreed, sighing.

The car rolled past the Falkland house. Its windows were boarded up. Wild morning glory veiled its porches. The elder Falklands had both died long before. Helena was somewhere in California, and had never come home after Denton died.

Beyond that overgrown plot there was another marked only by a crumbling chimney. Long before, when her father was a young man, Dorinda knew, the Moorhavens had lived in a house that stood there. She wished that they lived there still. That she had grown up in the house that once surrounded that chimney instead of in the great manor that overlooked the marshes.

At the Van Nuys house, Delaney parked. He took her hands in his. "Now, listen," he said. "There's nothing to be afraid of. We're just here for a visit. To talk to Dr. Peter and to Bettina. To get him on our side."

"I'm afraid we mightn't be able to do that."

Delaney's fingers tightened around her small clenched hands. "We can try. And if not . . ." He shrugged. "Then we'll do without."

She felt his warmth and strength flow into her from his touch. Yet she was afraid. She remained afraid. "They're going to ruin it, Delaney. Something terrible will happen."

And she thought of the night before. What had awakened her? Who had she seen walking in Jonathan's office?

Delaney said that was over and done with. But she knew better. Somehow she knew that it was not ended. It was only beginning.

She slipped from the car, hurried up to the front door with Delaney following her.

Bettina Van Nuys responded to Dorinda's knock.

"Come in," she smiled. "We've been expecting you. Dr. Peter's in his office, but he'll be right out."

Dorinda repressed irritation. Ralphine had said she would call, and call she had. She had managed her small contact with Dr. Peter, feeding the silly crush nurtured over the years. It was impossible for Dorinda to imagine that her aunt and Dr. Peter had ever been young. They showed no signs of it now. Dorinda didn't remember when they had shown signs of it. An impenetrable barrier lay between the two older people and herself. She supposed that one day she would breach it, but that day seemed far in the future. Whatever there had been between them once, Dr. Peter's wife Bettina seemed to Dorinda the only woman he could possibly have married.

She was one of those remarkable women whose warmth and good nature stamped themselves permanently on her features. She had round pink cheeks, dimples, and bright blue eyes. Her smile was open and direct. Her voice held laughter. She wore a green cotton dress that hung in loose folds around her ample figure to well below her shins. It was decorated with a high collar of white piqué, and covered her round arms to the elbow. Below the sleeves, the round arms were dusted with flour. Bettina had obviously been baking.

Now she said, in her laughter-filled voice, "I judge by your face that you're annoyed by Ralphine's calling. Don't be. She doesn't mean any harm."

"I suppose not," Dorinda agreed, but with no conviction.

Bettina chuckled, and led the way into the big living room.

It was long and narrow, dominated at one end by a huge bay window and at the other by a large white painted brick fireplace. The sofas were large and deep, each with antimacassars crocheted by Bettina herself. The chairs were large and comfortable, and Dorinda sank into one of them with relief. This house was the only one in Tembley in which she felt safe. In fact, it was, except for a few visits to the Falklands long ago, the only house to which she had been in Tembley. It had always been a retreat to her, and now it seemed even more so. It was not only a relief to be off Tembley's single street, to be shielded from those watching eyes, but a relief to have escaped Moorhaven, too, for a little while. The recognition was a painful one. Moorhaven was home to her. How could she feel that way?

Bettina interrupted her thoughts. "You must forgive Ralphine, Dorinda. She's very anxious about you, I gather."

"There's nothing wrong with me so there's no need for her to be anxious." Dorinda heard the stiffness in her voice and tried to soften it by adding, "Though I know she means well."

"Of course she does," Bettina agreed comfortably.

"But," Dorinda rushed on, unable to hold the words back, "she's determined to keep me a child. No matter how. And at whatever cost."

Delaney, silent until then, asked, "Dorie, do you really think that's what's behind it?"

"Behind what?" Bettina asked.

But Dorinda knew that she must have been well briefed. "Oh, let's not pretend. Ralphine was sure to have told Dr. Peter about our plans."

Bettina's dimples deepened, and her round face flushed. "Of course. Foolish of me to pretend otherwise." She looked as if she might have continued, but Dr. Peter entered the room.

He was still tall and very thin, but his shoulders had developed a permanent slouch, as if they had carried too many burdens for too many years. His light brown hair was white now, and very fine, barely covering his pink scalp. His amber eyes had sunk so deeply into the hollows of his face that they were hard to see.

He grinned at Dorinda, at Delaney. "It's good to have a diversion," he said, sinking into a big chair, and stretching out his long blue-clad legs. "There's so much sickness in this town now, and so little to do for it."

"So little to do?" Delaney asked.

"Malnutriton, for two generations, doesn't cure with a pill or a dosing," Peter explained.

"Things are very bad," Bettina said. "It was bad

enough when I came here more than twenty-five years ago. Oh, yes, the town was plainly dying of no way to earn a living . . ."

"From when the shipyards were closed," Peter murmured.

Bettina went on, "But now . . . with the whole of the country brought so low . . ."

"What existed forty years ago is made worse," Peter agreed. "And there's no help for it. None that I can see."

But Dorinda wasn't interested in a discussion of Tembley's economic problems. She moved impatiently. She said, "I know that Ralphine must have told you, Dr. Peter. Perhaps Jon has, too."

He nodded, his look becoming sober. "Yes, Dorinda. Not that it was necessary. I've seen it coming with my own eyes, you know."

"And?" she asked challengingly.

He hesitated. Then, "I brought you into the world, Dorinda. I gave Delaney his first check-up when he was five. I . . ."

"Yes, yes," Dorinda said impatiently. "But that has nothing to do with it!"

Delaney cut in, "Dorie, please. Let's hear Dr. Peter out."

Peter said, "I love the both of you. You know that. Nothing that I say implies any question in my mind about you, Delaney."

Dorinda felt her face grow pale. "You're siding with them, aren't you?"

"I'm siding with no one." Peter's voice hardened. "There are facts though. Scientific facts which must be considered. You can't ignore them, Dorinda. Or wish them away either. They exist."

Now she couldn't look at Peter's face. She fixed her eyes above the fireplace. Peter's two sons looked back at her. The older, called Pete, was in his last year of medical school. The younger, Jack, was just beginning.

Delaney asked quietly, "Then you believe that I'm Gregory's bastard?"

Bettina gasped, "Oh, Delaney ... to use that word ... oh, no ..."

"If it's true then my only legitimacy is the one conferred on me when Jonathan adopted me. And perhaps that's why he did."

"You're just repeating all that awful stuff Jon said," Dorinda cried.

Dr. Peter said coldly, "No, Delaney. Jonathan never really believed that you were Gregory's son. Not for a moment. Nor did Cordelia. The adoption was as much for you, as for Gregory, as much for Gregory as for you. He loved you and died, and they loved you, and they adopted you."

"Then why ... ?"

"The possibility exists, you see. That's where the trouble comes in. None of us know the truth. But belief isn't enough. There is still the possibility. Gregory said he found you in a railroad station in Chicago, a year before he brought you here. He said he reported it to the police. They knew nothing of you. Rather than turn you over to an orphanage, he kept you and raised you."

Dorinda said, "What difference does it make anyway? If he's my first cousin, or not, I love him. And I'm going to marry him."

"But marriage to a first cousin is a risk that you can't take. The mixing of two sets of genes, possibly very similar, with the same weaknesses and the same strengths, can produce predominating weaknesses. It's hard to think of that now, but you must. If you ever expect to have children."

"It's a risk I'll take," Dorinda flared.

But Delaney said, "Wait, Dorie." And to Dr. Peter, "How much of this is scientific fact, and how much old wives' tales?"

Peter shrugged his hunched shoulders. "It's all scientific fact."

Dorinda put her hands over her face. She said, "Delaney, are you turning against me, too?"

"No, Dorie. But we have to know what we're doing. And that's what Dr. Peter is trying to tell us."

"I don't care," she whispered. "I don't care about his genes, or whatever they are. You're not related to me by blood, Delaney. And since that's the case nothing else matters."

"But we don't know for sure," Peter said. "I don't think so. But I don't know. And neither does anyone else."

She rose to her feet, green eyes flashing in her white face. "Guesswork based on conjecture, born out of gossip. It amuses me that anyone, least of all you, should think that I could be swayed by it. I'm over eighteen. I'm legally of age to marry. No one can stop me. No one. And no one will. Delaney and I are going to be married."

She repeated those words to the family that evening.

She had waited until after dinner. Mary had served them coffee in the lounge. Ralphine sat on the sofa, with Estella on one side of her and Jon on the other. Dennis and Harris were playing chess, and Sam and young Denny stood peering over their shoulders. Dorinda said the words, then waited defiantly.

There was an instant silence.

Then each of them began to speak at the same time.

Jon's voice cut through the others' sharply, clearly, harshly. He said, "Dorinda, we all understand how difficult this is for you, but you must see that we're not going to permit you to make such a ghastly mistake."

She looked at him angrily. "You can't stop me, Jon."

He ignored her. "What about you, Delaney? Don't you owe the rest of us something? Don't you owe Moorhaven something? How can you let Dorinda ruin her life and yours?"

"It'll not be ruined," Delaney answered.

Jon retorted, "You don't know that. Nor does she."

The staring eyes, the walls of the big room, seemed to swell. The air was suddenly thin, choking.

Dorinda burst into tears and screamed, "Nothing can stop us, Jon, nothing," and ran from the room.

Chapter 19

Afterwards, Dorinda told herself that she should have guessed.

There had been a peculiar emptiness in the house, a stillness like the quality of death itself.

But that morning, when she went downstairs, she was completely unprepared.

Ralphine was alone in the breakfast room, sipping coffee, toying listlessly with a piece of toast. Her thin face was sallow and even more hollow than usual. Her gray bun was askew, as if it hadn't been rolled with the usual care.

She said, "Good morning, dear. Are you feeling better now?"

Dorinda nodded. She was about to speak, but Mary came in with a pot of coffee.

She poured a cup for Dorinda, served her, and then with smiling concern, said, "I'll make you some eggs right away."

"No, thanks, Mary. I'm not hungry."

Mary put hands on her round hips, bent her gray head. "It won't do for you to starve yourself to death. Nothing's worth that. And if you want to make a fight for it then you'll need all your strength."

"I'll wait," Dorinda answered. "Later, when Delaney comes down . . ."

"Then you'll have a . . ."

Ralphine cut in dryly, "Mary, thank you. I'd like very much to have a few words with Dorinda."

Mary's dark eyes narrowed. "Alone, you mean."

Ralphine simply looked at her, mouth straight, eyes veiled.

It was, Dorinda thought, just the way she had looked when she spoke to Dr. Peter the day before on the phone. Uncompromisingly sure of herself. It occurred to Dorinda then that although Ralphine told Dr. Peter what she and Delaney planned, she had said nothing about her having gone out of the house in the night. Dorinda asked herself why Ralphine hadn't mentioned it, but could find no answer.

Mary turned away from Ralphine to give Dorinda a compassionate look. "I'll be in the kitchen." She went out, banging the door emphatically behind her.

Puzzled, Dorinda asked, "What's the matter? Have you and Mary been feuding?"

"She's a good soul, our Mary. But she takes too much on herself," Ralphine said. "She's been with us for so long that she thinks of herself as a Moorhaven."

"As she ought to."

"Hardly. Or at least within limits." Ralphine drew a deep breath. She said, "But never mind that. Now, about Delaney . . ."

"We won't discuss it," Dorinda said quickly.

"But I'm afraid we must."

Something in Ralphine's tone made Dorinda put down her cup. There was a sudden dryness in her throat. She felt the pulses begin to pound in her temples. She asked, "Ralphine, what is it? What's happened?"

"Delaney's gone," Ralphine said quietly.

"Gone?" she said in an unbelieving whisper.

Ralphine nodded. "Very early this morning. He took young Denny out to San Francisco for a small trip."

"For how long a small trip?" Dorinda demanded.

Ralphine's thin shoulders moved in a shrug. "Why,

I'm not quite sure. Jon gave him some commissions . . . business . . . the offices . . ."

"Impossible," Dorinda retorted. "We all know that our offices and depots have been sold out. We have no . . ."

"Odds and ends, further details," Ralphine explained.

"Alderson and Alderson takes care of the details," Dorinda said coldly. "Jon has simply sent Delaney away. And he had no right to do it. Delaney has a legitimate legacy here. He can't be driven off."

Ralphine's shoulders moved once more in that uncaring shrug. "My dear, of course he has a legitimate legacy. That's not in question. But he has his responsibilities to the family. Which is why he agreed to go."

"It was because of me," Dorinda cried. "You know, and I do, too, that Delaney was sent away to separate us."

"That may be. But if you both love each other as you claim, if you can't give that love up, then a month or two, or even longer, won't matter. Even a year won't matter."

A wave of dizziness swept Dorinda. The room seemed to sway and spin and the sunlight to turn into darkness. She held tightly to the edge of the table, with the chair, the floor, shifting under her rigid body. At last she murmured, "But he didn't come to tell me himself. He didn't even say goodbye."

"We thought it best. And he agreed."

"Did he?" Dorinda asked, unbelieving again.

"My dear child, you've been behaving so oddly, and you must know it yourself. It began when your father died. We've all noticed it. We do understand. All this, even your unseemly love for Delaney, is related to your father's death. But you seem to be walking on the thin edge of hysteria. As if you might, at any moment, slip over it. We didn't want to precipitate a great emotional upheaval unnecessarily. You must be reasonable. It's for your own good, you know."

Pain stabbed through her chest. It became a suffocating breathlessness.

Dear beloved Delaney, who had never been separated from her except for those months at the time during the school year, the painful stretches through which they had both agonized, would never have gone away without first telling her, without making plans with her for his return, without holding her in his arms, pressed to him, and promising her with kisses.

She got to her feet stiffly. The abrupt movement knocked over her coffee cup, spreading a dark stain on the white linen cloth. She stared down at it.

She said, "I don't believe you, Ralphine. I don't believe he's left. He's here somewhere. You've done something to him. He's here. I know it. I must go and find him."

"Dorinda!" Ralphine gasped.

But Dorinda had turned toward the door.

Sam stood there, blocking her way. He asked, "Dorie, what's wrong?"

"Don't call me that," she answered. "Nobody calls me Dorie except Delaney. I don't want you to mock me."

He stared at her, his jowls pink, his brows drawn down in a frown. "What's this?"

She put out both hands in a thrusting gesture. "You've done something to him. I must find him."

Sam moved aside, still staring at her. She was aware of his narrowed gaze as she stumbled from the room.

She was aware, too, of his deep voice saying, "Do you remember, Ralphine? How Jonathan was when Cordelia died?"

She paused for an instant, checked by a need she didn't understand. She heard Ralphine say sadly, "Sam, don't!"

Then she went on, down the hall, across the vestibule and into Jon's office.

Her three brothers were there, gathered around the desk in low-voiced conversation.

They were, she supposed, talking about her, about Delaney.

She moved up to them stiffly, her face set. She demanded, "All right. Now tell me. Where is Delaney? What have you done to him?"

The three faces swung toward her, identical in their questioning stares.

"Done to him?" Jon echoed finally. "What an odd thing to say, Dorinda."

"Don't fence with me, Jon. Where is he? I know he wouldn't leave without telling me goodbye."

"But he did," Dennis said, his face breaking into a kind smile, while the red smear of paint on one cheek made him look like a half-made-up clown. "You were asleep. We knew you needed your rest, so . . ."

"No. It's a story you've made up. He's here. Somewhere. I know it. So you might as well tell me."

Jon and Dennis always stood together, and always had. Perhaps it was because they were the two oldest. But Harris had once had something of a rebel streak. He had run away, hadn't he? And stayed away for three years? Even today he went more frequently into Tembley than any of the others. She appealed to him. "Harris, you tell me."

He grinned at her. "You're making too much out of nothing, love. He'll be back. You'll be hearing from him. Nothing terrible has happened."

But something had. She knew. She was sure. She turned, left her brothers without a word.

Delaney was somewhere in Moorhaven. She would find him.

She spent most of the morning in a useless search.

She checked the storerooms below, and the kitchen and pantries. She looked into the drawing room, the dining room. She was finally satisfied that he had not been hidden away on the lower floor.

She went slowly up the steps, and without shame, or even thought of it, she checked each of her brothers' private quarters. She examined every closet, every wardrobe, every chest. She went into the unused schoolroom, the nursery that had been hers, the small room that she had used as a child.

At last, at the very last, she went to Delaney's room.

It was stripped bare. His comb and brush were gone from the dresser, his clothes from the closet, his books from the bedside table, his suitcase from the storage shelf.

And still, oddly, she thought later, she wouldn't believe it; accept it. If Delaney were not in the house, then he must be in Jonathan's wing.

She went down the steps, moving like a wraith through the hallway, past the framed photographs of Jon and Delaney, of Dennis and Harris, and herself. She didn't even glance up at them as she slipped into the kitchen, took the key from behind the door, then slipped out through the back.

Estella, wearing a big floppy sunhat, sat curled up in a chair. She glanced up at Dorinda. "Good morning. I thought I'd get myself out of the way. You and your brothers . . ." Her smile faded as Dorinda passed without speaking. "I told them there'd be trouble," Estella grumbled. "You needn't blame me. I told them."

Dorinda went on, turned the corner of the wing, and followed the path along the terrace, past the lilacs, to the front door.

The windows that flanked it were dark, but glints of reflected sun winked at her like malevolent eyes.

She unlocked the door, stepped inside, thinking of the day before when she and Delaney had stepped inside together. It seemed so long ago now.

It was with a strange reluctance that she began her search. She told herself that she was frightened because this was the last place she could look for Delaney. If he wasn't here, then he had left Moorhaven without saying goodbye. Without explanation, without promising to return. It was the last place . . .

She paused to look back, over her shoulder across the terrace and down the slope to the dike that held back the marshes. She shuddered, and closed the door behind her.

She stood still, holding her breath, listening.

There was something here. Some watching presence. She felt eyes on her. She heard the beating of pulses that matched her own.

Then, with a shake, she told herself to stop imagining what wasn't there, what couldn't be there. She told herself to look for Delaney.

Jonathan's office was empty. The scuff marks on the rug that she and Delaney had seen were gone. She stared at the place where they had been, her slanted green eyes widening.

Had the marks been there? Or had she imagined them, too? Had she imagined Jonathan's shadow as well?

She backed from the room, went swiftly through the three others, no longer checking closets and chests.

Delaney wasn't here. If he were, she would have felt it. She would have basked in the warmth of his love. She would have sensed the power of his protection. Instead she was overwhelmed by a malign emptiness, an emptiness that mocked her.

She went out, closed and locked the door behind her, and sat on the step.

Delaney could not have left her. Then where was he? Her eyes went to the tree-covered cliff behind the house, and then swung down to stare at the slick, shining marshes. She buried her face in her hands.

Some time later a shadow fell over her. She looked up.

Harris said, "Dorinda, love, you mustn't do this to yourself, you know."

"But you, Jon and Dennis, have done it to me."

Harris shook his head. "We've done nothing."

"Then tell me where Delaney is."

"On the way to San Francisco with young Denny. You know that, love."

"But I don't believe you. I can't." She got to her feet. Suddenly it was clear. If Delaney and Denny had gone off, it would have been either by car or by train. She said, "How did they leave, Harris?"

"How?" He blinked at her. "Why, I drove them into town myself, and they took the morning train."

"Will you drive me in now?"

"What for?"

"Will you, Harris?"

"I don't understand." His dark eyes were narrow, his mouth faintly smiling. "Tell me what you're thinking, love."

"I want to find out if he and Denny really left, really got on that train."

"But I just told you . . ."

"Harris," she said coldly, "it's easy enough to understand. If you want to. I no longer believe any of you. I think Delaney must still be here. Denny's gone, I grant you. He could have gone on the train alone. I want to find out."

A peculiar expression crossed his face. It seemed, almost, as if he were frightened.

Dorinda was even more certain that she had guessed right. She said, "Take me, Harris."

"All right, love," he agreed. "If you insist on making an ass of yourself, then I'll be glad to help."

"Now?"

"Why not?" he shrugged.

He drove as fast as always, slewing around the sharp curves and shooting over the rises, but she urged him on, sitting on the edge of her seat with her face raised to the warm wind.

He stopped before the small shed that was the Tembley station.

"Go ahead, if you insist. I think, after all, that I don't want to be a witness. I'll use this wasted time to pick up the mail and come back for you in a few minutes. You won't need any more time than that."

Without a word, she slipped from the car.

She went quickly into the shed. It was dim, the air hot and malodorous.

Arley Jones sat with three other men on a wooden bench near the pot-bellied stove.

He raised his white head and smiled broadly, while the other men murmured among themselves.

She waited a moment at the barred ticket window, then turned to ask, "Who sells the tickets, please?"

After a pause, one of the men rose. He was past middle-age, thin. He growled from the corner of his mouth, "No more trains today."

"I just wanted to ask you a question," she explained.

"Then ask."

Old Arley Jones smiled broadly at her again. "Don't be bashful, Dorinda Moorhaven. You're among *friends*. Surely you know that."

There was another unpleasant murmur. Cold eyes glared at her. Friends? she thought. What a strange word to use. Why was he mocking her?

"I wanted to ask ..." she faltered, "... do you happen to know ..."

"Yes," the man said. "Well, what?"

"Do you know if a man ... tall, sandy-haired ... and a twelve-year-old boy ..."

"We know the Moorhavens," the man said dryly.

"Too well," another added.

The first went on, "You're speaking of Delaney, of course. And the boy, Sam's son, Denny, aren't you?"

She nodded.

"Well, what?"

"Did they get on the train this morning? Both of them? Did you see them, did you see them yourself?"

The man's eyes narrowed. He seemed to weigh her question for a long time, though it should have been easy enough to answer. Was that, too, a kind of mockery? she wondered.

At last he said, while the men behind him murmured, and Arley Jones grinned, "Yes, he did. And the boy, too. Bought tickets for New York. Heading west to San Francisco, he told me. Though I didn't ask. Did you want anything else?"

She shook her head numbly. She stumbled outside into the sunlight, all hope gone from her.

From nowhere, it seemed to her, a group of children

in ragged clothes had gathered. She moved toward them, and they shifted back like waves parting to allow her to pass without coming close to any of them.

She walked between them, and heard one say, "That's another one of them. The Moorhavens. Doomed. That's what my mother says. Accursed Moorhavens. They're high now, but one day they'll be brought low."

Harris was coming toward her, hurrying.

She fixed her eyes on his face. She tried to breathe. But the sunlight faded. The world turned dark. She fell into his arms.

Chapter 20

"Vitamins," Peter Van Nuys said, "And rest. That's all you need, Dorinda." He smiled at her.

She nodded. She thought bitterly that he didn't understand. She needed Delaney. Neither vitamins nor rest would help. Nothing would. Only Delaney. She felt like a sleeping princess. He must return to awaken her to life with a kiss.

He said, "Are you listening to me?" in a suddenly stern voice.

She nodded again, tried to focus her attention on him. He meant well. He had brought her into the world, hadn't he? He must mean well.

"This fainting? Has it happened before?"

"No. I was just upset. It's nothing."

"A doctor who treats himself has a fool for a patient," he said irritably. "A patient who treats himself is just as much a fool. Will you kindly allow me to diagnose your problem for you?"

"But there is no problem. Harris shouldn't have brought me here."

Peter shrugged his thin hunched shoulders. "I suppose you think he ought to have left you lying in the middle of Washington Avenue with everyone standing around and staring at you, and whispering their idiotic superstitions over your unconscious head."

She smiled faintly. "No. But he should have taken me home."

"You're suffering the delayed shock of your father's death, Dorinda. You do understand that, don't you? You must allow yourself time to recover from it."

"It's not that," she said impatiently. "It's because the boys have sent Delaney away. They've separated us. And you know why."

"A month or two won't matter," Peter said slowly.

"But maybe he'll never come back," she cried.

"He will."

"You don't *know*."

"I'm sure." Dr. Peter smiled at her again. "You should be just as sure." Then, "In fact, though I don't want to hurt you, I think this delay, and separation is very wise indeed."

Her face tightened. Her eyes glittered, but she said nothing.

"You don't realize yourself how difficult these past five years have been for you, Dorinda. You were only fifteen when your mother died. An age when a girl needs her mother very much. Bettina and I were aware of it, and did what we could. I know Ralphine tried, too. But still, your mother was gone. You tried to be wife and daughter to your father, mother and sister to your brothers. It was more than you could be, of course. And you know very well that Jonathan wasn't himself in these past years."

Her glittering eyes widened. "He wasn't?"

She had taken for granted her father's grief. Men behaved so, she thought, when they lost the women they loved. It hadn't seemed particularly odd to her, though she had found him difficult to deal with after he had withdrawn to the wing, to live alone, sit alone, eat alone, pace the floor alone.

But now Peter said, "Surely you can see that such a denial of life is . . ."

She rose to her feet. She didn't want to hear any more. It was too frightening. She wouldn't listen. She said, "Never mind. I'll take your vitamins and I'll get plenty of the rest you prescribe for me."

"And you'll try to calm down?"

She nodded. She felt strong now, and steady on her feet. The woolly dizziness had gone from her.

She said goodbye to him and to Bettina, conscious of the bright blue eyes that anxiously searched her face. Then, going out to Harris, she told him that she was ready to go back to Moorhaven.

"You're all right now? What did Dr. Peter say?"

"Something about delayed reaction over father's dying," she said briefly.

But Peter was old. He didn't know. It was Delaney, his leaving without a word to her, that had been the mortal blow. Only later, did she think of her father again.

She was dressing for dinner. She put on a sleeveless dress of pale green voile. It had a dropped neck decorated with a soft full bow, and came just to mid-calf. Her shoes were of pale green kid and neat little heels.

She did her face carefully, then brushed her auburn curls.

Mary came in, closed the door gently behind her. "Dorinda, what's this that happened in Tembley?"

She put down the brush, turned from the mirror framed in gilt plaster roses, to face Mary. "What do you mean?"

"Arley phoned to say you'd fainted at the train station and set the whole town talking again."

Dorinda said, "I fainted, yes. But the town always talks, so that doesn't matter."

"And you were asking if Delaney left," Mary persisted.

"Yes."

Mary sank down in the small rocking chair, hugging her plump body with plump arms. "What happened to you?"

"Just a dizzy spell. It's nothing. I went to see Dr. Peter afterwards."

Mary's worried face relaxed slightly. "It scared me. Arley calling to tell me. We don't see much of each other. He's as daft as the rest of them. Though I suppose he has reason enough. Old Arley . . ."

"Have you told everyone in the house?" Dorinda asked.

Mary looked indignant. "Not me. You know better. But Harris has. I've heard them talking about it."

It was just as well that Mary had warned her, Dorinda reflected. Now she would be prepared to have a lecture served along with her meal.

She said, "I ought to have known that Harris would."

"He, we all, are concerned about you," Mary said gently.

"Yes, yes. I know." She turned, took up her brush.

"It'll come out all right," Mary said. "Have patience."

Dorinda didn't answer her.

After a moment, Mary sighed, and left the room.

When she came downstairs, Harris was fixing predinner cocktails in the drawing room. She took a packet of Camels from her pocket, lit one, and blew smoke in his direction.

Ralphine frowned at her. "Are you quite well, Dorinda? Wouldn't you have preferred Mary to serve you in your room?"

"I'm fine," she answered.

Jon said heavily, "You seem very pale."

She gave him an exasperated look. She did not look pale, and she knew it. She had applied rouge liberally to her cheeks, and lipstick to her mouth. If anything she looked like a painted clown. Ordinarily Jon would have told her so, for he hated women to look obviously made up.

She wondered why Mary, he, Ralphine were determined to pretend that she was ill when she was not.

She understood almost immediately.

Sam said, "A very peculiar thing to do, Dorinda. To go into Tembley to ask about Delaney and Denny. We told you exactly how it was. How is it that you didn't believe us, refused to believe us?"

Estella patted her curls into place and smiled at Dorinda, "Tell them never mind. Tell them to leave you alone."

Dorinda ignored her. "I just didn't believe you."

"But isn't that strange? And the way you tore up the house, searching for him." Sam's florid face was hard, stony, no longer pudgy. "As if you thought we'd tied him up and hidden him. Is that what you had in mind?"

"I don't know. I was just looking for him."

"Oh, come on," Harris said. "What's done is done. She looked. So what? She understands now, don't you, kiddo?"

And she did. But not what Harris meant. She saw that from the point of view of the others, her behavior had been extraordinary. She had refused to believe the truth. She had searched the house, insisted on checking in Tembley. She had fainted there when she had finally been convinced that Delaney was gone.

A chill touched her. From the point of view of the others . . . But wasn't that the only point of view? Why had she behaved that way?

She finished her cocktail, followed the rest in to dinner.

After Mary had served, Dennis said, with a smile at Dorinda, "Still and all, I'm very glad that you went to see Dr. Peter, Dorinda. I feel better about it. Knowing that he knows."

Dorinda looked at his paint-smudged face, then forced her attention to the plate before her. She ate stolidly, chewing the thick roast beef without tasting it.

There had been something very odd about her father in those five years before his death. What she had taken for granted before was suddenly no longer the normal thing that she had supposed it. There had been something very odd about him.

And now . . . she herself.

She put a stop to the thought before it was truly born.

She rose, excused herself, and fled to her bedroom.

There, pacing the thick rug, she faced what she had not allowed herself to face squarely.

Delaney was gone. For however long, she did not know. He was gone. She must learn to live without him.

Her brothers, Sam, Ralphine, had all conspired against her to separate her from her love. To separate her from joy, and from life, forever.

Then she would separate herself from them, she thought bitterly. She wouldn't speak to them, nor acknowledge them. She wouldn't admit to their existence. Not until Delaney returned.

She buried her face in her hands and wept.

That night there was a summer storm. Thunder rolled down the cliff behind the house, and echoed through the marshes beyond the dike. Lightning laced the sky, forking across the horizon in great silvery bolts. Rain, wind-driven into heavy slanting sheets, lashed the windows.

She lay still, clutching the coverlet to her trembling body, her eyes wide open, staring at the ceiling.

The white curtains billowed out between the blue draperies, then sagged again. The movement caught her eye. She turned her head to watch. It was almost as if there was, behind them, a body, thrusting and then retreating. She saw it from the corner of her eye, then directly. She saw it take shape and fade. The curtain writhing and sinking, and writhing again.

At last she couldn't bear it. She slipped from her bed, went to the window. As she stood there, the room suddenly glowed with a flash of lightning. Cold blue ran up and down the walls, touched the mantel, glimmered on the pewter candlesticks, dyed the ceiling.

Below, on the windswept terrace, leaves torn from the trees in destructive gusts, rustled on the dark stone.

But the stone was not all dark.

She stared at the rectangle of pale yellow light for a long moment, recognizing it, yet refusing to believe that she was seeing it again.

A pale rectangle of yellow light. And then, moving through it, the slow, limping shadow of a man.

She gasped with terror, and fell back.

It was Jonathan, pacing the study in his wing, walking the floor lost in grief and guilt, as he had done for the five years before his death.

She drew back from the window at last. She turned her back on the shadow, her fists clenched at her temples.

It was then that she began to gather her things together, the few belongings that she decided she would need. A brush and comb. Some toiletries. A number of dresses. The books she loved. Then, with the lightning still dancing on the walls of the room, she began to ready herself.

It seemed perfectly clear that she must do as her father had done before her.

She must retreat to her own place, and live her own life. She must turn her back on the others as he had done.

By morning, she was ready, and set out to complete the task.

Mary found her laboring down the steps, arms loaded, barely able to manage the weight of what she carried.

"What are you doing?" Mary cried. "Where are you going?"

"I'm moving to Jonathan's wing," Dorinda said coldly. "Would you please get out of my way."

"But that's daft!" Instead of giving ground, Mary blocked the way even more firmly with her bulky body.

Dorinda smiled faintly. "Now you know perfectly well . . ."

Mary gave her a look of horror. "What do you want to move to Jonathan's wing for? There's a great big house here for you to live in. Why should you go there? What do you want to for?"

"Must I have a reason?" Dorinda demanded.

"Of course you must. What is this nonsense?"

Dorinda simply stood there, waiting.

Mary's tone softened when she said, "It's not a good idea, Dorinda."

"Why not?"

Mary flushed. "Oh, you know. You must know. It's just silly, that's all." And then she smiled, as if struck by inspiration, "And besides, I have enough work to do without having to run over there every day to do up after you. And there's Ralphine complaining that I've mislaid her silver box, and somebody, I suppose it was young Denny, made a terrible mess in the playroom, and . . ."

"I'll take care of myself, Mary."

"What for?" Mary cried. "Why do you want to stay there?"

Dorinda shrugged. "I do want to. That's all you have to know, Mary."

She moved forward, and Mary fell back, stepped aside muttering to herself. She had barely passed on down the steps when Mary rushed off.

Dorinda was opening the door of the wing when Ralphine caught up with her.

"Mary says . . ."

Dorinda didn't wait for the rest. She edged her way through the half open door, and walked down the hallway to the room that she had already decided she would use. She emptied her arms of the things she had carried so laboriously, and looked around.

The room was only medium-sized, wallpapered in pale gray. The double bed was brass. An easy chair was under the window. Over its back there was draped a shawl, black, fringed, and embroidered with fading red and yellow roses. It was peculiarly put together. She gave it a closer look, and saw that it had been torn into four pieces, and then carefully mended. She was still studying it when Ralphine cleared her throat, signifying that she had followed Dorinda, was there, politely waiting for Dorinda to offer her attention.

Dorinda looked up. "The shawl was torn somehow, and then put together again."

Ralphine nodded. "It was your mother's. She brought it with her when she came to Moorhaven." And then, in the same even tone, "I never thought that you would allow yourself to behave like an hysterical child."

Dorinda smiled faintly, "I'm sorry you were wrong about me."

"You punish no one but yourself by copying your father's behavior. Even if he was my brother, I'll tell you that he was wrong, and his wrongness destroyed him. Are you determined to do the same?"

"But was he wrong?" Dorinda asked.

"Women sometimes die in childbirth, Dorinda. No one must be blamed. Yes. He was wrong."

But Dorinda was no longer listening. She nodded, then left Ralphine. She went down the hall to the office.

The scuff marks were on the rug again!

They had been there after the first time she had seen Jonathan's shadow.

They had been there after the second time she had seen Jonathan's shadow.

She stood still, staring at them, her head cocked to one side, as if she were listening. But she heard nothing. Not then.

It was only later, when she was all alone, that the humming began.

Chapter 21

It took her only a little while to store what she had brought with her. When that was done, she went into the office. She stood at the window, looking onto the sun-filled terrace.

Dr. Peter had told her that she was suffering from delayed shock at her father's death, from the strain of the five years before that.

Ralphine had said that she was punishing the family for sending Delaney away by copying her father's behavior.

Only she herself saw her retreat to solitude as what it really was. A refusal to live among her enemies. She would wait for Delaney here. No matter how long it took for him to return, she would wait for him in the place where Jonathan's shadow walked.

She had loved her father, and he had loved her. If he was present in some shape that she couldn't see, she mustn't feel threatened. He wouldn't harm her. Yet she sensed something ugly in the air . . .

That evening Mary came with a tray. She set it down, sighing heavily. "I'm not as young as I was, Dorinda."

"Nor are any of us."

"But at twenty, you still have good legs. You could

use them to take you to your meals with the others instead of making me bring your meals to you here."

Dorinda didn't answer.

"Why won't you? A good, reasonable girl like you, making this extra work for me. You know perfectly well I've already more to manage than I can. Estella drifts in and out, expecting to eat when she's hungry. Dennis, too. I just don't . . ."

Dorinda found herself smiling. "All right, Mary. That's enough now. You've managed to change my mind. For your sake, of course. Now. Does that make you feel better?"

Mary's relief that her ploy had worked was obvious. Her black eyes sparkled with triumph. "I do feel better. I should think you'd go daft, all alone all day in this place."

"Why should I?" Dorinda demanded.

Mary openly winced. "That's just a way of talking. You look at me as if I actually meant it."

"But didn't you?"

Mary let herself down into the sofa, her black dress spreading around her. She fixed her eyes on Dorinda's pale heart-shaped face. "I was there, at the door, when your mother first came to this place, Dorinda. I opened it to her knock, and led her in. She was about your age then, small, pretty and with a look of fear in her green eyes. I see the same look in your eyes now. I was with her through all the troubles, and with her when the good times came. I held you just moments after you were born. So can't you tell me? What's come over you, Dorinda? What is it? What are you trying to do?"

Tears stung Dorinda's eyes. She blinked to hold them back. "I'm waiting for Delaney," she answered.

She lay awake in the unfamiliar bedroom, staring at the ceiling. No matter how she examined it, studying how it had been from every angle that she could see, she still didn't understand why he had gone without telling her. He should never have slipped away while she slept, leaving no word to comfort her in his ab-

sence, to warn her to wait and be patient. She supposed
that her three brothers had united against him, coercing
him somehow into going. But they could never have
kept him from seeing her one last time. Then why had
he gone as he had?

She found herself thinking suddenly that perhaps he
had gone, not because he was forced to, but because he
wanted to. Perhaps, deep in his heart, he had always
wanted to escape the small narrow world of Moorhaven, and to escape her as well.

The pain of that thought was hard and hot in her
chest. She began crying aloud into the dark.

It was as her own sobs faded away into stillness that
she heard the humming.

A soft sound, barely audible in the beginning, it
swelled until the room fairly sang with it.

Frozen, numb with terror, she stared into the shadows. And then, at last, gathering her strength, she
slipped from the bed. She reached for the lamp and
knocked it over. It thumped onto the floor, and as she
stepped over it, the humming stopped.

She could hear her own heavy breathing, but nothing
else. She could see the unmoving shadows, but nothing
else.

She went to the wall, found the switch, turned on the
overhead light.

There was a movement somewhere beyond her left
shoulder. She spun around. And found herself staring
at her own reflection in the mirror over the dresser. Her
green eyes glittered in her gaunt face. Her touseled
auburn curls gave her a wild look, a madwoman's look,
she thought.

She took her robe, belted it tightly around her narrow waist.

There had been a sound. Something had caused it.
She must find out what that something was.

But at the door, she hesitated.

What waited in the hallway for her?

Who waited there?

It took an effort to ease the door open, to peer out

into the darkness. She waited, listened, heard nothing. She tiptoed out, made her way to the hall switch. Light bloomed. There were no shadows now. There was nothing but emptiness.

She went on, into the office, again turning on the light. Again there was nothing but emptiness.

She tried the front door, and found it locked. She went through the shadowless hallway to the back door, and found that it, too, was locked as always.

At last she went back to bed. Towards dawn, she fell asleep, with every light in the wing ablaze.

She was roused by a banging. She sat up, heart beating quickly. She didn't know that it was day, the night behind her. She didn't realize that she had slept.

The banging stopped.

Moments later she heard the door open, then quick footsteps.

Harris called, "Dorinda, love, where are you?" and appeared in her bedroom doorway at the same time.

She stared at him.

He looked frightened, upset. His hair was disheveled, his collar open.

"What's the matter?" she demanded. "What do you want, Harris?"

"The lights," he snapped. "You've got every light in the place on. I was having a walk on the terrace before breakfast and I saw them, and I thought . . ." He let the words trail off. "Are you okay?"

"Yes," she said tightly. "But how did you get in? I had the door locked."

"The key behind the kitchen door," he told her.

"But I have that one," she protested. "Look there on the dresser. You'll see that I have it."

"There must be half a dozen of them around, Dorinda. Tell me, why did you leave on all the lights?"

She was tempted to tell him about the sounds in the night, about her search for the source of it. But she forced the need down.

It must have been her imagination. She had better not speak of it.

And the pacing, limping shadow? she asked herself. Had that, too, been a hallucination? A hallucination she had had twice?

No. She wouldn't tell Harris. He, Dennis, Jon were all against her. They had rejected Delaney, which meant that they had rejected her. They could talk about her welfare all they wanted, but they couldn't deceive her.

She daren't provide them with this new weapon against her. They mustn't know what had happened.

It was only later, much later, when terror was behind her, that she began to wonder why she had permitted herself to be so easily manipulated. She never knew the answer. Perhaps there was no answer.

But now, with Harris looking at her worriedly, saying, "Listen, Dorinda, are you sure you're okay? You look very peculiar to me," she answered briskly, "Get out, Harris. I want to get up. I'm hungry."

Relieved, he backed out of her room, closing the door behind him.

She rose and dressed. She put on a pale yellow dress with a dropped waist. She did her face carefully, brushed her hair. The familiar routine was soothing. Then, finishing her toilette, she searched the wing, room by room, closet by closet. She examined each piece of furniture, looked under the rugs. She didn't know just what she was looking for, but she hoped that when she saw it, whatever it was, she would recognize it.

There was nothing to explain the hum in the night, nothing to explain Jonathan's shadow passing by the window, either.

Although she knew that no one had entered her bedroom, for she had been awake, thinking, when the sound started, she even went back to look at the closet there. On the top shelves there were big hat boxes. Hats that her mother had saved.

Dorinda sighed, closed the closet door.

She paused to turn out all the lights in the wing and went to the breakfast room in the main house.

Mary had apparently already told the family that she was coming. But Mary was lingering there, watching for her, too.

Now she gave her an approving smile, said, "I'll get you a big breakfast," and hurried into the kitchen.

The family had apparently decided to humor her.

Jon said, "Good morning, Dorinda. Did you rest well?"

She nodded.

She was thinking that right after breakfast she must find a way to slip unobserved into the kitchen and get all the keys to the wing, front door and back. How could she protect her privacy if anyone could come in? How could she protect herself? The very thought frightened her. She forced herself to reject it.

Ralphine said, "I'm going in for the mail. Do you want to come along?"

She answered, "No, thank you."

Harris asked, "Did you turn off the lights?"

"Yes."

"What lights?" Dennis asked, mopping a smudge of yellow paint from his forehead.

"She had left some on by mistake," Harris said quickly.

She allowed herself the luxury of a smile. "Thank you, Harris."

"For nothing, love," he retorted.

Sam finished his coffee, pushed back his chair. He glanced at Dorinda, then said, "I'll be in the workshop, Ralphine. If there's anything from Denny for me."

"There wouldn't be, not this soon," Ralphine answered.

"You never know. Anyhow that's where I'll be."

Dorinda knew that the others were looking at her, too. They wondered if she expected to hear from Delaney. They waited for her reaction.

She would have been prepared to let them wait, to leave them asking themselves questions without answers. But she couldn't bear it. She had to know.

"Did you force Delaney to promise not to write to me?" she asked.

Jon said heavily, "Dorinda, of course not. I'm sure you'll hear from him soon."

"Why, surely," Ralphine put in, "we all will."

"I wonder," Dorinda said softly. "I wonder if that's so." Yet in her heart she was certain. There would be no letters from Delaney. She would never hear from him again, never see him again.

After dinner that evening she walked down to the dike. It had been, she'd found, the only way she could escape Estella. The slim blonde girl had apparently been delegated by Jon to try to keep Dorinda from isolating herself. So Estella patted her spit curls, and wistfully spoke of the wonderful times she had had the year she came out in Boston and in Newport. When Dorinda stirred impatiently, Estella dropped the subject, and turned to politics. Mr. Roosevelt could never be elected. Even if some women were said to be charmed by his smile. When Dorinda audibly gritted her teeth, Estella began to talk about clothes.

Dorinda muttered an apology, and went down to the hump of the dike. She climbed through the overgrown weeds to the stony path, and looked over the marshes. The shallow black water seemed to heave, breathing in long slow inhalations and expirations. An occasional greasy bubble broke free with a strange sighing sound. A dark patch of quicksand glistened emptily, hungrily.

Her life, Dorinda thought, was like that patch of quicksand. It was closing in around her, thick and clinging. She was sinking in it, with no strength to fight, and no foothold for purchase. Soon she would be gone, leaving nothing but the same smooth emptiness behind.

Doomed. That was the word the children of Tembley whispered. The Moorhavens were doomed. High now, but one day to be brought low.

The sun set slowly, turning the swamps pink, then

carmine. The shadows of the dark stunted trees became long and black.

She climbed down from the dike, and turned her back on it, her small shoulders rigid, feeling as if she had made a narrow escape from a danger she couldn't name.

She started up the long slope to the house. It lay in the shadow of the cliff now, almost in darkness. The big brass lamps at the black front door were lighted and gleaming. Otherwise there was no sign of light, or of life.

As she reached the terrace, she saw the window of Jonathan's office. It glowed with pale yellow light, and something moved back and forth before it. A tall limping silhouette passed through it and then disappeared.

She gasped, hesitated, frozen to the spot. But then she broke free of the invisible cords of fear that held her. She raced for the door.

She had nearly reached it when Sam suddenly appeared from around the corner of the wing.

He called out to her, came towards her quickly, moving fast for a man of his weight.

She couldn't hear his words. She ran on as fast as she could.

But before she reached the door, he caught up with her. He seized her arm.

"Dorinda! Stop. Wait a minute. What's the matter with you? Why are you running?"

She stared at his florid apprehensive face. Then she looked past his shoulder.

The light was gone now. The shadow, too.

He said, "You're pale as a ghost."

She choked out, "It's nothing, Sam."

"Come along," he said. "I'll get you a drink."

"No," she protested. "I want to go in."

But somehow he moved her. He drew her with him into the big house. He sat her in a corner of the sofa, said, "Just wait a minute. I'll mix us both something. We need it."

She sat still, panting. She closed her eyes when he left her.

He had been there when it had happened. But he had seen nothing. He would have mentioned the light, the shadow, if he had seen it. But he hadn't mentioned it. So he hadn't seen it.

Then it had not been real.

She shuddered. It had not been real. Which must mean that she was mad.

Why else would she see light and shadow when there was none? Why else would she see Jonathan's walking ghost?

Sam returned in what seemed to be seconds. He put a tall, cold glass into her trembling hand.

"There now. Drink up. It's the best bootleg whiskey money can buy."

She took a cautious sip, thanked him.

He said, frowning, "I saw you down on the dike. I was going to walk down and join you. And then suddenly you came back, and started running as if you thought the devil himself was after you."

She remembered the first night she had seen the limping shadow, and gone down to the wing, and then been unable to get back into the house. He had said much the same thing when she finally got the door open, and burst inside to find him standing on the steps, staring at her.

She finished her drink quickly, then rose. "I think I'll lie down and rest now, Sam. Thanks again."

"But why you would run . . ."

She shrugged, left him.

She watched the window as she crossed the terrace under the light of the brass lamps. It was dark. Nothing moved there.

But, of course, she told herself, it was always dark, always empty.

What she had seen existed only in her own mind. She was now certain. The only thing that troubled her was that she didn't know when it had happened, or why, or how. She assumed that she ought to feel different, be different. Wouldn't someone be different if he had gone mad?

She unlocked the door, and relocked it behind her. It was a useless precaution, she told herself. Gathering together all the keys to the wing, carefully locking the doors, was pointless. No one had come in to trick or threaten her. It was all in her mind.

She started for the office, and that was when she heard the humming again.

Chapter 22

She crouched against the wall, covering her ears with her hands. She waited through what seemed an eon, waited, hardly breathing, for the seizure to pass. For, yes, that was what she now considered it. A seizure. The shadow didn't exist. Nor the humming. She only thought they did. It must pass, and then she would be free for a little while at least.

The hall was in total darkness, the last vestiges of twilight gone. At last she dared to take her hands from her ears, to raise her head, listening.

The deep angry humming was gone.

She started down the hallway, through the dark to her room, feeling her way, her fingertips brushing the wall. As she moved, she felt a cold wind blow around her ankles, a cold touch lift her curls.

She cried, "Who is it? Who's there?"

No one answered.

She hadn't expected a reply, so she wasn't surprised by the silence.

She found the light switch in her room, and turned on the light. Just as she did, she heard music. Soft, tinkling music, faraway and sweet, that seemed oddly familiar. Music that had a haunting quality, that touched her and made her smile even though she was filled with terror.

Swaying, she listened, listened until the sweet sound faded away. And then she made her way to the bed and collapsed.

The June sun was very hot. It shimmered on the stone of the terrace, and glinted on the windows of the house. It covered the marshes with a slick of molten gold.

Dorinda sat at the window, watching. At the bottom of the long slope, Jon and Dennis and Joshua stood together talking.

She smiled faintly. The old man had at last had his way. He always walked the dike himself. For weeks he had been insisting that Jon do as Jonathan had done before him, and inspect the dike, too. That, Joshua insisted, was how it had always been. It must remain the same. The point was made once, twice, three times. He finally had stirred the others to unwilling action. Only Harris had managed to evade the old man. Dorinda supposed that Harris had left early for Tembley with Sam.

She closed her eyes. She hadn't been to town since the day that Delaney had gone. The others had suggested she visit the Van Nuys, a pretext, she knew, to allow Dr. Peter a look at her. But she had refused.

She had been away from Jonathan's wing only for her meals, and for very brief walks along the dike. She had been determined to outwait, or outlive, the madness that had assailed her the day Delaney left.

For, although she had seen the limping shadow before, she marked the real beginning at the time that she made her wild search of the house, oddly sure that Delaney must still be there. That the family had somehow hidden him from her. And since then . . .

She knew that the others suspected that something was wrong with her. Hadn't Sam reminded Ralphine of Jonathan's behavior after Cordelia's death?

But, Dorinda reminded herself, they didn't *know*. No one *knew* her secret.

Her brothers had decided that she was sulking, and would best be ignored.

Ralphine was satisfied that she was mourning her father, and Delaney's loss, too, and needed only time to recover her spirit.

Though Mary watched her with anxious black eyes, her plump face showing new wrinkles under her white cap, she said nothing.

Dorinda was satisfied that they should be deceived, and hoped they really were. The longer she could conceal her illness the better it would be.

She accepted it now. She believed in it.

She heard the humming in the night with terror, but with composure. She listened to the tinkling music with anguish, but with calm. On those rare occasions when she saw Jonathan's shadow from a distance cross the yellow-lighted window, she would race toward it, knowing that it would be gone before she reached the office.

It was all a part of some weak strain in herself, a strain that she must have inherited from her father. He himself had shown the signs of the same weakness. Hadn't he retreated to the wing to live alone, to pace away the nights? Hadn't he gone mad when he lost Cordelia? And now, his daughter Dorinda had taken the same path in the same way. How else could she explain humming that didn't exist, music that didn't play, a shadow that wasn't there?

How else could she explain her conviction that her Moorhaven ancestors looked down at her from their gilt-framed portraits, watching her with knowing eyes? How else could she explain her certainty that some evil lurked within Moorhaven itself?

She opened her eyes to see that the men on the dike had separated.

Jon and Dennis continued walking along the path. Joshua made his way up along the slope, moving slowly. When he reached the terrace, he paused to rest.

He was still robust, square-shouldered and heavy set. His beard was white but neatly-trimmed. He wore the same kind of work clothes that he had worn for as long as she could remember.

She saw that he looked her way, and hesitated. Then he approached slowly and stood before her window. He tipped his head back, squinting against the sun.

She leaned forward, smiled. "How are you, Joshua?"

"Pretty good, Dorinda."

"I see you finally got them down there."

"You'd think they'd know the need themselves," he said dryly. "Not have to be driven to it like stubborn mules. It's Moorhaven's protection."

"Oh, Joshua, what could happen after all?"

"Plenty. These old eyes have seen it, and they know." He shrugged. "Never mind. Maybe that's my trouble. Getting old."

"No. No, you're not," she said.

"Seventy-five last birthday," he answered. "Not that that's so old, I guess. I'm still hale enough in body to do what I've always done. But it's my mind. That's what worries me. I worry about my mind."

"You?" She forced a laugh. "You're steadier than all the rest of us put together."

He came closer. "Steadier than some, I'll admit that," he agreed. "But it's this forgetting things that bothers me. Put a thing down and never find it again. Pick it up days later some place else. Can't remember how it got from one place to another, or why."

"You've lost something?"

"Nothing that really matters. Just bits and pieces of things. Now you take that turntable I had for the victrola. I was set to fix it. I had it up in my rooms, working on it, and that thing is just gone now. I don't know when it went, weeks maybe, but it's gone."

"It'll turn up, Joshua."

He sighed. "Oh, I know that. But what about the forgetting what I did with it? That's what bothers me. For most things, my mind is sharp enough. I remember everything, Dorinda. I even remember a lot I'd as soon forget." He gave her a quick blue-eyed look, then turned abruptly and disappeared around the corner of the wing.

She sat back in her chair, sighed. If poor old Joshua only knew.

There was a cloud of dust over the road where it turned toward Moorhaven, a dangerous curve that offered the first view of the house and the marshes below.

She watched. Most likely it was Harris, returning from Tembley. He was certain, no doubt, that Jon and Dennis would have finished the tour of the dike.

The cloud of dust came closer and closer. It glowed golden in the sunlight. Then the car appeared below it, streaking toward the driveway.

Yes, Dorinda thought. It was Harris all right. No one else approached Moorhaven so recklessly.

The car disappeared in the direction of the garage.

She heard the slam of its doors. Not just one. But two. Two. She found herself suddenly on her feet.

There were voices.

She strained, listening.

She heard Delaney's laughter.

She held herself still. She told herself that she heard humming, and music, and saw shadows. Now she was hearing Delaney's laughter.

But then Harris came into view. He stood at the edge of the terrace. And Delaney was with him.

Not a shadow. Not a beloved imagined form. But real. Delaney, flesh and blood, with laughter on his face, his sandy curls aglow.

She cried his name and rushed outside. She started toward him, and he toward her, and then, midway, with her arms out and her face shining, she suddenly stopped.

Realization hit her. She let her arms fall. The brightness faded from her face. She stood still, stiff, waiting.

She had, somehow, never thought ahead. She had never planned for this moment. Now it was all there in her mind. In the month since he had gone, she had changed. She was not the Dorinda that he had left behind. She mustn't mislead him. She mustn't hurt him. She must be honest and tell him the truth, no matter what the truth cost.

He didn't seem to notice that she had stopped in mid-flight to his arms. He came on, clasped her to him. He hugged her hard, saying her name over and over again.

It was wonderful to feel the warmth of his body against hers, to feel alive again. It was momentary surcease from pain. She allowed herself to accept it for only a few long moments. Then she stepped back. She said, "Delaney, are you all right?"

But he was staring down at her, his dark eyes filled with concern. "Dorie, what's happened to you?"

Her heart pounded with dread, though she knew that she ought to be glad. They had always been so close. He could see it. He knew at first glance. He would understand what she had to tell him.

"Nothing," she said finally. "Nothing's happened that bears talking about."

He hugged her to him again. He whispered, "Don't worry. Everything is going to be okay. I can prove it. I have the papers. Do you understand me, Dorie? They can't stop us now."

She shivered within the circle of his arms. She stepped away from him. "We have to talk, Delaney. Let's go inside."

Harris, standing aside, looked disappointed. He muttered something that she didn't hear, and then wandered off.

Delaney turned toward the main house, but she shook her head.

"No. I'm in Jonathan's wing. Didn't Harris tell you?"

"He said something. I didn't understand. I guess I was too excited to pay attention." Still smiling exultantly, Delaney followed her inside to the office. "I took Denny to San Francisco as Sam wanted, and then, instead of following that made-up tour that Jon had laid out, the two of us went to Chicago and stopped there for a bit. Longer than I'd thought would be necessary."

She was only half listening. She sank into a chair. He sat on its arm, a hand on her shoulder.

"And then we went back to Boston. I left Denny with his mother's people. Which was what Sam had told me to do. Poor kid, he didn't want to stay there. He was as anxious to get home as I was."

She asked, "Why did you go, Delaney? Why didn't you tell me first, talk it over with me first?"

"Didn't you know? Didn't you understand? I was sure that you would. Oh, Dorie, you know how the three of them can be. They said they wanted to give you time to think, to get over the shock of father's death. To calm down ... then ... then ... if you still felt the same way ..."

"But you should have told me."

"You were asleep when it was decided, when I left. And they asked me not to waken you. For your own good. You know how absolutely logical they can seem. They made me feel I didn't care about you. So ..."

"And you never wrote ..."

He said suddenly grim, "That was part of it, Dorie. I promised I wouldn't. They leaned on me so much I just gave in on that, too. I was certain you'd understand." He put his head back and laughed. "But the thing that they didn't count on was that I had my own reasons for wanting to go anyway. As I told you, I spent some time in Chicago. I checked with the police. Remember that Gregory said he reported finding me in Dearborn station? And then kept me when they said they had no information about who I belonged to? Well, he was telling the truth, Dorie. He *did* check with the police. They still had a record of it after all these years. And that means I wasn't his bastard. If I had been, he wouldn't have gone through the pretense of having found me. So ..." Delaney's grin slanted across his face. "They did us a favor by sending me away. But now I'm back. And they can't stop us."

She stared at him. "Delaney, is that the truth? You're quite sure?"

"Of course. And I have a copy of the paper to prove it. The original foundling report." His grin faded. "There's just one funny thing. Somebody else was there before me, asking the same question. Would you believe that? It seems so strange. The officer I spoke to remembered it well. It was just a few months or so before I was there, and that's why they were able to locate the report without half a year's delay. They had already done it quite recently."

"But what does that mean?" she asked.

"I don't know. Except that someone was interested in me. In my antecedents. That much we can be sure of." His grin came back. "Listen, Dorie. It doesn't matter. Don't you see? We can be married immediately."

She took his hand, held it tightly. This was the moment. Now she must tell him. She said, "You must listen to me. We can't be married. We're not going to be, Delaney."

All the light and color drained out of his face. He sat absolutely still.

She went on, "I love you. Remember that. I *do* love you. That isn't changed. It'll never change. But . . . but something has happened. It makes marriage out of the question for me. It . . ."

"What's happened?" he asked hoarsely.

She drew a deep breath. She released his hand and folded her own together in her lap to keep them from trembling. It never occurred to her to dissemble with him. With the others, yes. But not with him. He must know the truth. She began slowly, carefully picking the words, trying to control her tone of voice. She finished incoherently. But she had somehow managed to tell him everything that had taken place. She spoke of the limping shadow, the light in the window, the humming, the music. She reminded him of Jonathan's last five years. She built up the case against herself.

She managed, somehow, not to use the word she

feared. But she told him the facts. She told him how she felt. She told him what she knew the facts meant.

"Oh, no," he gasped, "Oh, no, Dorie, you're not mad."

She winced. "Delaney, please . . ."

"You are not mad," he cried.

"I can't marry you. I can't pass on what must be the tainted blood in my veins." She smiled faintly. "Isn't it funny almost? Dr. Peter was telling us about the dangers of first cousins marrying. He didn't bother to tell us about the dangers of a madwoman marrying."

"Stop it," Delaney said harshly. "I won't listen to you."

"But you must," she answered. "If you love me, you must listen."

She sat at the window. The main house was dark, still. She looked at it now because Delaney was there. He had come home again. He had returned for her.

She knew that she mustn't allow her resolution to weaken. But, even though they couldn't be man and wife, it was a joy to have him close by. That was why she sat looking at the darkened house.

The moon streaked his window with silver, and glistened on the darkened brass lamps beside the door.

Was he awake now? she wondered.

She deliberately turned her gaze away from the house. And it was then that she saw the light in the marshes below.

She studied it, at first taking it for more moonlight, but it moved, and then moved again. It reminded her, faintly, of something, but she forgot the fleeting memory when she saw the flicker more clearly.

She rose to her feet, and went outside. From the terrace, she could see more clearly. Now she was absolutely certain. There was a light near the dike.

She hurried down the slope, through the warm empty silence. The light was gone by the time she had climbed the hump of the dike. But by the silver glow of the moon she could see below her, in the bog, something dark, still, unmoving.

She clambered down on hands and knees, unmindful of the sharp-edged stones, the thorny brush. She crept close, then closer to the dark sprawl. It was a body, big, dark-haired.

Jon lay there, and he was dead.

Chapter 23

The cortege was a short one. The long black hearse bearing the flower-banked coffin led the way. It was followed by the family limousine. Dr. Peter, driving his ridiculous electric brougham, completed the procession.

Dorinda sat well back in her seat, with her eyes lowered as they drove down Washington Avenue past the fire-blackened Moorhaven warehouses. Still she remained conscious of the stares, the whispers, the shrugs. She felt the waves of hate that flowed out from hunger-sunken eyes. Six weeks before Jonathan Moorhaven had died, and today, Jon, his oldest son, was to be buried. She refused to look up, to see the exultation. The Moorhavens were doomed. Another had been brought low.

But to withdraw into her own thoughts was equally painful.

She had run screaming to the house, knowing even then that it was too late. Nothing could save Jon.

Delaney and Dennis had met her at the big black door, shaken her out of wild incoherence into broken but at least sensible speech.

"Jon's down in the marshes," she cried. "Hurry."

Sam, coming from the steps, went directly to the phone, while Dennis and Delaney raced down the slope

217

with flashlights. Gray-faced Ralphine went for Estella, and Mary held Dorinda close, crooning wordless comfort, while she gave way to hopeless tears, remembering what had happened earlier that same evening.

Jon, a tall drink in his hand, leaning against the big fireplace, had given Delaney a hard-eyed look. "You've returned sooner than you were supposed to. What's your explanation?"

Delaney grinned, ran a slim hand through his sandy curls. "There was no longer any need to stay away." His tan-colored eyes moved around the room, then fixed on Dorinda. "I've found the proof, Jon. We're not blood kin." He drew a white document from his inside pocket. "See for yourself."

Jon accepted it, glanced through it. Then he placed it deliberately on the mantel. "This proves nothing. Gregory might have done this himself to cover his guilt."

Delaney looked thunderstruck. His eyes glittered. His sensitive lips set hard. "You know that's not so. You're simply fishing for another way out. But Dorinda and I love each other, and you can't stop us from being married."

It was as if she had not told him of her decision, of the reasons for it. It was as if he had not listened to her desperate words.

Dennis put in, "Delaney, you can't expect us to . . ."

But Dorinda drew a deep breath, said, "This is a useless discussion. I've already told Delaney that we'll never be married. There's nothing more to talk about."

Now the others looked thunderstruck. Ralphine whispered, "Dorinda! What's this?"

Estella's blue eyes opened wide. "My goodness, kiddo, after all the fuss . . ."

Dorinda felt a painful blush on her cheeks. "I have my reasons. I don't want to talk about them. But I won't change my mind." She expected Delaney to reveal what she had told him. But he said nothing, only looked at her.

"There's no more to be said." Jon smiled faintly.

"You'll have your allowance, Delaney. You can leave again at once."

"I'll not go," Delaney retorted. "I'm staying here in Moorhaven."

Dorinda knew that nothing would move him, nothing. He wouldn't go away and leave her even now. A part of her exulted. She would see him every day. She would hear his voice. But a part of her ached with pain. It would be hard not to hunger for his kiss, to withhold herself in spirit and body from all that she wanted.

She said quietly, "Jon, remember, you can't force Delaney to do what he refuses to do. He has the same right to Moorhaven that you have."

"We all know that," he answered impatiently. But there was no conviction in his voice, and she knew he was considering how to accomplish what he wanted.

It was later that night that she had found him dead in the marshes.

Though they had discussed it futilely for hours, first with Dr. Peter and among themselves, and then with the sheriff from Tembley, they had not been able to figure out what had happened.

No one had heard Jon leave the house. No one knew why he had gone down to the marshes. They had found a lantern, in the reeds near his body, which accounted for the flickering light that Dorinda had seen. They had found a bloodied rock near his head which accounted for the terrible wound. But they found nothing to explain how the accident could have happened.

Dorinda tried to accept the verdict. She concentrated mind and soul on believing it. Yet, it was like when Delaney had gone away, and she had searched the house for him, unable to believe that he had left her. She had not articulated aloud, nor even in her own thoughts, what she feared. Now it was the same.

This dread suspiciousness, she supposed, was one more sign of the madness that had so suddenly assailed her. It was of a piece with the humming in the night, the tinkle of music, the shadow of Jonathan limping past the yellow-lighted window. Somehow she had suspected her brothers of doing something terrible to Delaney to prevent a marriage of which they didn't approve. And now she somehow suspected that Jon had been lured into the marshes and murdered.

She gasped aloud at the thought. There. It was out for the first time.

Delaney leaned forward to touch her hand.

She looked at him through the small black veil she wore.

Estella whispered, "I don't believe it," and broke into sobs.

Within moments, they stood in the sunlight while the coffin was lowered. The minister spoke a few words.

Jon was buried beside Cordelia and Jonathan, and it was over.

Back at the house, after the Van Nuys had gone, Dennis said with new authority, "I think you'd better reconsider, Delaney."

Harris put in, "Maybe we ought to talk about it another time."

Sam said heavily, "What has to be done is done better sooner than later." And to Delaney, "You don't want to upset Dorinda any more than necessary, do you?"

"I won't," Delaney answered. "But I'll stay here."

Later, when Dorinda had withdrawn to the wing again, he followed her.

She told him that she wanted to be alone, had to be alone, but dreaded the night, dreaded what she might awaken to hear, to see.

He stood over her, smiling faintly, "I just want to tell you. I'm going to change your mind, Dorie. I'm going to persuade you that there's nothing wrong. You *can* marry me. And you will."

It was weakness, shameful and inexcusable, that made her lean against him, taking a moment's strength from him. It was sudden terror that made her start back, turn away, with her heart beat frozen.

Delaney had returned with the evidence that proved he could marry her. Jon had refused to accept it. He had told Delaney he must leave. That night Jon had died.

Delaney caught her by the shoulders, stared down at her. "Dorie, don't pull away. Don't look at me like that. Tell me, honestly, what are you thinking?"

She closed her eyes against his searching gaze. She struggled against an overwhelming need to weep.

But he'd known her too long, and too well. He'd loved her too long and too well. She couldn't deceive him. He read the fear in her eyes.

He let her go. He said slowly, "No, Dorie. Oh, no. Never think it," and went away and left her alone.

It was a week later.

Estella, weeping still, had packed her bags, promised to keep in touch, and returned to her home in Boston, accompanied by Dennis who had business with Alderson and Alderson.

That business accomplished, Dennis had returned, shrugging over his responsibilities, and speaking wistfully of his painting.

Dorinda sensed something latent lurking below the air of normalcy that surrounded Moorhaven now. A stillness, a waiting.

She was thinking of it as she sat watching Mary.

"I've too much to do," Mary told her. "The house gets bigger as I get older. I can't stand the dirt, and I can't keep it out. I don't know what your mother would say. Mud on the carpet. Mud, mind you. From the marshes, you'd think. Now who would do that? Who'd be so careless?"

Dorinda murmured a noncommittal reply.

"Yes. I know. I need more help. But try to get it. Do you know, Dorinda, I even lowered myself to call Arley about it. I did. I must have been daft to think of it. But I thought one of his sons, somebody, might know . . ." She sighed. "I should have known better. He laughed at me. He said they'd starve to death in Tembley before they'd work out here. I don't know what the younger generation's coming to. I don't, and that's a fact. I can remember when I first came. It was the same thing. I was sixteen then. And I knew the talk. My mother, God rest her, believed Moorhaven was cursed."

Dorinda smiled faintly. "And you didn't?"

"I was hungry, and so were they." Mary banged the vacuum cleaner into position, and pushed aside the table under the window. It caught and she gave it a jerk and bent down grunting. "What's this now?" She turned a strand of wire in her fingers, then pressed it back against the wall. "No telling where it goes. I'd better leave it lest I blow every fuse in the house." She shifted the table, turned on the cleaner and set to work. With voice raised over the din, she continued, "And then there's Ralphine ... why, you'd think she was in her dotage, but she's not all that old. But she's running all over, looking for that silver music box of hers. 'Have you got it, Mary?' she asked me. And what would I want with her music box? She's put it some place, of course. And can't remember where. Just like old Joshua, but he has an excuse at least. He's well over seventy. Ralphine's just sixty." Mary's shrill voice faded, then rose again. "But it all makes work . . ."

Dorinda was very still.

Music box.

The tinkle of familiar music that couldn't possibly be there in the darkness of the night. Music box.

No wonder that sound had been so familiar to her. How many times, over the years, she had sat with Ralphine and listened to the haunting tune.

Mary said, "It'll turn up. Things do. Still, I do wish she'd stop complaining."

Dorinda made some agreeable response, then went down the hall to her bedroom. She leaned back in the easy chair, the Spanish shawl at her shoulders. She closed her eyes, her fists at her temples. They felt as if they might burst beneath the pressure.

She couldn't think. She couldn't explain the sudden

certainty in herself. The tinkle of familiar music she heard in the nights was real. Real. Not imagined. It was from Ralphine's old silver music box.

And then light broke through the shadows and broke her heart at the same time. She saw her delusion for what it was. For if someone had deliberately set the music going for her to hear when she was alone, then it was a deliberate attempt to drive her mad. And to believe that must be madness itself . . .

Later that afternoon, to avoid her thoughts, perhaps drawn by Delaney's presence there, she went to the garage.

She watched Delaney and Sam confer over the motor of one of the cars, with Joshua offering advice.

"Maybe we'd better give up," Sam was saying. "Harris told me he wants the car in a little while."

"We can get it adjusted," Delaney protested. "Just get your hands out of the way and let me at it."

"Let you?" Sam's florid face broadened with a wide grin. "I'm the one that knows engines."

Joshua grumbled under his breath, "Knows engines, does he? Well, maybe. But not enough to leave a man's tools alone."

Dorinda asked, "Haven't you ever found your turntable, Joshua?"

He pulled his white beard angrily. "No. I haven't. But I plan to. If it's the last thing I do, I plan to."

It was Dennis who suggested they have drinks on the terrace, and sent Delaney to gather chairs and small tables. And it was Dennis who served the chilled martinis, while Ralphine sniffed disapprovingly.

"It's against the law," she said. "And I don't care if everyone does it. That doesn't make it right. It remains against the law."

"But not for long," Sam told her. "You'll see. In just a few years, maybe three or four, there's going to be a constitutional amendment."

"And in the meantime," she said coldly, fingering the

pearls at her throat, "you allow Harris to buy from
Arley Jones. Arley Jones, mind you."

"More likely Arley's sons," Dennis answered with a
shrug. "And what difference does it make anyway?"

There was a smear of blue on his chin, and his eyes
looked tired. He glanced at Delaney. "If I were you,"
he went on, "I wouldn't argue. I'd be gone like a shot.
The whole world to see . . ."

Delaney answered, "What I want is here."

Dorinda looked down at the marshes. She had seen
the flickering light there, and discovered Jon's body.
And years before, in nearly the same place, Marty
Brown had been found after nights of other flickering
lights. Marty Brown, and Lena . . . the whispers about
Harris that had stopped whenever her parents realized
that she was listening.

Now she looked up at the cliff, and saw the cloud of
dust rise that meant a car was speeding along the road.
"Here's Harris now," she said, and then she sat forward, spilling her drink on her knees.

The car was going too fast.

Harris, always a reckless driver, was even wilder
than usual. The car suddenly appeared from beneath
the trail of dust, careened in great swerves, and then
slid off the road and bounced in what seemed dreamlike
slow motion from rock to rock and then disappeared
from view.

She heard her own voice from a long way off, her
own voice screaming, and saw the others leap to their
feet, while she remained frozen in the chair, her eyes
fixed on the air where the car had been, but was no
longer. And the screams went on and on, coming
closer, closer.

Mary flung herself from the house, her face as gray
as her hair, and her plump body suddenly small. "It's
Joshua," she screamed. "Help me with him. Come help
me with Joshua."

Chapter 24

The two deaths within moments of each other, and so close together, left a terrible pall over Moorhaven.

Joshua's death was clearly suicide.

Harris' death was clearly an accident.

Yet Dorinda did not believe it.

Now, a week later, sitting in Jonathan's office alone, she went over it in her mind.

She had seen Harris' car speeding along the curve, seen it fly out of control, spin off the road, and tumble down the rocks.

Dennis said that when the men had finally gotten to him, his limp body had been covered with shards of broken glass, glass from the whiskey bottles he had been bringing back from Tembley.

It was ironic, Dorinda thought, that Harris, whose connection with Marty Brown she had always suspected, should have died carrying liquor after so many years.

And while the men had made their way to him, Dorinda and Ralphine had scurried after Mary into the workshop.

Joshua's old body dangled from a noose. A stool had been kicked away from his feet. It was plain that he had looped the rope over a beam, climbed up, then pushed the stool away.

Dr. Peter, and later, the sheriff from Tembley, had had no questions.

Harris had been drunk, missed the curve.

Joshua, old, tired of life, had hanged himself.

And yet Dorinda did not believe it. She could not.

But her further suspicions terrified her. She spoke to no one about them.

If the others, too, had questions, they were as careful not to ask them aloud as she was.

But there was a strange new wariness in everyone.

Dennis sat in his study in the main house, sighing over his papers, or looking out of the window. He seemed to have given up his paints, and was now uneasily waiting for something, though Dorinda had no idea of what it could be.

Ralphine's tall thin body seemed to have grown smaller in each dimension, her sallow face even more pale. She walked like a disconsolate ghost through the rooms of Moorhaven.

There was wariness in Dorinda, too. For as the first shock wore off, she had begun to think, to remember.

Delaney and Sam and Joshua had been working over the car. Joshua had left them, and complained to her that he had still not found the turntable for the victrola. He had sworn that he would find it if it took him as long as he lived. But he hadn't lived long after that. Why, Dorinda asked herself, was the turntable so important to him? Why, concentrating on such a triviality, would he suddenly decide to die? No. That was impossible.

Delaney and Sam had been working on the car. Harris had driven it into Tembley. On the way back he had lost control.

She shuddered, clenching her hands. Delaney? Sam? What terrible thing was in her mind. Was this the symptom itself of her illness? Was it the same madness that had made her refuse to believe that Delaney had left her that haunted her now, not allowing her to believe that Harris had died by accident? That Joshua had hanged himself?

And what of Jon? She had, she admitted to herself, never been able to believe that he had died accidentally in the swamp.

Jon. Who knew the dike and marshes, grew up with them. He couldn't have stumbled and fallen as it seemed.

Joshua. Who had lived seventy-five years in acceptance. He couldn't have suddenly decided to end his life.

Harris. Who had driven the road to town, drunk and sober since he was fifteen years old. He couldn't have had such an accident.

There were only three Moorhaven men left.

Who was next? Dennis? Sam? Delaney?

She clutched her hands even more tightly, nails biting into the flesh of her palm. She was mad. It was madness only that made her heart cry out that murder had been done. That murder was the doom of the Moorhavens.

As she sat there, shivering, her face beaded with perspiration, her limbs trembling, she heard a faint whisper of sound.

The room was in twilight now. The sun had sunk beyond the cliff, throwing long dark shadows on the terrace.

The hot summer air was still, breathless. There was a faint whisper of sound in the stillness. A click, a small snap.

She raised her head, waited.

She told herself that it could have been anything. A bird coming to rest in a drain gutter on the roof. A leaf sliding along the slate. A vibration in the wood of the floor. It could have been anything. But she waited.

The sound was repeated. A faint small click.

She rose slowly to her feet. She knew that her hallucination was about to assail her again. She didn't know what form it would take. But soon, soon now, she would hear the great humming of swarming bees echo at her from the wall, or she would hear the tinkle of familiar music.

It came just as she thought of it. It came clearly, though from far away. The sound was not in this room with her, but it was here.

Yes, yes. She was sure. It was not just in her head. But here, somewhere in the wing where the ghost of her father sometimes seemed to walk.

She fought down hysteria. She found a calm within herself that she could cling to. And clinging to it, she made a slow careful systematic search of the room. In her mind was the memory of the last time she had done the same thing. But she didn't allow that to deter her. She peered under the furniture, moved the heavy chairs, examined the bookcases. She found nothing unusual. She checked the underside of the table, and noticed the loose wire that Mary had found some time before. She didn't touch it, thinking, as Mary had, that it must be necessary somehow to the lighting system.

When she had convinced herself that there was no possible source for the music in the office, she followed the sound, as an unwilling dancer, to someone else's pipe, along the hall and to her bedroom. It was just as she went in that she heard the click again. The faint tinkle of music faded away and was still.

She repeated her search in the bedroom, and then, climbing on a chair, she began to examine the hat boxes on the top shelf of the closet. She had looked at them before, but she had never looked inside them.

Now she opened one. Hats wrapped in tissue. A black cloche with a tiny nose veil. A big white straw over-burdened with violets. She put them away, took down another box. A blue straw sailor hat, nothing more.

She had given up hope by then, but was moving automatically. What had been begun must be finished. But her heart was sinking within her. She no longer expected to find the answer to her search. She was already beginning to believe that the sound had been in her head, her ears, after all. Then she took down the third box. She drew out the big white hat and knew it instantly. It had belonged to her mother. Cordelia had worn it, the pink roses on the brim, the trailing light green ribbons. She took out a big blue hat of floppy chiffon, and beneath it, nesting in soft paper, was Ralphine's music box.

It was as if a strange nightmare was swiftly receding.

The music box had been deliberately hidden in her room. In some way that she couldn't imagine it was wound and went off, perhaps like an alarm clock, at set intervals.

She got down from the chair suddenly. If the music box had been left here, deliberately set to torment her, then what had caused the terrible humming? What of Jonathan's pacing shadow?

Quickly, she walked down the hall. Into her father's office.

She stared around it, trying to see it with fresh eyes, with eyes that took nothing for granted. She saw, in the mirror against the wall opposite the window, her own image. White-faced, thin, the cheekbones standing out. Eyes that glittered like polished green stone. Tousled red curls on her white forehead. And now she remembered another time she had looked into her own image in this same mirror, this same room. She had come into her father's office and he had been standing there, but the mirror had been displaced. He had moved it quickly, shielding whatever was there with his big body. She had asked him about it and been told it was adult business and nothing for her to concern herself with. She had looked into her own eyes, shining green, at that time, too.

Now she went to the mirror. She tried to lift it down, but could not. It was too heavy. It seemed not to hang by a hook. But to be affixed to the wall. As she tugged at it, it suddenly moved aside.

She could hear her father saying, "Adult business, Dorie. Don't worry your head about it."

She peered into the hidden safe in the wall. There was a turntable there. The one Joshua had been seeking? she asked herself. Attached to it there was what appeared to be the cut-out figure of a man. And there was a huge red and white child's top.

The silver music box ... the child's top ... the victrola turntable with its small figure ...

The explanation for all her hallucinations was here at hand, material, measurable.

Delaney ... Sam ... Dennis ...

Which one of them had tried to make her believe she had lost her mind?

Which one of them hated her, concealed that hatred behind a smiling face?

No, her heart whispered. No, not Delaney. He loves me. He refused to believe me, to accept what I thought was my madness. He could have no reason. But Dennis ... was he so opposed to her possible marriage that he would have taken such terrible steps to prevent her?

Was Sam?

There was a sound behind her.

She whirled.

Delaney stood in the doorway. "What's that, Dorinda? What have you there?"

She turned to fumble at the mirror, to swing it into place.

But he was too quick for her.

He lunged across the carpet, caught her hand. He stood over her, sandy head bent, to stare into the safe. His eyes were narrow, unreadable. His mouth grim, almost bloodless.

Finally he said, "That's the turntable Joshua was complaining that he lost."

She nodded numbly.

"Why are you saving the child's top?"

She raised her eyes to his. "I'm not saving it, Delaney. I found it there, just now, in the recess."

"I seem to remember it. One of us had it when we were kids."

She took it down, set it into motion. It moved slowly at first with a light easy humming sound, and then it picked up speed. The humming increased until it seemed as if bees were swarming in the room.

If she had needed proof after the silver music box, she had it now. This was the humming that had haunted her nights.

Delaney stopped it with his foot. He nodded slowly. "Yes. I hear it. I understand, Dorinda."

He reached with a lean finger to touch the turntable. Then he suddenly pulled it out. He took it to the table under the window and set it down in front of the lamp. He bent to the floor for a moment. As he rose, the turntable began to spin slowly. He closed the curtains and switched on the lamp. A shadow fell across the curtains.

"Father's shadow," she gasped. "Delaney! How did you know?"

"I didn't know," he said evenly. "But it occurred to me that it might work that way. It's a sophisticated version of the shadow play we used to do when we were little. Don't you remember?"

"Yes," she whispered. "I do remember. Now. But I never thought . . ."

He smiled faintly. "I never believed that you were mad, Dorie. You know that. I didn't know what had happened to you, but I just couldn't accept your explanation." He sighed. "I'm afraid that it's my fault Joshua died."

"But he didn't know anything about it, Delaney. He couldn't possibly have. I never . . ."

"He knew some," Delaney told her. "Because I told him myself. About the humming, and about the shadow. He agreed with me that there was some explanation for them aside from your own. He was just as certain as I that nothing in you could have produced such hallucinations. That they must have come from something outside. He was determined to find out the truth."

"You think then that he did?"

"I think he must have come pretty close, Dorie."

"But who then? Who did he suspect?"

Delaney shrugged. "I don't know. Dennis. Sam. Possibly Ralphine, though I can't really imagine it. Dorie, someone at Moorhaven *is* mad, you know. Not you, but someone else."

The moving shadow suddenly slowed and stopped.

Delaney took up the turntable, pulled the plug free, and returned it to the recess. He put the child's top in with it, and then slid the mirror into place.

"I think we can safely leave all this paraphernalia alone. Whoever is responsible will have no more need for it. Not as long as that person believes that you are still set on not marrying me."

She shook her head. "No, Delaney." She led him to her bedroom, and showed him the silver music box.

"Ralphine's," he grunted.

"Yes. But Mary told me that it had been misplaced some time ago. Perhaps Ralphine said that to cover for herself. Yet I don't see why she need have mentioned it at all. I had no idea about it until Mary mentioned it, and then I began to think of the music I'd heard."

He packed the music box under the hats, put it back on the shelf. "Just leave it there for the time being."

"It played tonight, Delaney. That's how I happened to find it. It played, and I recognized the music, and thought of the box, and started to look. But by playing it tonight, the person who did it showed that he's still intent on keeping me in terror. Even though he knows I'll never marry you."

"Perhaps so that you won't think too much of Jon, and Harris, and Joshua," Delaney said thoughtfully. "So you won't begin to examine everything that's happened."

She let her breath out in a long sigh. "Yes. You must be right." And then, "But what can we do? How long will this go on, and how will it end?"

"You have to move back into the house at once," he answered. "That's the first thing. To be sure that you're safe."

She shook her head. "No, I can't. If I do, it will seem as if I'm no longer afraid of being insane. Don't you see? It will seem as if I've discovered something here in Dad's wing."

"But you can't be alone here, Dorie. Unprotected, unwatched. We don't know what's in store for any of us. You can't risk it."

She thought about it only for a moment. Then she said, "No. I'll stay here. There must be an end to this ... this madness, Delaney."

Though he argued, he couldn't change her mind.

But when he left her alone, she felt the fear move in her again.

It was no longer a fear of herself, of the sounds she might hear, of the false shadow she might see.

Now she listened for a corporeal footstep, for an opening door, for human malice to reveal itself.

She listened through most of the long night, but nothing happened.

By the time the sun rose, she knew what she must do.

Chapter 25

There was madness at Moorhaven. But it was not her madness. She suffered from no mental weakness at all, except the willingness to doubt her own stability, to accept without adequate question what seemed to be for what was real.

Her mind was whole. She must use it to save Moorhaven.

It all began with her father's death, when Jon became the head of the family. She had announced that she was going to marry Delaney, and immediately, the attack on her, on her sanity, had begun. And, at the same time the family had united to send Delaney away. She saw no purpose in that as yet, but she did not doubt that there had been purpose in it, and that she would, one day, discover what it had been. With Delaney's return, Jon had died. Then, because he suspected someone, or knew something, Joshua had been killed. And, at the same time, Harris. Had Harris known, suspected, something? Dorinda couldn't be sure.

Jon had died, and Harris, and Joshua, too, after Delaney's unannounced return. What had his presence to do with those deaths? Had his slender hands been responsible? Had he lured Jon down to the marshes, and struck him? Had he, while working on the car

234

with Sam, tampered with the mechanism somehow? Had he, after speaking to Joshua and learning of the old man's suspicions, then hanged him in what appeared a suicide?

A wave of sickness washed over her. She loved Delaney. She must trust him. What were these awful thoughts? How could she doubt him?

But how could she doubt either Dennis or Sam, she asked herself. Dennis was her brother, Sam her first cousin. They had all grown up together in Moorhaven. She had no answer.

Then it occurred to her that the things that had happened to her in Jonathan's wing could not have been arranged by Delaney. He had been away during that awful mouth.

Her relief was so great that it shamed her. It made her see forcibly how deep her fear was of what he might have done. Might have done for her. But no. No, Delaney was not mad. He hadn't tried to drive her insane. He had not murdered to wipe out the opposition to their marriage.

So then . . . Dennis . . . Sam . . . She tried to imagine Dennis, wearing on his face the mask that hid hatred and jealousy. Dennis, with yellow paint on his cheek, and blood on his hands. Then she tried to imagine Sam, his florid flesh hiding dark yearnings.

But both pictures gave her only pain, neither understanding nor certainty.

And yet, one part of what was happening at Moorhaven was horribly clear to her. Someone among them was determined to destroy the others. Someone among them was determined to take his place as head of the family. It was the only explanation for Jon's death and Harris's.

It was with those thoughts whirling in her mind that she went to the main house for lunch the next afternoon.

She found that Bettina Van Nuys had driven out from Tembley to visit with Ralphine. The two older women were in the drawing room together. They both turned anxious faces toward her when she joined them.

"Are you all right, Dorinda?" Bettina asked. "Dr. Peter requested I return with a full report on you. He's concerned about your health in these unhappy days."

Obviously Bettina was concerned, too. Her bright blue eyes examined Dorinda critically. There was hardly a sign of her dimples now.

Dorinda smiled faintly. "I'm fine."

Bettina frowned, as deeply as she was able to frown, that is. "I must tell you, child, that you don't look fine to me. I thought Ralphine was exhibiting aunt-like exaggeration, but I see now that she wasn't. If I didn't know better I'd believe that you'd been dissipating disgracefully for weeks on end."

"I don't sleep too well. But I'm sure that will pass," Dorinda told her.

It was, she knew, her terrible thoughts marking her face that Bettina could see so clearly. As counterpoint to the conversation of the two women, she heard the awful questions in her mind again. Dennis? Sam? Which one of them was responsible? Or which one would be next? Who had already been chosen to die, but walked unknowingly in that danger?

She knew that she must stop it. She must break the pattern. She was afraid of what she must do, yet she saw no other way except the single one open to her.

Bettina was saying, "I've had a most disturbing letter from Estella since she went home. Poor girl. She's been badly affected by Jon's awful death."

"So have we all," Ralphine said dryly. "But she's shallow enough. She'll overcome her sorrow and be married within the year to someone else."

"Perhaps not," Bettina answered. "She harps so on the impossibility of an accident. It isn't a good thing for her, you know. Dr. Peter considers it morbid."

"Impossibility of an accident," Ralphine snapped. "She ought to be ashamed of herself!"

But Dr. Peter didn't know, Dorinda thought. And apparently Ralphine didn't either.

If they thought Estella's suspicions morbid, what would they think of what lay in her mind?

She was more certain now than ever that she must not spell out her suspicions to Dr. Peter, and certainly not to Ralphine. If she did, if she told them everything that had happened, and what she believed had happened, they would surely think her insane.

Dennis and Sam came in, and no further mention was made of Estella.

Dennis asked how things were in town, and about the Van Nuys boys.

Bettina was happy to complain about the situation in Tembley, and happier still to boast about her sons.

She was still at it when Delaney joined them.

He gave Dorinda an anxious look, his thin face questioning her. But she smiled at him. She waited until there was a pause in the conversation, and then she said, "I have something to tell all of you. And I hope you'll be glad." She rushed on as the faces turned toward her, inquiring, still, expressionless. "Delaney and I are going to be married in two days."

This was what she had known she must do.

This was the only way that she could see to force the hand of her secret enemy.

After a pause, Ralphine said, "Dorinda, I don't know what to say or think. This is hardly the right time to . . ."

Dennis said dryly, "You're as changeable as a chameleon. First you said you would. Then you said you wouldn't. Now you say you will again."

"What made you change your mind?" Sam asked.

Delaney's cheeks were flushed, his tan-colored eyes bright. He said, "Dorie, I thought we'd agreed . . ."

She cut him off, smiling brightly, although her heart was pounding against her ribs. "Oh, darling, there was no point at all in keeping it a secret. No one can oppose us now." She shrugged. "And if anyone does, then I'm sorry. It can't be helped. You have the proof that the only objection posed was based on silly gossip by silly people years and years ago."

Though she spoke lightly, it took all her strength to

get the words out. Now that they had been said, she felt weak, light-headed with relief. There. It was done. She could not take it back. She would not. If her marriage to Delaney was in some way related to the plot in which they were entangled, then someone would be forced to act.

It was only then that she realized what she had actually done. Only then that she saw the danger into which she had put each of the three men before her. One was a murderer, but the other two were possible victims.

She wanted to scream out that she had been joking. She didn't mean it. She would never, never marry Delaney. But she realized, in the same moment, that Jon had died, and Harris, too, after her refusal of Delaney. After. Then somehow it was not just the marriage. There had been some other catalyst. She knew at once what it was, had to be. Jonathan's death. That had been the beginning. The possibility of her marriage was in some way connected to the murderer's motive. But she didn't know how. She only knew that something must happen soon. Very soon. And that she must be on the alert for any clue which would reveal his hidden identity.

After they had had lunch together, Delaney followed her out onto the terrace.

His voice was deep, nervous. He said, "You shouldn't have done it, Dorie. It's too much of a risk."

"Do you have second thoughts now?" she asked. "Have you changed your mind? Do you want to back out?"

He didn't smile, though from her tone, he must have known that she was teasing him. He said simply, "I'm afraid, Dorie. For you."

She gripped his hands tightly, whispered, "I'm more afraid for you, Delaney."

"What do you mean?" he demanded. "Why? Why should you be?"

But she shook her head. She couldn't explain. She

didn't dare. No one must know what her true thoughts were. No one. Not even Delaney.

He said tightly, "You don't trust me, do you."

She leaned her head against his shoulder. "I do. I do. But you must trust me, too."

Sam came outside then, stood watching them, a grin on his florid face, a gleam in his black eyes. "A loving scene," he said at last.

Dorinda drew back from Delaney, but slowly, with no embarrassment. She refused to let the gleam in his eyes affect her.

He went on, "I suppose you haven't noticed, with all you have on your mind, Dorinda, but I'm very concerned about Dennis these days."

"About Dennis?" she asked. "But why?"

"He's so . . . well, the only word I can think of is restless. He sits in the office and stares out of the window, pretending to be at work when he really isn't at work at all. It won't do, you know. As head of the family, he must carry on. There's no good his brooding about what might have been. Or what he might have done."

"Aldersons handles most of it anyway, Sam," she said. "So that part of it will be all right regardless. And so much has happened. It'll take time for us to come to our senses again."

He nodded agreement. "You're right, of course. And I realize that it will take time. That's why I've written to my Denny to stay on where he is for the next few weeks. Moorhaven is just not the place for him now. Perhaps, later . . ."

"Yes," she agreed. "Perhaps later, Sam."

She heard the sound the moment she opened the door.

It drifted toward her down the shadowy hallway. It was the sweet soft tinkle of familiar music.

She paused for just a moment. Her heart gave a quick hard leap in her breast and then steadied. There was nothing to be afraid of. It was only Ralphine's silver music box. She went down the hall slowly, and then into her room.

It was empty, of course, and she'd expected it to be. But the music continued. It continued while she got a chair, climbed up, and took down the hat box from the top shelf of the closet. It continued while she opened it, moved aside the hats, and lifted out the silver box.

As she looked at it, the music suddenly stopped.

A quick exultation swept her. She had struck at the nerve of her enemy at lunch time. And now, in this way, he had struck back, testing her, trying her. But he would not succeed. He would not. She would save herself, save Moorhaven. She must.

But the exultation was suddenly lost in a wave of fear. She was not only moving herself toward danger, but two others as well. Could she risk it? How would she expose the plotter?

The music box seemed to throb within her fingers. She took a long slow breath. She must let the plotter know that his tricks were discovered. That part of his game was lost. Then let him make his next move.

She didn't wait. She went directly to the main house. She found Ralphine in conversation with Dennis and Sam.

Ralphine spotted the box, cried, "Oh, Dorinda, where did you find it? I'm so glad. Really. It meant so much to me, and I never thought I'd see it again."

"Don't ask me how it came to be there, because I don't know. But it was in the top of my closet, under some of Mother's old hats that I was going to try on just now."

She said nothing about the long nights of horror when she had listened to the faint familiar music, thinking that she was going insane. She said nothing of what she suspected. It was not necessary. The person who had put the box there would know. He would understand. He would make his next move.

Though she studied them carefully, she saw nothing in Dennis' face, nor in Sam's, that was in any way revealing. They were both more amused than anything else.

"A sentimental attachment?" Sam asked, examining the music box.

"In a way, yes." A spot of color appeared in each of Ralphine's cheeks.

"Fancy that," Dennis said. "Where did you get it?"

Ralphine did not answer. She took the box from Sam, and then turned and went slowly up the stairs.

Sam grinned. "She's remembering the past I expect. Poor thing. What a shame to live only with memories."

"What do you mean?" Dennis asked.

"I suspect you mean 'whom'," Sam answered. "Why, Dr. Peter, of course. I'm sure he brought that to Ralphine some time or other. Back in the good old days, when she was in love with him."

"She was?" Dorinda asked. "What makes you say that? And what happened?"

Sam shrugged his thick shoulders. "Don't ask me. I don't know. Except that they didn't get married. I think Dr. Peter was interested in your mother for a while. But she had eyes for nobody but your father. Nobody but Jonathan. And then Dr. Peter married Bettina, but that was later, I'm sure."

It was hard to imagine Ralphine in love, young and in love, hard to think of Dr. Peter as having been drawn to Cordelia. Of course they had been good friends, her mother and Dr. Peter. Even Dorinda could remember that. But anything else? No. She found she couldn't picture any of them as having been young enough to be in love. Not love as she and Delaney knew it. But then she remembered the sudden flush on Ralphine's cheeks, and the unaccustomed brightness in her eyes, and realized that somehow, even now, Ralphine continued to be in love. And yes, it must be love as Dorinda and Delaney knew it.

It was an insight that opened doors in her mind.

As she returned to the wing, she found herself wondering if what was happening now at Moorhaven could be a continuation of the past which seemed so distant to her, but was, in fact, a part of the present. She didn't know then how close to the truth she was.

Sighing, she dismissed her speculations. She couldn't search through a time before she had been born for something which could help her now. She could only be wary, and hope, hope that somehow she could save herself, and Moorhaven, from further horror.

The faint click sounded loud in the night's heavy silence.

Dorinda was instantly awake. It was as if her sleeping senses had been attuned to some whisper of sound, and responded to it in the moment it came.

She sat up quickly, listening for further proof that someone had entered the wing. When she heard nothing more, she got out of bed, slipped on a robe and a pair of mules.

She listened at the closed door of her room before easing it open, then listened again.

She went through the dark hall toward the office.

As she reached the door, hearing only the sound of her own beating heart in her ears, there was a sudden thump, then the rasp of a window thrown open.

She lunged for the door, flung it back.

The office was in darkness, empty.

Chapter 26

But, by the faint light from the lamps outside, she saw that the mirror had been moved aside, and not replaced. The safe was open now.

The red and white top, and the turntable with its small figure, were gone.

She stared at the receptacle only briefly, then raced to the open window.

There was no one on the terrace. In the long night shadows, nothing moved.

But she had, from the corner of her eye, the impression that someone had ducked behind the end of the wing.

She ran to the hall, fled down it to the back door. She flung it open and stepped out into the night.

She realized her mistake, but realized it too late. She was alone, defenseless. Even as the shadow lunged at her, the raised fist striking her down, she tried to retreat.

But the blow caught her on the side of her head. The lunging shadow seemed to explode with brilliance. She went down into unconsciousness . . .

The air tasted bitter. There was a sour cloud over her face. She tried to move her head from side to side. Pain lanced through her drooping body. Dimly, she knew that time passed. She sensed that much even though she was barely conscious. Time passed, marked by the deep aching throb that held her, by the pulses that seemed to scream in her temples, by the recurring waves of nausea under which she sank. It passed, and slowly she became aware of the bitterness again. The sour cloud that seemed to be sucked into her with each breath. At last, struggling for strength, she raised her head.

She was in darkness. Where she was, how she had come there, she didn't know.

Darkness. Enclosure. A faint humming. And bitter air.

She reached out blindly, her hand fumbling for some familiar object, for some material thing that would identify for her where she was. Her trembling fingers encountered cool glass, then metal, and at the same time, she became aware of the coarse nap under her cheek.

In that instant, she realized where she lay. She identified the bitter smell. She forced herself to sit up. The bitter air was overwhelming now. And she recognized it.

She was in the garage. In one of the cars.

The air was fouled by motor fumes.

As she managed to open the door, step out, she saw the thin pipe that hung in the very nearly closed window. She didn't understand what it meant. But she knew that she must get out, out into the fresh air.

She crept softly through the darkness. The garage door opened silently when she bumped it. She fell through it into a clear bright dawn.

She gulped in hungry breaths, and struggled unsuccessfully to rise.

There were sudden running footsteps. She cringed against the cool earth.

With her returning memory, came fear. She had stepped outside into darkness. She had seen a lunging shadow and been struck down.

She hadn't been able to recognize the person who had been there with her. It had all happened too quickly. Her instant descent into unconsciousness had protected him against discovery.

And now he was returning to finish the work not quite done.

Delaney bent over her. "Dorie! What is it?"

She raised dazed eyes to his face.

He was pale. White rimmed his lips. His tan eyes were fastened on her. "Dorie!"

Had he struck her down to keep her from recognizing him? Had it been he who had removed the top and the turntable from the safe? How could that be when most of the attempts against her sanity had taken place during the month when he had been away? Still, he was here now. He, and no one else, was here.

He gathered her into his arms, drew her to her feet. "What happened to you?"

She whispered, "I heard something in the wing. I went to look. The safe had been opened. Someone rushed out of the window as I went in. I thought to head him off, and hurried outside, and just as I . . ."

She stopped then. She shook her head. "Delaney, I've lost hours and hours. I can't understand it. It was dark when I rushed outside. And now . . . now look. The sun is rising."

"If you were unconscious . . ."

Now she remembered the car, the pipe fitted into the window. She said, "Let me show you where I was."

He helped her as she took him back to the garage. His face went even more pale when she showed him the car, the almost-closed window, the pipe.

"I was here. And I couldn't breathe. If I hadn't awakened, I don't know what would have happened. But I just couldn't seem to . . ."

"I know what would have happened," he said grimly. "You would have been dead. The pipe was feeding noxious air into the car, and into your lungs as well. It would have killed you, Dorie."

"Then I was left here to die," she whispered. "Struck down and carried here, and left here."

"And it would have appeared to be suicide." A grim

smile touched Delaney's lips. "As if you would ever have figured out how to do that. You don't even know how to drive a car."

"But who?" she breathed. "Who?"

Delaney's eyes did not quite meet hers. He said, "I don't know. I only know one thing. I must take you away from here. And I'd better do it right away."

She had been slated to die as a suicide. The same way that Joshua, who had lived so long in the rooms above where she stood at the moment, had died. She had come so close to Moorhaven's enemy that he had turned and struck her down.

"No," she told Delaney, "I won't leave. You oughtn't to expect that I would. This is my home. I was born here. I belong here. I won't allow anyone to drive me away."

Even as she spoke, she realized that Delaney had not told her how he came to be in the back of the wing at dawn. He had not told her what had brought him down, out of the house, to find her.

Dennis said, "I think I'd like to take a trip." His voice was low, his head bent over his paint-stained hands. "Maybe out to San Francisco," he added, plainly trying for a nonchalance he didn't feel.

"You?" Sam frowned.

Dennis gave him a curt nod. "Me."

"What for?" Sam went on. "Alderson and Alderson is handling it all."

"Well, Jon sent Delaney . . . it might . . ."

Sam laughed. "Now, Dennis, you know just as well as I do that that was nothing more than an excuse, a ploy that didn't work. You'd do better to stay right here in Moorhaven, studying the reports, and keeping in touch with the market."

"Stay right here," Dennis sighed. "The old castle bit, the center of the patriarchs. Old-fashioned. Uselessly old-fashioned. We'd all do better to move out of Moorhaven. There's nothing here for any of us. Yes. That's what we ought to do. Give up Moorhaven."

"Give it up," Dorinda cried. "But Dennis, Moorhaven is home. What are you talking about?"

He gave her an embarrassed look. "I guess what I'm saying is that I feel . . . well, I feel as if I'm in a prison. The walls, the marshes, the cliffs. Don't you understand me, Dorinda? I thought surely you would."

"No," she said slowly. "No. I don't."

But she wondered how candid he was being. Was it truly that he simply felt too cut off from the world in Moorhaven? Or was it that he was afraid? Did he suspect that he was the next Moorhaven to die? Was that what made him want to get away? Was he covertly eyeing Sam and Delaney, wondering which of them would strike at him from the dark? And if that were so, if he had begun to suspect the circumstances of Jon's death, and Harris's, and Joshua's, how was it that he had not told her, told anyone else? Why was he keeping it a secret?

Dennis went on, somewhat shamefacedly, but stubbornly, "I find myself thinking these days that Tembley is right, and we're wrong."

Ralphine, silent until then, raised her thin brows, "Dennis, what nonsense is this?"

"Nonsense?" He shrugged. "Well, maybe you're right. Maybe that's what it is. But just the same, the facts suggest that nonsense may not be the right word. Have you ever considered everything that's happened?"

Sam said, "We've had some bad luck, of course. But that's all it is. A man may slip in the marshes, you know. A man may have an auto accident. And poor old Joshua . . ."

Dorinda folded her hands together. *Doomed. The Moorhavens are high now, but they'll be brought low.*

Dennis looked at Sam. "I'm not talking about now, not particularly. Sam, what about the years past? Don't you realize, your own mother . . ."

"Of course," Sam cut in, "I remember. And I know more about it than you do. It was well before you were even born. And that was an accident, too. Though I suppose it fed the superstition of the foolish people in town who insist on thinking of us rather than facing their own problems."

Ralphine said coldly, "The whole thing started when my parents built the house here. It had nothing to do with anything but that. They built the house and gave up the shipyard and closed the warehouses, and Tembley was hard hit. They had to find some way to explain the terrible times that began then so they blamed them on us."

"Then they might as well blame the Depression on us," Delaney said.

"In a way, I suppose they do," Sam answered.

Dorinda was watching Dennis. He seemed tired, uneasy. At last, she asked, "But Dennis, are you really serious about leaving Moorhaven?"

"I am." He rested his head on his hands. "I must admit that I find it hard. The weight of it on my shoulders. It was different when Jon was here. The weight was on him then, the responsibilities on him. But I," a faint grin touched his lips, "I don't like it, nor want it. I'd prefer to go to Paris, for instance. Forget San Francisco. Sam's right about that. Nobody needs me there. But in Paris, where I could study . . ."

Sam laughed abruptly, "Paris is a long way from Moorhaven interests, Dennis."

"I know," Dennis said. "Perhaps that's why I mentioned it."

"I think that he's frightened," Delaney said. "I don't know what's happened. It may be that he has his reasons. It may be that he's guessed or seen something. Or that he's begun to think and add two and two. Anyway, I'm sure that he's frightened, Dorie."

"But he can't know what you and I know," she protested. "How could he? I never said a thing to him."

"He knows Jon and Harris and Joshua are dead. He knows that two of those deaths were designed to look like accidents."

"But how would he know that?"

"Perhaps in the same way that we do."

She shook her auburn curls firmly. "I don't think he actually realizes what's happening." She wondered if Dennis' real reason was not fear of being a victim, but fear of going on . . . of going on with some terrible plot.

The thought pulled her up sharply. But why would he have to continue, if he were the plotter? With Jon dead, Dennis was master in Moorhaven. There need be no other deaths. There need be no plot against her herself. Then why had Harris died? It could not be Dennis.

Then Sam.

Her first cousin. Son of Captain Dennis whose portrait hung in the vestibule. Dennis the older brother of her father Jonathan. Sam. Son of blonde, cool-faced Elena, who had died in the swamps so many years before.

Sam.

A shiver went over Dorinda. Could it be that Sam had planned the death of each of the Moorhaven heirs? Was that why Jon had died, and then Harris? Had Joshua been killed because he knew or guessed? Could Sam have tried to keep her from marrying Delaney by driving her insane? Would that keep Delaney himself from being an heir, too? Jonathan had adopted Delaney, but did he automatically become the head of the Moorhaven empire if the others died before him?

A faint glimmer of an idea moved in her mind. She tried to seize it, examine it, but it was gone before she could bring it into focus. She told herself to forget it and perhaps it would return later, like a memory one sought too hard and chased into oblivion with the effort.

Delaney put his hand on her shoulder. "Better go in, Dorie. And be careful, will you? Don't go wandering around in the night."

She smiled faintly. "You sound a little like Dennis. Are you thinking of Tembley's superstitions, too?"

He shook his sandy head. "No, I'm not. I'm thinking only of real danger. Real danger to you, Dorie."

"Yes," she agreed soberly, "it's real enough."

"And you will be careful?"

"I will. But will you?"

"Yes." His finely-cut, sensitive mouth firmed into a hard line. "Believe me, I want to live to be your husband."

Inside the wing, with the front and back doors bolted, she sat down beside the window to read, the lamp light a yellow circle around her auburn head.

But her eyes could not follow the print. Her mind did not hold the words she read.

Her thoughts continued, circled, searching for meaning, for understanding, in the few concrete facts that she knew.

Jon and Harris had not died by accident, but by design. Dennis had become heir to Moorhaven then. How was it that Harris had been killed while Dennis was allowed to live? Since he was next in line it would have seemed more likely that he would have died in the car rather than Harris. But somehow that had not mattered. Perhaps if all the Moorhaven men must die the order didn't count. Her oldest brother and youngest brother were each dead. That left Dennis, and herself, and possibly Delaney. Delaney, surely, if he married her. When he married her. But what if there was no marriage? What if, while still single, she herself died. Who then would inherit Moorhaven?

She knew the answer to that. It was Sam. Sam, the son of Dennis. Sam . . .

A shudder touched her. She had come back to his name again. Was he the madman who sought to be master of Moorhaven?

Or was she wrong? Was it Dennis, pretending now to fear, to displeasure with responsibilities that he had sought while Jon was alive?

There was a faint sound from outside, from the shadows on the terrace.

She immediately switched off the lamp, and sat very still, staring into the dark.

Chapter 27

Dennis walked by, his head bent, his hands clasped behind his back. He reached the edge of the terrace, and then stood there, a tall dark shadow in the night.

Dorinda, watching, wondered what thoughts were in his mind. Was he frightened now? Had he begun to see in the events that had taken place a pattern? Or, as he stared down into the marshes, was he merely thinking of all the cities he hadn't seen, adventures he hadn't had?

She rose to her feet, without knowing why. Slowly, carefully, she edged back from the window to a point where she couldn't be seen by anyone outside. Later she would realize that it was instinct alone that moved her. Once freed from the fear that she might be insane she could trust her judgment.

Long moments passed. A warm breeze stirred the lilac bushes. The moon rose high, silvering the terrace and the slope below.

Then she heard the sound of the front door as it swung open and then shut. She heard footsteps on the stone steps, then on the terrace itself.

Sam passed below the window, paused to look up at it, then went on.

Dennis turned, his silhouette tall and dark against

the moonlight. When he spoke, his voice was a whisper. "That you, Sam?"

"Yes. Having some air?"

"A last cigarette before turning in," Dennis answered.

"I'll join you," Sam said.

A moment filled with the soft footsteps. Then the two shadows joined.

Dorinda could no longer hear what was said. She watched uneasily for the space of two breaths. Then, moving quickly, silently, she went into the hallway, and unlocking the back door of the wing, she went outside and around. From the shadows there, she peered at the edge of the terrace where she had seen Dennis and Sam stand together.

But it was empty now. They were both gone.

Panic swept her. She had, by announcing that she would marry Delaney so soon, set in motion the force which must mean death to another of the Moorhavens. She could not stand here in the shadows. She must separate villain from victim. She must know the truth.

The terrace was empty, the house dark and still.

She set out after Sam and Dennis.

She knew they had not turned off the terrace and gone back to the cliff. She would have been able to hear them making their way along the stony paths upward. No one could walk there in such utter silence as surrounded her now.

But once off the terrace, on the soft grainy earth of the slope that led down to the dike, all sound would be muffled. The marshes . . .

She ran that way after another anguished glance at the house where all was still silent, still dark. No one was up, watching. And there was no time now to go for help. No time now to seek out Delaney in his room, to beg Mary to come, to cry out for Ralphine.

She ran lightly down the steps from the terrace, and then onto the slope itself. She kept well in the shadow of the brush, pressing on into the dark, though every fibre in her body urged her to go back into light and safety.

But from somewhere ahead, she heard mingled voices and muffled footsteps. The voices faded away briefly, and then, as she hurried on, became louder.

Suddenly she froze.

Dennis and Sam were at the foot of the dike, deep in the shadows of the rounded hump.

Here her father had walked. And more recently, her brother Jon, driven by Joshua's insistence, had walked, too. Here was all that held the marshes back from Moorhaven. She shuddered suddenly. What if some day the marshes rose? Would they creep up the slope toward the cliff to engulf Moorhaven?

Dennis and Sam ... She could hear the sound of their voices, but not the words themselves.

Crouching low, she wondered what they were talking about. Could they have somehow joined together in murder? Was Sam the puppet master who pulled the strings to make Dennis dance? Had they, in concert, murdered Jon, Joshua, and Harris? Had they sought to drive her insane to keep her from marrying Delaney?

Now she drew her breath in slowly. Or was she, even at this moment, believing in herself, her sanity, at last, completely misled. Was she mad? Were her suspicions signs of an illness she could not recognize for what it was?

In her imagination, she tried to conjure up the sound of the humming, and reminded herself of the red and white top. She tried to remember the faint and familiar music and thought of the silver box. She pictured the turntable and its small silhouette cutout of a man, and saw Joshua dangling from the rope that had strangled him.

These things were proof of her sanity. What she had thought of as hallucination was real. She drew new strength from that.

The voices once more faded briefly. Dennis and Sam suddenly emerged from the shadow of the dike and were silhouetted against the sky.

She could see them clearly. She rose, took cautious steps, angling closer to them as soundlessly as she could.

She wondered if Sam, as he stared into the oily heaving water, at the black stunted trees, was remembering his mother who had been lost in the marshes. Under what circumstances, or why, or how, or even exactly when, Dorinda was not sure. But Sam, twenty years older than she was, might know. Was he thinking of Elena now? Or was he remembering his sister, Lena, who had fallen in love so desperately with Marty Brown, shot in the sinister darkness and brought to the house to be cared for? Was Sam thinking of how Lena left with Marty Brown, and was killed among strangers?

And Dennis, was he daydreaming about Paris? Was he thinking of himself working in some light-filled attic? Was he chafing under the burden of Moorhaven?

She heard the whispering voices, and mixed with them, from somewhere very close by, another sound that was no more than a faint rustle in the reeds. The silhouette of Dennis stood with head bent. The bulkier one that was Sam stood close, head thrust forward, talking, talking earnestly.

He raised his hand, apparently pointing to the eastern horizon. Dennis turned to look that way.

At the same time, she became aware of a presence near her. She felt rather than saw or heard it. She froze, waiting. And then knew that it was Delaney. She knew it before she could see him. He pressed close to her, shook his head, turned her face toward the slope and the house and gave her a slight urging push.

In that instant, when her attention was completely centered on him, she heard a dull thud. It was faint, but in the thick silence it was clear.

A thud first, and then the sound of reeds being crushed by a falling weight.

Delaney swore under his breath, and lunged for the dike. She scrambled after him.

When they reached the top, they saw Dennis

sprawled, unmoving. Sam was hunched over him, his hand raised, his fingers curled around a rock.

Dorinda's scream was shrill, carrying.

Its echo seemed to stay Sam's hand, to hold it in mid-air for a moment.

Then he looked up. His hand fell. The rock slipped from his fingers into the water.

At the same instant, Delaney hurled himself at Sam.

The two men became a mass of struggling arms and legs, of grunts and curses, while Dorinda watched, sobbing.

Sam . . . her first cousin . . .

Dennis got to his feet groggily, looked around him in bewilderment, and wiped mud from his face. Then, with a bellow of anger, he threw himself into the melee.

It was over in another moment. Between them, he and Delaney subdued Sam, and rose to their feet, dragging him with them.

He was still, no longer struggling. His baleful eyes glared at Dorinda.

"Now you know," he said. "You know what Dennis is. I've suspected him for months. He wanted to be master of Moorhaven. His interest in painting, in travel, in getting away, was all just a front. It was Moorhaven. So he killed Jon and Harris, and Joshua figured it out, so he killed the old man, too."

Dennis cried, "Sam. Don't. You pushed me off the dike, and came at me with that rock. You'd have killed me if Delaney hadn't stopped you. You . . ." His sickened voice faded away.

Sam laughed bitterly. "That's how it was all right. Except for the cast of characters and what they did. Dennis pushed me . . . he . . ."

Delaney said quietly, "Never mind. We saw what happened. Dorie and I both saw it, all of it. It won't work. Don't try it, Sam."

There was a moment of silence. The marsh reeds rippled faintly around them. A frog somewhere began to croak.

Sam's shoulders squared. He raised his head. His

mouth was an ugly twist under his mustache as he rasped, "But it very nearly did work, you know. And it would have been justice. It would have been as it was supposed to be. The portraits. My father. Dennis in his uniform. My mother. Elena with her sad eyes. He was the oldest. When he died, I should have inherited Moorhaven. But no, that's not how it was. Jonathan was the heir instead. My mother would have married him, and that would have made it right again. But he married Cordelia instead. Cordelia, a nobody from nowhere. A governess brought into this house because my mother wasn't well. My mother tried to prevent it. Did you know that? She broke her heart and her health trying. That's why she died. If she'd been able to prevent that awful marriage, you wouldn't have been born, Dorinda. Nor you, Dennis. She'd never allowed Jonathan to adopt you, Delaney. But my mother died. Cordelia became mistress of Moorhaven in her place. And I lost what would have been mine. All because Jonathan murdered her. Yes, yes. Murdered my mother. That's what I said. He drove her into the swamps. They thought I didn't know. Cordelia and Jonathan. All these years, they thought I didn't know. I was only ten. But I did know. I remember. I remember it still. The Moorhavens killed my mother. And it was only just that I kill them. This was to be all mine. But Jonathan took it away from me."

Dorinda's voice, shaky, a stranger to her own ears, asked, "Sam, it's not true? They didn't . . ."

"If it hadn't been for Cordelia, my mother would have married Jonathan. She would . . ." Sam's raspy voice grew more hoarse. "But I'm avenged now." His ugy smile grew wider. "And I almost won back what is rightly mine for me and for young Denny."

"That's why you sent him away," Dorinda said.

"Why I sent him away and kept him away," Sam agreed. "It was all for him. But I didn't want him to witness it. Jon's dead. Harris. No one left but Dennis and Dorinda. A few easy steps . . ."

"Dennis tonight," Delaney said softly. "And then

Dorie? What of her? Why did you try to make her, the rest of us, think she was mad?"

Sam laughed harshly. "Oh, that was so easy. Much easier than I expected. She was already upset about Jonathan's death. It was all there in her mind, just waiting to be touched off. And I was always good with my hands. I designed the mirror safe for Jonathan myself years ago. So I knew about that. I collected the top, the music box, the turntable, and worked over them with timers. It was clever, I think, the way I did it. Dorinda fell right in with my plans. She moved to the wing, which made it even easier for me. She took the key to the doors, but I had already made a copy for myself. I was in and out of there, back or front, with no trouble at all. But, eventually, she figured it out. Didn't you, Dorinda? That's why you gave Ralphine the music box. So I'd know."

"Yes," she agreed. "I found your little gadgets. But I didn't know they were yours, Sam. I didn't know you'd set them up. I just knew that someone had." She drew a deep shaky breath. "Sam, tell me. Tell me why you did it? Why try to drive me crazy? Why frighten me in such a terrible way?"

He rubbed his chin on his collar as if it were too tight for him. Then he looked up at her. "I didn't want you to marry Delaney. You couldn't marry Delaney, Dorinda. If you did, you'd spoil it all for me."

Dennis asked, "But why? What's that got to do with it?"

Sam laughed. "Kiddo, none of you realize what's really involved. You forget that I worked for Alderson and Alderson until not so very long ago. I had an opportunity to study Jonathan's will. And I did. You can be sure that I studied it carefully, and since I'm a lawyer, I knew what it meant. The rest of you have always taken Moorhaven for granted. You've never bothered to think about what it is. An empire to be passed down, to be kept intact. Which proves none of you has any right to it." Sam paused, then went on, his voice rasping in his throat, "Delaney was adopted when

Gregory died. But Delaney could not inherit the hold-ings. Never. Never. Jonathan specified it. But ... and this is the thing ... if Delaney married Dorinda he could gain control through her. Because she could in-herit. So I couldn't allow the marriage. With Jon, and Harris, and Dennis dead, Dorinda would be the heir. And I, as her kind old first cousin, would have had control, through her. And then, poor thing, all her peculiarities would be established. If she survived them, Dr. Peter would agree with me that she should be put into an institution. I would have had Moorhaven, and after me, young Denny."

"But you tried to kill me," she cried. "That night when you put me into the car, the motor running ... you did intend to kill me, didn't you?"

"A clever improvisation. You very nearly caught me in the wing. I thought you'd actually seen and recog-nized me. So I did what I did. Then later I knew that you didn't know who had attacked you and kept on with the original plan."

Disgusted, sick with understanding, Dorinda bowed her head, remembering those moments in the smother-ing air. "Moorhaven," she said bitterly. "It *is* cursed. They say we're all doomed. And they're right. They're right."

"No," Delaney told her. "Moorhaven isn't at fault, Dorie. There was Elena. Now Sam. These are people. Human beings. Greed, hatred. Those are the faults. Not an old house that your grandfather built with love for his family to enjoy."

"To enjoy." Sam laughed. "There's nothing left of the Tembley house but the crumbling chimney. Noth-ing left of the warehouses but the charred walls. That was the beginning. Wait and see. Let time tell you the rest. Then you'll know the truth."

He moved then. He jerked away from between Den-nis and Delaney. He flung himself backward, shouting with hoarse laughter, and disappeared instantly into the moon-streaked shadows.

Dennis yelled and plunged after him. Delaney swore and raced into the dark.

Dorinda followed, shouting, "No, no. Come back. Don't chase him. Let him go. Let him go, Delaney. Dennis, listen to me." Her voice was whip-sharp in the softness of the night as she followed the sounds they made. "Do you want him to go to a trial, and tear young Denny to pieces? Do you want him to hang? No, no. Come back, both of you."

But the men didn't heed her. She heard their thrashing through the reeds, the splashing and struggling, and oaths echoing through the night.

Finally, she stopped, stood ankle-deep in the mud of the marshes, and waited, trembling.

A long time later, the sounds faded away.

Two of them returned to her. Just two of them.

Dennis and Delaney.

They were mud-covered, wet from head to toe, panting with exhaustion.

Dennis went past Dorinda, and climbed to the top of the dike, and then disappeared into the dark.

Delaney said, "It's no good, Dorie. We'll have to wait until daylight."

"I'm glad," she cried.

"You may be right," he said, passing a muddy hand through his curls. "I don't know. I just don't know any more." And then, "Dorie, let's forget Sam. Forget everything that he said. Let's make something wonderful of Moorhaven." He took her into his arms, and she leaned against him.

"Oh, we will, Delaney. I promise you that we will."

Something cool, damp, touched her cheek. She tipped her head back. The thing glimmered at her. A bit of chain, a locket. She drew it free from the button on which it was caught.

"Look," she said.

He took it from her, turned it in his fingers. "I wonder who it belonged to. I wonder how it came here in the swamps." He made as if to toss it away, but when she protested, he put it into his shirt pocket.

Then they climbed to the top of the dike, and from there, they stood looking at the house.

As they watched, the brass lamps that flanked the big black door were suddenly aglow.

Dorinda knew that Dennis must have turned them on, but she smiled. It was an omen. Life would be good again.

Chapter 28

"You mustn't be nervous," Dr. Peter said, patting Dorinda's hand. "I brought you into the world, though you wouldn't remember it. And now I'll be here to do the same for your son."

He was as thin and tall as ever, but now the slouch in his shoulders was very pronounced, and though his amber eyes were bright, they peered from between thick wrinkles of tired flesh. The wisps of white hair were sparse and the pink flesh of his mostly bare scalp seemed wrinkled too.

Dorinda smiled up at him. She wasn't nervous. It was just that the waiting seemed to be the hardest part for her, for Delaney, too.

And they had already waited so long. Ten years of prayer, and hope. Ten long years. They had been, were still, happy together. But she had begun to believe in her secret heart that she would never bear Delaney's children. She had begun to wonder, though Dr. Peter always insisted otherwise, if something was wrong with her, or with Delaney, that would keep them from becoming parents. To keep them from filling Moorhaven with the young life and laughter that it needed, with the young blood that would carry on the future.

Sometimes in the sleepless dawn, with Delaney's lean warmth against her, she had begun to wonder if, after all, she and Delaney were too close, with blood and genes so the same, that they would not, could not mingle. Perhaps Sam, the others, had been right, and she and Delaney wrong. Perhaps Gregory had tried to cover Delaney's illegitimacy by filing a false report with the Chicago police, and making the boy appear a foundling. She had never really known Gregory. She couldn't imagine what he would have done. She only knew that Gregory had brought Delaney to Moorhaven, and then gone to France and died there so long ago.

But now, with Dr. Peter beside her, she knew that all those wonderings were finished. Soon, very soon, she was sure, she would have Delaney's son. There would be a new Moorhaven.

"I know that everything is ready," Dr. Peter was saying. "I've just checked with Mary. Fortunately there's plenty of space here. We're all set up. And I'm sure that my boy will be along any time. If he's not, we'll just go ahead."

She chuckled, as she knew he expected. "I doubt that we could wait. And that you need any help either."

"I doubt it myself," he agreed with a young man's grin. "But you see, the boy is beginning to take over for me now. I wouldn't want to affront him by not inviting him in on this."

"You're proud of Pete," she said. "You've the right to be proud."

"I am. Yes. And I'm relieved, too." He sighed. "A man grows old before he expects to. I'm seventy years old, Dorinda. Tembley needs a younger doctor."

"And a hospital," she said.

"That, too," he agreed. "But where's the money to come from for it? The WPA passed out a few jobs for a while. We got a new post office, and hardly any mail coming in. We've got a new park, and a few hungry kids to play in it. But that's not enough."

"Yet there are a number of bars," she said dryly.

"Agreed. Where men are poor they need their bars.

Since the end of prohibition, though, I doubt there's more drinking in Tembley than there was before. Old Arley was a good supplier in his own day, you know."

"And still is, I guess," she said tartly.

"Not any more. He's retired. His sons carry on though. Only legitimately."

"Then they must have the only money there is in Tembley by now."

"Yes. But that isn't saying much, Dorinda. You can't get blood out of a turnip, you know. So what they make is small pickings compared to what they'd make if there were jobs in town."

"Mary says they do all right."

"Oh, yes." Dr. Peter turned away, went to look out of the window. "I see Delaney's checking the dike."

She laughed. "It's an obsession with him these days. He says the marshes are rising, and there were some cave-ins during one of the spring storms."

"I doubt the marshes are rising, or ever will."

Dorinda didn't answer him. She was concentrating on the sudden pain that had struck her.

Dr. Peter, perhaps noticing her silence, swung around to look at her. He smiled, "Well, what do you think?"

"I think that maybe the waiting will soon be over."

"I think so, too." He went to the phone, picked it up. After a moment, he spoke briefly.

She listened to his low voice, thinking how glad she was that he was here to attend her. He had been her mother's doctor, now hers. He would be, for a while at least, her son's doctor, too. He was a part of her life continuing on to be a part of her son's.

He put down the phone, grinned at her. "The boy's on his way. I was sure. But I thought I would check. We won't mention to him that I did." He glanced at his watch. "Tell me when the next pain comes. We'll start timing now."

The baby was born at midnight.

There had been moments during that day when Dorinda wished that she had not become pregnant, others when she swore loudly that she would never go through this again.

But at last it was over, and when Dr. Peter put the tiny boy into her arms, she forgot the sweat and blood of the hours before, and looking down into the small face, she smiled and whispered, "We'll name him Delaney."

They called the boy Dell. He was a good infant. He ate when he was fed. He rarely cried. It was six months before Dorinda began to wonder why he showed so little response, and at the same time began to realize that Mary was watching him with concern in her black eyes.

Dorinda promised herself that she would speak to Dr. Peter when she took Dell in for his check up. But she found that she couldn't. She was afraid to. It was unnecessary for her to raise the question.

Dr. Peter checked Dell thoroughly, and then, with a sober face, he told Dorinda to call Delaney in. "I must speak to the two of you together."

"What's wrong?" she gasped. "Tell me now. Tell me quickly, Dr. Peter. What . . ."

He didn't answer. But his hand, pointing toward the door, was trembling.

Delaney was talking with Bettina. He rose, followed Dorinda when she called to him.

They sat across from the old doctor, in the office they had known all their lives. Dell was plump, but limp in Dorinda's protective arms.

He said, "I'm sorry. I have to tell you. There's simply no other way. You must know the truth. Dell will never be a normal child. He shows every sign of being a mongoloid."

Bewildered, Dorinda stared at the doctor. "A mongoloid? What's that? I don't understand."

"He'll be retarded. Always. He'll not grow up as a normal child, but will gradually fall further and further behind."

Delaney made a strangled sound, and put his face in his hands.

Dorinda shrank back in her chair.

Dr. Peter said quickly, "We don't know how it happens. But it does sometimes. Some chemistry goes awry during the development of the foetus most likely. It affects the correct development of the brain, those controlling the intellectual powers, I'm afraid. I can't tell you yet just how severe Dell's condition is, nor how it will develop. But I can tell you that with love and help and care, you'll have a son to be proud of."

Delaney straightened up, his face white, his tan-colored eyes dull. "You warned us not to marry, Dr. Peter. You told us, I remember it quite clearly, about the genes, and how first cousins . . ."

"No," Dorinda whispered. "No, no. Now stop it."

"But you are not first cousins," Dr. Peter cut in quickly. "You've been sure of that for ten years. There is no reason to change your mind now. This has nothing to do with that, or your suspicions of that. Mongoloid children are born to families not even remotely related. So it couldn't be, even if you and Dorinda were blood kin, the cause of this."

"That's what you say," Delaney whispered. He went to the door. "Come on, Dorie."

She hugged Dell against her, as if the small body so limp, so warm, so completely helpless, was a protective armor behind which she could hide. She looked at Dr. Peter, her green eyes burning with held-back tears.

He said gently, "I know it's a shock. But it will wear off. Be trusting, and accepting, have faith. And have another child."

"I wouldn't dare. I couldn't," she said huskily. "After all this time . . . after what we've hoped . . ."

"You must," Dr. Peter told her. "You'll understand me some day, even if you don't understand me now. You must have another child."

Delaney was waiting behind the wheel of the big Buick. His lean fingers twitched and trembled as he pushed the door open for her. He didn't speak.

She slipped into the car, sat back, cradling Dell protectively. "He's our son," she said. "We must love him."

"Can you imagine," Delaney said. "Can you just hear what Ralphine would have told us if she'd lived to hear this news?"

"It doesn't . . ."

"Oh, she would laugh. Oh, she would . . ."

"Dr. Peter just told you . . ."

A bitter grin twisted Delaney's mouth. He ran a lean hand through his sandy hair. "I heard him. But reassurance comes cheaply when there's nothing else to give."

Dorinda's small heart-shaped face tightened. Her eyes flashed. "I love Dell," she said softly. "You love him, too. He's all we have. Do you understand me? He's ours. Born of our love."

"A moron," Delaney retorted. "Sam would say . . ."

"No!" Her denial was very nearly a scream. "No, Delaney. Don't you ever say that. Don't think it. Forget Sam, and Ralphine. Just think of our son. Our Dell. Some children are less bright then others. There's room for all in this world."

He didn't answer her.

"And in my heart," she added.

A shadow fell across her. An elderly man looked in, leaned closer, then grinned.

It was Arley Jones. Arley, who must be in his eighties, who had normal sons, normal grandchildren, too.

"This is the heir I've heard about," he said. "And how does Moorhaven suit him?"

Dorinda forced a smile, was about to speak.

Delaney started the motor with an impatient roar. The car leaped forward as he released the brake.

Arley Jones fell back, almost as if knocked aside.

"Delaney!" Dorinda cried. "That was a terrible thing to do. You must be careful. You could have hurt the old man."

"Damn him," Delaney retorted.

The baby, as if sensing her anguish, began to cry.

When Dell was four, he had curly red hair and wide green eyes and a sweet open trusting smile. He crawled as fast as other children could walk. He laughed and crowed when other children could talk. He recognized his mother, and his father, and even knew young Denny who came down from Boston on occasional visits. But best of all, he knew Mary. When the boy was with her, Dorinda was easy in her mind.

There had been a certain estrangement between Delaney and herself since Dell's birth. It wasn't that they blamed each other. How could they? Dr. Peter first, and then Dr. Pete, too, had assured them that what had happened was an accident of chemistry. One which had happened to others, and would again. But there was a question still in each of their minds, a niggling sense of guilt that troubled them and lay between them, holding them apart instead of drawing them closer together.

That was what made Delaney drink, made him sullen and sombre. That, and the war. . . .

They had been having Sunday afternoon dinner. The December sun was lemon pale on the silver flatware and the crystal goblets.

Dell was a year old then, plump, tiny, grinning, able to sit only by being propped in his high chair with pillows.

Mary said, "Dorinda, everything will be cold. Can you get that man to the table? He's in the office, hanging over the radio."

Dorinda bent to kiss Dell's cheek. She thought, with a tug of the heart, that he would seem like any other child as long as she didn't know the truth.

"And you won't be finished before Dr. Peter comes. Not if you don't . . ."

Dorinda went to the office.

Delaney stood over the radio, his face pale, his eyes glittering. "It's come," he said. "They've attacked Pearl Harbor."

"You always said it would happen," she answered.

She thought of the day he had insisted that she drive in to Tembley with him. He had parked across from the old, crumbling walls of what had once been the Moorhaven warehouses.

"I have a big thing in mind, Dorie," he'd said. "I want to know what you think of it." He drew a deep breath, then smiled. "It's for Tembley as well as for us. Keep that to yourself though."

"What do you want to do?" she had asked. She was uneasy. She had felt, as long as she could remember, that the less the Moorhavens had to do with the town the better it would be. She couldn't forget what had gone before, though she wanted to.

"It's the war in Europe, Dorie. It's going to spread. As sure as I'm sitting here with you, Hitler is going to try to take all of Europe and then England. We can't allow the English to fall. So we'll have to get into it ourselves."

"But Delaney, that . . . why, that's just crazy," she'd cried. "We've nothing to do with that madman. And there's an ocean between us."

"It isn't as wide as you'd think," he said soberly. "We'll have to be in on it. We'll need goods, guns. What it takes to fight a war." He drew another deep breath. "I want to build a factory. Right here in Tembley, Dorie. It will save the town."

"But does the town want to be saved by Moorhavens?" she'd asked.

"That's all in the past, Dorie. I'm thinking about the future now. I think Tembley will think of the future, too."

That Sunday Delaney refused dinner, stayed crouched over the radio the rest of the evening, listening solemnly with Dr. Peter and Bettina, while Dorinda sat with them, Dell in her arms.

She remembered now that she had been filled with a hot defiant shame, but she was glad that Dell was a child, glad that he was what he was. He wouldn't have to go. He wouldn't be faced with the terrors of war, with the possibility of death in some faraway place. She had risen, gone into the vestibule. She looked up at the portrait of Dennis, Sam's father, lost in Cuba. Her own father, Jonathan, whose dark brooding eyes looked down at her. He had carried the faint scar and walked with the limp gotten in the same war. Gregory, not shown in the gallery, had died in France. She had turned away with a shudder.

She hadn't thought of how Delaney would feel then. But one day soon after she had sat on the terrace, dressed warmly against the cold. The sky seemed dark, ominous, heavy. She waited, full of foreboding, for his return.

He had said nothing of his intentions, but she had known him too long not to know what was in his mind.

She had seen him examining his face in the mirror. She had seen him stand at the window staring into the night.

He had refused to share the reasons for his preoccupation, but she had guessed them. And when he had gone to Tembley that morning, she had begun to wait.

Now a cloud of dust appeared on the curve at the top of the road. It came careening down, trailing the car that sped before it.

She remembered Harris, driving much the same way, recklessly taunting death, and finding it because Sam had willed it so. Her heart had seemed to slide upward into her throat, cutting off her breath.

Delaney pulled into the new driveway and passed around the terrace without even a wave to acknowledge her presence.

She rose, hurried to meet him at the garages, knowing what he had to tell her, feeling a mixture of pity and relief.

"I'm too old," he had said bitterly. "Thirty-one years. And just plain too old."

Chapter 29

She could tell by his eyes, by the way his hands shook, that he had stopped in one of Tembley's bars. Perhaps he had stopped in one before as well as after. Not that that would have mattered. Everyone in Tembley knew that Delaney Moorhaven drank, had started drinking when his son Dell was born.

He lurched by her. She put a hand on his arm. "Tell me what happened."

He stared at her. "I just did."

"Don't feel too badly," she told him. "We need you here. And the factory . . ."

For Delaney had managed to have the factory in operation before the Japanese struck. And in Tembley he had been seen reeling from car to factory and car to bar. They had shaken their heads, and grinned, she supposed. But they said little enough. The factory had brought the beginnings of prosperity. They were willing to accept that, if not the Moorhavens. The war boom had brought changes. New store fronts, and new stores, too. But everything in Tembley moved slowly, and always had. She supposed there was the fear that what had happened before could happen again. If the ships could fail them, the yards close, as Mary had once told her, then the factory could, too. She supposed she didn't blame the town.

"The factory can run on its own. With a good manager. Damn the factory anyway."

"And we need you. Dell does. And I do, too," she had gone on.

"But my country doesn't," he said angrily.

He closed himself away from her in the office that night. There was the steady clink of bottle against glass.

She had listened and sighed. She knew that he wanted to help, to serve, to share in what was to come. But she knew, too, that he wanted to get away from Moorhaven. From the sight of Dell. Perhaps even from herself.

A few days later, she heard from Denny. He had volunteered, was going immediately into basic training.

Delaney made no comment when she told him about it. The following year, when he heard that young Denny had died on Guam, he buried his face in his hands.

Now Dell was four, wordless, but full of laughter, and Delaney avoided his son in work, and after work, in drink.

She had news for him that she hoped would make him happier. But she was nervously keeping her secret until she could find the right time to tell him.

She was glad when he suggested that she ride in to Tembley with him. Just the two of them together. That trip, she thought, might provide the right opportunity.

But they reached Tembley just as a funeral procession turned into Washington Avenue.

Delaney stopped to allow it to pass.

Dorinda caught a glimpse of two of the Jones boys in the family car, and said, "Why, Delaney, I think Arley Jones must have died. Those are his sons. I wonder why Mary didn't say . . ."

"Because she works at Moorhaven," Delaney told her. "You know that. The family has been estranged for years."

"But still . . ." Dorinda watched as the long cortege moved by slowly. She remembered the day she had searched for Delaney at the station, and the children had moved back from her when she emerged. *Doomed.*

The Moorhavens are doomed. High now. But they'll be brought low. She told herself that she mustn't think of that. Not now.

Delaney's fingers drummed the wheel. "You'd think the old man was mayor of the town."

"He was. In his way," she told him. But now she was remembering the day that Dr. Peter had told Delaney and her that Dell was a mongoloid child, and would never grow up to be normal. She was remembering how Arley had leaned in the window to talk to her, and Delaney had driven away, thrusting him back.

It was more than three years, closer to four, and she realized now that she hadn't seen Arley since then. Of course she herself did not come into Tembley often, and never had, and Arley was an old man, perhaps ill. So he might not have been up and about. But still she wondered uneasily if Delaney's carelessness that day was one more mark against the Moorhavens.

The procession finally came to an end.

Delaney drove on, parked before a shop. He grinned at her. "You wait here."

She wondered, but not for long. He returned in a few moments, thrust a round teddy bear into her arms. "It's for Dell," he said.

That was when she told him that they were to have another child.

She saw the sudden panic flare in his eyes. But then, smiling, he leaned over to kiss her, and getting into the car, he took her into his arms.

"It's going to be all right," she said quickly. "You know it is, Delaney. It's what I've been hoping, waiting for . . ."

"Sure," he agreed. And then, softly, "Don't worry, Dorie. I'm very glad. I am very, very glad."

"I know," Mary said. "They told me."

"But if you'd only mentioned it, Delaney would have brought you in," Dorinda said. "Why, Arley's your brother. Your brother, Mary. I just can't imagine . . ."

Mary's narrow mouth folded in. She settled herself in

the easy chair, the Spanish shawl wrinkling at her back. "But you don't understand, Dorinda. It goes back a long way. Such a long way . . ." Her face was wrinkled with thought, with a wry acceptance, too. "I was sixteen and your mother was just barely twenty. I took my side then, and I haven't changed it."

"But there's no side, Mary. And no reason to feel that there is," Dorinda protested.

Mary gave her a faint smile, then went on. "When the shipyards were closed, my father went to work in a mine. It was some ninety miles away. He never got back. In those days it was hard. He was killed there. My mother had six children. Arley was the oldest. I was the youngest. Arley stayed in Tembley. The four between us went away, one by one. And each of them died. Each of them, Dorinda. And I came out to Moorhaven. It made my mother . . . well, they called her crazy. And I suppose, in a way, she was. And Arley, he took it over, you see. That was what was always wrong between us. Because I wouldn't. And so . . ." She shrugged. "That's why I didn't go to his funeral. I'd not have been welcome. Not by his wife, nor his sons, nor his grandchildren either. So what was the use to go?"

The day that Dorinda gave birth to the tiny redheaded girl that she and Delaney named Cassandra, but always called Cassie, was one of the happiest Dorinda ever remembered.

Delaney smiled at the tiny girl in her arms, and then offered his cupped hands. She put the baby into them, and he laughed aloud.

"It's going to be good from now on," he said. "I know it's going to be good."

A year later, she was pregnant again. She had no reason to be troubled about telling Delaney. She thought she had proved, with Cassie, that they had nothing to fear.

But from that evening on, she noticed that Delaney spent more hours alone in his office when he finally came back from the factory. She noticed that he moaned in bad dreams, and came half awake, soaked with cold sweat, and saying, "No, no."

She was in her eighth month when she had the fall that brought on the premature birth of her third child.

It was late one night, too late, and Delaney had still not come to bed.

She went down to the office and found him, head down on his arms, snoring against the desk top. The newspaper he had pushed aside had a big black headline. ATOM BOMB DESTROYS NAGASAKI. She didn't know what it meant. She didn't care.

She shook Delaney, whispered, "Come on. It's late. You need some sleep."

He reared up, and threw her aside.

She stepped back from him, and tripped on her robe, and then, unable to catch her balance, she fell heavily.

An hour after that she called Mary. Mary took one look at her and ran to the phone.

Dr. Peter came very quickly, driven out by his son.

The both of them worked over her for hours. Hours in which an August storm pounded the house, and seemed to pound at her resisting body, too.

The last thing she remembered for a long time was the two of their faces, one young, one old, but so alike that it was like staring at amber-eyed carbon copies bent close to her.

Then she sank down into darkness, thinking somehow of that time she had been in the garage, the fumes hissing from the pipes, spilling death unseen around her, and somewhere in that same dark, Sam seemed to be waiting, holding his breath, waiting for her to die.

When she finally awakened, the older Dr. Peter sat by her bed.

She stared into his face, whispered, "Tell me. Tell me quickly. Is the baby gone?"

Dr. Peter smiled at her. "No, Dorie. No. He's safe and sound. Now go to sleep."

She wanted to ask more, but she didn't dare. And her tongue was too tired. Her body was bone weary. Her mind seemed to have come to a stop.

It was the next day before she held her son in her arms and saw the malformed hip with which he had been born.

Dell, she thought. And now Mark.

She and Delaney never spoke about what had happened the night their third child was born. It was as if that moment had been blotted out of time, but she knew that it lived within them. In her, and in him as well. She promised herself that she would never have another child.

She had had three. She had Dell, and Cassie, and Mark. She loved them all, but only Cassie was unblemished. She would have no more.

There were times in the next few years when she stood in the hallway of Moorhaven and listened to the peculiar silence. She would stare at the portraits of her parents, of Cordelia and Jonathan, of her Uncle Dennis and Aunt Elena, and remember that Sam had said Moorhaven and all that belonged to it was his by right. She would shiver a little, and wonder if the house was having its revenge against her.

And then, squaring her small shoulders, she would go to play with Dell, pick up Mark when he fell, brush Cassie's hair, and consult with Mary about the week's menus.

One afternoon Delaney came back early from Tembley where he still spent most of his time at the factory.

He looked pale, grim. He fixed himself a drink before he said, "I have something to tell you, Dorie."

She waited, holding her breath. This would be another blow. This would be the unbearable blow. She had accepted what had come before. But this she would not be able to accept.

He went on, "Dr. Peter died today."

Relief, and then quick pain, jolted her. She sank back in her chair. "Oh, Delaney, I'm sorry. Is Bettina all right?"

"Yes, she is. And young Dr. Pete is with her, and his boys are on the way."

"Do you know what happened to him?"

"The same thing that happens to everybody. If they live long enough. He just wore out."

"But I didn't even know he was ill. He seemed fine when I saw him last week."

"He wasn't ill. He and Dr. Pete went on a call this morning. He came home, and had his dinner, and went to take a nap. That was it."

Dorinda rose. "I'll tell Mary to let everything go and spend her time with the children. I want to go in to Bettina now."

One day they had a letter from Mexico. Dennis wrote that he was settled there, had been since the war forced him to leave Paris. He promised to return for a visit when the war was over, and to bring his son and wife with him.

Dorinda imagined him painting happily under blue skies, painting too happily to leave them. But she knew that he couldn't face Moorhaven yet. If he could have, he would be at home now. His checks were sent to him from Aldersons as they had been since he left fifteen years before.

The war ended, and Tembley seemed almost immediately to collapse into its old patterns, for the Moorhaven factory was closed.

Dennis still didn't return.

In 1955, they heard through Aldersons that he had died, leaving his son Henry as his heir, and the checks went out to him. Dorinda wrote, invited Henry to Moorhaven, but never received an answer.

Four years later, while walking with Dell along the dike, she felt a sharp explosion in her chest, and gasped, "Dell, get Daddy for me."

He was nineteen then, about the same height as Dorinda herself and with her auburn hair. He had a round child's belly that hung over his belt, and a sweet plump child's face. He tugged her arm. "Mama? Mama?"

"Get Daddy," she gasped. "I need Daddy, Dell."

He stared at her, fright blooming in his green eyes.

She gave him a small directing push with the last of her strength.

His lip came out, tears ran down his cheeks. "Love," he whispered.

"Love, Dell," she gasped. "Now get Daddy for me."

He turned, trotted away.

She sank down on the path, listening to the heave and crackle of the thin ice in the marshes, and to her own rasping breath.

The pain was red and hot. It hung in a haze around her, so that even the slope, the terrace, the house itself, and the cliff behind, were misted with it.

Dell, she thought. And bright-eyed, sensible Cassie. And Mark ... How would they fare? What would Moorhaven hold for them?

She saw Delaney running, and with him, Mary, and thought that Mary was much too old to run so fast, and that Delaney, too, ought to be more careful.

But when he reached her, she had forgotten that. She was completely in another time. She smiled at him, and put out her hand. "I knew you'd come back," she said, closing her eyes.

Chapter 30

Washington Avenue lay empty and still under the scorching July sun. Shimmering heat rose from the tarred road and swirled like steam from the gaping potholes.

Cassie stood with Dell just within the post office door, conscious of the hard-eyed stares that focused on her back, and of the silence of unspoken words. She knew the moment she stepped outside there would be an eruption of surly comment.

Dell tugged her hand, asked plaintively, "We go, Cassie?"

There was a thick phlegmy chuckle behind her. Someone switched on a transistor radio and Bob Dylan's bittersweet voice broke the silence.

She managed to smile at Dell. "Yes. Let's go."

They stepped out into the sunlight together. The heat instantly enveloped her, bringing a flush to her high cheekbones.

She was twenty-two years old, but she looked younger. There was something not quite defined or settled about the slenderness of her body, though a thoughtful look in her green eyes suggested a certain maturity. Her deep chestnut hair glinted with streaks of auburn, and she wore it long, straight to very near her narrow waist. This morning she had on a white shirt tucked into

faded blue jeans, and scuffed white sneakers. Around
her throat she wore a gold chain that held a locket. The
pictures that it had once held were gone. But she knew
that they had been of Cordelia and George Davis, her
great-grandparents. Mary had told her that when she
gave Cassie the locket just after her mother's sudden
death. "It was Cordelia's, your grandmother's," Mary
had said, black eyes shining with held-back tears. "It
was lost for a while, and then it was found. I know that
Dorinda would want you to have it." Cassie put it
around her throat, and had worn it every day since. It
had become her talisman, her good luck piece. She
touched it quickly as she led Dell outside.

"Ice cream?" he asked.

"Of course. I haven't forgotten," she answered.

"Chocolate?"

"Certainly," she agreed, and then added quickly,
"Unless they're all out of it, Dell."

She was never quite sure how much he understood
and how much passed him by. But she had learned,
growing up with him, to speak with him as naturally as
she could. He might not always know the words, or the
concept even, but he knew the sound of her voice, and
that seemed, always, to be enough for him.

They started down the street together, their shadows
falling before them. The length was roughly the same.
Dell was very under-sized for a twenty-six-year-old
man. But the shape of their shadows, and the width,
was very different. His was thick, heavy, shambling,
with a slight side to side roll. Hers was slim, tiny at the
waist, and very straight.

"Cassie . . ." Dell murmured. "Cassie?"

She said, "What?" and he laughed.

It was extraordinary to think that men could build
capsules that sailed through space beyond the stars,
that one day they would send ships to the moon, but
that they had never figured out how to help someone
like Dell.

She dismissed the thought and raised her eyes from
the shadows falling before them. Her throat suddenly

tightened. Her fingers crept to the locket beneath her shirt. The street had been empty before, but suddenly, as if from nowhere, a group of teen-agers had gathered.

There were six of them, four boys and two girls. Both boys and girls wore patched blue jeans, worn shirts, and long tousled hair.

"Look," one said, "here comes the Moorhaven re-tard," and then blew a large pink chewing gum bubble that hung from between his lips like an extra and over-large tongue.

"And there's his keeper, the Princess Moorhaven," another said. "You'd think she'd know better herself than to come to town with her dummy brother."

"But which is the dummy?" one chuckled.

"The fat one, stupid. Can't you see his slanty eyes?"

"They both have slanty eyes, if you ask me."

Cassie walked steadily on, with Dell beside her. But her heart began to beat very fast as the circle before her tightened and did not give way.

"Re-tard," a boy shouted. "Just like all of them. Can you imagine, a great thing like that. Wonder who helps him dress and go toidy. Wonder who feeds him."

Dell's face began to change. The happy glow went out of it, but he sang, "Hi, there," and waited hopefully.

"Re-tard," the group chanted.

Dell's big soft hand reached for Cassie, fingers curled into the waist of her pants, and his whole body, shivering now, pressed close to hers. He didn't know the words, but he knew the malice.

She said reassuringly, "It's okay, Dell. We're going to get your ice cream," and continued walking.

But the tight circle grew tighter still. She was surrounded now, and after another two steps, she was forced to come to a stop.

Dell shivered harder, and his fingers clutched her.

"What about it, princess?" one grinned. "How are things these days at Moorhaven?"

"Let me pass through please," she said coldly, reaching for an evasive dignity.

"Sure, princess. Sure. Why not? You own the town. You own the street. You own the air. Why shouldn't you pass through? Just go ahead."

But no one moved.

She didn't dare try her slender strength by using force to thrust against them. She didn't dare frighten Dell.

He whimpered, "Ice cream, Cassie?"

"Buy your dummy some ice cream," a girl laughed. "Go on. Get it for him. We'll wait right here. We'll keep him company. We'll make sure he doesn't get run over by a car."

Cassie sent a quick searching look up and down the street. No one was there. She was surrounded by these six with nobody to help her.

She said coldly, "You're blocking the way. We want to go through."

But no one moved.

Dell whispered, "Bad, Cassie?"

A boy dropped to his knees, rolled about, screaming with false laughter. "Bad, Cassie! Bad, Cassie!"

Another asked, "When is your father going to open the plant again, Cassie? When is he going to put something in our pockets?"

She refused to turn to look down the avenue toward the big building closed for so long. She wouldn't give them the satisfaction of acknowledging the shattered windows, the obscene graffiti on the blistered walls.

"How about it, Cassie? When?"

"You'd have to ask him," she answered, licking her suddenly dry lips.

She was older than they were. They should, at least, have been a bit afraid of her. But they were afraid of nothing.

"He doesn't come to Tembley any more. That's why we're asking you." The answer came sharp and fast and bitter.

"I don't know anything about it, and never did," she retorted. "And now . . ."

"How's your brother, the cripple?" That question

came from a small, dark-haired, dark-eyed boy, who danced even closer than the rest.

He was one of the Jones children, Cassie realized with disbelieving horror. Arlene's youngest brother. Mark's brother-in-law now.

A wave of sickness passed over her. She fought to control it. She must not give way here. She must not allow these children to see how mortally those words had wounded her.

Dell whimpered, "Cassie, go now. Ice cream."

And took a single shambling step.

The circle drew tighter in sudden silence.

Cassie felt herself begin to vibrate to Dell's trembling. She didn't know what would happen now. She didn't know how to stop whatever was to come.

But a small red Volkswagen rattled down the street and jerked to a stop beside her.

Mike Van Nuys slid over, then climbed out. "Cassie. Hello. What are you doing here?"

He moved through the circle as if it were invisible. Though he was a big man, over six feet tall, his wide shoulders touched no one. His arms hung at his sides. But he seemed, somehow, to have shoved the teen-agers away. They retreated a few feet, then re-grouped, watching avidly.

Dell cried, with the glow back in his face, "Mike! Hi, there, Mike."

Mike tousled the curly auburn hair, grinned, "What are you up to, Dell?"

"We're going to get some ice cream," Cassie answered around a sudden lump in her throat.

"Chocolate," Dell put in hopefully.

"If they have it."

"Watch out that you don't catch it, Mike Van Nuys," one of the boys sang out, annoyed because he had interfered with the game.

Mike gave him a brief glance from under dark straight brows. "Go on about your business, you kids."

"You could catch it, you know. You hang around

with the Moorhavens long enough and you'll be drooling, too."

Mike's hard, chiselled twenty-eight-year-old face suddenly looked old. For a brief moment, Cassie saw Dr. Pete, tired, annoyed, saddened by the folly he saw around him.

Then he became Mike again. He put his hand on her shoulder. "Where's your car?"

"Back at the post office. I guess I shouldn't have . . . but I thought . . ."

"Then let's just leave it there for the time being. Okay? Come back to the house with me. My grandmother would like to see you, I know."

"But I promised Dell . . ."

"We'll get it," Mike said. "I haven't forgotten the ice cream."

"It looks good on the outside," one of the boys yelped "Nice hair, nice shape. But you better watch it, Mike. She's got a cripple for one brother, and a dummy for another. It might run in the blood. You never know what you could get from her."

A line of red rose from below Mike's open collar and dyed his tanned muscular throat red. His amber eyes glittered like polished stone. He hitched his suntans over flat hips, then completely turned his back on the group.

"Ready?" he asked Cassie.

She had had enough, more than enough. She said, "Dell, we'll go in Mike's nice red car for the ice cream. All right?"

His whole face lit up.

It reminded her of earlier when she had asked him if he wanted to ride into Tembley with her. He had grinned, and trotted out of the room in his rolling shamble, and when she had, after her argument with Arlene, finally gotten to the car, he had been sitting in the front seat, waiting patiently. He loved to ride. He loved to go any place. And more than anything, she suspected, he loved to get away from Arlene.

She climbed into the small seat in the back, and

Mike put Dell beside him, and then carefully made sure that the door beside him was locked.

As they pulled away, the teen-agers hooted with bitter laughter.

"You should have called me," Mike said. "If I'd known you were coming in to town, I'd have been waiting for you."

She didn't answer him. It would have taken more strength than she had at the moment to explain to him that she couldn't rely on him for protection against the town. She had no right to. And she had no need to either. And more than that, she considered it best that she not see him too often. She couldn't explain why to him either.

He slid an amber look at her in the rear view mirror. "They got to you this time, didn't they?"

"Well," she said uncomfortably, "you know how it is. And Dell . . ."

"You mustn't pay too much attention."

"I don't. Not when it's directed at me. But when they start to pick on Dell. And on Mark . . ."

"That was Arlene's kid brother in with them. Did you recognize him?"

Cassie nodded.

"That's a good part of the trouble, I suspect. They don't like it. Her living at Moorhaven. The cars, the swimming pool. Whatever it is that Moorhaven stands for in their minds."

Cassie didn't say so, but she thought that the people of Tembley, the Jones family itself, could hardly like what had happened less than the Moorhavens did.

"In a way, too, you can't blame them. Why should she have all that luxury when they have nothing?"

"The luxury doesn't much please her, Mike."

He didn't answer. He pulled in, parked before a small shop. "Chocolate for Dell. Right?"

"Right," Dell crowed, peering lovingly at Mike.

"Coming right up," Mike said. He glanced up and down the street as he left the car, and then disappeared into the shop.

He moved with a quick lithe grace that left Cassie somehow breathless. But she didn't forget to watch the street from the moment he was gone from sight.

She didn't want Dell to hear any more malice. She didn't want to hear any more herself. It had always been an ordeal to come in to Tembley. For as long as she could remember, she had dreaded it. Now, since Mark had married Arlene, it had become even worse.

She had not realized just how bad it would be when it had happened that Thanksgiving Day. But over the past eight months she had come to believe that the mistake Mark had made would bear a fruit more rotten than she could imagine now.

Mike came back. He handed Dell his ice cream cone, and Dell settled back, licking happily, and crooning his joy through sticky lips.

Cassie accepted her ice cream cone, too.

Mike got in. He finished his ice cream in three bites, then started the car. "Grandmother's now. Okay?"

She nodded. Then, "How is she feeling?"

Mike grinned. "For an old girl in her nineties she's going fine. At least that's what my father says. But I think that something's gone out of her since Grandfather died. That's why she wants to close down the house. That, and, if you ask me, though she won't admit it, she's had all of Tembley she can take."

"But your father's still here," Cassie protested. "She wouldn't want to leave him, and you, and . . ."

"He's a busy guy, Dr. Pete. And I guess it's no secret that Grandmother and my mother never got along too well. Which is why Dr. Pete built his own house years ago."

A wave of dismay swept over Cassie. She bit her lip, trying to hold back her anxious question.

Mike seemed to read her mind. He said, "I don't know just what I'll do. Grandmother and I have always been compatible. As you know. But I don't think I can live with my father. Not any more."

She nodded silent understanding.

"He never could see why I wouldn't go to medical

school." Mike chuckled softly. "Dr. Peter, Dr. Pete, and Dr. Mike. That's how he saw it. As if I weren't my own man. My own heart. My own soul."

"But you're doing well enough, Mike. And by now . . ."

"Oh, sure. I'm doing fine. But to Dr. Pete there's something not quite respectable about being a writer. I think he has the suspicion that I'm the next best thing to an almost respectable con man." Then, soberly, Mike went on, "But it's not the writing. Nor the books. Anything I did, except doctoring, would make him feel the same. It actually has nothing to do with me, Cassie. It's him. His sense of dynasty, and my grandfather's, too, I guess. Maybe ego. I don't know. Call it whatever you want."

"Whatever you do call it, you can say that the Moorhavens seem to have it, too."

"True enough." Mike paused as he pulled into the driveway of the old Van Nuys house.

Cassie turned to look at what remained of a chimney in the overgrown field just beyond. Mary had once told her that when the Moorhavens were shipbuilders they had lived there. She found herself wishing that they lived there still. Beyond it, the boarded-up Falkland place seemed to be crumbling to the ground.

Dell crowed happily, bobbing up and down in the front seat.

"Then if your grandmother closes the house," Cassie said at last, "you'll be leaving Tembley, won't you?"

"I don't know."

She tried to keep her face blank. She shuttered her eyes, and searched busily in a pocket for tissue. She found it and wiped Dell's mouth clean of chocolate as Mike leaned across to unlock and open the door for him.

He got out, stood waiting, smiling joyfully into the hot sunlight.

Cassie climbed down, took his hand.

As they went up the steps together, Mike said, "But I don't want to leave, Cassie."

Chapter 31

Cassie smiled as she leaned down to kiss the wrinkled cheek that was as soft as rose petals still. "How are you, Grandma Bettina?" she asked.

"As well, or better, than can be expected," Bettina Van Nuys answered. She tipped her head back on her thin neck, peering up at Cassie through bright blue eyes. "You look . . . well, dragged out. That's the only word I can think of. Yes. Dragged out. You ought to stop in and see Dr. Pete one of these days. And soon."

"It's just the heat," Cassie told her quickly.

"The heat? Well, it's been with us this time of year as long as I can remember. We all managed. We ought to be able to manage still. And without looking dragged out, too."

"Grandma," Mike laughed. "Don't drum up business. My father wouldn't like it. You'll have him called an ambulance chaser pretty soon."

Bettina gave an inelegant snort. "He would like it. It's your mother that wouldn't. She's protocol prone. I'm not, and never have been." Bright blue eyes shifted to Dell. "Come here, boy, give us a sweet kiss."

Dell shambled to her side, leaned down cautiously. She reached up with two small hands as delicate as baby bird wings and cupped his cheeks.

"I won't break, boy," she said gently. "And I won't bite either."

"He had ice cream," Cassie said.

"Ice cream," he repeated happily. He gave Bettina a careful kiss, then settled down on the floor, leaning against her knee.

"Does he want television to watch while we talk?"

"Yes," Dell cried.

Mike switched on the set, the volume down.

"It's a comfort," Bettina said. "And I do like the color. But I think you can see too much, more than you want to even." She patted Dell's curls, then looked at Cassie. "How's Mary?"

"She's all right, I guess.

"But getting older."

"Yes, of course. Though it's hard to believe. She's just Mary. She doesn't really change."

"That's miraculous." Bettina grinned. "She's eighty-two, you know. Though I expect she lies about it."

Cassie grinned, too. "That depends on her mood."

"Is she getting along all right with Arlene?" Bettina demanded.

"It's not easy for her," Cassie admitted. "I don't know how much longer she'll be able to take it."

"But she has to take it. Either that or leave Moorhaven. And where would she go? I think it would kill her to have to leave."

Cassie said gently, "I know. But what I worry about is that it might kill her to have to stay."

"That bad? Because of Arlene?" Bettina asked.

Cassie nodded.

"Well, it's an odd situation. Arlene being her great-niece. Old Arley's grand-daughter. The family falling out all those years ago."

"I don't much care what happened all those years ago," Cassie said tiredly. "It doesn't matter."

"Perhaps it shouldn't, but I'm very much afraid that it does."

"It's Arlene that matters," Cassie said hopelessly. "And I don't know what to do."

"I don't see that there's much that you can do. Except maybe hope for the best," Bettina answered.

But, as Cassie drove back to Moorhaven with Dell chattering his happy gibberish at her, she thought that hoping for the best would not help.

If Bettina closed up the house and moved from Tembley, Mike would leave too.

It seemed as if the bright sun grew dimmer, the thick hot air more suffocating.

She had known him all her life. He had been the only child that had come from Tembley to play with her and her brothers. His was the only birthday party she had ever gone to. But he was six years older than she was, and it wasn't until the Thanksgiving weekend three years before that she had suddenly seemed to have caught up with him. She had not only caught up with him; she had fallen in love.

It was just moments after she had returned from school. Dell had been watching television then, too. A flash had suddenly filled the screen. A flash from Dallas. The president had been shot. She had gone straight to the phone and called Mike. She had realized only later that she had felt that the one thing that would assuage her sense of terror and bereavement would be the presence of someone she loved. Of Mike. He had come out within half an hour, sat with her and the others, through the horror of the hours that followed. That was when it began. But nothing happened. She wouldn't allow it to.

And then this past Thanksgiving weekend, in all the confusion and pain, she had realized that she couldn't put him out of her heart no matter how she tried.

She had told herself that she had been particularly vulnerable at both times, and that she must forget him. She had assured herself that she would forget him when she returned to school to finish her last term. But those next months until she graduated had proven her wrong. She had continued to think of him by day, dream of him by night. And when she had returned in May, she had realized that she still felt the same. There was no other man for her. There never would be.

What Mike felt, she didn't know, couldn't imagine. She supposed that he viewed her as casually as he would have a younger sister. There was a peculiar pain in that thought, but she knew that she must accept it.

Now, at the top of the cliff, at the curve in the narrow road which gave her the first view of Moorhaven, she pulled off and parked.

"Home?" Dell asked quickly.

"In a moment."

He shifted his thick body closer to hers, and took her hand.

She wondered if he, too, felt the odd resistance that she had in herself.

Moorhaven.

The house was long, three stories high, built of weathered gray stone. Jonathan's wing, haunted by his limping ghost, she had heard in town when she was only a child, was only one floor.

Black shutters, built sturdily against autumn storms, glistened in the hot sunlight, and between them the curtained windows gleamed emptily. The big black door with its rarely used brass knocker gleamed like a mirror, flanked by the two big brass lamps that were always lighted at night.

Great stands of graceful lilacs covered the foundations. In April and May they were covered with falls of purple that scented the air. Now their green leaves were limp and dusty.

The terrace was rimmed with planters where petunias bloomed in gay reds and white. The long slope down to the dike was smooth and green, landscaped with juniper and boxwood, split by a single, shell-covered path.

The cliff rose up behind the house, a strong backdrop that dominated the whole view down to the hump of the dike.

Beyond the dike, the marshes were brown and oily, rippling with underground springs and gasses, overgrown with cat-o-nine tails and marsh grass, and sprinkled with small stunted trees that stood on unreliable hummocks.

She sighed. Now she wished that she could have stayed in town longer. Not in town itself. But in the Van Nuys house, visiting Mike and his grandmother.

Always, no matter where she had been, or why, no matter how long she had been absent, she felt this strange reluctance to return to Moorhaven. It was as if an invisible wall lay between her home and herself, a strong barrier, not seen but felt, that pushed her back.

"Home?" Dell asked.

She started the car, swung into the curve. "Yes, Dell," she answered. "We're going home."

When she had parked in the garage, and started across the back patio for the house, with Dell trudging along at her side, Jim Hooten, the handyman, stopped her.

"Mrs. Abel's been looking for you, Cassie. There's been another to-do up at the house, I think."

She smiled, thanked him, then hurried on uneasily, while Dell went with the handyman into the garage.

Jim Hooten had come to work at Moorhaven about a year after Cassie's mother had died. He was about forty-five now, a lean, weathered man, with squinting blue eyes, and a quiet manner.

Mary had found him, and the housekeeper, Mrs. Abel, at the same time. She had needed someone to help her, and with Delaney's permission she had gone in search of them. She had refused to look in Tembley, but had written to a Boston employment agency with some trepidation. That hadn't worked. But when she contacted Alderson, Alderson and Kinney and told Mr. Kinney the problem, he had suggested that she leave it to him. Within two weeks, Jim Hooten and Mrs. Abel had come for interviews. They had remained ever since.

The housekeeper was at the front door when Cassie opened it.

"Oh, there you are, thank heaven," she said, her pink

round face sagging with relief. "They've been at it again. And something terrible, too. And I just didn't know what to do. After all, Mary's an old lady. She mustn't, you know. Cassie, she just mustn't."

"Where is she now?"

"I talked her into going up to her room. And I must tell you," Mrs. Abel went on, "it won't do. Really, it won't."

Cassie nodded, raced up the steps.

She found Mary sitting in a rocking chair near her window. She wore a loose-fitting black dress with a collar of white lace at her wrinkled throat. Her hair was white and thin, done in a braid. She was shrunken to doll-size but her black eyes were sharp, and glowing now with anger.

"Cassie," she said. "You must listen to my side of it. And not just Arlene's. There's my side, too. I can't, I won't . . ."

"Now, Mary, please, you know you mustn't upset yourself over small things."

"Small things," Mary sniffed. "Arlene is no small thing. Unfortunately. No, no, she's not. Why, my own brother Arley's grand-daughter, and she insists that I call her Mrs. Moorhaven. As if she were mistress here. Mrs. Moorhaven indeed! She looks down her nose at me. She even had the gall to say I was nothing more than a servant in this house. Of course I was a servant, and am, but what does she mean 'nothing more?' All the wickedness that was there in the town, she's brought to the house with her. She . . ."

Cassie sat on the floor, took both Mary's hands in hers. "I know," she agreed softly. "There's only one side, Mary. And it's yours. But what can we do? You tell me. What should we do?"

"Not we. I," Mary retorted. "I'll do what I should have done the awful day Mark brought her home with him."

"But I need you," Cassie protested gently. "And Dell does, too."

Mary's lined face crumpled. "Don't I know it? Isn't that all that's kept me?"

Cassie got to her feet. "I'll talk to Mark again. I promise. And I'll have a word with Arlene, too. Another word with Arlene."

She was at the door when Mary stopped her. "Oh, Cassie, I forgot to tell you. There's company. Arlene drove it clear out of my mind, but there's company in with your father."

"Who?" Cassie asked curiously. She couldn't remember when there had last been guests at Moorhaven. Except for the Van Nuys, of course.

"Dennis's boy, Cassie. Your mother's brother. The painter in Mexico. His son . . . Hank . . ."

Cassie stared at Mary. "Are you quite sure? Hank Moorhaven was listed as missing in Viet Nam. Don't you remember? Mr. Kinney wrote and told us about it."

"That's where he was," Mary answered, "but he's here, in Moorhaven now. Just traveling, he was, with a friend of his, he said. Stopped off in Boston to give Alderson and Alderson and Kinney a look at him, and then drove down here past the Tembley sign, and decide to stop and say hello."

"Funny. I've never seen Dennis, much less his son. I can't imagine . . ." She shrugged. "Well, I'll go right down."

"But don't forget about Arlene and Mark," Mary muttered. "They come first, if you're really going to talk to them."

"She's nervous about the baby coming," Cassie said hopefully. "Maybe that's all that it is, and then, when it's over, she'll be . . ."

"She's a mean-hearted snippet. A Jones if I ever saw one," Mary retorted. "And I should know. Since they're my own."

Arlene wore a turquoise chiffon birdcage that floated around her, concealing the huge curve of her belly. Her matching shoes were spike-heeled and ankle-strapped. Her black hair was piled high in a mass of shiny curls.

"The old cat's made her complaint, has she?" she asked, curling her red lips spitefully.

"We should try to get along with each other," Cassie said gently.

"Oh, should we?" Arlene tossed her head. "You make me sick. Everybody here makes me sick. Mary's going to learn that I'm Mrs. Moorhaven. Just me. Me. Nobody else. She's going to treat me with proper respect."

"Then you must understand that she means to, Arlene. But she's an old lady now. You probably don't realize . . ."

"I realize well enough," Arlene said sourly. "She's against me, and always will be. And I won't put up with it. I won't have it. She's not going to call me a daft girl. She's not . . ."

"Mary doesn't mean any harm," Cassie said.

"Oh, yes, she does." Arlene turned on her spike heels, spinning the dress around her. "She means me all the harm in the world. But never mind her. I can handle her all right. How do you like my dress? I ordered it from Lord and Taylor. Mark thinks it's the greatest."

"Very pretty." Then, "Mary said my father has guests."

Arlene grinned suddenly. "That's right, and you ought to see them. If I had, before I married that crippled husband of mine," she laughed as Cassie winced, "if I had, then you'd probably have been in luck. I'd have picked Hank Moorhaven any time. Or, if not him, then his friend. They're both real men."

Cassie made herself smile. "Dolls then."

"Right," Arlene agreed. "Go and have a look."

The male laughter was rich and thick.

It stopped Cassie at the door. She stood there for a moment, listening.

It had been so long since she had heard her father

laugh. It was almost as if he never had. She thought back over the years, and realized that Moorhaven had never been a place where there was much laughter. The very atmosphere stifled joy. It was as if a heavy shadow lay over the house, the marshes, and its weight crushed everything beneath it.

She pushed the door open, savoring the cool air that touched her hot cheeks.

Her father was sprawled on the sofa. He raised his sandy-gray head, and grinned. "There she is. There's my girl Cassie. Come on in. Meet Hank and Ed."

Delaney's tan-colored eyes were bloodshot, his skin sallow, his flesh sagging under the pressure of his hard-lived years.

Cassie looked at the somewhat stocky man who rose to his feet, smiling lazily at her. He was of middle height, but he had great thick shoulders and arms. His hair was cropped very short, a reddish-brown. His eyes were brown. He wore well-pressed suntans, and a white sports shirt.

She said, "Welcome to Moorhaven," and put out her hand.

Hank's smile widened as he squeezed her fingers, then let them go after a moment that lasted just a shade too long. "Your father was saying he had a daughter. But he didn't say what kind of a daughter. I'm glad to meet you, first cousin." Without waiting for an answer, he gestured at the man beside him. "This is my friend. Ed Parmenter. He's an Army buddy. We just got back. A couple of weeks ago. Thought we'd take a small trip, and saw the name of the town, and I remembered Moorhaven, so here we are."

"Hello, Ed," she said, giving him a long careful look. He was a big dark man, lean as a whip, and just as hard. His tanned face was hollowed at the cheek and temple, his eyes deepset.

He nodded to her, smiling faintly, but didn't speak.

"My father, Dennis, you know, always spoke of this place," Hank went on. "Beautiful, beautiful."

Delaney said thickly, "He left here in . . . when was

it? 1930? Yes. That's when. Thirty-six years ago. And
never came back. We always thought he would. Some
time. For a visit at least. But he never did."

"He wanted to. But you know how it is." Hank
shrugged. "You get so set in your way, in your life."

"He liked Mexico, didn't he?"

"Sure. That's why he stayed. And why not? With his
allowance coming in from Alderson, Alderson and Kinney four times a year."

Delaney gave a great shout of laughter. "Of course,"
he agreed. "You're absolutely right. Why shouldn't he?
It's what we should all have done. Gone and never
come back. Like Dennis. And I always knew he
wouldn't. He was afraid to. He never got over being
afraid of what happened to him here in Moorhaven."

Hank raised his brows questioningly.

But Cassie asked, "Afraid to? What do you mean?
Why should he have been afraid to come back?"

Delaney shrugged, his eyes suddenly dulled. "Never
mind your pretty little head about that," he said. "It's
ancient history now."

Chapter 32

It was the next morning.

Cassie was having her coffee in the breakfast room. She sat near the yellow-curtained window, looking down the slope to where the early sun turned the marshes to molten gold.

Her brother Mark came in, limping awkwardly as always. Of the three of them, she thought, he was the real Moorhaven. She and Dell both had their mother's coloring, but Mark was his grandfather and great-grandfather all over again. His hair was very dark, his eyes, too. He was lean and tall. He was exactly like the two older Moorhavens except for his deformed hip. The hip, which she thought, had affected not only his gait, but his very soul.

Now his thin face was filled with repressed excitement, but she knew she must wait for him to tell her what caused it. If she asked, he would find her prying, and close up like a clam. His dark eyes would become sullen, burn with anger, his lips pout. He was twenty-one now, but he had been that way ever since she could remember.

He lowered himself into a chair across from her, helped himself to coffee from the silver pot.

At last he said, "We're going this morning, Cassie. As soon as Arlene gets herself ready."

"Going?" Cassie hadn't known that he and Arlene planned a trip, and it seemed that the eighth month of pregnancy wasn't exactly a good time for Arlene to be traveling. Not, Cassie admitted to herself, that she cared what Arlene did. But after all, there was the coming baby to be considered. Mark's baby. She found herself trying to imagine what the child would look like, but couldn't. It just didn't seem real to her. She supposed the whole thing, marriage and all, didn't seem real to her.

"We're going to Boston," Mark said defiantly. "To wait until the baby comes."

Cassie blinked at him. "A month ahead of time?" And then she wished that she hadn't spoken. To cover the slip of acknowledging what she didn't want to acknowledge, of accusation that she didn't want to express, she hurried on, "I mean, is Arlene going to have the baby there?"

"That's right," Mark said stiffly.

"But I just assumed . . . We've all been born in this house, Mark. It never occurred to me that ..."

Mark looked as if he might answer, but just then Arlene came in. Her yellow cotton shift billowed as she sank heavily onto the edge of a chair. She tipped her head back, her piled high glossy curls shining in the light. "I heard you," she told Cassie. "Maybe that's what's the matter with the Moorhavens. Being born here, I mean. But anyhow, that was before. Now is now. I'm going to have everything just right. And that doesn't include getting stuck upstairs until it's all over."

"But Dr. Pete's hospital in Tembley . . ." Cassie murmured. "I'm sure you'd have everything there. And he's a wonderful doctor . . ."

"That hick doctor? And that dump?" Arlene sneered. "Fifteen beds, and every one of them filled with the dying. No, thank you. We're off to Boston. We'll see some shows, maybe, and get to some fancy restaurants." She grinned slyly at Cassie. "Don't you wish you were coming along, too?"

"Not exactly," Cassie answered. "It's going to be hot there."

"But air-conditioned," Arlene retorted sweetly. "With just as good central air-conditioning as here."

"Of course," Cassie agreed. She rose to her feet. "I wish you both all the luck in the world. Let us know when there's news."

"Thank you," Arlene said sweetly. "I'm sure you do wish us luck, and Mark will surely call you." She giggled, "To tell you if it's a boy or a girl."

Cassie nodded, went out to the terrace. She was standing there, looking down the slope, following the white shell path to the dike when Mark joined her.

"The reason we're going so soon," he said awkwardly, "well, maybe I ought to tell you, Cassie. It's because of Mary. She really bugs Arlene. You know what I mean?"

"I know," Cassie said dryly. "I could hardly avoid knowing. But that works two ways."

"Mary always starts it. You've got to get her to quit."

Cassie shrugged her slim shoulders. "I'll try. If you promise to try to get Arlene to quit, too."

Mark ignored that. He went on, "And it's Dell, too. She worries about Dell. That's why she doesn't like him. It gives her ideas about the baby. Our baby."

"It's all right," Cassie said gently. "You don't have to apologize to me. Not for anything. Arlene ought to do what she thinks is best about it. If she'll feel better away from Moorhaven, away from Tembley, then . . ."

"Just until the baby is born." He flushed again, and fidgeted with his hands. "And I doubt it'll be very long," he added quickly. "The way she looks, and the way she feels . . ." He ducked his dark head, then turned and walked away.

Cassie, watching, felt her heart contract with pity. He dragged his left leg, then swung it out for balance at each step, before shifting his weight to make headway. Yes, the deformed hip with which he had been born had marked him in every way. It had been a burden he had carried all his life, and would carry until he died. He had been a lonely, a quiet boy at home, a misfit at preparatory school. When he graduated, he had refused to go to college. Nothing Delaney said could change his mind. He had come back to Moorhaven and settled down. But he hadn't stayed there. He had gone in to Tembley, at first to spend time with the Van Nuys, then later, he just didn't bother to say.

Cassie didn't know under what circumstances he had met Arlene, or where, but she supposed it had been in one of the shops or bars.

It was Grandma Bettina who had written her that he was being seen regularly with Arlene, that all of Tembley was talking about it. But Cassie, at school then, wrapped up in her own interests, with the ache of loving Mike so hopelessly, simply frowned and forgot about it. And then she had come home for the Thanksgiving weekend.

They were all in the drawing room, having drinks before the big dinner that Mrs. Abel had prepared under Mary's supervision and instruction.

Mike, and his parents, and Grandma Bettina had been there.

She watched the reflected glow of the fire on Mike's face, and thought of the sad Thanksgiving weekend three years before when she had first seen him with new eyes, and wondered if he would ever realize that she was now grown up.

She had dressed so carefully that day, brushing her gleaming hair carefully. She knew her black peau d'ange dress with its tiny waist and bell skirt was marvelously becoming to her. She knew her new French black patent leather heels showed off her slim ankles. But Mike had come in, grinned, given her a very big brotherish wolf whistle, and immediately begun to talk to Delaney.

She told herself to forget that other Thanksgiving, and smoothed the crepe over the small curve of her hips, and began to wonder where Mark was, and if he would return in time.

He had been away the night before, and all that morning. And while she was thinking of him, just at that moment actually, he came in.

He came in, holding hands with Arlene.

It was the first time Cassie remembered seeing her.

She wore a narrow black velvet sheath with a high waist that pushed her small breasts up and out of the deep neckline. A strand of pearls glowed at her throat. Her black hair was piled high in curls. Her mouth was shiny red and curved in a provocative smile.

Mark swallowed so that his Adam's apple leaped in his throat. He said, "This is Arlene. Arlene Jones. We got married last night."

It was so still that the hiss of the burning logs in the fireplace was suddenly audible.

Then Delaney leaned his head back and laughed. "Maybe you've got the right idea, Mark. If you find you can't lick 'em join 'em."

Grandma Bettina's bright blue eyes moved from face to face in nonchalant appraisal. She was clearly unsurprised.

Dr. Pete and his wife seemed to wish themselves elsewhere, but politely sipped their drinks in silence.

Mike drew deeply on his cigarette and then exhaled, retreating behind a cloud of blue smoke.

But Mary got to her feet slowly. She was hunched and old and withered, but she had remarkable force. She said, "You can't do it, Arlene. How dare you? What are you doing in this house?"

Arlene's laugh was high, shrill and venomous. "But I have, Aunt Mary. I'm here." She thrust out a thin hand. "This is my wedding ring. I'm here, and here I stay."

"Even if you are my own brother Arley's granddaughter," Mary began, ". . . even if you are, you have no right to use that tone to me."

"And you're nothing to me, Aunt Mary," Arlene flared. "Nobody says your name. You turned your back on them, and they on you."

"And you're about to do the same," Mary answered.

"That's right." Arlene sauntered into the room. She sank down on the big burgundy velvet sofa, and grinned. "That's just what I'm going to do. But unlike you, Aunt Mary, dear, I'm Mrs. Moorhaven now. And you . . . who are you? What are you?"

Cassie had known, even then, that Mark had made a terrible mistake. But she didn't know how much of one until she returned from school a month later for Christmas.

Only then did she understand how Mark's need had trapped him, and how, through his marriage, he had brought the generations-old resentments of Tembley into Moorhaven itself.

Sickened, she had heard Arlene call Mark her "crippled sweetie."

Enraged, she had heard her call Dell, the "grinning dummy."

Ashamed, she had heard her call Delaney the "drunken old man."

But Arlene was Mark's wife. There was nothing Cassie could do except bite her lip and bear it, and seethe inside. There was nothing she could do but try to protect those she loved from Arlene's malice.

She thought it was one reason why she had given up the secret dreams she had nurtured within her for as long as she could remember. The dream of going to Boston to live and work after graduating. Of escaping Moorhaven forever.

Delaney, with the holdings managed by Alderson and Alderson and Kinney, could get along well enough. And then there would be Mark. Mary and Mrs. Abel did very well with Dell. Cassie had always thought that she would be free.

But then she had finished school, and come home for what she thought would be only a brief visit, a face to face explanation to Delaney of what she planned.

She had seen Arlene settled in Moorhaven, the mistress there, and in action. She had seen Mark's helpless and infatuated response. She had realized that Mark had neither will, nor sense, as far as Arlene was concerned. And she had learned of Arlene's pregnancy. She had immediately understood that she could not leave Dell, the others, to Arlene's unchecked malice. She had stayed.

But Arlene was only one reason, she knew. She thought that she must always have deceived herself. She had been drawn back to Moorhaven, as the family always was, by some mysterious cord that she had not broken. She had come back and stayed on because she had to. The spell of Moorhaven was on her, and she could not break free of it.

So she hid her love from Mike, the love she had hoped to run from, and busied herself with everyday tasks . . .

Now Mary's thin old voice broke into her thoughts. "You've heard, I suppose," she said bitterly. "What's good enough for everybody else just isn't good enough for her."

Cassie turned, smiled. Mary's hair gleamed like pewter in the sunlight. Her pale face was like an old sheet of parchment. "Now, Mary," Cassie asked, "what difference does it make anyway?"

"Plenty of difference. And all to the good." Mary's narrow lips smiled, too. "I'm glad she's going, and I hope she stays. Though you can't tell me it'll be for a month. I know what I know. She's just about ready to deliver. I give her three days, four at the most."

Cassie said nothing. She thought Mary was probably right.

Mary went on, "And I can count as well as the next one. She trapped poor Mark into it. An eight month baby. They'll say it was premature, of course. That's what people have been saying since Adam and Eve."

"It doesn't matter," Cassie said.

"Just wait. You'll see it does matter. She'll come back, lording it over the rest of us. I know that bunch. I ought to."

"We'll all do the best we can," Cassie said soothingly.

In spite of the heat, Mary shivered suddenly. She

folded her thin black-clad arms across her chest, hugging herself in an oddly young gesture. "I was sixteen when Jonathan brought Cordelia to this house. She was a worthy mistress for Moorhaven. And later, after so much trouble, your mother Dorinda took her place. And now, now look what Mark brought home. Look what he's done to us. Arlene! Arlene Jones!" Sadly, she went on, "I'll have to go. As big as Moorhaven is it isn't big enough for the two of us. Not for Arlene and me, Cassie. You know that, don't you?"

Cassie took the old woman's hands in hers. "Don't talk that way," She said. "You can't go, Mary."

"I'm old enough to see the handwriting on the wall," Mary answered. Her trembling hands shivered in Cassie's fingers. She went on, whispering now, "And old enough to act on it, too. But I'm afraid. I don't know where to go, or how, or what to do. I've always been here. In Moorhaven."

"Don't think about it," Cassie said.

Mary sighed. "And did you know? With all the trouble we've already got, we've got some more, too?"

"What do you mean?" Cassie asked quickly.

"Your father," Mary said. "Delaney. Did you know what he did last night? He invited Hank and that friend of his Ed, to stay on. To stay here. In Moorhaven."

"He did?"

"He did, and they jumped at the chance. If you ask me they jumped too fast. Why would two young men like that want to hang around here? What's in Moorhaven for them?"

Cassie shrugged. "Now don't go paranoid on me, Mary. After all, Hank is Dennis' son."

"That makes no difference," Mary retorted. "And you know it as well as I."

"I wonder why Delaney did it," Cassie mused. "It's not like him."

"He was probably in his cups," Mary said wisely. "And they put the idea to him instead of the other way around." She went on with no change of tone, "And

Cassie, you tell him to walk the dike. He hasn't done it for a long time."

"Oh, Mary . . ."

"You tell him, that's all," Mary retorted. "Just make sure he does it."

Later, Delaney sheepishly confirmed Mary's guess that Hank had suggested the invitation.

Delaney said, "I don't quite know how it happened. We were sitting around last night, talking, and the next thing I knew it was settled. They'll stay on for a couple of weeks, that's all. And then they'll continue their trip to wherever it was."

Cassie didn't answer him.

He narrowed his bloodshot eyes at her. "What's wrong? Why are you so displeased about it? Hank's a nice guy. And Ed is a very personable young man. I should think you'd be pleased to have somebody like him around."

"I'm not exactly displeased," she answered. "I just wondered about it. I thought surely they were leaving last night. And . . ."

"Well, they didn't. And it doesn't make any difference. We've got plenty of room."

What she thought, but didn't say, was that she feared it *would* make a difference. Her father's eyes were bloodshot, as they always were in the mornings, and his hands shook. But she feared it would be worse now that he had companions to drink with. She could imagine all-night carousing, the trading of tall tales about war until morning. She could imagine the effect of that on Delaney's already shaky health.

She said gently, "I hope you'll take it easy."

His eyes flashed up at her from between swollen lids. "I suggest you mind your own business. I don't intend to have my twenty-two-year-old daughter tell me how to live."

She grinned, "And here I was, just saying I hoped you'd take it easy."

He put his gray-streaked head in his hands. "You don't know what it's like, Cassie."

Outside, a car door slammed. Cassie went to the window. Mark and Arlene waved as they drove by.

"They're leaving now," Cassie told Delaney.

"Good riddance. I hope the witch never comes back. But she will. I know she will." He frowned at Cassie. "Do you know what she wants now? A convertible, Cadillac, no less. Red, with leopard seats. She put in her order to me yesterday morning. She said it would be a lovely present for the baby. Her words."

Cassie grinned, "Well, why not?"

"Because I say not, that's why not. And something else. A tennis court. To give her something to do while she's stuck out here. And through Mark, she made another small request. His allowance isn't big enough. I ought to tell Alderson to get Kinney to increase it."

Cassie grinned. "Maybe she'll get tired of us and leave."

"No chance of that," Delaney sighed. "I know that family from way back. Now that she's got a toehold here, she'll hang on forever."

"How do you suppose the Joneses feel about it?"

"I know what Arley would have said. Don't ask me about the rest of them."

"I expect they're as displeased as we are."

"Maybe. And maybe not. But I'm pretty sure she hasn't been to see them since the marriage. I'm pretty sure she hates them as much as they hate us."

"But why do they? And why does Tembley?"

Delaney didn't answer. He turned abruptly, went to the mantel. He picked up the silver music box and wound it, and then, with head on one side, he stood listening to its tinkling tune.

Chapter 33

"I think," Ed said deliberately, "that that is just about the funniest sight I ever saw in my life. And I've seen a few, too."

He stood over Dell, hard and fit-looking in green Army fatigues, dark eyes narrowed with amusement.

Dell was crouched in a big sand box, busily building a sand castle that looked suspiciously like Moorhaven itself.

"How old is the kid anyway?"

"Twenty-six," Cassie said coldly. "And I'd very much appreciate it if you wouldn't make fun of him."

Hank put in, "Sorry, Cassie. He'd not making fun, you know. He's just surprised." Hank, too, wore Army fatigues, and his brown eyes were filled with amusement that hadn't come through in his voice.

"Was he just born that way?" Ed asked. "Or did something happen to him?"

"He wasn't born twenty-six years old," Cassie answered dryly.

She was stretched out in a green and orange beach chair beside the pool that had been built years before when the doctors, unable to do any more for Mark, had suggested swimming as the best possible exercise for him. He didn't use it as often as Cassie would have liked, but she no longer suggested that he take a daily swim. For that seemed to bother him, too.

She was aware now, of Ed's dark eyes, Hank's brown ones. She found herself wishing that she had worn something more conservative than her tiny blue bikini. The men seemed to find nothing to look at besides her, and, of course, Dell.

Ed squatted down next to her, said softly, "I'm sorry, Cassie. I didn't mean to get your goat. Nor hurt the kid's feelings either. I didn't realize that he might understand me, you know."

"He knows when people talk about him," Cassie said. "See?" She moved her head in Dell's direction. He had looked up, an inquiring expression on his face.

"Yes. He sure does know," Hank agreed. He yawned, stretched. "Do you suppose it would be okay if I had a drink? I've got me a mighty thirst. I'm on vacation these days."

"Of course. Just ask Mrs. Abel. She'll show you the liquor cabinet in the morning room. And she'll get you a bucket of ice, if you like. I'd go and see to it, but I don't want to leave Dell near the pool alone."

"We'll watch out for him," Ed assured her.

"He won't stay with you," she explained.

Hank grinned at Ed. "You're elected, buddy. See what you can do for the three of us, will you?"

Ed nodded, rose, walked across the concrete pool area, and disappeared around the end of Jonathan's wing.

"It's very nice to have a buddy, isn't it?" Cassie observed. It struck her that the relationship between the two men was an odd one. Ed was obviously the older, the more experienced. Yet Hank gave the orders.

Hank laughed now. "Yes, it is nice. But maybe I ought to explain. He's reacting out of habit, the way people do. I used to rank him."

"Oh," she said. "I see." But she wondered privately if that was the real explanation. Somehow she didn't think so.

"And besides, he just likes to oblige me."

She didn't answer him.

He said, smiling faintly now, "I hope it's okay with you. I mean Ed's and my staying on for a little while." And he went on when she still didn't speak, "Your father thought it was a good idea. And I sure didn't mind."

It wasn't, Cassie thought, that he actually was lying. But the way he worded it suggested that the visit was Delaney's idea. And Delaney had led her to believe that the idea had been entirely Hank's. Maybe, in a way, they were both right. But the thought left Cassie wondering even more.

He said, "You don't have any idea of what it's like. Seeing a place you've heard about all your life. You begin to think of it as if it was a monument." He raised his reddish head, looked up at the house. "And I guess it is."

"It's just a house," Cassie said dryly. "With the same features that all houses have."

But even as she said it she wondered if that were true. Was Moorhaven like all other houses? Did they, too, seem to have living pasts, shadowy secrets?

Hank grinned. "I wouldn't say Moorhaven is exactly like other houses. Most of them don't have private swimming pools, and central air-conditioning, and their own personal cliffs behind them."

"I suppose not," she agreed, her eyes on Dell.

"And you know, it's hard to believe," Hank went on, "but it's just what my father said. He talked about it every day of his life, I guess." Hank's grin widened. "I think maybe that's why my mother left him. She probably got her fill of Moorhaven, how things were done there, the way people were . . ."

"But he never came back," Cassie said thoughtfully.

"Oh, I guess he had his reasons. Besides, what would he have done here?"

"The same as the rest of us, I suppose."

"Oh, he enjoyed living. Believe me, the old man knew how to live all right."

Cassie thought that it was odd that she didn't have a

picture of her Uncle Dennis in her mind. She had heard his name mentioned, of course. She knew that he had lived in Paris for a time, then moved to Mexico. She knew that he had always been interested in painting. But it seemed to her that that was all. She decided that Mary must know more.

"It's a Moorhaven quality, isn't it?" Hank laughed. "I've got it, too."

Cassie looked at him from under her long lashes. "You said you went to the firm, didn't you? To let them know that you'd come back after being missing."

"I sure did. What did you think happened? When I was scratched, they put a hold on my income. So, when I got out, I had to let them know I was still alive." Hank chuckled. "And what a thing Mr. Kinney put me through. Papers, identification, the works. I tell you, I was beginning to doubt myself even. I was beginning to think I'd never gotten out of Viet Nam after all."

"Were you there long?" she asked.

"Eighteen months. Eighteen months too long, for my taste. I went in early, really early. It didn't look like it would be much then. I was captured by the gooks after about nine months, then held in a compound for six months, before I broke out with a couple of other guys, and got back to our lines. And then," he shrugged his heavy shoulders, "a few months in a hospital, then back and out, and here I am. And glad to be here, too."

"It must have been rough," she said with sudden sympathy.

"It was," he said, "And believe me, it's going to get worse. A whole lot worse before it gets better. I don't like to think about it, nor talk about it. And Ed feels the same way."

"Was he with you all the time?"

"Yes. Yes, he was."

Just then Ed brought the loaded tray, set it on a white wrought-iron table. "Here's sustenance," he said. "Name your poison."

Cassie shook her head. "Nothing for me, thanks."

She was glad her father was inside now, glad that he

wouldn't be here to join in the early drinking. Not that
he needed company, she knew. He had, alone or with
guests, always had more to drink than he needed or was
good for him. It was a fact of life about Delaney
Moorhaven.

Hank was saying, "I'll have the usual, you clown.
You don't have to ask, do you?"

Ed filled two tall glasses with ice, poured dark shots
of bourbon over them, and gave one glass to Hank.

They toasted each other silently, then both of them
drank.

Cassie considered that it was still pretty early in the
day for straight bourbon, and sighed, thinking of her
father again.

"How long do you plan to stay?" she asked.

Hank shrugged, chuckled. "We're not planning.
We've put in a long time with everything figured out for
us, planned, enforced, right along the dotted line. Now
we're just living. Just waiting for the spirit to move us."

She hesitated, then, "I'm afraid you're going to find
it very quiet here."

"Quiet?"

"There's nothing at all in Tembley."

"So we noticed yesterday." Hank chuckled again.
"But, you know, that doesn't matter. After where we've
been peace and quiet suits us oaky, more than okay."

Ed, giving her a meaningful look that swept her
bikini-clad body from head to toe, said, "And what
we've seen around here, at Moorhaven, suits us both
fine, too."

But Hank released a loud mock sigh. "If only we
weren't first cousins, Cassie."

She ignored Ed's glance, Hank's words.

She closed her eyes, and leaned her head back,
thinking about Mike.

They were still at the poolside when he arrived an
hour later.

By then, both Ed and Hank had begun to show the
signs of the whiskey they had consumed. They were
bright-eyed, and somewhat over-animated. Though

Hank had said they didn't like to talk about the war, they had begun busily trading anecdotes about it for Cassie, while she pretended to listen to them.

She made the introductions, while Dell, pulling at Mike's arm, fought for his attention.

He nodded at the men, then allowed Dell to draw him proudly to the sand castle. He spent a few moments with him, then, patting his auburn curls, he returned to sit with Cassie.

Hank said, "Are you a relative? Or just a friend of the family?"

"Old friend," Mike said briefly.

"I was wondering. Because my father never told me about you."

"I wouldn't expect that he would have," Mike answered. "He left here before I was born by a good number of years."

"Oh. Yes. That's right. I guess he must have."

But Cassie found herself wondering again. Wouldn't her Uncle Dennis, if he'd talked so much about Moorhaven, have at least mentioned the Van Nuys? Dr. Peter, and Dr. Pete . . . Grandma Bettina . . .

Ed eyed Mike speculatively. "Where do you stand in the draft? Are you going to have to go, do you think?"

"I've already put in my two years," Mike answered. "Now I'm in the Reserves. Maybe, maybe not. I don't know."

"Lucky," Ed told him. "You don't know what you're missing."

"That's right," Mike agreed. "I guess I was lucky." He turned to Cassie. "Arlene and Mark went to Boston, didn't they?"

"This morning," she answered.

"My father must be relieved," Mike told her with a grin. "She's not the most patient patient. And he's got his hands full as it is."

"But she's sure a good-looking girl," Hank said. "When she gets that melon out of her belly, I'll bet she's going to be a knockout."

Neither Mike nor Cassie answered him.

"How long have they been married anyhow? Arlene and Mark, I mean."

Cassie said, "Since Thanksgiving."

"And she's a town girl, isn't she?"

Cassie nodded.

Hank finished his drink, studied Cassie and Mike over the rim of his empty glass, then handed it to Ed, gesturing for a refill. When he had it, he said, "And what about you two? Are you engaged?"

Cassie blushed. "No," she said quickly. "Certainly not."

Mike, unperturbed, arched a dark brow. "Why do you ask?"

Hank shrugged, his brown eyes suddenly veiled. "Well, I'm just trying to get the family sorted out, kind of."

Ed laughed heartily. "I had a better reason for wondering than that," and gave Cassie another meaningful look.

She pretended not to notice. Stony-faced, she hid her embarrassment. Poor Mike. What a position to be put into. He certainly had no more than a brotherly interest in her. She just hoped that he had never suspected how she felt about him. But he seemed completely untroubled.

He asked, "Where are you from originally, Hank?"

"Mexico," Hank told him. "A hick town you'd never have heard, I'm sure. That's where my father settled when he came back from Paris just before World War II. And he never left it. My mother did. She divorced him and took off. I stayed with my father, of course. Then I came back to the States to go to school. He died some time in there. And the next thing I knew I was drafted and that was it."

It was, Cassie thought, just what he had told her earlier. But somehow, as he spoke, she had a feeling of uneasiness. It sounded as if he had memorized a speech, was rattling it off as if he had rattled it off too many times before. Perhaps it was because he was bored with explaining. But perhaps it wasn't.

"Are you interested in painting, too?" Mike asked.

Hank shrugged. "Afraid not. The old man got all the talent."

"What happened to his paintings, I wonder," Cassie asked. "Are they still around some place?"

"I guess so. Probably in storage. Or in galleries. I wasn't there. I don't know who took care of that part of it."

"It would be interesting to see them now," she said. "That's why I was asking."

"There was one I remember he did," Hank answered. "Of Moorhaven. Now that would be interesting to see again. Because it seems different now. The pool, I think. I'm not sure what else. I don't remember it all that well."

"That sounds like one he did when he was a boy. Of Moorhaven, too. A view from the dike," Cassie said. "I'll ask Mary where it is now."

"Good," Hank told her. "I'm interested. Really interested, you know. When you're a kid, you don't pay much attention. The old man talks, who cares? But then, you get older, and family, history, all that stuff, it begins to matter."

"We've lots of photographs," Cassie said idly. "Pictures of our grandparents. Everybody, I guess. I'll see if I can find them for you, too."

"I hope you can."

"And there are the portraits in the house, of course."

"Yes, I saw them. In the hall. Quite a family." Hank grinned again. "See, that's the thing. The old man talks. You think it's mostly daydreams, fantasy. You don't really believe him. Who could? But then you find out it was all real. Moorhaven was actually real."

Ed choked on his drink, and laughed, "That's a fact, Hank. That's how it is."

Mike asked, "Didn't you see your father's portrait along with the others in the vestibule, Hank?"

Cassie blinked at him. There was no portrait of Dennis, and Mike knew it. But he must know what he was doing. She said nothing.

Hank gave Mike a bewildered look. "If he's there, then it was of when he was a kid or something. And he must have changed a lot since it was done."

Just then Delaney came out of the house. He came toward them, smiling ironically, his sandy gray hair bristling and uncombed. "News from Boston, believe it or not. They made it just in time. The trip must have been too much for Arlene."

Dell got to his feet, went to his father, and tugged at him.

Delaney looked at him, then winced. "Well, what is it now? What do you want?"

"He wants you to look at his sand castle," Mike said.

Delaney didn't seem to have heard. He drew away from Dell, said absently, "Mark said the baby's okay. It's a boy," and walked away quickly.

Later, Cassie thought she should have guessed what was happening when Mike brought Bettina out to the house, and she and Mary got together behind closed doors for a long talk.

But at the time she was no more than selfishly pleased because the visit had brought Mike back to Moorhaven after he had spent a good part of the day there. And more than that, it had distracted Hank and Ed from their excessive attention to her. They had singly or together dogged each step she had taken all that day. She had already had more than enough of her first cousin and his friend, too.

It was not that she was adverse to the admiration of men. It was just that she had no interest in them, and didn't expect to develop any. Besides, she sensed some hidden motive. They might already be bored, and thus amusing themselves. But they might also be assuming that the length of their stay depended on how well they entertained her. She didn't like the thought.

When Mike had suggested she take a walk along the dike with him, she agreed with alacrity.

Hank and Ed hinted that they, too, would like some

fresh air, but Mike said bluntly, "Why don't you guys take a look around town?"

Hank laughed. "Excuse me, Mike. Didn't mean to butt in. You've got a good idea."

Ed, plainly less willing, suggested that they make up a party, and all four go.

Mike said, "No, thanks," and didn't give him time for further discussion.

He drew Cassie outside, and across the terrace.

They walked down the slope together. It was a still night, with frogs croaking in the marshes, and a soft warm breeze.

When, once, their arms brushed, she drew herself away quickly. His warmth troubled her. The wish to experience it again was so strong that she found herself breathless.

She tried to think of something to say, but her mind was filled with Mike, with a three year-old hunger. At last, she said uncomfortably, "I was surprised you came out again this evening, Mike. I thought, since you took time off during the day, you'd want to work on your book."

"I'm doing more thinking than working these days. And besides, Grandma wanted me to drive her. She still has a bee in her bonnet, Cassie."

"Oh? What's that?"

"She *is* going to give up the house and move to Boston. She wants Mary to go with her."

"Is that what they're in there plotting about now?" Cassie asked.

Mike laughed softly. "Part of it."

"And the rest?"

"Grandma feels that she has to dispose of me, you know. She can't put her rebel grandson out in the cold."

"In July?"

"In the heat then, Cassie. I might as well tell you everything. It depends on Mary. If Mary will go with Grandma, then Grandma's going to inveigle Delaney into inviting me to stay at Moorhaven."

Cassie gasped, "But Mike, you can't."

He gave her a lazy smile. "Why not, Cassie?"

"Because . . . well, because you don't belong here," she finished lamely. "And in Tembley . . ."

"Let's not use Tembley as an excuse, Cassie." His smile widened. "Let's just be honest with each other. Okay?"

But she had no intention of telling him what she felt. The quick quiver of half joy, half fear that assailed her. Mike, in Moorhaven. But he didn't belong there. What was wrong with Moorhaven must never touch him. And there was something wrong. She had always known, sensed it. That was why she buried her love for Mike deep inside her. Because whatever was wrong must never touch him. He wasn't a Moorhaven.

Finally she said, "You know you'll always be perfectly welcome here, Mike," and turned back toward the house.

Chapter 34

"His name," Arlene said, "is Jones." Her red lips widened in a challenging grin. "Isn't that gorgeous? Jones Moorhaven?"

No one answered her.

She moved languidly across the terrace and sank into a wrought-iron chair.

Her figure, good even in pregnancy, had become sleek but curvy at the same time. She had on a tight-fitting white dress, with a low scooped neck and no sleeves. Her high-heeled shoes were of white patent leather. She wore earrings formed of linked gold bells, and a bracelet that matched.

She crossed her long slender legs, and smiled slowly around her. She noticed Cassie's gaze centered on her earrings, and she touched them with a red-tipped finger. "Tiffany's. Mark got them for me." And then, "Well, I could have named the baby Arley. I was thinking of it. But somehow . . . Jones . . ."

Mark, holding the blanket-wrapped infant, shifted his weight from his bad leg to his good one, and awkwardly allowed Cassie to peer into its tiny face.

"He's a doll," she announced.

Arlene laughed raucously. "But of course. What did you think? That I'd have a Moorhaven with horns and a tail? Or one with a no-good hip? Or one with no

318

brains at all? Not me. I can do better than that. And I
have." She turned to Mark and said irritably, "Well,
don't just stand there, hanging on to your son and heir
as if you haven't the faintest idea what to do with him."

Uncomfortably Mark asked, "But Arlene, what did
you . . ."

Cassie said quickly, "Mrs. Abel fixed up a nursery,
Mark. The room next to yours and Arlene's."

She didn't mention her own labors. In the ten days
since the phone call from Boston, she had been in a
frantic rush to prepare for the coming of the baby. For
the coming of Jones, she said to herself. Jones Moorhaven. All the things that Arlene had never bothered to
do, that Mark had never even thought of, had to be
done.

Mrs. Abel had grumbled, "Who's going to care for
the child?" as if she already knew that she would end
up taking most of the responsibility on herself.

Mark started for the door, giving Cassie a grateful
look. "Thanks."

Dell lurched to his side, peered at the small bundle,
and put out a tentative finger.

Arlene cried, "Listen, you. You quit that, you dummy. Mark, don't let him touch the baby. You hear me?
I want him away from my baby."

Cassie said quickly, "Dell, come here to me. I have
something for you."

Dell backed off, his green eyes moving between Cassie and Arlene.

He was, Cassie knew, afraid of Arlene, and always
had been. It might be because he recognized the dislike
in Arlene's voice. It might also be because Arlene took
any opportunity she could get to hurt his feelings.

"Come on, Dell," she repeated.

He finally obeyed, circling widely around Arlene. He
sat down next to Cassie, leaned against her, rocking his
body back and forth on his haunches.

Arlene made a disgusted sound, and he slid his hand
into Cassie's and clung to her.

"I suppose we should get a nurse for the baby,"

Arlene said. "I'm not going to be able to manage. Not on my own." She gave an exaggerated sigh. "But the trouble is, who is there to get? Nobody'd want to come here. And, of course, there's not a soul in Tembley I'd ask anyway. I wouldn't have any of that bunch around my son."

"I suppose Mrs. Abel can manage," Cassie said. "Though she does have a great deal to do."

"I'm afraid she'll just have to manage," Arlene retorted.

Delaney, silent until then, raised his head. "Have you let your parents know yet?"

Arlene's brows rose in arcs of astonishment. "What's the sudden interest in my family?"

Delaney's bloodshot eyes narrowed. "Why, I just thought . . . your first child . . ."

She laughed. "You're the living limit, old man. You just leave my family to me. When I want to take up with them, I will."

"It suits me," Delaney answered. "I don't care what you do."

"I know," she said sweetly. And then, to Cassie, "But where's Aunt Mary, the old sweetie. You'd think she'd be out to welcome the boy. After all, he is a Jones."

"She's gone," Cassie said.

"Gone?" Arlene repeated blankly. "You're kidding me, aren't you?"

Cassie shook her head.

"But I always figured she'd be able to take care of Jonesie for me, too. I figured she'd love it. I mean, after all, one more Moorhaven to notch on her belt, and a healthy one, too. As well as a Jones."

Cassie said gently, "I doubt Mary would have been up to infant care any more, Arlene. But in any case, she has gone to live with Mrs. Van Nuys. Mike's grandmother is closing the house, and the two of them are going to share an apartment in Boston."

"Well, so I finally got through to her," Arlene said. "I never did see why she was still hanging around. Her work here was finished a long time ago." She transferred her gaze to Delaney. "Well, father-in-law, dear, what are you giving Jonesie as a present?"

He didn't answer her.

"How about a nice Caddy?" she grinned.

"Forget it," he said shortly, and went into the house.

Arlene laughed softly. "I'm not likely to forget it. And I won't let him either. I'll have my Caddy, a nice bright red one. Just wait and see."

Ed laughed admiringly. "I'll bet you will, Arlene."

She turned a long, unsmiling look on him. "I'm surprised you're still here. I didn't realize you were planning on hanging around this long. I mean, ten days in Moorhaven . . . oh, wow!"

"We've been having a pretty good time," Hank told her.

She raised her brows. "At what?"

"This and that," Ed answered quickly.

She gave him another long stare from under mascara-thick lashes, then transferred her attention to Cassie. "When did this about Auntie come about?"

Cassie shrugged. "Oh, a few days ago. Mary moved into town yesterday."

"Just before I got back, huh?"

Cassie didn't answer her. She was remembering those moments just before Mike had come to collect Mary.

Mary had been rechecking her room with Cassie's help. Closets, drawers, bookshelves were emptied, put in order, and scrubbed. Mary was determined to leave the place spotless, ready for Mike when he wanted to move in.

With a final satisfied glance around, she sank into the rocking chair that had been hers for so long. She was silent, catching her breath. Finally she said, "It's a strange feeling, this. To be leaving now. To be leaving like this, too. Sometimes I think I'm daft to go away because of Arley's child. Which is why I am, of course. But I'm old now. I can't fight her. And two Joneses in Moorhaven is one too many." She smiled faintly. "Do you know? I always thought I would die here. Oh . . .

perhaps not always. I didn't think of death when I was young." She raised white brows at Cassie. "Don't stand there looking at me like that. Sit down somewhere and listen to what I want to tell you. And listen well, Cassie."

Cassie pulled over a hassock, sat at Mary's knee. "You're not going away forever, Mary. And you're not going far. We'll see you. I'll come to Boston, and you'll come here."

Mary's faint smile widened. "You talk as if I have a whole life before me. When I have a whole life behind me instead." She held up a small withered hand. "Never mind. Never mind that. When I first came to this house I was sixteen. I thought to be here a year, or maybe two, and earn the money I needed, and the family accepted it though they didn't like it."

"Mary, tell me something. How did all that begin. What do I feel when I get to Tembley? Why is . . ."

Mary's bright black eyes seemed to turn inward. "Well, you know the story about the shipyards. They were closed down, and then the harbor was closed because the ships could no longer come in. It happened, and that was the end of it. But the people in town didn't understand. So . . ." She shrugged her thin shoulders. "You see, my mother, Daviette, lost her husband and four children in those hard times. She blamed the Moorhavens. She was crazy, crazy with sorrow. She swore that the Moorhavens pushed back the sea when they built the dike at the foot of the slope, and that one day the sea would return. My brother and I fell out over that bit of nonsense. For he agreed with her, although he knew better. But that isn't what I have to say to you. Although there's a connection. Cassie, when I'm gone from this house, and not here to protect you, you must be careful."

Cassie stared at Mary, seeing her in a new way. The shining black eyes, the broad white forehead, the straight steady mouth. They were all the same, familiar. What was different was the expression. It held an earnestness that Cassie had never seen before.

Mary's warning struck some sympathetic note that vibrated inside her. Recognition of danger, sharp, and cold welled in her. Yet what was the danger?

Mary said, "Arlene ... she's a Jones. Never, never forget it. I'm one, so I know. You must be careful of her. Aways remember what I tell you. She's for herself, and for no one else. Be on your guard with her. For you, and for Dell."

Cassie nodded in sudden relief. Arlene was not what she would consider a cause for fear, only a cause for concern. She must be handled. She must be dealt with. Like the people in town, she must be treated politely but firmly, and ignored when necessary.

Mary went on, "And Hank Moorhaven, and his friend. Now you listen to me, Cassie. I know nothing of them, and never have. Do you take my meaning? I have never known anything of Hank."

Cassie blinked. "Hank? But why should you? He was born in Mexico, and Uncle Dennis never ..."

"I said I know nothing of Hank." Mary's straight wrinkled mouth grew tight. "But Dennis I knew. I knew well. And he never loved Moorhaven. He hated it. He feared it. He fled from here with relief, and left your parents behind. Believe me, I know."

"He was afraid, you say? Afraid? But of what? Why, Mary. Why did he leave Moorhaven?"

"He had good reason to be, and don't you ever forget it. But you're not listening to me, Cassie. You must. For your own protection. I tell you, those two boys are up to something. Dennis never talked of Moorhaven with love. How could he when he hated it? So they must be up to something. They want something. And you mustn't let them have it. Whatever it is, they mustn't have it."

"I don't understand you, Mary."

"I'm telling you only to be careful." Mary drew a deep breath. "There has been trouble in Moorhaven. Terrible things have happened in the past. Perhaps they would have happened no matter what. But now, now that I'm an old woman, I see a pattern. Perhaps I'm as

daft as my mother before me. But I *do* see one. She
said that the sea would return, and that the Moorhavens were doomed. And when she was gone, Arley,
who should have known better, took over her prophecy
as his own. Tembley took over her prophecy, and his,
too, for its own. Perhaps it's only coincidence. But
perhaps the prophecy itself, and the belief behind it,
create what would not have been there. Anyway," now
her voice lightened, "it was that over which Arley and I
fell out. I wanted an end to it. And Poor Arley . . . he
would hold on the past as if he needed it to breathe by.
And now there's Arlene. Arlene. In Moorhaven."

Soon after Mike had come for Mary. She had cried
when she kissed Cassie and Dell and Mark and
Delaney goodbye, and allowed Mike to help her into
the car. She had cried as they drove away together . . .

Now Arlene said, "How about a drink somebody?
I've been off the sauce for as long as I'm going to be."
And she slanted a look at Cassie. "Don't you dare ask
about Jonesie. Mark's got the formula for him. Mrs.
Abel will take care of it for me."

Cassie smiled, but said nothing.

Ed said, "You name your poison, Arlene, and I'll get
it. I know where everything is now. I've made myself at
home."

"Gin and tonic for starters," she laughed. "And
make it quick."

Hank laughed, too. "You're like a kid out of school,
Arlene."

"Like a girl out of the hospital, you mean," she
answered.

She rose, took a few quick paces across the terrace,
then swung back. "Oh, I feel good. Oh, I'm so glad it's
over, and I can be myself again."

"I'll bet you are," Hank told her. "And no wonder.
Look at what yourself is."

She preened happily. "Yes. It was easy. I didn't have
to do a thing. Except buy a bunch of new clothes. And
you can bet I did that. We'd have been back yesterday

except for my shopping. Mark nearly had a fit. But I told him if we didn't get my shopping done, he could come back alone. Without me, I mean. And without the kid, too. So that shut him up."

Mark came out then, empty-armed, moving with his limping gait. "He's sleeping, Arlene."

"Well, what would you think? Of course he's sleeping. That's all he ever does. Sleep, eat, and mess."

Mark said anxiously, "But maybe you ought to have a look at him."

"You look at him," she said. "Ed's getting me a drink and we're going to have a party."

Mark hesitated for a moment, then limped inside, his shoulders sagging, his dark head bent.

He was, Cassie thought, too young, and too vulnerable to deal with Arlene. He didn't know where to begin, or how to begin.

Ed brought the drinks out, and Arlene, accepting hers, leaned back with an exaggerated sigh of pure pleasure. "Oh, this is going to be good," she said. "At last. Finally. It's going to be good. Now that Mark's got something to concentrate on besides me, I'll be able to live again."

Cassie saw a car glint in the sunlight as it rounded the cliff.

She watched it appear and disappear and then finally make the full turn into the driveway.

She knew, even before she could recognize the car, that it was Mike.

He had said he would be back today. Part of her had been waiting for him.

Hank said, "I tell you, Arlene, if you're really so hot for a party, then we ought to celebrate tonight. We ought to paint the town red, what there is of it."

Arlene leaned her dark head back, considered. Then she laughed. "There's three, maybe four bars in Tembley. And none of them are exactly oases of joy. But if you want to try them, then I'm your girl. We'll do it tonight."

Ed grinned hopefully at Cassie. "You'll come, too, won't you?"

"No," she answered. She rose to her feet. "No, thanks. I don't do the bars in Tembley."

A memory of the circle of teen-agers rose to her mind. Their sneering laughter, their mocking eyes. That was what she would find in Tembley.

Arlene giggled. "You can bet she doesn't. And you wouldn't want her along. You might get yourself a face full of whiskey, and a kick in the head for the company you keep."

"I'm pretty good at taking care of myself," Ed said shortly to Arlene. "And I choose my own company." To Cassie he said, "Don't worry. Just come along. Try me."

She shrugged, walked across the terrace to where Mike had stopped the car. She hoped Arlene would have second thoughts about her projected trip to town. Arlene was, Cassie knew, no more likely to have a comfortable welcome in town than she was herself, perhaps even less likely.

Mike, getting out of the car, grinned at her. "You look as if you're glad to see me," he said.

"I am. It gave me an excuse to walk away from the drinking party on the terrace. Arlene's back, as you can see, and full of beans."

Mike pulled a long sad face. "Oh. Is that what it is? I hoped, for a minute, that all that joy was for me myself." But his woe was exaggerated, and his eyes were smiling.

She said lightly, "Of course it was for you, Mike." Then, "The room is all set. Why don't you take your stuff up?"

"I will. But later. Right now I want to sit in on the party. Just for a few minutes. How about joining me?"

"Do as you like," Cassie told him. "But I've had enough of it. I'm going to collect Dell from Jim Hooten, and take him for a swim in the pool."

"I'll join you pretty soon," Mike told her.

But he didn't.

The party on the terrace went on until dark, and then it adjourned to a car and roared off to town.

Chapter 35

Mark's dark hair was disheveled from the many times he had nervously run his fingers through it. He repeated the gesture once again as he limped to the window and peered past the glow of the brass lamps to the shadowy darkness beyond.

Delaney, observing through bloodshot eyes, laughed malevolently. "You won't bring her back by watching for her."

"They'll be along any time now," Cassie said quickly, repressing a sigh.

It seemed that they had been waiting hours for the others to return, pretending that they were watching television. Now the pretense was dismissed.

Mark answered, "Sure. I know they'll be back soon." He turned to give Cassie a false grin. "You understand, don't you, Cass? She's been tied down for so long, pregnant and all. And she's young. So alive. She needs some diversion."

"You'd think the baby would be adequate diversion," Delaney retorted.

"He's okay," Mark said quickly. "Mrs. Abel's got the formula all fixed up. And she'll hear from him when he's ready for it. Arlene wouldn't have gone out if she wasn't sure of that."

Delaney ignored the defense. He said, "As for being

328

young . . . Well, she's twenty-one years old. Exactly the same age that you are. That's adult enough to be a parent. It ought to be adult enough to act like one, too."

"But I've always been old," Mark said slowly. He glanced down at his bad leg, with lines suddenly showing in his face.

In a thick, heavy voice, Delaney said, "You were a fool to marry her. For whatever reason. A fool to bring her here. And even more of a fool to keep her here."

"But she *wants* to live in Moorhaven," Mark cried. "Do you think I'd care? I'd go anywhere. Anywhere at all for her. This is where she wants to be."

Delaney didn't answer. He took the whiskey decanter, and a glass with it, from the table beside him. He rose and walked out of the room.

Mark, flushed with anger, burst out, "He doesn't even care about the baby. I thought it would be different. I thought he'd be glad, proud. What's the matter with him, Cass?"

Cassie didn't answer him. She didn't know how Mark could have deceived himself with such an impossible hope. Delaney had made it quite plain from the first moment he met Arlene that he disapproved of her, and violently disliked her. He treated her with minimum courtesy and maximum indifference.

Arlene responded in kind, but Cassie wasn't sure the girl would have been different if she had been welcomed with open arms. She was arrogant, gleeful, and flauntingly triumphant. She knew her power over Mark, and delighted in proving it over and over again. The escapade this evening with Ed and Hank and Mike was a perfect example.

Mark said, "He's determined to break us up, Cass. He'll do anything he can to accomplish it."

"Oh, no, he won't, Mark. It'll get better. I'm sure that gradually, given time, he'll begin to accept her."

Even as she said the words she knew she was lying. It wasn't just Arlene herself, however obnoxious she was. It was that she was a Jones. Mary had put it in the

simplest of terms. Arlene Jones was Tembley's hatred
for the Moorhavens. That was what Delaney felt. It
made no sense to Cassie. All those things that had
happened so long ago . . . how could they matter now?
The past was dead and gone, she told herself. But she
knew at the same time that somehow the past still
lived. She had seen it in the eyes of those teen-agers
who had taunted Dell. She saw it every time she walked
into the Tembley post office.

Mark laughed briefly. "You know Delaney won't
ever accept her. It's just wishful thinking. You're almost as bad as I am." Then, slowly, he went on, "But I
need her, Cass. More than you can imagine. I've always
been alone."

Cassie kept herself from looking toward him, from
allowing her face to show what she was thinking.

But Mark went on, expressing what she had held
back. "And I'm alone now, too, of course."

"But you have a son to be proud of, Mark."

"Yes. That's true. Only he can't take the place of
Arlene. How could he?" His face grew even more
flushed. He turned his back, peered out the window
again.

Cassie wondered if he were concealing tears.

He said, "Did I ever tell you how I first met her?"
He didn't wait for an answer. He went on, his voice a
hoarse whisper. "It was just about a year ago. A few
weeks after the Fourth of July. I was fed up. It seemed
as if Moorhaven was a prison, and I would never
escape it. I began to think I was going crazy, Cass. I
kept imagining I heard whispers in the night. I found
myself listening to the silence and hearing sounds that
weren't there. It seemed as if every little thing in the
house was trying to tell me something. I mean things
that I've seen all my life . . . the pewter candlesticks . . .
the music box . . . the Spanish shawl in Delaney's office
. . . When I touched those things, I sensed a secret
offering itself. I couldn't stand it after a while. So one
night I went in to town, thinking I'd visit the Van
Nuys. Then I changed my mind. I decided to stop

somewhere for a drink. I parked in one of the back lots. A bunch of kids started lobbing firecrackers at me. You know, for a minute, I thought they were shooting." He gave a wry grin. "It scared me, Cass. I just froze there. Arlene pulled up in that jalopy she had. She jumped out and gave them the devil." Again he grinned wryly. "She can. As you know. Only you don't know the half of it. Arlene speaks a language neither of us ever learned. I guess maybe she grew up with it. Anyhow, she ran the kids off, and slipped her hand under my arm and told me I looked like I could stand a drink. I didn't know her name, or anything about her then. Except that she waited tables in that joint. And when I did know I didn't care."

Cassie swallowed hard against the lump that had risen in her throat. She found that her fingers were clutching the locket she wore under her dress. She didn't want to hear any more. She was afraid that she would break down and weep if she did. And she knew that she musn't weep for Mark.

She yawned deliberately, looked at her watch. "Well, it'll be okay," she said. And then, "It's pretty late. We ought to turn in."

"I'll wait for a little while longer."

But she decided not to. She didn't want to be sitting before the blinking television set in the empty room when Mike returned. And she suddenly found herself wondering why, if he were so enamored of Tembley, he hadn't found a room there, instead of inviting himself to live at Moorhaven.

It was much later when she heard Mark go limping past her door on his way up to the third floor. She knew his step, the thud, the faint hesitation while he shifted weight, the lighter sound of his good leg. It seemed to take him a long time to negotiate the second flight. She supposed he was pausing to listen between each step. To listen for the sound of Arlene returning.

Cassie hoped he wouldn't have to listen much longer. She finished brushing her hair, then turned away from the mirror. It was an old one, framed in gilt plaster roses. It reminded her of what Mark had said earlier. He had felt as if the old things in the house were whispering to him. It had frightened her to hear him say that. To know that he, too, had had the same feelings about Moorhaven.

She switched off the light, curled in the easy chair near the window. She was still there when, much later, she heard the rumble of deep laughter on the path below, and Arlene's shrill giggle. After a few minutes, she heard a splash that she instantly recognized.

The beach ball that Dell had been playing with that afternoon had been thrown in the pool.

She straightened up, waiting. The second splash was that of a body cleaving the water in a flat dive. One of the men had decided to take a swim, she supposed.

Then, clearly, on the warm air, Arlene's words floated up to her. "Hey, be careful. Don't wake up the old man."

"Mark?" It was Ed's voice. "Oh, come on, he's dead to the world by now."

"Not Mark, you dope. I can handle him any time. No, no. I mean his father. He wanders around half the night. And that's all we need. For him to come out right now. He's been waiting to get something on me ever since I came here. And if he can he will. And I'm not about to let that happen."

There was another ripple of laughter, a whisper, then silence.

Cassie rose, retreated from the window. She crawled into her fourposter bed. It was a long time before she fell asleep.

The morning sun was golden, filtering through the yellow curtains of the breakfast room.

Cassie watched the dance of dust motes in the light, and sipped her coffee.

"Let me ask you something," Ed said seriously. "And don't think I'm prying. That's not my intention. But I couldn't help but notice, and wonder about it. So I thought maybe you could enlighten me."

He was wearing his green fatigues again, with the collar unbuttoned, and a wedge of black curly hair showed at his throat. His lean face had shadows under the eyes, making him look older this morning.

He was an attractive enough man, Cassie thought, and she wondered what it was about him that made her feel so uncomfortable.

"Enlighten you about what?" she asked, concealing her discomfort.

"About Arlene."

Cassie raised her brows.

"Last night," Ed said. "When we went into town, well, it was really pretty funny. Arlene said she was a native. Knew every spot, and every soul in every spot. But you know, it was obvious that if they knew her, they didn't want to."

Cassie didn't answer.

"I'm the sort of a guy who doesn't look for trouble, but if it comes I figure I can handle it. Still, last night was peculiar. There we sat, the four of us in a booth, and the center of every pair of eyes in the place. Arlene acted as if she didn't notice. But nobody said hello to her, and nobody said goodbye. And if looks could have killed, then you wouldn't have a sister-in-law any more. She'd have been dead, and the rest of us along with her."

Cassie made no comment.

Ed went on, "Mike talked to a couple of people, and they answered. But it was a noticeably hostile atmosphere." A wide grin softened his hard face momentarily. "The thing is, I was wondering. Was it us? Hank and me. Because we were with her? Or was it Arlene herself?"

"Neither," Cassie said finally. "It's Moorhaven. Tembley doesn't like us. Nor our house."

"Why not?"

She shrugged. "Oh, it's ancient history. I don't even know the whole story myself. And I don't care about it either. It's just something that is, and always has been. We don't pay any attention to it."

"Then you've got to have a pretty thick hide."

"It helps," she agreed, thinking of Mark.

"Now Mike," Ed said, "he's a pretty good guy. Is he yours?"

"Oh, no," Cassie said quickly. "I told you. An old friend. A good friend."

"Fine." Ed grinned. "I've been wondering about that, too."

Dell peered around the edge of the door, smiling hopefully.

"Come on in," Cassie said. "Breakfast for you, Dell."

He came in, slipped into the chair closest to Cassie. "Juice, Cassie."

"It's coming. Did you have a good sleep?"

"Good sleep," Dell answered, and smiled happily.

"You should have come along with us last night," Ed continued as if there had been no interruption. "I mean, even though the air was pretty strained, we had a good time. But it would have been better, for me, if you'd been along."

She smiled at Ed, then rose. "I'll get your juice, Dell."

She was at the door when he suddenly cried, "Cassie!" and came shambling after her.

"Hey," she said. "What's the matter? I'm just getting your orange juice. You wait at the table. Okay?"

But he wrapped his fingers around a fold of her skirt, and pushed himself against her.

Ed said, "I guess he's not used to me yet."

She nodded, and followed by Dell, she went into the kitchen.

Mrs. Abel was preparing a tray with a glass of juice, a bowl of cereal, and a glass of milk. She passed the tray to Cassie, and turned back to the stove.

Cassie started for the breakfast room, but Dell hung back, insisting he wanted to eat at the kitchen table.

"Leave him," Mrs. Abel said, "I'll keep an eye on him."

"But he always eats with me in the breakfast room," Cassie said. "What's wrong with you, Dell?"

His green eyes went to the door, the brightness faded from his face.

She knew what that meant. Dell didn't like Ed, or he expected that Arlene would soon be down.

She patted his hand, and left him to his meal.

Ed was still at the table, sipping coffee. He asked, "Isn't the kid going to eat?"

"Inside," she said briefly.

"You've got your hands full with him, haven't you? It surprises me that a girl like you would tie herself down with her brother."

"Why not?"

"Because most girls your age, as good-looking as you, with your kind of money, could do anything." He grinned at her. "How's that for reasons?"

She didn't answer him.

After a moment, with his grin gone, he said thoughtfully, "You know, Cassie, I get the funniest feeling about this place. I was telling Hank about it, but he just laughs at me."

"What kind of a feeling?" she asked, interested in spite of herself.

"It's like when you walk into a room full of people, and they all stop talking when they see you." He chuckled. "Secrets. Do you know what I mean?"

"Oh, yes," she answered. "I know just what you mean."

It was that conversation, as well as what had happened the night before near the pool that led her to search for Delaney.

She found him in his office. He was leaning back in his chair, his face toward the window. She thought, at first, that he was sleeping. His finely-cut mouth was relaxed, his eyes closed. But as she hesitated, he sighed, turned to look at her.

She perched on the corner of the desk, swinging one sneaker-clad foot. "Have Hank and Ed said any more about moving on?"

"Not yet."

"Don't you think you ought to talk to Hank then?"

"Why should I?"

She hesitated, not quite knowing how to put her unease into words. Finally she said, "We've got our hands full as it is. I just don't see . . ."

Delaney cut in, "But Hank's a Moorhaven. We can't turn him out, Cassie."

"I don't see why not."

Delaney shrugged. "Why not just leave it to me? Maybe I have reasons . . ."

"What reasons?" she asked quickly.

He gave her a faint smile. "My reasons," he answered, and then would say nothing more.

Cassie sat in her room, listening to the stillness. Its oppressive quality weighed on her spirits, sapping her strength. She yawned over the book in her lap, and leaned back, closing her eyes.

In the two weeks that had passed since Mike had moved in, she had seen surprisingly little of him. He spent his mornings pecking away at his typewriter. He spent his afternoons with Ed and Hank. He spent his evenings with them and Arlene.

But if she had seen little of Mike, she had seen too much of Ed. Though he seemed always to be occupied with Hank and Arlene, in odd moments, he managed to corner Cassie. He sought her out most often when she was alone, or with Dell, and seemed to enjoy asking her about Moorhaven, its history and its occupants. She knew little about it, having taken it for granted all her life. And what she did know she considered too dull to repeat. Thus their conversations always ended in fencing matches, with him pursuing a subject that she evaded. When they came to a stop, because there was nowhere to go, he would tell her how pretty she was, and that it was a shame for her prettiness to be wasted at Moorhaven when she could do whatever she wanted with her life.

Hank still had not mentioned leaving, and Ed never said anything about it either. She felt that she couldn't ask directly, lest her query be taken as a hint that she felt they were not welcome. Such a move was her father's prerogative. But he had said he had his reasons for doing nothing, and he did nothing. She wondered if his reasons were simply that he enjoyed Hank and Ed. He spent hours drinking with them on the terrace until Arlene appeared. Then, no matter how much laughter there had been, he immediately withdrew, glowering if he was still sober, muttering under his breath, if he was not. He muttered more often than he glowered, Cassie had been sorry to notice.

She stirred restlessly in her chair.

She reminded herself that she had never allowed herself to believe in intuition. From her earliest youth she had always insisted on the solid, the real, the factual. She had had to. In self-defense. For she had always, as far back as she could remember, been hag-ridden by Moorhaven. If she had allowed herself to believe in the feeling of doom, in the feeling that evil lurked in the shadows, she would have gone mad long ago. But now Mary's warnings rang in her ears. Mark, too, had had these strange thoughts. And even Ed . . .

Cassie's pulses began to beat too quickly. She didn't believe, but a vague uneasiness came over her.

She got to her feet and went to the window. She looked down on the terrace, and at Jonathan's wing.

It was empty, still.

Delaney had closed it after Dorinda's death, and moved back into the house. It had not been used since, although Arlene had hinted, and then demanded, that she and Mark take it over, and laughed when Delaney informed her that Jonathan's wing was haunted, and that if she slept there one night she'd never sleep there again.

Now Cassie thought it really did look haunted. The windows were shuttered. The long stone wall was striped with shadows. Then one of the shadows moved.

It separated itself from the others and silently slid away.

She watched it until it disappeared into the dark.

She supposed it was Delaney, taking one of his midnight walks. But Delaney, by that hour, was rarely so quiet, so stealthy. Then she began to wonder if it had been Dell. For he, too, sometimes woke in the night and slipped out of the house. Dell, like Delaney, however, was never careful to make no sound.

Uneasiness spurred her. She went into the hall, then down to Dell's room. She gently opened his door and peered in. He slept soundly, his face turned toward the small lamp that always burned at his bedside.

She backed out, closed the door.

It was not Dell out there, then it must be Delaney.

She went to the head of the stairs, stepped to listen.

The house breathed and sighed around her. A place full of secrets, Ed had said. And he was right. Too many secrets. If these walls could speak they would tell all, explain. Perhaps they would banish the shadows forever. But the walls could not speak. And something had been lost with each generation. Some truth forgotten, some wickedness buried.

She told herself that she must return to her room, go to sleep. But the thought of her father, wandering about in the dark below, perhaps going down the shell path towards the marshes, was too much for her.

She went down the steps, and through the dark vestibule under the gilt-framed family portraits. She stepped outside, into the pale light of the lamps, and looked around the terrace. It was empty.

She walked slowly to the corner of Jonathan's wing, and looked down the slope to the dike. Nothing moved there. She rounded the corner of the wing.

Then, as she hesitated, she heard a whisper of movement.

She called out, "Father? Is that you? Who's there?"

But no answer came out of the dark to reassure her.

She heard a faint splashing sound, a lapping, a rippling. She went directly to the pool, running now, filled with sudden terror.

And then, caught on the rim of the pool, hanging there, balanced but rocking on her feet, she stared at the moonlit water, and screamed.

Chapter 36

The sound tore the silence, and echoed back from the gray stone of the house and the cliff behind it.

Even as it faded away, there were running footsteps.

Mike burst from the darkness. "Cassie!"

"In the pool," she gasped, pointing with a hand that shook.

A shadow lay on the still water, a sprawled form floating on the faint silvery reflections.

Mike made some sound deep in his throat, kicked off his shoes, and dove into the pool.

Cassie waited, her hands clenched at her sides, fighting to retain her composure. She did not allow herself to think. She simply waited, overwhelmed by pained terror.

Mike disappeared for a few seconds. Then, suddenly rising from the water, he began to swim, towing the heavy shadow with him.

With her eyes fixed on him, Cassie was aware that Jim Hooten was running from the direction of the garage. She knew that the lights went on in the kitchen behind her, and the door slammed open. She heard Hank and Ed come out together.

"What's the matter?" Ed asked. "I heard you yell."

She nodded at the pool.

Ed squatted down at the edge, his arms out to receive Mike's burden.

Between the two of them, they managed to lift the heavy dripping shadow from the water.

They placed it on the concrete apron.

Mike climbed out, knelt and turned the body over.

Bloodshot eyes were open and staring. Mouth and nose ran gleaming rivulets.

It was Delaney, and he was dead.

Three days after Cassie found her father floating in the pool, he was buried beside Dorinda in the Tembley cemetery. Afterwards, with Mark trailing her, Arlene hanging on his arm, Cassie slowly walked from one headstone to another. Here lay the first Jonathan Moorhaven, shipbuilder, and beside him his wife, Janina. And here lay Cordelia next to the second Jonathan. The third Jonathan had been unmarried, and, like his brother Harris, lay alone. There were monuments for some who were not actually buried there. Dennis, who had died in Cuba, and young Denny, who had died in Guam. And others, so many others.

Dell tugged at Cassie's arm, whispered, "Cassie? Sad?"

She smiled reassuringly at him. "It's okay, Dell. We're going home now."

"Cassie cry?" he asked.

"No more," she said. "I'm through crying, Dell."

She walked slowly, Dell clinging to her arm, back to the car.

Settled inside, she slipped off her black straw hat. She took Dell's hand in hers. "It's going to be okay. Don't worry, Dell."

He nodded, but his mouth tucked down, and his childlike eyes narrowed when Arlene, followed by Mark, climbed in beside him.

"I'm glad it's over," Mark said.

"And so am I," Arlene agreed. "It's so depressing. Funerals, I mean. But now we can go home and forget

it. We don't have to think about bad things any more."
She twisted in her seat. "Are the others coming?"

"Hank and Ed are just waiting for us," Mark said.
"And here comes Mike with Mr. Kinney now."

"What's he doing here anyhow?" Arlene asked. "I
was amazed when he turned up." She blinked behind
her black veil. "I never knew he was such a good friend
of Delaney's."

Mark shrugged.

Cassie clung to Dell's hand. She tried not to listen to
Arlene. But she, too, was wondering why Mr. Kinney
had come to Moorhaven. It was the first visit of his she
could remember. In the past, Delaney had always gone
to Boston when there was something special to discuss.
But now . . .

Mike and Mr. Kinney got in, Mike behind the
wheel. He glanced back at Cassie, his amber eyes full
of concern. "You okay?"

She nodded, her throat too tight with held-back tears
for her to speak aloud.

He drove slowly out of the cemetery, followed by
Hank and Ed, then by Dr. Peter and his wife.

On Washington Avenue, a group of loitering men
looked up and stared as the three cars went by.

Arlene made a small sound, a repressed laugh or a
cough, then said, "Look at them, staring at us."

"It doesn't matter," Mark answered. But then, as if
he couldn't hold it back, he burst out, "Only they have
no reason to hate him. He opened the factory to help
them, and he kept it going as long as he could. It
wasn't his fault that he had to close it down."

"Tell them," Arlene jeered.

Mr. Kinney turned in his seat, tipped his white head
forward. "Cassie, we're going to have to have a talk.
Would it be convenient for you if we were to settle
down to it when we get back to the house?"

"Me?" she asked.

"Yes, Cassie, you."

She felt her heart shrink within her. What did Mr.
Kinney have to say to her? Why didn't he speak instead

to Mark. Mark would need his help, advice. She
wanted no part of Moorhaven, nor the responsibility
for the holdings that her grandfather had built up and
her father perpetuated.

She knew that Mark was looking her way, but didn't
raise her eyes to his, nor to Mr. Kinney either. She said,
"If it's necessary, we'll make time."

"I don't like hurrying you on such a day but I want
to get back to Boston this afternoon. So . . ."

"I understand."

But she didn't understand, nor did she want to. She
kept her eyes on her hand, linked with Dell, and
thought of Delaney.

Delaney . . . wandering about the grounds of Moorhaven, thinking thoughts she didn't dare imagine, driv-
en by memories that even his nightly drinking didn't
wash away. Delaney . . . who knew his way through the
property by night or day, eyes closed or open, falling
into the pool and drowning there.

Mr. Kinney sighed, "A terrible accident, of course.
But we must go on. There's the future. The past must
be forgotten."

Cassie didn't answer. She bit back the words that
rose to her lips.

Delaney's death had not been an accident. It could
not have been. He would never have fallen into the
pool. And if he had, his angry bellow would have been
heard half way to Tembley.

She told herself that she must be mistaken. She must
not give credence to the ugly whisper that she had
heard in her mind. It was, she told herself, an odd
feeling. One that she had tried all her life to outgrow.
She must not, in the grief over her father's death, allow
it to seize her.

Yet against rationality, against what appeared to be
fact, what Dr. Pete, the sheriff had agreed, she was
convinced that Delaney's death had not been an accident.

As the car left Tembley behind, sped along the narrow curving road back to Moorhaven, she allowed

herself, for the first time, to think through to the conclusion that must be faced.

If Delaney's death had not been an accident, then it must have been murder.

A shudder moved through her.

Dell shifted uneasily. "Cassie?"

She forced a smile for him. "It's okay, Dell."

"Then where's Da?"

"He's gone away," she said gently.

Arlene asked, "Do you suppose he knows what's going on? Does he realize that he's just lost his father?"

"You can tell that he knows something," Cassie answered.

"What you ought to do, Mark," Arlene went on, "now that your father's gone, is to send Dell away. There's plenty of good places for him. Where he'd be better off than he is now. Places for people like him, too."

"He's fine where he is," Mark said quickly.

"Fine, is he?" Arlene's forehead creased in an ugly frown. "Maybe he is. If you say so. But what about Jonesie? You ever think of that? Dell's . . . well, after all, let's face it. He's not right in the head, is he? Suppose he decides to hurt Jonesie? What would you do then?"

"He's never hurt anybody, or anything, in his life," Cassie said sharply. "Forget it. This is Dell's home. It will be his home as long as he lives and it stands."

Arlene sighed, leaned against Mark. "Somebody has to care about Jonesie," she said softly.

Cassie stopped listening. She was too angry to bear the sound of Arlene's voice, the import of her words.

Delaney had been murdered.

But by whom? Why?

How could she find out what had happened to her father? How could she avenge his death?

She glanced quickly at Mark.

Now he would be the head of Moorhaven. He would hold in his hands the power that the generations before had passed on to him.

Her heart seemed to climb into her throat. Had Mark, in a moment of anger, of mad anger, thrust his father into the pool, and run limping away from what he had done? Mark and Delaney had quarreled bitterly and repeatedly over Arlene. Had there been a last quarrel? One that had ended in death for Delaney, and terror for Mark?

She found it hard to accept. Mark was her younger brother. She had known him all her life. She had seen nothing in him to suggest possible violence.

But then she reminded herself that she had seen nothing in him that suggested that he would fall in love with Arlene, be controlled by his abject and hungry need for her.

And what of Arlene herself? Could Arlene have shoved Delaney into the pool? She had the wiry strength that would have made the physical act possible. And she had disliked Delaney because he so markedly disapproved of her. She had disliked him because he refused to respond to her charm or her whims. But was that reason enough to kill? Could it explain murder?

She thought of the two men riding in the car behind them. Hank and Ed. She couldn't understand why Delaney had seemed so enamored with their presence, why he enjoyed drinking with them, listening to their stories with rapt attention. When she had spoken to him a second time, about them, he had laughed and said, "Why not have them? Hank's your mother's nephew. He's as much a Moorhaven as you are. Why shouldn't he visit here for a while, if he wants to?"

"But why does he want to?" she'd asked.

Delaney's eyes hadn't quite met hers. "Most probably just marking time, Cassie. You ought to understand how it is. After being in Viet Nam, I think, they both need a while to readjust."

She'd said, "Oh, I understand that," but she noticed that he hadn't mentioned again that he had reasons for wanting them to stay on, and she had continued to wonder uneasily when they would leave.

She was wondering that now as the car rounded the last curve above Moorhaven.

The house looked the same as usual in the shadow of the cliff. The long slope down to the dike was a bright green, dotted with junipers and divided by the white shell path. The hump of the dike rose, brown and stony, weed-covered in some places, pitted and gullied in others. The marshes beyond it were streaked with sunlight. Overhead, the sky was a clear hot blue, and yet something dark seemed to lie over Moorhaven. Something heavy and still.

It was suddenly as if she saw not the house itself, the stone and wood and glass of which it was built, but beyond them to its basic spirit. And what she saw was terrible to behold. What she saw was death.

Dell whimpered suddenly, "Home? Home, Cassie?"

She hugged him, and forced herself to look back at the house as Mike guided the car around the last curve, and then down into the driveway.

Once again, she was swept by a strange reluctance to return. Now she saw that the big black door was opening slowly. She held her breath.

Mrs. Abel stepped outside, followed by Jim Hooten.

Cassie let her breath out again. She didn't know what she had been expecting, what she had imagined would be waiting on the stone steps between the brass lamps.

But Mrs. Abel and Jim Hooten were normalcy, and good sense. They were waiting only to welcome the funeral party back, to offer a cold lunch and tea.

Mike stopped at the foot of the terrace. Arlene, Mark and Mr. Kinney followed Cassie and Dell out of the car, and then Mike drove on to the garages, trailed by Hank and Ed, and by the Van Nuys' car.

"All right?" Mrs. Abel asked Cassie.

She nodded.

"I've a bite in the dining room. If you'll send everyone in there ... Just a buffet, Cassie. People need a little something at a time like this."

Cassie said, "Thanks, Mrs. Abel. I'll see that every-

one goes in." She dropped her straw hat on the big
table in the vestibule, and then paused at the door,
waiting for the others, with Dell still clinging to her.

Jim Hooten asked, "Want me to take Dell for a bit?
We could have a climb on the cliff. It would do him
good, Cassie."

"Oh, yes, Jim, thanks," she said, smiling gratefully.
"I'm going to be busy for a while." And to Dell, "You
go with Jim. Okay, Dell?"

He didn't answer. He was staring down the steps to
where Mark and Arlene were standing, talking earnestly. His mouth twitched, and he pressed close to Cassie.

"With Jim?" she asked. "To go climbing?"

"Come on, boy." Jim grinned, put out his hand.

Dell carefully released his grip on Cassie's fingers,
transferred his hand to Jim's. "I go," he said, but he
was still watching Mark and Arlene.

Mr. Kinney accepted a sandwich of thinly sliced
ham, and a glass of ice tea. He stood at the window,
peering out at the slope while he ate.

Dr. Pete said, "It's a sad day, Cassie. Your father
was still a young man. Though fifty-seven mightn't
seem that to you now."

Cassie nodded, but didn't answer. She let her eyes
travel around the room.

Hank. Ed. Mike. Arlene. Mark. They had all been
here, here at Moorhaven, the night Delaney died.
Which one of them covered triumphant joy at murder
undiscovered? Which one of them, now that Delaney
was safely buried would believe their secret purpose
accomplished? Which one of them must be watched,
finally exposed?

Mr. Kinney said gently, "And now, Cassie, if you
don't mind . . ."

"Of course," she answered, and then blurted out,
"But why me? After all, I won't have anything to do
with it. I don't think . . ."

"But you will. You'll have everything to do with it,"
Mr. Kinney told her. "You're the heir of Moorhaven."

Chapter 37

A breathless silence followed those words.

The spell was broken when the cup that Cassie held danced in its saucer, making a faint tinkle of sound, and she turned to the table to put it down.

Hank pursed his lips in an ear-piercing whistle. Ed's eyes narrowed in amused surprise.

Mark's thin face went red, then white, and his shoulders slumped.

But Arlene cried shrilly, "Why, that nasty old fool! How could he do a thing like that to spite you, Mark?"

Mr. Kinney gave her an open look of dislike and disapproval. He said, "How extraordinary that you should entertain such an idea." His raised brows straightened, and his mouth thinned. "The will is one that Dorinda herself wrote originally. Delaney has been scarcely more than executor these past years."

"But I had no idea," Cassie said. "I ... we all always thought ... the oldest sons always ..."

"Perhaps that's what Dorinda, and then Delaney, too, wanted you to think." Mr. Kinney went to the door, "Now, Cassie, if you will ..."

She gave Mark a single beseeching look. He smiled at her faintly.

Relieved, she followed Mr. Kinney to her father's office.

She took the big chair behind the desk, uncomfortably aware that she had never sat there before. It was too large for her. Too large in many many ways, she thought.

Her eyes glanced toward the bookcases, the rows and rows of leather bindings that she had browsed through when she was younger, the Mark Twain with its mended cover, the Emily Dickinson.

Mr. Kinney seated himself across from her and folded one thin black-clad leg over the other. "I realize that this is a shock, Cassie."

"But why didn't my father tell me, warn me? Why didn't he prepare me?"

Mr. Kinney sighed. "I believe that he planned to. This summer. You must realize that he didn't expect to die. He was young enough to expect to live many more years. But I have reason, from what he said, to believe that he would, this summer, have begun to give you some idea of what's involved."

"And he waited too long," she said sadly.

"Perhaps. But perhaps he wanted to. I think he believed that your growing up years shouldn't be clouded by the expectation of heavy responsibilities. Or ..." He stopped himself. Then, "Well, never mind. There is one thing that I want you to understand quite clearly since you seem troubled, and your sister-in-law foolishly brought it up. You were in no way chosen over your brother Mark. And you must never think that. You were next in line, you see. Because of poor Dell."

"But Mr. Kinney, we always assumed that Mark, being the son, would ..."

"It was that way. In the beginning. Mr. Alderson tells me that the rule held in your grandfather's generation. After Dennis's death in Cuba, Ralphine was the oldest child. But your grandfather Jonathan inherited. Perhaps in those days a woman was not considered capable enough. In any event, it was changed in your parents' generation. Your father was an adopted son, you know. The holdings went to Dorinda, the oldest surviving child. And now, to you. And it will go to your oldest child, I am sure, whatever its sex. Is that clear?"

She nodded unhappily, noting how Mr. Kinney took for granted the fact that she would marry, have children. She thought of Mike then. A quick pain touched her. She told herself not to think of him. She asked, "What about Mark, Mr. Kinney?"

He raised his brows. "Oh, he has the income, of course. Just as all the Moorhavens have shared in the income for three generations now." He frowned suddenly. "Which somehow reminds me, Cassie. Your father had queried me about Hank Moorhaven. Dennis's son."

"Yes," she said. "We discussed it."

"His papers are quite in order, you know," Mr. Kinney said. "We have absolutely no reason to believe that he is not Henry Moorhaven."

She stared at Mr. Kinney blankly. "Is that what my father had suggested?"

"No. Not exactly. But he seemed rather . . . let's say curious about the boy's background."

"I see," Cassie murmured. "He never spoke about it to me." Now she found herself wondering if Hank had known of Delaney's curiosity. If Hank had guessed that Delaney was asking questions about him. And then she wondered what had made Delaney curious in the first place. Could Mary, before leaving, have spoken to him? Could she have said to him, 'I never knew Hank. But I knew Dennis. He always feared Moorhaven.'

Mr. Kinney went on, "How long does Hank intend to stay on at Moorhaven?"

She hesitated. "I don't really know. It hasn't been discussed. Perhaps now . . . with Delaney's death . . ."

She thought, but didn't say, that she would not suggest that Hank and Ed leave at once. She didn't want them to go. Not until she had the true facts of her father's death.

"You will continue to maintain this house, Cassie?"

"Of course." She stared at him, slanted green eyes widening. "It's home to me, to Dell, to Mark."

"Yes. Three generations of Moorhavens have lived here. But the world is different now. Help isn't easy to get, I understand. I thought, perhaps, that you would decide . . ."

"I might give it up. Some time." She shrugged uneasily. "But I don't have to think about that now. And I don't intend to. Not yet."

He nodded, made a tent of his fingers. "You have to decide only one thing, Cassie."

"And that is?"

"Aldersons have been handling Moorhaven affairs all these years. But you do have an option, you know. If you wish . . ."

She leaned back in the chair that was too big for her. Her face was pale above the black of her dress and under the gleaming chestnut of her hair. She said, "Mr. Kinney, you know . . . without your help . . . I couldn't . . . I don't have even the faintest idea . . ."

"Then we go on as we always have before. Is that it?"

"Of course," she said quickly. And then the thought struck her that it might be that Aldersons preferred to make some change. She added, "Unless, that is, you, the rest of you feel, that Moorhaven is no longer . . ."

"My dear child," he smiled, "set your mind at ease there. I felt that I had to, in honesty, point out that you are in no way obliged to continue with us. If you had suggested that you did not want to, however, we should have had a most vigorous discussion about it."

"I'm glad that's settled then." She waited. And finally, "But you must tell me exactly what I must do."

"Must do?" He smiled at her. "These things virtually run themselves. You are, at the moment, not directly involved in any business, you see. In your great-grandfather's day there were the shipyards. He sold them out, and your grandfather switched to land transport. Just before the Great Depression he sold out, lock, stock, and barrel. We invested in the best securi-

ties at the right time. Then Delaney built that factory in
Tembley. It was the only enterprise which we couldn't
consider successful. Because he refused to close in time.
But then, that didn't matter. The loss wasn't meaningful in our terms. You'll receive quarterly reports from
us. I want you to read them and understand them.
We'll have papers for you to sign on occasion. You
must read and understand those, too. If you have any
question at all, you must consult us."

"And?"

"And that's just about all, Cassie. Moorhaven holdings virtually run themselves at this point."

She sighed with relief. "Then I needn't have been so
afraid that I wouldn't be up to the task that my father
left me."

"No," Mr. Kinney agreed. "You need not have been
afraid of that, Cassie."

But there was something in his voice that suggested a
reservation, a train of thought which she was unable to
follow.

She was considering how to frame the question she
felt when he said, "Cassie, you know very little about
your family, don't you?"

"Little?" She raised her dark brows. "Why, I think I
know what there is to know. Or as much as anyone
knows about his family. After all, Cordelia and Jonathan lived here in this house, and built the wing. Both
my parents always lived here."

Mr. Kinney nodded his white head. Then, "I haven't
seen Mary about. Is she ill? I would have expected her
to be at the funeral, you know."

"She's in Boston with a friend. Mrs. Van Nuys. Dr.
Pete's mother."

"Oh? Is that so? I never thought that Mary would
allow herself to be retired from Moorhaven."

"It was more or less her idea. And not one that she
was overly happy with, I'm afraid," Cassie said. "She's
Arlene's great-aunt. Moorhaven just wasn't large
enough for both of them. Poor soul, it was hard for her
to decide what to do. After all, she raised us, and my

mother before us. But it was simply too difficult for
her. And, of course, she's quite old now. She couldn't
do very much, and that troubled her, if no one else."

"I see. But she knows of your father's death?"

"Of course. We notified her immediately. But I ad-
vised her not to come back for the funeral. I was
worried about her health, making the trip so soon
again. You see, she's barely settled. She only left a few
weeks ago. And what could she do here?"

"You were wise, I think. When I return to Boston,
I'll look in on her."

"I'd appreciate that, Mr. Kinney."

He got to his feet. "Do you have any other questions
now?"

She shook her head.

"The formal reading of the will can wait, can it
not?"

"Of course. It's up to you, Mr. Kinney."

"The necessary papers will be signed, filed, and so
on, immediately." He nodded, then said quietly, "I
hope you will consult me should anything arise to
trouble you, Cassie. We are all old friends, you know.
Try to remember that."

"I will," she promised. But even as she said the
words, she knew that she was already breaking that
promise. She had not told Mr. Kinney her suspicions
concerning her father's death. She had not told him of
her certainty that Delaney had died, not by accidental
drowning, but by evil design.

He gave her a last searching look before he went to
join the others in the drawing room.

Soon afterwards the Van Nuys drove him to the
station.

After she had waved him off, she retreated to the
office again. Mike found her there, looking out the window at the long slope that led to the dike and the
marshes beyond.

It was a view she had known all her life. She had
seen the marshes with the skim of winter ice glittering
between the stunted black trees, seen them gray and

heaving under spring skies, seen them glow like molten gold under summer sun, and seen them black and bottomless in autumn storms.

But now she looked at them through different eyes. The slope, the white shell path that led to the hump of the dike, the marshes themselves . . . They were Moorhaven.

She felt the weight of it on her shoulders.

With Delaney's death, the fear that she had known and fought all her life became reality . . .

From behind her, she heard, "Looking at your new domain, Cassie?"

Startled, she swung around.

Mike stood in the doorway. He had taken off his tie, unbuttoned his collar. He looked easy, relaxed.

She answered, "Not at my domain. At my headache. My responsibility. I don't know if I'm up to it, or want it."

"Then suppose you just walk away from it," he said, suddenly sober.

"I don't know what you mean."

"Of course you do. I mean simply send everybody away. Mark and Arlene can live wherever they want to. Hank and Ed don't belong here in any case. You take Dell, get yourself a nice apartment in Boston. You'll be near Mary and my grandmother. You'll be more in the center of things. This backwater has nothing to offer a girl like you. So, now that you're really your own boss, get out."

She stared at him thoughtfully. "I never knew you felt that way about Moorhaven, Mike."

"But I don't feel any way about it. Not for myself. I'm thinking about you."

"Me?"

"Yes, Cassie. You."

"But this is home," she said simply. "All other considerations aside, it remains that to me."

And it was true. The other considerations, her reluctance to return to Moorhaven, her dream that she would one day leave, were small compared to that fact.

"I know that," Mike was saying. "But home isn't necessarily the best of all possible places, Cassie. Song and story, notwithstanding. And Moorhaven . . ." He shrugged his wide shoulders.

She asked, "Are you thinking of what you've heard in Tembley? Is that what you're driving at?"

"In Tembley? Maybe. But just a little. It's what I've heard in my own family. And it isn't a particularly superstitious family, is it?"

She smiled. "One of the least of them, I should imagine."

"Right. And Dr. Peter always said that there was something unhealthy about Moorhaven. He never liked the site, nor the marshes. And that had nothing whatsoever to do with Tembley either."

"Tembley . . ." She tried to grin, but the muscles refused to respond. She looked down at her hands. "Mary told me a little about it. Her mother saying the sea would return . . . all the terrible things that happened to her . . . the way Mary and her brother quarreled . . ." She raised her eyes to Mike. "But that has nothing to do with Moorhaven. How could it?"

"I'm talking about something else entirely."

"And that is?"

He sighed. "Listen, Cassie, do you realize that every time Moorhaven has changed hands there's been death?"

She raised her brows, bewildered, questioning. "Of course. How else would anyone inherit, except from the dead?"

"Elena Moorhaven . . ." Mike's voice was very deep, slow. "You know who I mean, don't you?"

"That cool-looking blonde," Cassie said promptly. "Some kind of an aunt. I think she was the first Dennis Moorhaven's wife."

Mike nodded. "She was. And she was left when he died with two children. Lena and Sam."

"Yes, of course. I heard my mother speak of Lena. She ran off with a gangster or something, and got herself killed. I outraged my mother by saying I thought it was very romantic. To run off with a gang-ster, I mean."

"Elena was lost in the marshes. Did you know that?"

She said, "If I did know it, I've forgotten it, Mike."

"She was lost at the time that your grandparents married."

Cassie stared at him.

"And her son, Sam ... many years later ... he was lost in the marshes, too. That was just before your parents married, Cassie."

"Why are you bringing it up now, Mike? It's old old stuff. Who cares about it? What has it to do with me?"

"I don't know," he answered uneasily. "I was just thinking about it."

She eyed him curiously. Then, "Mike, what's really on your mind?"

"If you have to know, it's what I suggested before. Why don't you make a big change for this family? Why don't you just close up Moorhaven?"

"But why should I?" she demanded.

"So you can start out fresh and new, Cassie. With nothing hanging over you."

"But what's hanging over me?" she asked. "Or rather, what do you think is hanging over me?"

"Moorhaven," he said curtly. "The weight of it, the history of it. You know that as well as I do. You've been aware of it all your life."

It was true, of course. It had always been true, though she had always tried to avoid facing it. She had tried to pretend that she had no intuition of evil. But always she had had a sharp awareness of some strange quality in Moorhaven, the cliff behind the house, the heaving marshes. She had known that secrets hung on the still air, hidden in the ever-present shadows. She had always felt the burden of an invisible weight, press-ing against her, stifling ease and laughter and joy.

And now there was her certainty that Delaney had been murdered.

She drew a deep breath, and asked, "What do you think the burden is, Mike?"

"It doesn't matter. As long as you don't allow it to destroy you."

She suddenly found herself wondering what reason he could have for wanting her to leave Moorhaven. Was there some way he could benefit from her closing of the estate?

He was one of those that had been in the house when Delaney died. He had been the first to reach her side in fact. He had pulled the limp body from the pool.

Had he killed Delaney, and then, lurking near by, rushed out when he heard her scream?

Pain touched her, abrupt, unbearable.

No, no, not Mike. There was no reason for Mike to have killed Delaney.

She said quietly, "I don't have the faintest idea of what you're talking about. This is home to me, no more, no less. It won't harm me."

"I hope so," he said in an equally soft voice. "You may be right."

But she realized that there was no assurance in his tone.

From where she stood on the cliff, the marshes appeared to have been dyed a deep blood red, punctuated by the black gnarled silhouettes of the stunted trees.

The stone of the house was a faded pink, and the still air was a faint mauve.

Distance offered perspective. The house and dike and marshes were material, concrete. They had neither souls, nor secrets.

She smiled to herself, approving the insight. She had been wise to climb the cliff alone, to look down on Moorhaven. It was a good thing to clear away the cobwebs of intuition and imagination. Material things have no souls or secrets, she repeated to herself. She must have a clear head for what she was determined to do.

Now she swung away from the vista below her, and returned to the path that she had taken to this particular point. It was narrow, shaded by the giant blue spruces, and so overgrown that it was hard to follow in the fast-sinking mauve twilight.

She rounded a huge towering rock, then stopped suddenly, turning to look behind her. She thought that she had heard something. She didn't know what. Perhaps a bird rustling in the brush, perhaps a footfall. She peered into the hazy shadow of tree and falling night.

A quick, chopping blow sent her reeling.

She fell and rolled into absolute darkness.

Chapter 38

Nearby whimpering, and small frightened tugs, made her open her eyes, struggling through waves of pain to surface in confused bewilderment.

Dell crouched beside her, his head bent close to hers, his wide-open eyes regarding her with anxious pleading. "Cassie? Cassie sleep?"

She blinked at him. "Dell, what are you doing here?" And then, "Where's Jim, Dell?"

He looked over his shoulder into the shadows of the trees.

"Where's Jim?" she repeated.

"Cassie sleep?" Dell demanded, and his fingers brushed tentatively at her temple.

She winced, pulled away quickly, as pain became a great burst in her head. "No, Dell," she told him, "No. Don't touch now."

He made a small gasping sound, and got to his feet.

She looked up at him, realizing suddenly that he was a man. He had the mind of a child, but he was a man with a man's physical strength.

Jim suddenly came out of the shadows. "Dell. You Dell, where did you get to anyhow?"

"He's here," Cassie said, rising laboriously to her hands and knees, and then pushing herself to her feet. "He's here with me, Jim. What happened?"

Jim's outdoorsman's eyes examined her dirty and torn jeans and stained shirt. "Is something wrong?"

She didn't answer his question, but asked, "What happened?"

"What happened indeed? That's just what I'd like to know," Jim retorted.

Dell made a plaintive sound. Jim looked up and down the boy, then slowly smiled.

"Well, he looks all right," he said, in a voice heavy with relief. "You can't imagine what a couple of hours he's given me."

"What do you mean?"

"Why, he slipped off. It's the first time he's ever done a thing like that, Cassie. We were climbing on the trail. Him just behind me, the way we always do it. I stopped to light a cigarette, and when I looked back for him, he was gone. He stepped off the trail, and into the trees, and I couldn't see him. I heard him all right, and hollered out, thinking he'd be scared, and instead of coming to me, away he went. And what a chase he gave me. I'd hear him first on one trail, and then on another. I've been up and down and around until my bones fairly gave out. The truth is, I was about to come down for help, when I heard him, again, and . . ." Jim stopped suddenly. "Cassie! Is that blood on your face?"

She put her hand to her temple. "Just a little. I . . . I took a fall."

"A fall?" he repeated, frowning. "And how did you catch up with Dell?"

"I didn't. He found me."

Jim stared at her silently for a moment. Then he said, "Let's get you back to the house, and see just how bad that is."

"It isn't much."

Jim squinted at her. "It's enough," he said briefly. He put his hand out to Dell. "Come along, boy. Let's get Cassie home now."

Dell regarded him anxiously, then allowed himself to be led back to the trail.

They made their way down the cliff slowly, their footsteps echoing through the dark.

Cassie, her head thumping with each movement of her body, watched Dell, and wondered.

Someone, she was sure, had stood behind her in the shadows. Stood there, watching her, and then flung a stone at her. It had brought her down, stunned her into unconsciousness. When she had next opened her eyes, had been herself again, Dell had been squatting beside her.

Had he deliberately slipped away from Jim? Had he caught a glimpse of her through the trees, at the point, or on the path, and tried to catch up with her? Had he flung the stone to attract her attention, and then, seeing her fall, squatted beside her to whimper in fright?

Was it possible that Jim, usually so careful, hadn't really been able to find Dell immediately? Was it possible that he'd searched for two hours without coming upon him? Or had Jim simply slipped away from Dell, left him alone, and sent the stone through the air that brought Cassie down?

She shivered.

Delaney had died in the pool.

And she had just been attacked. A hand had reached at her from the shadows.

She remembered now those few moments before she left the house. Arlene and Mark, Hank and Ed, and Mike had been in the drawing room together.

Mike had seen her pass the door and called out to her. "Where are you going, Cassie?"

She'd paused to say she was going to take a walk on the cliff to clear her head. He'd invited himself along, but she'd told him she'd only be a few minutes, and hurried away.

So they had all known where she was going. Any one of them could have followed her.

Now her eyes went back to Dell. Could he have been responsible? And then on to Jim. Or Jim?

She was glad now that she hadn't told Jim what had really happened. It was better that no one know of the stone that had come suddenly out of the dark. She could already imagine what Arlene would say. Arlene who had begun to complain that Dell was not to be trusted. She would surely seize this incident and expand on it. And hurt Dell.

But Dell could not have been responsible, Cassie was sure, except by accident. That much she was sure of, if nothing else.

She imagined him seeing her through the trees, tossing a stone to surprise her.

That was when she realized with absolutely certainty that Dell had not struck her down. If he had, and seen her fall, he would have cried out. He would have rushed to her side. She would have heard him as she fell. She was certain that she would have heard him even as she spun into the black whirl of unconsciousness. But no. There had been nothing but that rustling in the trees that had made her turn. Dell must have come upon her as she lay there, and not knowing what else to do, had crouched down beside her.

Then who had been on the cliff? Who had stalked her through the twilight, watched her, and then attacked her, hoping to create an accident?

Another accident, she thought grimly.

Was it coincidence only that Dell, for the first time, had run away from Jim? Or was there some connection between the two events?

Jim, leading Dell, emerged from the trees, at the back of the house. Cassie followed them across the pool area, and around Jonathan's wing, to the terrace, where the brass lamps cast a pale yellow glow on the empty chairs.

She was glad that no one was there. That she would not have to face the others, to attempt to explain what could not be explained.

She said, "Jim, you needn't mention that I had a fall, you know."

His eyes narrowed. "Why not? What's there to hide about that?"

She shrugged, smiled stiffly. "It just makes me feel so silly."

"Well, it's up to you. But you'd better do something about that cut."

"Yes, I will." She took Dell's hand. "Come on. Mrs. Abel probably has your supper ready for you."

She led him inside, hoping that he had forgotten what had happened on the cliff by then.

But when Mike stepped out of the drawing room, Dell promptly said, "Cassie fell down."

Mike's face paled. "You're bleeding, Cass! What happened to you?"

"Nothing really," she said lightly. "I tripped over my own feet and bumped my head."

But he wouldn't allow it to be nothing. He led her into the kitchen, fussed with ice packs. Finally, he pressed a small patch into place on her temple.

She felt a thrill at the touch of his gentle fingers. She tried to ignore it, smiling, "I think you've wanted to be a doctor all along. Why did you make yourself give up what was obviously your true calling?"

But he refused to respond to her levity. He asked grimly, "Cass, how did it really happen?"

She had no intention of telling anyone, anyone at all, that there had been an attack on her.

First she must protect Dell against even the possibility of an accusation. She could imagine too easily Arlene's outraged remarks. Second she must trust no one. She must watch, wait. She must learn who could have been on the cliff, who had left the house in the past few hours, and tracked her silently through the trees.

"I've told you what happened," she told Mike. Then, "Where's everybody?"

"Arlene is upstairs, I guess. Getting ready for a big evening."

"Tonight?"

"She doesn't believe in phony mourning it seems," Mike shrugged.

"And Mark?"

"He's in the drawing room mixing drinks. The others

. . ." Mike grinned. "They went out exploring the marshes some time ago."

"What about you?" she asked.

"Me?" He raised his heavy brows. "I'm here. What do you mean?"

"How did you spend your late afternoon?"

He frowned at her. "What's that in aid of? Why all these questions?"

"I just wondered."

"Since you made it plain that you didn't want my company, I went up to my room for a while, and did some work."

"Did you get anything done?"

"Not much."

"Maybe this isn't the best place for you to work, Mike. You might well be better off in town."

"I might?" He was staring at her, his brows drawn in a frown. "Are you delicately trying to suggest that you want me to leave Moorhaven?"

"Oh, no," she protested. "Why would you think that?"

He grinned at her. "I think it's a reasonable suspicion, Cass."

She looked up at him, then glanced away. She said, "Not reasonable at all. The thought hadn't occurred to me."

He laughed softly. "That's good. Because, unless you throw me out bag, baggage and typewriter, I intend to stay on for a while." He paused a moment, then went on, with all laughter gone from his voice, "You might consider Hank and Ed though. Just what do they contribute here?"

"Not much," she said promptly.

"Then . . . ?"

"I'll make the decision when the time comes, Mike."

"There speaks the new mistress of Moorhaven."

She rose, touched her bandaged temple lightly. "Thanks for the first aid. Mrs. Abel will be calling us to dinner soon. I'd better have a shower and change."

He didn't answer her, but as she left him she knew that he was still staring at her, a question in his eyes.

As she climbed the broad staircase, she asked herself whether she could trust him. Her heart told her that she could. Everything that she felt toward him promised her that she could. Yet the sequence of events presented her with a series of ugly suspicions.

Mike had moved into Moorhaven very soon after Hank and Ed had turned up. He had been present when Delaney died. He had been at Moorhaven when the stone had come out of the foliage. He had said he had been working, but accomplished little.

The trouble was that the sequence of events not only presented her with suspicions, but with an explanation as well. Delaney had died, and she had become his heir. The mistress of Moorhaven, as Mike had just said. She had not known that she would be, nor had anyone else. All had assumed that Mark was next in line. Could Mark have argued with his father over Arlene, thrust him into the pool? Could he have deliberately allowed his father to drown? And then, finding himself not the master of Moorhaven after all, could he have decided that she, Cassie, must die? She tried to picture him limping quietly through the trees, climbing the rocky trails. But it was impossible. His crippled hip would never have allowed him to accomplish it.

Hank and Ed had been out of the house, exploring the marshes, Mike had said. They might have gone to the cliff instead. But they had absolutely no interest in Moorhaven that she could see. Hank's income would continue through Alderson, Alderson and Kinney no matter who was the Moorhaven heir. Neither of them would have any reason to move against her.

By the time she reached her room, showered, and changed into a dark blue pants suit, her head ached not only from the small cut on her temple, but from the pressure of the whirling questions that swirled through her mind.

She gave herself a final glance in the rose-framed

mirror. Her eyes were too bright, and her cheeks were
flushed with repressed excitement.

She stood very still. It seemed that the room was
suddenly filled with whispers of old voices that offered
wordless warning.

Somewhere in Moorhaven a murderer planned and
watched. Delaney had been killed.

And Cassie knew that she was the next victim.

Ed grinned at her. "I didn't expect this to happen,
Cassie," and added, "Not that I'm not delighted."

They were on the terrace together, looking toward
the road where the red taillights of the car winked
before disappearing around the curve of the cliff.

After dinner, Arlene had tossed her dark head and
said, "I can't take this grim atmosphere. I feel like a
night in town, and I'm going to have it. Who's game to
go with me?"

Cassie thought that Arlene simply could not resist
the need to lord it over Tembley, to drive in in the big
Moorhaven car, and walk arm in arm with Moorhavens, wearing dresses that had cost the equal of two
weeks' pay for most of the town men. She couldn't
resist telling the town that she had won Moorhaven and
escaped the stultifying life into which she had been
born. It was, Cassie considered, something of a shame
that Arlene couldn't relax and enjoy what she had, and
forget what she had escaped.

Mark's thin face was expressionless. "I can't go with
you, Arlene. Not tonight. You ought to know that."

She pouted, "Oh, that's just an excuse, and you know
it. All you want to do is sit and stare at the dike. I
didn't marry you to become a prisoner of this place."
She gave an exaggerated shiver. "I love it, of course.
But I feel something funny here. I need a respite from
it." She grinned at Hank. "You need a respite from it,
too, don't you?"

"I don't feel anything funny," he answered, with a
sidelong glance at Cassie that she caught and wondered
about, "but I'll be glad to go into Tembley with you.

Why not? I'm always for some music, some drinks, a couple of laughs."

"Oh, sure, there are lots of laughs in Tembley," Mark said.

"What about you, Cassie?" Ed asked.

"No thanks."

"Does your head hurt?"

She touched the bandage on her temple lightly. "Not really." She thought of Delaney. No, no, she couldn't go in to Tembley that night.

Ed said, "Then I'll stay and keep you company."

"Oh, that's not necessary," she protested, wondering against her will what Mike would do.

Finally he said, "I'll go along for the ride, Arlene."

Soon after he and Hank and Arlene drove off, Mark excused himself and went to his room. Cassie sat on the terrace with Ed.

Now he was saying, "As a matter of fact. I'm more than delighted. I figured Mike would insist on staying behind. Just to protect his proprietary interest in you."

Chapter 39

"Mike has no proprietary interest in me," Cassie retorted coldly, "as I've already told you."

His dark eyes narrowed with open amusement. "So you have. But I've noticed a few small things here and there."

She felt an odd sense of pleasure and a refusal to believe at the same time. It would be wonderfully exciting to think that Mike did care for her. But it would be impossible to allow. Then she found herself wondering suddenly why Ed was so insistent about some relationship between her and Mike. What difference could it make to him?

She said stiffly, "I don't know what few things you've noticed, but since we've known each other for years . . ."

"Childhood sweethearts and all that stuff?"

"Not sweethearts," she snapped. "Friends. Just friends."

"Good. I'm glad to hear it." Ed's grin flashed in his lean face. "That clears up part of it anyhow."

Cassie gave him a long deliberate look, but didn't answer him.

"The thing is," he went on casually, "for a young girl you've got an awful lot on your shoulders, haven't you?"

"I'm twenty-two," she told him. "That isn't exactly infantile."

Ed laughed aloud. "No, no. You're not infantile." His eyes moved over her, assessing her body openly. "I didn't mean that at all. I just meant that Moorhaven, the family, all of it, must be a great deal of responsibility. You need a good strong shoulder to lean on, don't you? Somebody who could help you."

She didn't answer him. She needed help all right, although not for the reasons he suggested, but she knew nowhere to turn to find it.

Ed lowered his voice to a whisper, "And let's face it, Cassie. Mike is really in a perfect position. You said it yourself. Childhood friends. Practically a member of the family. All that. Well, why shouldn't he try to move in on you now? When there's so much to gain, and nothing to lose."

She sat back in her chair and stared at him. She took a deep breath before she asked quietly, "Are you by any chance hinting that you believe Mike is interested in me because of Moorhaven?"

"Not exactly. I'm just pointing out to you that he could be." Still whispering, he went on, "And I want you to keep that firmly in mind."

She didn't point out to him that he himself could be as easily suspected of what he suggested Mike's motives were as Mike himself. Perhaps more easily. Since it was Ed, rather than Mike, who seemed now to be pursuing her.

"Anyhow," he said easily, "I'm glad to have a chance to be alone with you. I'd never try to cut into a relationship, to break it up, I mean. But your saying there isn't one makes me feel better about it. The only thing is, you don't make it easy for a man to try."

She raised her brows. "Why should I? When I'm not interested in the man."

He gave an exaggerated sigh. "I was afraid of that, Cassie. But what can a man do except hope?"

She decided that his frankness was a cover for something else. She didn't believe anything he said. Though

he had been open in his admiration for her, and seemed
to arrange to be with her as much as she allowed, she
knew that she wasn't his type and never would be. Any
more than Arlene was Mike's type. Then what was Ed's
real purpose in his pretense at candor?

She waited a moment, then deliberately changed the
subject. "Have you known Hank long?"

"Just since the Army. That's where we met. First in
a staging area, then . . ."

"Then you never knew my Uncle Dennis?"

"No," Ed said. "And from what I understand neither
did you."

"That's right. He left here when my parents married.
And never returned."

"That's funny," Ed mused. "Why not? Do you
know?"

"I don't know," Cassie said, thinking of Mary again.
Dennis had been afraid, afraid of Moorhaven. That was
what Mary had told her. Was Dennis' fear the same as
Cassie's own? Had he all his life felt the surging of
secrets around him?

"Ask Hank," Ed was saying. "He can probably tell
you."

"He seems to know remarkably little," Cassie answered.

"That's how it is. People don't tell their kids things,
you know. I expect that's one of the reasons Hank was
so curious about Moorhaven. I mean, he probably
thought it was funny, the family all here, and his
father, there, staying away, as if he were a black sheep,
or maybe not wanted around here for some reason."

"Do you suppose curiosity is what made him come
here?"

"Oh, we were just having a little trip," Ed said. "I
told you that. Or Hank did. And passing through. We
were figuring on riding out to Haight Ashbury, to have
a look at the flower children, but then he saw the
Tembley sign, so . . ."

"Just saw the sign," Cassie echoed.

"Sure," he laughed. "What else? That, and we

weren't trying to make a train, you know. And here was Hank's family. All he has in the world. You, Mark, Dell . . . just the three of you."

It should have been perfectly straightforward, but somehow, it didn't ring true. Later that evening, when she was alone, Cassie considered it further.

There was something about Hank Moorhaven that just wasn't right. About Ed, too.

The intuition in which she refused to believe was whispering to her. Certainly Mr. Kinney had done as he said, checked thoroughly to be sure that Hank Moorhaven was who he had said he was. Yet Mary had warned her about him. Mary had said Dennis would never have spoken of Moorhaven with longing. He had run away from it because he hated it. He had never returned because he hated it. Then Hank had lied about his father's feelings. If he had lied about that, he could have lied about everything else. Or . . . he simply might not have known Dennis' true feelings. He might not ever have known Dennis.

But if Hank hadn't known Dennis, then who was he? And who was Ed? What were they doing at Moorhaven?

Was it coincidence only that led to Delaney's death after Hank and Ed's arrival? Or had he learned something about them? Something they were determined must be kept concealed? Had they murdered Delaney for that reason?

The questions plagued her, kept her awake long after she went to bed. She heard Arlene come in, her heels making a quick muffled tattoo on the carpeted steps. She heard Hank's whisper, and Mike's. She thought tiredly that at last Mark would be able to sleep.

The house slowly settled into silence.

She shifted restlessly, punching her pillows in search of the comfort that continued to evade her.

Her temple throbbed beneath the bandage and itched at its edges.

Someone had sought to kill her on that cliff that

afternoon. She wondered when that someone would try again.

The dream was a familiar one. Many times before, since her early teens, she had struggled with it. She supposed that her mother had struggled through it, too. It was a natural by-product of unexpressed fear.

Dell was whimpering. He was alone, weeping, and there was no one to comfort him.

Cassie's throat was tight with tears. She went swiftly through the house, looking for him. She stood on the terrace and called his name. She . . .

The whimpering grew louder. She found herself sitting up in bed. It took her only a moment to realize that what she had thought was a dream was, in fact, reality. Dell was weeping in the night.

She grabbed her robe, belted it around her, and stepped out into the hallway.

Dell's sorry little cry was louder there, but still faint.

She hurried down the dark corridor to his room, and went inside quickly.

"Dell? Dell, it's Cassie. What's the matter?"

She saw by the light that always burned near his bed, that his sheets were thrown back. His bed was empty.

"Dell," she cried, suddenly frightened. "Dell? Where are you?"

She ran to the big wardrobe, jerked open the two mirror doors.

Dell was crouched in the bottom, hiding beneath a stack of clothes.

"Come out," she said softly.

He looked up at her, his tear-streaked face full of fright.

"What's wrong? Why are you hiding?"

His lips stuck out. He rocked back and forth.

She reached in, offering her hand. He took it, and she could feel his trembling. She squatted down and slid her arms around him. She held him tight, crooning,

"It's okay, Dell. Tell Cassie. Did you have a bad dream?"

But he wouldn't answer her, although, finally, she was able to draw him out, to lead him back to his bed.

It took her half an hour to quiet him, and by then, she was wide awake, but she knew no more of what had disturbed him than when she had first heard him cry out.

She sat with him until, still holding her hand, he finally dozed off, his trembling body slowly sinking into sleep, the wide fearful eyes closed. Then she gently disengaged her hand. She covered him, and tiptoed out.

The hallway was empty, dark. She walked toward her door. It was partly open, the room beyond now touched with the first pale glimmer of dawn.

She moved the door back, and had an odd impression of glinting brightness, and at the same instant, the whole of the room seemed to explode with glittering fragments and shattering noise.

She clung to the door frame, her knees weak, her breath caught in her throat.

There were shards of glass, sharp as daggers, within inches of her toes.

A curved bit of gold rose, its inner plaster showing, lay among the glinting slivers.

In the moment it took before the others came, she knew just what had happened in a series of pictures that went through her mind. A shadowy form went silently into Dell's room, moved quickly to frighten him in some way, perhaps only whispering in a disguised voice, perhaps touching him. Then when he crawled from bed whimpering to hide in the wardrobe, the shadowed figure withdrew, watched while Cassie went to see about him, then slipped down the hall to her room. There, in seconds, it lifted the mirror from its place over the dresser, balanced it on the partly open door and its frame, and slipped away.

She knew now that someone had tried to kill her once again.

Mike was the first to reach her. His thick brown hair

stood on end, his eyes were shadowed. He cried, "Cass, what happened?"

She pointed at the shattered mirror.

"I don't understand. What happened?"

She had no time to answer him.

Hank, then Ed, came bounding down the steps from the floor above. "It sounded as if the house was falling apart," Hank said.

"Or we had a fragging," Ed added. "It's a good thing this didn't land on your head, Cassie."

"But how did it get there?" Mike asked thoughtfully.

Arlene, yawning, stood on the steps. "What's going on? You woke up Jonesie. Why are you all standing around in the middle of the night? We've hardly been in bed for two hours." She stopped abruptly. She stared at the debris on the floor, then at Cassie. "Boy, this family. What a time to start re-arranging your room. I never thought you were as crazy as the rest of them, Cassie."

Mark brushed past Arlene, limped slowly down the steps. "Cassie, are you okay? Are you sure?"

She nodded. There was no use pretending any longer.

One of the people now surrounding her had deliberately set a death trap for her, just as a death trap had been set for her father.

She said wearily, "I'm all right. Dell was disturbed. I went to see what was the matter. When I came back, and started into my room, this is what happened."

It was utterly still for a moment. Her words seemed to echo back, like the ancient whispers, from the walls.

At last Arlene cried, "You really are crazy. What are you talking about? What happened?"

Mark said horsely, "Cassie . . . are you suggesting . . ."

Mike put a big hand on her shoulder. "Explain, won't you?"

But Hank was grinning. "Looks like Cassie had herself a little party while we were in town, Ed. What did you feed her anyhow?"

Ed frowned, "Don't look at me. I don't know anything about it. I was in bed where I belong, and asleep."

Cassie swallowed, shook her head. One of those questioning her now knew the truth. She stepped into her room, closed the door behind her.

She went carefully through the broken mirror on the floor, and sat down on the edge of her bed.

There was no need to explain. What had happened was as evident to her as to whoever had arranged it. No one else mattered.

She was to have died beneath the falling mirror when she returned to her room.

There were still voices outside her door, questioning and arguing voices. She ignored them, and finally, they receded. Silence fell.

She buried her face in her hands and wept.

"You," Ed said, "had better take it easy today." His eyes were narrowed on her face, watching her over the mug of coffee he held to his lips.

She raised her brows in a silent question.

"After yesterday, you ought to be careful."

She didn't answer him.

"You had a fall on the cliff, didn't you? And that's how you cut your head, even if you haven't said anything about it. And then, during the night, you had that crazy thing with the mirror."

Still she said nothing.

"Of course Arlene might be right, for a change. Maybe you were doing some furniture moving, and had a go at the mirror. But I doubt it. I think somebody pulled a kid's trick on you. Balancing that mirror on the door, and then when you opened it . . . pow! That's what I think."

"Interesting," she said softly. "And who do you think would have done that?"

"Maybe your brother. Oh, I don't mean Mark. I mean Dell. It's a kid's trick, see."

She didn't bother to point out that Dell was the only person in the house who couldn't have done it. He had been with her while the trap had been set. Only Dell had no opportunity. But any one of the others had had that opportunity. She wondered which one of them was hiding disappointment, which one was already preparing plans to try again.

"I'd not only take it easy if I were you," Ed went on, "but I'd be very careful, too. When people get a jinx on them, they've got to be careful."

She smiled faintly. "Thank you for the warning."

"Warning? I didn't mean it that way," he said quickly. "I only . . ."

"Is this a private conversation? Or can anybody join?" Hank's stocky form filled the doorway.

"Have a seat," Ed said. "We're discussing last night."

Hank sat down, poured himself coffee from the pot Cassie handed to him. "It was a funny thing to happen, but things like that do sometimes."

"Yes," she agreed.

Mrs. Abel brought in platters of toast, slices of baked ham, and scrambled eggs. She stood over Cassie, hesitating for a moment, then returned to the kitchen.

The men filled their plates, ate quickly and silently.

Cassie picked at her food without appetite. At last, she asked thoughtfully, "Hank, how can you find out where your father's paintings are stored?"

"I don't have any idea." He gave her a bewildered look. "Why? What difference does it make?"

"I was just wondering," she said. "But it would be nice if they could be returned to the family. To Moorhaven. I think he would have liked that."

"Sure he would, but who knows what was done with them?" Hank answered. Then he said quickly, "Ed, come in to town with me this morning. I've got a couple of things to do."

"Okay. As long as we get back early. I want a swim this afternoon. That pool is too good to go to waste."

Hank asked, "What about you, Cassie? Want to come?"

"No, thanks," she answered. "I've got a couple of things to do, too."

The first thing she would do, she decided, would wait until she had seen Ed and Hank drive away. Only until then, and not another minute longer.

Chapter 40

The voice speaking from the television screen was overly bright and smug, promising a cleaner wash. But Dell, staring at the sleek woman, didn't seem to object.

Cassie watched him for a moment, noting his tired eyes, the sudden tremors that shook his hands. Though he had on a clean shirt, and freshly-pressed blue trousers, he looked disheveled.

Someone had used him, once on the cliff, then again last night, used him and frightened him, making him the bait to lure her into danger.

Who could have been so cruel as to manipulate his pathetic vulnerability? Whose hate had created the plot which must surely damage him forever while it aimed to destroy her?

Anger fed the fear that burned through her. At all costs she must protect Dell. She must protect him, and live on to protect him. Because he had no one else to turn to.

She smiled at him when he looked up, yawning with sudden boredom. She said, "Do you want to watch more, or come with me to the kitchen?"

"Watch," he answered.

She nodded, and left him, thinking that he would be all right for a little while. Hank and Ed had gone to town. Arlene was still in her room. Mark was with

Jonesie, giving the infant the attention that his mother failed to give him. That, Cassie knew, was going to turn out to be a real problem. But she would face it later. Dell must come first.

Mrs. Abel was at the sink, washing the breakfast dishes, the transistor radio playing softly beside her. On the work table behind her, was a row of four pewter candlesticks, each holding a tall thick candle. She said, "I got them ready. In case the electricity goes. They said something about a storm. Alice, or Betty, or something like that, brewing down south."

"It'll probably swing out to sea," Cassie told her.

"Sure," Mrs. Abel agreed. "Only they've got storm warnings out from Nag's Head all the way up to Nova Scotia."

Cassie sighed. She had no interest in weather reports at the moment. She was about to put the first part of her plan into action. But she had no chance to speak.

Mrs. Abel asked, "Have you been into Jonathan's wing lately? Did you take the key from behind the door here?"

"No. Why? Is something the matter?"

"The key's gone. I don't know why I noticed it, it's not being used for so long, but I did."

"But who . . . ?"

"If I knew, I wouldn't be asking you, would I?"

"I'll have a look," Cassie said. Then, "Mrs. Abel, would you do something for me?"

"I will. If I can."

"When you're finished up here in the kitchen, I'd like you to pack some things and take Dell, and go into town to stay with Dr. Pete for a few days. Jim will drive you."

Mrs. Abel's lips tightened. "Take Dell, you say? For a few days? But what about you? How will you manage? This big house. All these people to feed. And the baby. Jonesie needs somebody. He's only had me, and his father. I'll give Mark that, he does keep an eye on the child, but still . . ."

"Arlene will just have to pitch in," Cassie said firmly.

Mrs. Abel gave a platter a vigorous swipe with a dish towel and then set it aside with an emphatic thump. "What's the matter, Cassie? Why are you sending Dell off like that?"

"I have my reasons."

"I know," Mrs. Abel retorted softly. "Which is why I'm asking."

Cassie hesitated. Then, "I don't like the way he looks. He seems ... well, he seems nervous. Something's bothering him, Mrs. Abel."

"Something's bothering him," the older woman repeated. She folded the dish towel carefully, hung it on a rod, then sank into a chair near the work table. She gestured to the one opposite. "Sit down for a minute, Cassie. I want to tell you, something's bothering me, too. And has been since your father died."

Cassie perched on the chair, as if ready to leap up. "Yes? What is it?"

Mrs. Abel folded her hands in her lap, and took a deep obvious breath. "It's as if history is repeating itself all over again, Cassie. History you don't even know about, and maybe I shouldn't tell you. I swore I wouldn't. I promised Mary on my mother's grave. But Cassie, it was a foolish oath to take. Only how would I know what would happen?"

"I don't understand," Cassie whispered, bewildered. But the collar of her yellow shirt seemed too tight. She reached up to loosen it, and her fingers touched the locket at her throat.

"Add it up," Mrs. Abel answered. "Your father died. Something is scaring Dell. Yesterday you came home from the cliff with that cut on your head and your face as white and hard as marble, too. This morning I found the broken mirror in your room. Oh, don't say no. Mike's told me what happened, and I know you could have been killed. Killed, Cassie. That's why you want me to take Dell away, isn't it? Because you're afraid for him. And I'll do it. Don't worry about that. But you must understand that this is a house bewitched."

"Mrs. Abel, no . . . no . . . you . . ."

"Bewitched," the older woman said firmly. "Or cursed."

Cassie forced herself to laugh. "Really, Mrs. Abel. This is 1966, how can you talk to me about curses. Why, it's . . ."

"Oh, I know how it sounds. Me, with my feet as solidly on the ground as anybody else, using that word to you. But use any word you want, only understand that it's true. Mary told me, and she knows. She's the only one left that does know, Cassie. It goes back a long way, three generations all told. In each one there has been evil, and death. And it all began when Moorhaven was built. The first Dennis died, and then his parents. Then Dennis' wife Elena was lost in the marshes. In the next generation, Jon died, then the old man Joshua, and then Harris was killed in the car accident on the cliff, and your cousin Sam went into the marshes, too, and never came back. And now . . ."

Cassie leaned forward tensely, "But Mrs. Abel, it's mad to believe . . ."

"If it's mad then I'm mad. And so is Mary. For she *does* believe there's a curse on this house."

Cassie rose, and a prickling ran up her spine. Murder in three generations? Was that what Mary, what Mrs. Abel, asked her to accept? Murder repeated, then hidden. It was hard to believe, yet she knew that she had twice been a hoped-for victim.

She said, "Well, never mind all that. You'll get Dell ready as soon as you can?"

"I will. But we can't never mind. I want you to come with us, Cassie."

She shook her head. "I can't leave Moorhaven."

"Some day you will. Some day you'll have to, Cassie."

"No, not now. Not some day either," she answered. But, oddly, the suggestion afforded her a certain sense of relief. She had once wanted to escape Moorhaven. Mrs. Abel was promising her that she would. In spite

of her denial, she knew that was still what she wished
for.

Mrs. Abel said insistently, "But you will, Cassie.
That's part of it. The end of Moorhaven."

The end of Moorhaven, Cassie thought.

What was it that Mary had said? The sea would
return. The sea . . .

She went into the hallway. The television set still
murmured softly at Dell, but she saw that he was
dozing when she looked into the morning room.

She passed down the corridor, into the vestibule, and
stopped to look up at the portraits that hung there.
Dennis, her grandfather's brother, in cavalry uniform.
Jonathan himself, with the scar on his forehead. Then
Cordelia, Harris, Elena . . . Had they all, in their own
ways, each been victim of the curse that lay over Moorhaven? Were they whispering to her now from beyond
the grave?

She forced the thought away and turned toward the
stairs. But then, after a brief hesitation, she went outside. The sky was faintly overcast. There was a hot
damp breeze blowing in from the marshes.

Mrs. Abel had said that the key to Jonathan's wing
was missing. It was important to know what had happened to it. Who had it. Why . . .

Both the front and back doors were locked, but
Cassie was able to unlatch the shiny black shutters. She
opened a window, and climbed through into the bedroom that had once been her mother's. She stood still,
looking around carefully. Nothing had been disturbed.
She went into the hallway, listening now, but hearing
nothing. When she examined the office, she knew why
the key had been stolen.

This room had been used. There was a ring on the
finish of the old well-polished desk, a ring left by a
glass. An ashtray was dirty. The sofa cushions were
wrinkled instead of plumped up. The rug showed scuff
marks. Mrs. Abel couldn't possibly have left the room
this way when the wing was closed.

But Cassie didn't know what it meant. She gave a

last look around, searching for a clue to whoever had been in this room, and remembering that, just moments before she had found her father in the pool, she had heard a sound nearby. A sound that could have come from this very place.

Finally, with a despairing sigh, she left the way she had come. She hurried into the house and up the steps.

She had spent more time with Mrs. Abel, more time in the wing, than she had meant to.

Hank's room was the same one that Dennis, his father, had once had. It was at the front of the house. She went to it, slipped inside.

The morning straightening up had already been done. The two beds were made, coverlets smoothed. The rug had been vacuumed, the heavy green velvet curtains drawn back.

It was hard to know where to begin, Cassie thought. But begin, she must. She examined the most obvious places only superficially, since, if he had something to hide, Hank would have made a real attempt to do so.

She was at the small kneehole desk under the big window, opening the drawers, when the heavy black shutters suddenly slammed shut.

She leaped with fright. Then, realizing what had happened, she very nearly laughed at herself.

She opened the big windows, forced the shutters back against the wind, then closed the windows again. Some papers had blown to the floor. She bent to pick them up, and noticed the edge of something hanging from the top of the kneehole in the desk. She got down on her hands and knees, and peered at it, then she carefully loosened the holding tape, and took it into her hands.

She opened the narrow white envelope carefully. Within it were army discharge papers and other identification papers. They were made out in the name of John Carroll. The description given easily fit Hank. There was also a blurred photograph of a slim young man in battle fatigues. Scrawled on the back of it was a single name. *Hank*.

What did these papers mean? Cassie asked herself. Was the Hank in the picture the real Hank? If so, where was he now? What had happened to him? And who was John Carroll?

Biting her lip, she read the papers again. John Carroll had been discharged in Boston, two months before. He was twenty-three, born in a small town in Maine. It just didn't make sense to her. She was so immersed in her thoughts that she didn't hear the sound of the door opening, the approaching footsteps. But suddenly a shadow fell over her.

She looked up. "Mike!"

"What are you doing in here?" he demanded.

She put the envelope behind her back. "I could ask the same of you."

"And I'll tell you. But first I want to know what you're hiding."

"Nothing," she retorted.

"Cass . . . please . . ." He put out his hand.

She shrank back from him. "Don't touch me, Mike."

He stared at her in disbelief, a flush on his cheeks, his eyes narrow and bright and hard as crystal. "You're afraid of me, aren't you?" he said slowly. "You're actually afraid of *me*."

She said, "You still haven't told me why you came into Hank's room."

He didn't answer her. He walked up to her, reached behind her back, and pulled the papers from her fingers.

Ignoring her angry protest, he scanned them quickly. He gave the photograph a single glance. Finally he said, "These are just what I was here for, Cass. To look for these."

"Then you've been wondering about Hank, too."

"Of course." He smiled faintly. "It was the main reason I moved out here, Cassie. Grandma Bettina got the word somehow, and passed it on to me, that Hank and Ed had been asking questions about the Moorhavens in Tembley. All kinds of funny questions. Before they came out here. Not after. Questions that it seemed to her, and to me as well, they wouldn't have needed to ask if Hank really was a Moorhaven. Now we both know that he's not. He's John Carroll, of course. The picture must be of the real Hank."

"But I don't see how . . ."

"Hank was listed as missing in Viet Nam, remember? Our Hank, John, told us that he and Ed had been captured, held prisoner for nine months, and then escaped. The odds are that the real Hank was with them, talked about Moorhaven, and then died. And when he died, John took his papers, passed himself off as Hank Moorhaven to the military, and then to Aldersons, and made his way here to see what good he could do for himself."

Her mouth tightened. She straightened her shoulders. "And then Delaney died," she said. "So soon after they came here."

"Yes," Mike said softly. "Which is just why we're not going to call them on this, not yet. We put this stuff back where you found it, and we wait."

He was so glib, so sure of himself. She found herself wondering if he had had that story ready about his suspicions of Hank and Ed just in case she had found him in this room. She wondered if he had some other motive for wanting to prove Hank and Ed impostors other than to protect her. She remembered what Ed had told her, and tried to imagine Mike plotting, and planning, and placing her life in danger. She couldn't. She just couldn't. Her mind could entertain the notion, but her heart would not believe it.

Then he said, "Cassie, come on. We're through here. I don't want them to find us, to think that we know this much of the truth anyway."

"But we don't know very much, do we?" she said.

"No." He took her hand, drew her with him. Out in the hall, he paused, said, "Not very much. But enough. You've been in danger ever since Delaney died, Cass. I've known it. That was another reason for my hanging around with them so much these past few days. With Arlene, and Hank, and Ed. It wasn't a particularly pleasant chore. But I had to find out as much about them as I could."

"And did you?"

"Just enough to whet my suspicions. Enough to make me frightened for you. That's why I told you to leave Moorhaven."

Was that why? she asked herself. Or had he had some other reason?

He went on, "And also to see that Arlene is less interested in her marriage than you'd expect her to be."

"What do you mean?" Cassie asked.

"She's a flirt," Mike retorted. "She loves to get men going, and going after her. Hank. Ed. Even me." He grinned wryly. "That's right, Cass. Even me."

"I should think you could adequately protect yourself," she said stiffly. "I haven't noticed that you tried so terribly hard to escape her wiles."

"I haven't. And I won't. Not until I know what's going on here," he answered grimly. "And you can think whatever you like about it."

She thought a great deal about it through the rest of the day.

The house was strangely, painfully, empty without Mrs. Abel and Dell.

Jim Hooten had returned, saying that Dell was content to remain with the Van Nuys, and that Mrs. Abel had been talking wildly about him keeping his eye on Cassie. He waited, blue eyes squinted hopefully, for some explanation of her remark, but received no answer. So he looked up at the sky and said that his bones told him a storm was coming from somewhere out of the south, and he'd better be sure that things were well secured.

Did Mike mean that he suspected Arlene was a conspirator along with Hank and Ed? That was the question she asked herself when Jim Hooten stamped off to do his chores. Did Mike mean that he thought Arlene and Mark were determined to kill her? Did he mean that he would do anything to unmask the source of the danger to her? Or had he simply been trying to divert her from seeing a truth too painful to consider? From seeing that it was he, he alone, who was determined to destroy her. Again her heart rejected the thought. But it could not force her mind to forget it.

She was alone, she told herself. She must trust no one. She must watch, wait. Hank was not a Moorhaven. He had come here only to enjoy what luxury he could while he collected from Alderson, Alderson and Kinney the inheritance that did not belong to him. Perhaps he had other plans as well, such as marrying her to Ed. Which would explain Ed's unwanted and persistent attentions.

Mark would inherit if she, Cassie, were to die. Mark and Arlene. And Mark could be twisted any way by Arlene's will. That had been obvious from the day of their marriage. Arlene had trapped him with a pregnancy, and gotten herself to Moorhaven. Perhaps she would stop at nothing, not even murder, to become its mistress.

At twilight, they all gathered on the terrace for drinks.

There was a strange bronze cast to the sky over the dike. The marshes were shadowed, uneasily heaving and straining against the black silhouettes of the stunted trees. The air was still and somehow ominous.

Mark, with Jonesie in a basket at his feet, said, "I hope Mrs. Abel will be back tomorrow, Cassie. I don't see how we can get along without her."

"Maybe she will be," Cassie answered.

Arlene yawned, and stretched. "Well, if she's not, my dear sister-in-law, then I'm going to be gone."

"Is that a threat or a promise?" Hank laughed.

"We'll work it out," Mark cut in quickly. "Meantime the baby's okay. He's doing fine."

"It's me, I'm worried about," she said. "Not him."

Once again Hank cut in, "We'll take turns with the baby, Arlene. Don't let him scare you."

She smoothed her black curls and burst into jeering

laughter. "What a bunch of squares you are. You thought I meant it, didn't you? Don't you worry, or wish for it either." She jumped to her feet, scooped the baby into her arms and cuddled him against her. "Nothing's going to happen to Jonesie. Nothing. You better be sure of that."

Chapter 41

It was as if in answer to her laughing words that the baby gave a loud choking cough.

She looked down at it. "Hey, what's that? Don't say he's allergic to his mama."

Mark rose, limped over to where she stood. He bent his dark head to peer into the baby's face. "Could he be catching cold? Can babies?"

"How do I know?" she demanded.

Cassie sighed. "Maybe it's this wind, Mark. Why don't you take him inside, and see if you can find the baby thermometer?"

Arlene gave Cassie a sideways glance, then sat down and picked up her empty glass. "I need a refill, Ed. The wind bothers me, too, I guess."

Mark hesitated, and Cassie rose.

"Come on," she told him. "I'll get it for you."

Indoors, beyond range of the hearing of those still outside, Mark muttered, "That's what Arlene should be doing. Coming in here to help me. Not you, Cassie."

She didn't answer him. She saw no need to involve herself in a discussion of Arlene's shortcomings. If she did, Mark would immediately begin to defend his wife. Cassie supposed that he had to, but knew that she lacked the patience to listen at that moment. There was too much on her mind now, too many questions to which she must find the answers.

They were in the baby's third-floor room when Mark said suddenly, "Cass, tell me the truth. Why did you send Mrs. Abel into town with Dell?"

"I thought he needed to get away for a little while, Mark."

"Away from what?" he persisted, holding the baby to him, and patting the small diapered bottom.

"From Moorhaven."

"But why? You still haven't told me why."

How much could she tell him? How much dare she trust him? It shamed her to look into her brother's face and feel that she must hide her terror from him. At her death, he would become master of Moorhaven. And there was something in the blood, something wicked that had shown itself over three generations. Mrs. Abel had told her, and Mary had hinted at it. She had sensed it in the whispering shadows all her life.

She drew a long shallow breath, said carefully, "Oh, Mark, you know how odd he's been behaving lately. So scared and uneasy. I just . . ."

"You think getting away would help?" Mark asked bitterly. "Nothing is going to change Dell. You know that."

"Nothing is going to change him, or hurt him either, if I can prevent it," she said firmly. "And that's why he's staying with the Van Nuys for a few days."

"You're scared for him," Mark said wonderingly. "That's what it is."

"Yes," she agreed.

She thought that if he had concentrated less on Arlene, and more on what was going on around him, he could have known it himself, known it before.

At that moment the baby gave a great hacking cough again, and when it had subsided, he burst into shrill laboring screams.

Mark gasped, "Cassie, what is it, do you think?"

"I think you'd better take him to Dr. Pete. And right now."

He looked as if he might argue, but then he grabbed

a blanket, a handful of diapers, and ran down the stairs.

Cassie hurried after him. But she paused and let Mark go ahead of her, when she saw Mike leave his second-floor room.

"What's up?" he asked.

She explained about Jonesie. Then asked, "You worked?"

He nodded. "Some," and grinned, "Don't start worrying about me, Cassie."

"No," she answered. "I just wondered where you were."

It was the truth, but she wished that she hadn't admitted it. She oughtn't to have told him that she wanted him under her eyes, where she could see him, know what he was doing. She felt the same about the others, of course.

He followed her down the steps, and out to the terrace.

Arlene was saying, "Why do you have to take him to Tembley?"

Mark answered, "Well, it's the cough. And I don't know what to do. I think you ought to come, too."

She tipped her head back, looked first at Mark then at Cassie. "Say, what are you two up to anyway?"

"Up to?" Mark demanded.

"Call Dr. Pete to come out here," she retorted. "If you really think it's necessary."

"No. I'm going."

"As you please." She sipped her drink, dark amused eyes on Cassie. "Tell you what, Mark. Give me a call when you get to town?"

"Oh, you don't mean that," Mark said disgustedly. "Jonesie is your son. Don't act that way."

"You just want to get me out of Moorhaven. You and that sister of yours," Arlene answered. "I can see right through the two of you. I suppose you cooked it up while you pretended to take the baby's temperature. But I'm not going to fall for it. You can't con me that way."

There was a brief silence.

Then Mark stalked away, his shoulders rigid.

Cassie sank into a chair, folded her hands in her lap.

Why did Arlene think that Cassie had been trying to get her to leave Moorhaven for a few hours? What made her suppose that it would be against her own interests to be away for a little while? Did Arlene think that Mark had finally decided to put his foot down, force her to give up her scatter-brained behavior? Did she think Mark was about to turn against her, and assert his rights as a man, as a husband?

And then Arlene sighed, said gloomily, "I guess I was wrong. I ought to go with him. It's just that he . . ." She jumped up. "Oh, he makes me so mad sometimes. He knows how I feel. It's one thing to go to Tembley for drinks, and laughs, not needing anything from any of them. But it's something else to go for help."

She fled after Mark, her red skirt billowing, and raced around the corner of Jonathan's wing, toward the garages.

Moments later, the car passed below the terrace.

Jim Hooten was driving. Arlene and Mark sat close together, their head bent over the baby.

"Now that's just what I like to see," Hank laughed. "A beautiful reconciliation scene."

"Mother love," Ed put in dryly. "You can't ever beat that."

Cassie glanced sideways at Mike.

He didn't appear to be listening to the others. He was leaning back, looking thoughtfully at the bronze horizon. "The weather," he said softly. "It's building."

"He's some doctor," Arlene pouted. "Of all the nerve I ever heard that takes the cake. We couldn't stay, he said. We couldn't help. And we'd only be in the way. Who'd want to stay in that dump of his if he didn't have to?" She shot an angry look at Mike. "Even if he is your father, he's a real stuffed shirt, and I don't know what else. As if I'd deliberately given the baby the croup."

"Dr. Pete didn't mean that, Arlene," Mark said tiredly. "It's just that there wasn't any place for us. You know how small the hospital is. Just those few beds. No real waiting room." Mark went on to Cassie. "Dr. Pete said it wasn't serious. But he wanted to watch him. So . . ." He shrugged.

Arlene smiled sourly, "So we're back and you can take your disappointment and choke on it, Cassie Moorhaven."

Mike said sharply, "Maybe you'd better explain yourself, Arlene. You came out with something foolish like that before you left, too."

"Oh, don't bother me," she shrugged. "I know how you feel. You're all against me. But it doesn't matter. It just doesn't matter, you see. Mark and I are married, and we're going to stay married. I'm a Moorhaven, for what it's worth, and I'm going to stay a Moorhaven."

"It's worth quite a bit," Mark retorted. "And don't you forget it."

Her face darkened ominously. "Are you threatening me?"

"Am I what?"

"Threatening me. That's what I said. And if you are, just forget it. I'm not afraid of you, Mark."

She looked from face to face, scowling in the heavy and embarrassed silence. Then she suddenly laughed, "Oh, what's the use? How come we're not one big happy family?"

No one answered her.

Hank whistled soundlessly between his teeth, and Ed grinned up at the darkening sky.

Mike got to his feet, stretched, then said casually, "I'll see if I can get the news on TV. Want to come, Cass?"

She went into the house with him, and flicked the switch for the two outside lights as she passed it.

Mike said, "I don't know how long Mark is going to put up with her after all."

"As long as she lets him," Cassie answered. "But he's burning inside. And ashamed, too."

Mike didn't answer. He turned the set on, then sat down to listen.

Hurricane Alice was swinging along the coast. Storm warnings from Nag's Head to Nova Scotia remained in force. Emergency driving conditions had been declared several miles south.

Cassie tried to concentrate on the news, but found that she could not. Her attention was centered wholly on Mike, on his hard-set profile, on the way the hair curled at the back of his head, on his lean hands resting on his knees.

Had he really moved out to Moorhaven because he suspected Hank and Ed from the beginning? Why had he urged her to leave? Why had he insisted that she delay unmasking Hank and Ed, and sending them away? Was he, as Ed had hinted, merely jealous of Ed, fearful that Ed, instead of himself, might gain Moorhaven through her?

She yearned to touch Mike, to lean against him, to confide her sense of growing terror.

It would have been easier to bear, she thought, if she didn't feel so alone. If she could trust him. If she could trust him above all others as she wished to.

But there were too many questions in her mind. She couldn't banish them. She mustn't allow cowardice to lead her into an error that could cost her her life.

Dell was gone from Moorhaven now. He was safe.

Jonesie was in Dr. Pete's hospital and would be well cared for.

Only Hank and Ed and Mark and Arlene and Mike were here with her. And among that group, there was one, perhaps two, who wanted to destroy her. One, or two, who must soon move again.

She knew that she could not bear the waiting much longer. She felt herself growing less strong and less sure. She must make certain that the attempt came soon. She must offer herself and be ready for the consequences, whatever they were.

Mike suddenly turned, looked at her. "What, Cassie?"

She shrugged, and smoothed the collar of her yellow shirt.

"You were staring at me, weren't you?"

She nodded.

After a moment, he got to his feet. "I'm going to make sure Jim has everything ready. It sounds as if it's going to be a good one."

"They're always good ones this time of year when they come, Mike."

"Yes. That's why it's better to be prepared. I notice Mrs. Abel thought so, too. She got out the candles before she left." He went to the door. "I don't know if you saw it this evening, with so much else going on on the terrace you might not have. But I had a good look at the marshes. It seemed to me they were rising."

"Tide," she answered. "Or maybe the wind."

"There wasn't all that much wind then, Cassie."

"Then it *is* the tides, I suppose."

He nodded, went out.

She remained where she was, with the television silent now, its blank face reflecting the faint glow of the light.

It seemed to her that the room was full of whispers again. Cordelia's voice, and Jonathan's. Her parents. Her uncles, cousins. Moorhavens. They all seemed to speak to her, those she had known and those she had never known, too.

At last, to evade them, she went into the kitchen to prepare supper.

Arlene had changed to black pants and a high-necked black pullover that hugged her small breasts. Her eyes were made up, her lips freshly painted. Now she raised her dark head, "What's that? That funny noise?"

It was while they were eating that the wind began a slow steady thrumming, and a sudden gust drove tapping fingers of rain against the glass.

"Storm," Hank said. "It's been building up all day and now it's here."

"We'd better see to the shutters," Mark said. He rose, limped slowly to the window.

Mike went to help him. Together they struggled to close the black shutters and hook them tight. When they were done, they left the room to secure the other windows.

Arlene suddenly shivered. "I wish I'd stayed in town after all."

"But you would have, if you could," Hank told her.

"You don't know anything about it," she snapped. "I could have gone to one of my brothers'."

But Cassie wondered. She knew of the estrangement that had occurred when Arlene married Mark. Would the Jones brothers have taken Arlene in?

Arlene said, giggling, "They're all ready to make up now. Now that I'm really married. And now that they see what I've got."

No one answered her.

She hurried on, "Well, you can guess how it looked to them at first. I mean, what they thought. But now they know different. So maybe that's what I should have done." Her eyes suddenly held a frightened, faraway look. "Yes. I never thought it would be like this. It sounds . . . it sounds so awful . . . It's never like this in Tembley . . ."

"It's too late now to be sorry," Hank told her. "And I'm glad you didn't stay in town. It looks as if this is going to be a long night. We're going to need all the company we can get."

Ed laughed. "Just what are you figuring on, Hank?"

"Some small amusement," Hank retorted. "Whatever we can find."

"Don't get your hopes up," Arlene warned him. "Moorhaven hasn't too much amusement to offer."

It was early when Cassie left the others.

With Mike, she had checked the doors of the house, making sure they were locked. She had seen to the distribution of candles, lest the lights should fail in the night.

Then Mike had gone to his room, to work on his book, he said.

But she wondered. He had seemed abstracted, restless. She wondered what he was planning, or if it was just the coming storm that had affected him.

Mark and Ed were playing chess, and Arlene and Hank were playing records, and dancing in the corner, whispering with their heads close together.

It was a relief to be alone at last, to step into the silence of her room, and close the door behind her.

She paused, looked back at it, then turned and locked it, too.

One of the five who had sat down to eat with her, one of those who had smiled at her, would be waiting for the opportunity to try again.

When she was removed, Mark would be the master of Moorhaven. And when he was, what then? Would he be struck down, too? Would Arlene inherit? Or did Hank hope to frighten Cassie into turning to Ed? Or did Mike hope to frighten her into leaving? Or . . .

She shuddered, feeling as if the pounding wind outside had forced itself inside her.

She turned off the lamp, lay down on the bed and closed her eyes.

She tried, at the same time, to turn off her thoughts. It was better to lie quietly, to rest. Soon now, her intuition told her, it would be over. It would be over and forgotten, very soon.

The sea will come to claim its own.

Silent words, whispering, like fluttering leaves in the invisible corridors of her mind.

The sea will come to claim its own.

Soft, familiar . . . the phrase spoke itself.

She had a picture in her mind of the marshes rising. Rising high against the dike, hurling themselves against the restraining wall that kept them from seizing Moorhaven.

Then, slowly, she sank into its darkness.

Chapter 42

Half awake and half asleep, conscious of the deep steady strumming of the wind, pictures formed in her mind.

She was very small, perhaps five. She wore a bright red raincoat, and a rimmed red hat, to protect her from the drizzle that slanted from the gray sky. She walked between her mother and father, each of her hands unpleasantly imprisoned between their larger ones. She wanted to hop and skip, and run ahead. But they held her back, locked her between them on the narrow path.

The marshes were gray, ruffled in places, and smooth in others. Black warped trees rose up against the sky.

"I remember," Dorinda was saying. "My father used to walk the dike every day. Particularly in August. I can see him now, limping slowly, with Joshua beside him. My mother used to tease him about his inspection tours." There had been a peculiar note in Dorinda's voice. "She didn't believe in it, of course."

" 'The sea will return to claim its own,' " Delaney said mockingly. "What delusions of grandeur, Dorie."

"But she didn't know," she answered. "No one really knows."

"Superstition. A crutch for weak minds," Delaney retorted.

Dorinda stopped, squeezed Cassie's hand. "But every

year the marsh nibbles away at the dike, and the marsh is fed by the sea, and . . . somewhere within it . . ."

Cassie felt the trembling in her mother's fingers. She pressed close to her hip.

Delaney said, looking down, his face glittering with tiny sparkles of rain, "Drop it, Dorie. Little pitchers have extremely large ears, and this one more than most. We don't want her to grow up with that fear."

Slowly, Cassie rose up in the darkness. Her memory of her father's words echoed through her. *We don't want her to grow up with that fear.*

Was the threat of the marshes one of the secrets whispered to her by the big old house?

Was that what Mrs. Abel meant? And Mary, too?

How long had it been since anyone had examined the dike? Surely, in all the years passed since her grandfather's death, weather and time would have changed it.

She told herself that if it had lasted this long then surely it would last forever. But she knew that was false reasoning.

She imagined the marshes rising, the stunted trees pulling free of their roots, crashing soundlessly into the syrupy muck that surrounded them. She imagined a thin finger of black water working its way into a crevice, a rock sliding, a gully opening . . .

She stood up, went to the window. There was nothing to see but the reflection of her own drawn and anguished face made by the dark backdrop of the closed shutters behind the glass.

She thought of opening the shutters, but knew that if she did the wind would take them, shatter them against the stone of the outside walls.

She turned away from her reflection, trying to fight her growing compulsion to go out of doors, to look at the marshes and convince herself that they were as silent and heaving as always.

But some strong need impelled her. She knew it was useless to fight it. She would have no rest through the long hours of the night that lay ahead.

At last she opened her door, stepped into the hall, listening.

It was a little past midnight, she saw by her wrist watch, but the house was totally still. The others, she supposed, had gone to bed, since she could see no light from the lower floor, nor hear any voices.

She went down the steps in the dark, and to the kitchen. There, in the cabinet drawer, she found the big flashlight kept for emergencies. She had just straightened up when the door slowly swung inward.

Chill wind gusted around her, and a swirl of leaves skittered along the linoleum, rustling loudly.

She thought she heard a sound beyond the rustling, and looked toward the hall. But it was dark, silent.

She fought the door shut as quickly as she could, and then stood there, her hand on the latch. The door had not been locked. It couldn't have blown open if the lock had been set. But she and Mike had checked it, thrown the bolt, just before she went upstairs. Then someone had opened it. Someone had gone out into the storm.

She slid through the door, shut it firmly behind her. With her finger on the flashlight button, she skirted the edge of the pool, and rounded the corner of Jonathan's wing.

There she stopped abruptly. A glimmer winked at her through the curtains of the window.

She stared at it, aware with some part of her consciousness of an unfamiliar sound mingling with the steady thrum of the wind. She had no time to consider it then, for the glimmer of light winked at her once more.

Her shirt and trousers were soaked through by then, her hair pasted to her head. The driving rain lashed at her face as she drew closer.

A shadowy movement resolved itself into two unidentifiable forms.

She watched them separate, then blend again into one.

It passed through her mind that she had heard that

Jonathan's ghost had once walked in the wing, haunting it for years, before being laid to rest.

And then she remembered that she had heard a sound near the wing the night she found her father's drowned body, and afterwards, Mrs. Abel had complained that the key was gone, and Cassie herself had crept in, found signs that someone had used the office. Now she knew that her speculations were true.

These were not ghostly shadows, she told herself. Not ethereal substances, but flesh and blood.

She stepped into the lilac bushes, thrusting herself closer to the window, but the drawn curtains shielded whoever, whatever, was inside.

She waited, straining to hear over the soughing of the storm, the pounding lash of the rain. It tore at her, hair, body. But she waited.

Then, in a brief lull, faintly, she heard Arlene's voice. She heard Arlene say, "But why, Hank? Everything's going okay."

"And that's how I want to keep it," Hank answered, laughing softly.

Cassie realized that Arlene and Hank had met, not just now, but several times before, in Jonathan's wing.

"But it *will* be okay," Arlene said urgently. "It will, I tell you. We've got nothing to worry about. I can handle Mark. Believe me, I can twist him around my little finger. He won't know if he's coming or going, when I get through with him. And besides, there's Jonesie. Mark won't want to lose Jonesie, you know."

"Maybe you can manage him. Or maybe you have a higher opinion of your persuasiveness than you should have," Hank answered hoarsely. "But believe me, you won't be able to handle Cassie. Not her. And she's the one who controls the purse strings. I notice you don't have your Cadillac, and you haven't mentioned those tennis courts recently. And you better not either. When she gets herself together, she's going to start looking long and hard at you, and what you do. You might find yourself on bread and water, no matter what Mark says. It might be she's already started looking. I saw how she watched you on the terrace today. You tipped your hand too far, Arlene, honey. You're letting your power go to your head. If there's any power. And any head."

"There is," Arlene snapped. "You better believe it, too. I know what I'm doing."

"I wonder," Hank said slowly. "You know, ever since that night Delaney walked in on us, I've been wondering."

"Then don't," Arlene said coldly.

"Well, you've got to admit, honey, it's peculiar how that same night he fell into the pool and drowned."

Listening, Cassie winced. She could imagine the scene too clearly.

Delaney, wandering about with his usual night restlessness, seeing a shadow, hearing a sound, in Jonathan's wing . . . Delaney marching in to confront Hank and Arlene. And then. . . ?

"What happened anyhow?" Hank asked softly. "You can tell me, honey. I'll be gone as soon as the storm ends tomorrow. Ed and I will hit the road for San Francisco, so you won't ever . . ."

"No," Arlene cried. "You don't have to, I tell you."

"He told me to get out, and I did," Hank said thoughtfully. "And then the next thing I knew . . ."

"Maybe you ran into him outside," Arlene suggested spitefully. "Maybe you didn't like it when he said you had to leave Moorhaven. Maybe . . ."

"Only that's not how it was. And I can prove it." Hank laughed. "You can't make me the fall guy. Ed was waiting up for me."

"So what?"

"He was on his feet breathing fire when I left. So how come the fire got put out in the pool?"

Arlene laughed softly, unpleasantly. "Questions, questions. Is that all you can do? Oh, come on, Hank. You know, it's you and me."

Sickened, Cassie wanted to creep away. She knew enough now. Almost enough. She took a cautious step back.

The steady thrum of the wind had risen to a shrill howl, and powerful gusts slammed down the cliff and over the marshes. Her body suddenly went off-balance and she staggered, reaching out to steady herself.

A heavy shutter broke free of its mooring. It slammed into the building, then tore loose. It whipped past Cassie's head, one end catching her on the shoulder, knocking her to her knees in the bushes.

She struggled to rise, hearing Arlene's, "What's that?"

"It's storming," Hank answered. "Remember?"

"Somebody's out there! Somebody's watching!" Arlene shrilled.

Light suddenly poured through the pulled-back curtains as Cassie regained her feet. It revealed her hunched body from head to toe.

She turned to run but the force of the wind held her. The door burst open.

"Get her," Arlene screamed. "Stop her, Hank. She was listening! She knows!"

Arlene fought her way out, onto the terrace, the wind whipping her hair wildly around her white face.

Hank followed more slowly, his hands in his pockets.

"Not me, honey," he said slowly. "I'll have nothing to do with this. I've seen all the violence I intend to see in my life."

"But it was all your fault," Arlene cried. "All yours. When Delaney walked in on us I knew he would have to die. I knew it. Because he'd have used it against me. He'd have made Mark send me away. So, when we started back to the house, I pushed him into the pool. He wasn't afraid of me. He didn't think I could hurt him. But I did. I killed him."

Cassie fought free of the grip of the wind, the grip of her own terror. She bent in a lurching racing run for the house. She made it as far as the broad stone steps, then with Arlene almost upon her, she felt herself swooped aside.

Mike lifted her, swung her away, and then set her

on her feet. In that instant, Cassie knew that he had always been there to protect her. He had moved to Moorhaven for that reason. He had watched over her for that reason. He had urged her to leave for that reason. And that night he had followed her from the house for the same reason.

In that instant, too, Arlene threw herself at him. "You won't stop me. You can't. You can't! Nobody can."

As he thrust her away, the two brass lamps flashed on, spilling yellow light around them. Then Mark limped out.

Arlene, staggering against a metal chair, knocked it over and fell with it. She leaped to her feet, and backed away to the edge of the terrace.

"Easy," Hank said, smiling slightly. "It's no use running away, honey."

She turned to face them, her hair blowing about her head, her white skin glimmering in the dull light.

"It's mine," she said. "All of it. Moorhaven's mine. I knew as soon as I'd killed Delaney that it was fated. It must have been. But Mark didn't inherit. So I knew what I must do. I had to earn Moorhaven. Me, a nobody. A Jones from Tembley, figured out how to earn Moorhaven. And I would have ... I would have ... with just a little more time ..."

A hundred questions sprang up in Cassie's mind, rose to her lips, but she didn't utter them. She leaned against Mike, hardly able to believe what had happened.

Arlene's cold laugh rang out as Mark appeared in the doorway. "Cassie ... It was all spur of the moment. I just had to take my chances when they came. I had to use what I could. She went up to walk on the cliff. I went after her. Dell got a look at me and ran away. I couldn't take the time to do it right, so I did the best I could. She wasn't hurt. And besides, she must have thought it was Dell that threw the rock at her. And the mirror ... that was easier. I woke Dell up, and waited. When Cassie went to his room, I went to hers. Easy again. Only it didn't quite work. After that I figured I'd better wait a while. When things quieted down, I knew I could do it. And Mark . . . you poor excuse for a man. You'd have been next. Yes, Mark. You. And I'd have been mistress of Moorhaven. The town was right, you know. Always, always. The Joneses always knew that the Moorhavens were doomed. And they were . . . they ruined the town, and us, and we . . ."

Hank shrugged, turned away.

She cried, "You and me, Hank . . ."

He said quickly, "Don't get me mixed up in this. I'm just a poor boy from Maine making my way. I've got nothing to do with your crazy schemes, Arlene." He gave Cassie a faint smile. "You figured it out, I guess. So I'll not only be making my way, but going my way. I wouldn't have hurt you. Never. Nor Ed either. I just thought it was something to try. And if it worked, good. If not . . ." He shrugged. "Nothing lost. And no trouble. Only remember, your Arlene is all yours."

Mark brushed by him, hunched and rocking against the wind. "Arlene," he said quietly. "Come away from there. We'll talk about it."

"Oh, no, thank you," she retorted. She took a step back and then another. Her slender black-clad body seemed to hang, swaying in the air, and then, with a scream, she disappeared.

Mark lunged after her, shouting wordlessly.

Hank grabbed him at the edge of the terrace, and they struggled together until Ed, appearing out of the dark, caught Mark's hands, pinned them behind him.

"Look, man," Ed said. "Look down there. What do you see?"

Cassie gasped, ran to them, and peered into the night.

The shell path down the slope had disappeared. The long landscaped slope to the dike was gone. The dike itself was gone.

As far as her eye could see there was nothing but heavy black water, marsh water, oily and slick, rising,

rising. Great long whitecapped rollers poured endlessly over where the marshes had been, and as she watched, they reached upward, their dark spray almost at the edge of the terrace.

The car, parked on the cliff, rocked in the gusty wind. The rain had stopped, and the thick cloud cover had parted. A pale moon streaked the horizon.

Beneath it, a once-familiar landscape was unalterably changed. Nothing about it would ever be the same.

Cassie sat within the circle of Mike's arms, watching the great white-rimmed rollers smash against the rock walls of Moorhaven.

Hank and Ed had driven Mark in to Tembley. Jim Hooten had followed in another car.

But Cassie had insisted that Mike stop on the last curve. From there, high above, she could see the devastation wrought by the storm.

As she watched, the house shivered under the onslaught and the windows and doors caved in. And where Moorhaven had stood for seventy-six years, the sea sucked hungrily against the base of the rocky cliff.

"It's gone," Cassie said in a wondering whisper. "All of it. The good and the bad ... The dreams and the hopes ... the love and the evil ... Mike ... how did it happen? Why? Why?"

Mike turned her face into his shoulder. "The love isn't gone," he said gently. "Never think that. We have it now. Between us. Forever. So don't look back any more, Cass. Look ahead, to the future, with me."

**THE SWEEPING ROMANTIC EPIC
OF A PROUD WOMAN
IN A GOLDEN AMERICAN ERA!**

*PATRICIA
GALLAGHER*

Beginning at the close of the Civil War, and sweeping
forward to the end of the last century, CASTLES IN
THE AIR tells of the relentless rise of beautiful, spirited
Devon Marshall from a war-ravaged Virginia landscape
to the glittering stratospheres of New York society and
the upper reaches of power in Washington.

In this American epic of surging power, there unfolds a
brilliant, luminous tapestry of human ambition, success,
lust, and our nation's vibrant past. And in the tempestu-
ous romance of Devon and the dynamic millionaire Keith
Curtis, Patricia Gallagher creates an unforgettable love
story of rare power and rich human scope.

   27649 $1.95

AVON

CIA 5-76

**A TOWERING MANSION
AND ITS TANGLED LEGACY
OF EVIL AND DESIRE**

THE STORMY ROMANTIC SAGA BY

FLORENCE HURD
ROMMANY

It began with Eustacia, first mistress of Rommany, whose love for Duncan Blackmore was not to be denied. But the innumerable rooms and sins of Rommany drew her into the grip of a sinister plot that spread its evil stain across seven decades. . . .

Until, in the life of Constance, her granddaughter, three generations of mystery converge in a fateful decision to love the hypnotic Leonard, a man cruelly linked to the shadowy past.

Suddenly, the gloom of Rommany is punctuated by ominous thumpings in the night, and Constance must pierce the veil that enshrouds her hopeless passion—so the ultimate secret of Rommany can be unmasked at last!

 28340/$1.75

ROM 6-76